BETWEEN EACH BREATH

Adam Thorpe was born in Paris in 1956. He has
written five collections of poetry and ten works
of fiction. His first novel, *Ulverton*, was published
in 1992; his most recent, *The Standing Pool*, is
published by Jonathan Cape in 2008. He lives
in France with his wife and three children.

ALSO BY ADAM THORPE

Fiction

Ulverton
Still
Pieces of Light
Shifts
Nineteen Twenty-One
No Telling
The Rules of Perspective
Is This the Way You Said?
The Standing Pool

Poetry

Mornings in the Baltic
Meeting Montaigne
From the Neanderthal
Nine Lessons from the Dark
Birds with a Broken Wing

ADAM THORPE

Between
Each Breath

VINTAGE BOOKS
London

Published by Vintage 2008

2 4 6 8 10 9 7 5 3 1

First published in Great Britain in 2007 by Jonathan Cape

Vintage
Random House, 20 Vauxhall Bridge Road,
London SW1V 2SA

www.vintage-books.co.uk

Addresses for companies within The Random House Group Limited
can be found at: www.randomhouse.co.uk/offices.htm

The Random House Group Limited Reg. No. 954009

A CIP catalogue record for this book
is available from the British Library

ISBN 9780099479925

The Random House Group Limited supports The Forest Stewardship
Council (FSC), the leading international forest certification organisation.
All our titles that are printed on Greenpeace approved FSC certified paper
carry the FSC logo. Our paper procurement policy can be found at
www.rbooks.co.uk/environment

Printed in the UK by CPI Bookmarque, Croydon, CR0 4TD

In loving memory of Frederick and Judy Busch

'We are dreadfully real, Mr Carker,' said Mrs Skewton;
'are we not?'

Charles Dickens, *Dombey and Son*

PROLOGUE

The vehicle, a battered ice-blue Saab with a front passenger door in matt violet, raced down the wide dirt road on the southern peninsula of the island as fast as a clattery engine could take it. The plume of dust the car raised was out of all proportion to its size. It was summer on Haaremaa. The northern light was the gold of ryegrass; where it penetrated the forest of birch and alder on either side, it made minor miracles out of fine spiderwebs linking branches ten feet apart. The dust left by the car rose into the sunlight and shaped it, made it touchable.

The young woman in the passenger seat was happy. She was holding a flat cardboard tray of eggs on her lap. She was happy because it was summer, it wasn't cold or wet (as it had been, in fact, for three days), and because this evening, in her parents' dacha, she would be making a huge cake out of the eggs for her husband's thirtieth birthday the following day. Her husband, who was driving, was also happy, but in the measured way usual to him; he was a specialist carpenter and had built up a reputation on the island, despite its relative poverty and ageing population, that ensured he was the first and natural choice for the most interesting of the EU-funded building projects. These included a pine-roofed spa hotel, a community hall converted from a Communist Party headquarters, and a farm museum.

The air rushed in through the open windows and caught the woman's long, tawny hair, rippling it out behind her or agitating strands of it over her face. She was — and he of course knew this — exceptionally beautiful, even by Baltic standards: she had high cheekbones, slightly polished like the curve of cowrie shells. Her husband sometimes joked that her beauty was wasted in her job, which was helping to run the island's community radio station. The car stereo – kept in place with brown tape – was playing a sample album by an obscure rock band from England called Castledown. It had been sent to the radio station as a promo. The present track was called 'The Attending', an ethereal, lyrical song that the woman loved for its simplicity: steely guitar, frail voice, English words she couldn't catch completely but whose sad poetry she appreciated and that reminded her of the old songs of Estonia.

> She is standing
> on the shore
> the girl I dream of
> no one more

Her husband's taste was different: it was for free jazz and hard rock. She would have preferred him to drive slower, but underneath his gentle carpenter's calm was this taste for the opposite, for speed and things scudding past on the surface, for distorted guitar and angry sax. He would race about the island on its dirt roads as wide as runways – built for Cold War bombers in its Soviet military days – as if he was starring in an American road movie, the stereo turned right up and his broad, sap-stained fingers tapping the wheel.

Up to now, he had never had an accident. There were relatively few cars on the island, and plenty of space to evade or spin in the event of an emergency. The monotony of the forest either side was the chief danger: drivers would nod off and wander and sometimes die against tree, especially after a night on the local vodka. Or they would simply take to the road drunk. But he was not a drinker. Apart from his tendency to push the old Saab too hard on its balding tyres, there was no reason why anything should have happened.

The door on her side was violet because it had been backed into by the island's snowplough, beaten out and repainted with the only can of metal colour – from the job lot her father had saved from Soviet days – that remotely resembled the original blue. Being good with his hands, and not able to afford professional help, her husband had done it all himself. The chief problem was the lock – the area most dented by the snowplough. It had taken him a whole day to fix. The door had to be slammed in a certain way to enable the tongue of the lock to come home.

Right now, the door rattled very slightly, but neither of them could hear this over the noise of the old engine and the gravelly dirt road and the lovely song on the stereo, let alone the rush of the warmish summer air in their ears. The door rattled because the tongue was not quite home: she had not slammed the door correctly, encumbered by the eggs on her lap, their shells still smeared with muck and feathers. They were not eggs from the dacha's hens, as they would normally have been; a fox had done its nasty work in an orgy of blood and feathers a few weeks ago, and they had not yet replaced the dead hens. But for this fox, she would not have been in the car at all, with the eggs from a cousin's farm balanced on her lap.

Now she was humming along to the song, the corner of her mouth puckered in a way he loved, like the very beginning of the happiest of smiles.

The curving bend in the road was familiar enough for him to take it relatively fast, right out on the edge of – but not over – the safe limit of control. The rules of weight and velocity meant that she leaned against the door (there were no seat belts installed, of course) and the tongue slipped and the door opened. She started to fall out of the car, slowly, the fifteen eggs on her lap jittering in their moulded cardboard tray.

Instead of putting a hand out to save herself, to break her fall, she tried to protect the eggs. It was an instinctive thing: she did not want the eggs to break, not a single one. He had already flexed his foot towards the brake and reached his hand out, but she had fallen too far away from him, and all he grabbed was air.

She fell away from the car with both her hands over the eggs, so that the back of her head hit the grit surface first. By the time the car had slewed to a dusty halt, she was lying on the road in a welter of yolk and glassy white, open-eyed and as if about to say something, her hair spread out like a fan. A black-bird, practising its scales a few yards into the wood, was disturbed by a great howling that felt dangerous, and fell silent as if in homage.

ONE

The pub, called O'Looney's, was thick with drunken Finns. It was playing the same screechy Irish number as two days back, at full distorted volume. The Finns were singing over it, football songs sol-faing over the Irish folk: starlings swirling onto and off the black wires.

I left the pub without ordering and went back down the street to the café-bar clocked on the way up. It was playing minimal lounge and had chairs of perspex with the names of French poets scratched on. I sat in the bay window on *Appolinaire*. I wasn't certain it was spelt right. Appolo. Appollo. Apollo.

Frayed by a morning in the flat spent making sense of a descending diatonic scale in four different tempi, I needed to chill out, but the chair was not designed for comfort. Still, it felt good in here, it felt Continental and far away, with a silvery northern light outside that fell through the glass onto the table and my hands, along with the etched name on the window: *Majolica*. I moved my hands and the name rippled over the knuckles, making them look as if they were caught in a sandwich bag.

The cobbled street was quiet, gusted by the cool October wind. This is OK, I thought to myself.

The house opposite was hidden behind scaffolding and green tarps that slapped now and again against the metal poles. The finished houses were brightly coloured, not looking in the least bit medieval. Those yet to be dealt with were grey and dirty, their brown stonework chipped and their balconies leaning. Part of me preferred these houses, as if I'd known them before. Maybe their neglect reminded me of Hayes.

What looked like a ghost with sunlit hands turned out to be the waitress, approaching my table from the kitchen. I swivelled to give my order, but her face was turned away – someone was calling her from the kitchen. I only saw the flange of her right cheekbone and a cataract of tawny hair.

Then she faced me and the corner of her mouth puckered.

'Hi.'

'Hi. A latte, please. Thanks.'

She called out something in reply to a yell from the kitchen. She was wearing tight jeans and a cutaway shirt.

I looked out of the window again. My outlook commanded quite a stretch of the street's vista. One of the Finnish drunks further up was performing a ballet, his T-shirt on his head like a wimple.

No great expectations of this trip, on my part, to be honest. Then the airport's sliding glass doors had opened to an expanse of marshy grey water, low wood-covered hills and some dilapidated buildings off to the right. Unspectacular, a bit like Cheshire or somewhere, but the air was different. So was the light. Birds dimpling the water beyond a blurry line of reeds. *Really* different, in fact.

I felt excited. Happy, even. I was like an old-fashioned little boy in a train, glimpsing the sea for the first time.

A driver with long sideburns was already opening the boot of a battered yellow Mercedes and wafting me towards it like a feather.

'Please, please.'

The front seat was occupied by the remains of a sausage in its wrapper, so I sat in the back on a torn tartan rug. The car was a fug of bitter, American tobacco. It instantly turned into a getaway car – although I had not yet negotiated my seat belt, which turned out to be broken – with a throaty roar that I thought at first was the plane taking off beyond the wire fence. We hurtled past abandoned factories, Stalinist housing schemes and construction sites with big gravel dunes.

Skeletons of big-box stores squatted in a waste of mud, yellow cranes and adland hoardings. I wondered whether I shouldn't shift across and try the other seat belt, despite a sharp rip in the plastic upholstery.

Life, I thought (clutching the broken belt to my chest), is an adventure.

The driver's identity card swung from the mirror, showing a younger man with burning eyes. *Olev.* Voices kept breaking in over the intercom as if something catastrophic was occurring. In the photo swinging from the mirror, Olev looked like a psychopath. Maybe Russian. Dirt-track detours around roadworks got Olev muttering savagely, as if they'd sprung into being in the brief time he'd been waiting for a pickup.

We were stopped at the lights when Olev's staring image suddenly reproduced itself between the seats: plumper, stubbled. The eyes were bloodshot.

'Hoor?'

'Sorry?'

'Hoor? Hoor?'

It sounded as if he was about to throw up. He was waving an unlit cigarette about. It was taking me a moment to cotton on.

'*Oh* – sorry! Thanks, but I don't smoke,' I said, at last.

Olev frowned at me. He wasn't offering me a fag, he wanted a light. I gave a little self-conscious snort, indicating stupidity, and tapped my coat's breast pockets. 'Um, sorry! *Nyet.* No light. No matches. *Rien.*'

The real Olev disappeared, his seat bouncing and squeaking on its bolts, leaving his photo to carry on glaring at me below an equally baleful, fleshier slice in the mirror. When the car suddenly filled with smoke – Olev steering with his elbows as we raced away – I had to confess I felt a bit at sea.

I did my best not to cough, keen not to appear effeminate.

We reached the edge of the old town's pedestrian area, bumping up onto the pavement as if it was in the way. Olev shouted something over his shoulder, conducting an orchestra;

it took me a minute or two to get it. A car could go no further without a special licence, the street was the next right. The meter declared a price in kroons that I couldn't begin to calculate; I handed over a thick wad of notes (the equivalent, I later checked, of about ten quid).

Olev got out and opened the boot and removed the suitcase with a grunt.

'Please,' he said, pressing a soiled little card into my hand.

Disko, Baar, Saun – 24 hr.

I thanked him without enough irony, then waved with unnecessary heartiness as the taxi accelerated off – as you would to an aunt who had stayed too long.

At the café table, only three days on, I contemplated the meaning of home. I certainly felt at home in Tallinn. I had felt the same about Berlin, even before the Wall came down, even after my one sortie into the Eastern sector for a glasnost music festival.

'Your coffee.'

'Oh, great. Thanks.'

The corner of her mouth puckered again as I looked up: the post-Soviet, Estonian smile. As minimal as the café's music. No, not true: it flickered over the whole of her face, like sunlight and cloud shadow over a field of ripe corn. And then she was off.

Some fat and elderly tourists were wobbling after a little flag on a stick. Apart from these and the drunken Finns, there was no one else on the street. I was picturing that very large East Berlin hall with its fitted carpet no one had bothered to glue, so it slid about under your feet; and the Soviet bloc composers with their fake leather jackets, chain-smoking even at breakfast. I couldn't remember what we talked about.

The tourists spotted the clutch of Finns, who were embracing each other as if on a storm-tossed ship, and turned up a side alley.

The latte was more than passable.

Calling out an order, the waitress played the ghost again in my view of the street.

I took another sip of my coffee and added half the paper tube of sugar, stirring once. A stroll around the castle, if the rain held off. I'm not a great one for novels, but I had brought along *Anna Karenina*. The Penguin copy was battered and creased, and a segment of some thirty pages had come unstuck – kept dropping out. So I had to be careful. This time I would finish it. The lounge music was scribbling two-beat figures in my head, semitonal oscillations that could have been interesting if crossed with something pentatonic in E flat major – a trumpet, maybe. A louche girl's voice had started up, something about *spending a lifetime with you*, weaving around the extremely down-beat bass.

The door squealed and the waitress went out onto the café's little terrace – just a couple of tables on rough planking, like a projecting medieval stage. A customer with a grey pony-tail and a long black coat was braving the gusts; she took his order, glancing up to where the Finns were attempting hand-stands. She seemed to know him – he was nodding, looking serious.

Sometimes you wish you could be like everyone else: at home in the world, as if they'd known about it before they were born.

Then the man laughed, and so did she.

There was a tower up at the castle, flying the Estonian flag for as long as the country was free. Until about ten years ago, it had flown mostly other people's flags: Danish, Swedish, Prussian, Russian, German. Then the Red Flag. I would now go up and sit there and tackle the lower slopes of *Anna Karenina* until the cold got through to the bone, like common sense.

She came back inside, animated by her encounter. I had considered growing a ponytail, like the telly Crusoe of my child-hood, but Milly had said *no way*. The slap bass of the new lounge track made me think, as it happened, of the slap of her groin against mine as she rode bronco on top, facing my flat feet and saying, over and over, 'Seed bearer, seed bearer, seed bearer . . .' Which I'd heard at first as 'Syd Barrett': original, if off-putting. Deborah Willetts-Nanda had told her to say it, apparently. A psychosomatic aid to fertility – which had definitely put me off. Anyway, it hadn't worked, so far.

One night I asked her who the seed bearer was, exactly.

'I'm not sure. I'd supposed it was me, but maybe it's you. It's all about fulfilment.'

'Could be both of us.'

'Probably. Night night.'

'Um, Mill, don't you think we should at least check ourselves over with a normal doctor?'

But she was already asleep. At that moment I felt about as fulfilled as a hole in the wall.

The waitress was taking out a cake and a coffee to Ponytail. As she returned, her tongue lying on her lower lip, she glanced over my side of the room – a just-checking, all-in-the-job look. I was in the way of it. Her tongue retracted and she smiled again with her whole face. Just a flicker. As a kid I'd look at the goldfish in Hayes Park's dark pond and they'd kiss the surface and the surface would change just the way her face changed when she smiled. To my surprise and embarrassment, I blushed. The blush made me blush even more. I opened my book and pretended to be swallowed up in it. I hadn't blushed since the fifth form. I'm not fair, so it's barely detectable, but I still felt like a ripe tomato.

I waited until the waitress was in the kitchen before going up to the bar, not waiting for the change. The barman was young with a shaven head and a big Roman nose pierced with gold beads on each flange. The piercings made his nose look like the head of a praying mantis. I was removing myself by force from the café, hand firm on my own shoulder. It had to be done.

As I was passing through the door, I heard someone call out *goodbye*.

I steeled myself not to reply, pretty sure the voice was hers and in a provocative register. It was a small victory.

Afterwards, of course, I felt stupid and English and rude.

★   ★   ★

I'd left my mate Tolstoy behind. This wouldn't have bothered me, if the book hadn't had some notes tucked into it.

I'd made them as I was examining the old cannon by the medieval wall, and they were technically complex, to do with an emerging melisma. I had decided to keep the five oboes and harp but to enlarge the voice to three sopranos, realising that Estonian was all long vowels and that was perhaps why Arvo Pärt sustained his notes to the extent that he did; stretching syllables in his *Miserere*, for instance, in a way that might not have been so unusual to his ear. I'd sketched the shape of the whole piece, leaning the paper on the cannon, and felt it was the melting of the ice.

Three days, and I was already thawing out.

I reckoned I might as well buy a new copy of *Anna Karenina* – there was an English section in the bookshop near the apartment. I imagined the waitress picking up my dog-eared copy and the thirty-page portion slipping out onto the floor. And perhaps my folded sheet of notes she would puzzle over in the privacy of her tiny but very cosy garret room. She would have posters on the walls – interesting posters. Experimental plays in Estonian, films by Tarkovsky. Or Marlon Brando playing pool, maybe. A photo of her family. Their farm, their horses. No man in her life right now.

I was sitting on a bench opposite the gold-domed Alexander Nevsky Cathedral. There was a nip in the air, it being October and on about the same latitude as St Petersburg or the Orkneys. It was really quiet and peaceful. I could see the palatial eighteenth-century parliament buildings to my left and the medieval city wall sloping down to my right. My hands were half hidden inside my duffel coat and my scarf was about my throat, making it itch. I wondered what the point of life was. Benches do this to you. Or maybe the date: 1999. The sustained syllables of wild flowers were sounding their melismata in my head: *hound's tongue, henbane, bugle, cross-leaved heath, marsh andromeda*. That was the entire libretto of my piece. I had taken the names from my old *Observer's Book of Wild Flowers*.

'But it's about Estonia,' Milly had pointed out. 'Why British flowers?'

This was a pleasant surprise: she was usually too busy with her own planet-saving work to comment on mine.

'They're also found in Estonia.'

'Shouldn't you check?'

'How do you know I haven't?'

'The way you said it.'

'The whole point,' I went on, irritated, 'is the relation. The relation *between* the two countries. It's not just a hymn in praise of Estonia. They're flowers in dramatic decline,' I added, eventually, hoping to impress her. But she was already on the phone.

The score was writing itself behind my eyes, second by second. I'm never quite sure whether the music writes the score or the score writes the music. Sometimes I feel I'm sight-reading a score that someone else has planted there. On the other hand, it remains completely my own, inasmuch as anything is one's own. I don't bother to write it down straight away, since I have excellent recall. This is not so much genius as the way my brain is made. Other living composers of like repute don't necessarily have this knack, they have to work harder, they have to toil and lick their pencils. But they end up in the same place, to be acclaimed or stamped on.

When I was seven, I wrote a score that featured cymbals and a bass drum. I'd only heard these on the radio (my parents would usually listen to Radio 2), but in this score they became something that sounded Tibetan. There was no discernible rhythm. Remarkably close, someone pointed out two decades later, to Arvo Pärt's use of the three notes of the triad. This was, presumably, why I was on a bench by the Alexander Nevsky Cathedral in the capital city of Pärt's native land, staring glassily into space: it wasn't just the commission – potentially a mega one, in terms of my 'career' – it was the arc of one's life, the patterns and the ripples, the ripples that hit the grassy bank and start to return.

For instance, I had left a book in a Tallinn café and could

not go back to get that book because I'd gone lush on a pretty waitress. I started grinning, and shaking my head, and a woman in a fur coat walking a cocker spaniel on a red lead glanced at me anxiously. Her high heels were getting a weirdly hollowed tone out of the slabbed square that reminded me of a log drum. Maybe it was the open side door in the cathedral, like that ancient quarry cave in Syracuse, throwing the sound about. Then there was a man in a long woollen scarf and floppy woollen hat that ought to have belonged to his teenage daughter, if he'd been a bit older; he was holding a tiny grey tranny emitting pop so badly it was white noise. And after him came a couple of Japanese male tourists, one in a pair of thigh-length boots and an expertly washed white cotton jacket; they looked very cheery, as if they had been born that way and would die that way, their digital cameras playing jingles after every snap, gnawing wormholes in my brain.

When it comes down to it, there is no one who is not weird.

I tried to conjure the face of the waitress, but failed. My visual memory is as bad as my aural is good, although I had a strong impression of her dimples, the way the right-hand corner of her mouth tucked in for a smile.

I played her voice several times to my inner ear. Slightly hoarse, from shouting out customers' orders.

I could leave Milly and stay in Estonia for the rest of my life. With this girl.

I gave a little self-satisfied grunt. The Finnish drunks aside, I found this city very civilised. I liked the idea of it hunkering down for winter. A real Estonian winter would clear the streets of everyone but the natives, who were hardened to it all, not even slipping about on the iced cobbles.

'Do you think you're depressed?'

Milly had asked me this a few months earlier.

'No.'

'You look it. Even Daddy's noticed.'

'I'm going through a creative slough.'

13

We were at her parents' in Hampshire, seated on the lower lawn by the lake, where the swans glide about on hidden runners. The grounds of Wadhampton Hall are so big that bits keep getting discovered: years ago, someone illegally jerry-built a cottage on the outer fringes, lived in it, died in it, and no one knew. The ground staff came across the cottage while brush-clearing a wood; there was a skeleton in the rotting bed.

'Isn't that depressing, a creative trough?'

'A slough. Not really.'

'OK.'

I loved her. She was experimenting with a bindi on her forehead. Her dad had been very rude about it, and about Asians, over lunch.

'Anyway, it's not really a creative slough. It's just that my imagination doesn't fit the shoe.'

'What shoe?'

'What it takes – to build a successful career. I hate that word *career*,' I added, before she did.

'As long as you don't crack up.'

I had expected her to say, 'But you *are* successful.' So I gave her another opportunity: 'Look, this success deal, it means you have to be doing these enormous great blockbuster works, operas, symphonies, with seriously sexy titles like, I dunno, *Heidegger's Last Kiss* or *Dark Woods, Funny Games*.'

'Did you just invent those? They're really good.'

'Or you go for film, like Glass. Or bootleg a pile of pop and classical, like Anne Dudley. Otherwise you're just part of this minuscule little self-congratulatory coterie. Who all hate each other. OK, I'm exaggerating. But.'

'Can't you put lots of your little things together, string them out?'

What I say out loud is different from what I think. So I don't like interviews. I look dark and moody in the photographs, but my interviews sound like a fifth-former who hasn't yet got it together.

I pretended to think about it, therefore. I didn't want a

14

scene, not at the Hall. I liked the Hall and its hundreds of acres of prime English cut, it kept reminding me how lucky I'd been in life. We'd all just polished off a 1962 Sauternes, my father-in-law holding its tawny gold up to the light and saying it was the only white that kept more than thirty years. 'Thirty-seven, to be precise,' he'd added, with that patented knowing chuckle of his.

Happy birthday, Jack!

Milly was still looking at me in a worried way. I was watching the swans on the water, how strict they looked. Dark death in their shadows.

'Well, I could just repeat the same note for two hours,' I suggested, at last; 'only varying the tempo. And call it *Following the Thread*.'

Now I was in a different country and the air was cold. The light wouldn't go for ages. I thought: were I to settle in Estonia, I would learn to skate on lakes, the ice groaning and banging under me − a very beautiful sound I'd first heard in Norway.

I spent the next two days fulfilling my vague suspicion that wherever you are, however exotic, gets submitted to your own level.

I worked away at the score in the flat at the very healthy rate of about a minute a day and walked in concentric circles around Tallinn, probing once beyond the old centre into the grim suburbs, where all the buildings seemed to be huge and wearing shabby grey overcoats with padded shoulders. When I thought about the waitress in the Café Majolica, a sort of golden age opened in my chest, starring Aphrodite. The piece wouldn't come right.

I avoided the actual street, although I came close when visiting the House of the Brotherhood of Black Heads. Milly had insisted I visit this, because of its name. 'I wonder how nasty your zits had to be,' she'd said, laughing. There was an alleyway near it that, according to the map, came out close to where I reckoned the café was. I found myself walking up this alleyway and then peering out; ancient merchant houses, a shop selling Indian stuff called Exotik, but no café. Perhaps it had been a dream. Perhaps I could write an opera based on the story of this young dude who falls for a waitress, but when he returns the next day the café has vanished. And then what?

It is always: *And then what?*

I walked a little way up the street in the direction of St Olav's Church, and saw the sign *Café Majolica* poking out on its curly wrought-iron frame where the street curved slightly to the left. Another blustery, autumnal wind that was playing havoc with the leaves on the trees – summer was finally throwing in the towel. The last summer of the twentieth century. The last summer ever, according to the optimists of a religious bent.

I didn't know why I was doing this.

I wanted to see her again, that's why. Just her face, as sometimes you want to test if something's real. I had to match the reality with the picture in my head, which was confused, like a triple exposure.

I stopped a few yards short. There was no one sitting out on the terrace. The windows were mirroring the street, from this acute angle. My legs started trembling. A power tool started up behind the tarp opposite the café, like the shrill condensing of all that was really sensible in the world. Then it stopped. Then it started up again, whiningly working the bit into masonry or concrete or whatever it was. The worst material being metal, like something composed by Roger Grove-Carey.

I turned on my heel and headed for the upper town.

I had already established a circuit, this animal run. I would take it from either direction, clockwise or anticlockwise; halfway round this circuit there was a view, a fairly amazing view at the foot of the castle. It was a panorama of the lower town, the harbour with its big ships, the Bay of Finland. Every evening so far I had stared and marvelled as the northern sun sank slowly, taking its time, turning the sky a deep greeny-blue as lights twinkled on the sea.

I decided I really liked northernness.

Yes, I could live here. I had done a lot of travelling in my career up to then, but it was always with other people and to do with performance, nerves, a certain exhibitionism. A certain placing of myself, not in the actual landscape, but in the landscape of contemporary music. I felt shut off from wherever I found myself.

Each evening, here, standing behind the low wall and looking out, with the odd stranger sharing the dying light and not speaking, or the odd pair of lovers canoodling with sloppy noises from their lips, I felt free. As if I could tear everything up and start again. Or as if my whole life up to now had belonged to someone else, and I could ditch it as easily as a book.

What helped was that, after I had waved goodbye to Olev's taxi a few days earlier, there had been this sudden slammer of a squall. The rain had billowed in a kind of mist, as if the wind wasn't allowing the drops to fall all the way, and people took cover under shop awnings. But I'd kept going. London, travel-fug, Olev's smoke: all blown away. Then the rain was switched off, and the sun gleamed like metal on the wet cobbles, and the air was scented with something I couldn't quite fix until I was waiting for the apartment's owner in the newsagent's below.

Almonds, that was it.

I was a new man. I felt it was all going to be fine. Graced by almonds.

The building itself was this old grey Soviet tooth in the done-up dentures of the street, described on the Internet as being 'a laughable distance from the Middle Ages center'. Sure enough, it joined the city's historic main square, Raekoja Plats, about fifty yards further up. A café and a jeweller's occupied the ground floor, along with the newsagent's.

The owner was not the cool, new-capitalist slicker I had been expecting: in his late forties, dressed in a comfortable woolly sweater, he looked like a bumbly don. His name was Koit, which I couldn't pronounce: a whiplash of a diphthong. Koit had laughed, dangling the keys from his finger.

'So you are having a nice time to Tallinn. Good luck. Any troubles, call this nomber.'

The steps up to the third floor were marbled and impeccably clean, while the apartment itself – two-bedroom, all mod cons – was surprisingly plush. In fact, I had expected jerry-built plumbing, wobbly chairs, really bad pictures of cats with big eyes. There was a damp smell of new plaster, the odd protruding wire and a packet of grouting next to the sugar in the kitchen cupboard, but otherwise it was fine. White fake-leather sofas, gilded bed-ends, curvy smoked-glass lamps and a supersize Sony television felt nicely alien. The hot-cold tap in the shower was dodgy, but they are the world over.

Someone – maybe the cleaner, maybe Koit – had sprayed the rooms with lavender air-freshener, so I opened the double-glazed windows after my shower. The sounds of the street poured in with the cold: voices, high heels, the thumping bass of a restaurant opposite, the usual instant-anxiety suppliers in the form of passing motorbikes, just as nasty as anywhere else. I watched the street action for ages, leaning on the sill, forgetting Olev, trying to forget London. I was here. I was not there.

A drawer in the retro dresser was full of red candles that rolled like the rollers in an airport baggage belt, but there were no matches or lighters anywhere: no *hoor*, if that's what the word meant. The fridge was empty, bar a single egg. A high-quality lithograph – forest at twilight, dark and menacing – faced the heavy dining table on which glass ashtrays were laid out as if for an executive meeting.

And all this, after just a few days' use, had come to feel like home.

Maybe that was the mistake. Is home that shallow? It was probably to do with being alone. I'd have quite liked a piano thrown in, but I was able to test out ideas on the baby grand in the musical-instrument shop, where the owner had a big hippy beard and spoke English. I've always found it hard nattering with strangers, and I hardly talked to anyone else.

I'd bought a bottle of Jameson's, rationing myself to a slug before supper. Tonight, in memory of my abandoned Tolstoy and maybe other things, the slug was generous. I sat on the white sofa, watching the news in Estonian. What did 'Majolica' mean, anyway? Men were crawling over great slabs of concrete, pulling out dust-covered bodies: I wasn't sure whether it was an earthquake, or a gas explosion, or terrorism. And no idea where.

Layer after layer of pain.

The next programme, about either dried-flower arranging or how to cope with grief (I wasn't sure, because there were occasional black-and-white head shots of pale-looking women), sent me off to sleep.

The following day, after breakfast, I looked up *majolica* in a dictionary in the bookshop next door. A fine kind of Italian glazed earthenware, from the former name of the island of Majorca. Nothing to do with flowers. The bookshop didn't have *Anna Karenina*, or only in French, German, Estonian – and Russian, of course. Milly had told me it was even better in French (her French is good), but it would be too much effort. Instead, I bought a newish biography of Handel and a trash thriller to help me sleep.

There was a phone in the apartment, but I wasn't phoning Milly because that was what we had agreed, outside an emergency. I really felt like talking to her, though.

Either that, or I would go back to the café for the book.

Yer what?

The waitress had served me a latte. We had exchanged two glances, lasting a total of three or four seconds. One thing I really wanted to avoid was to act like a prick to myself, let alone other people, just because I was abroad.

Milly was not in when I tried her. I didn't leave a message.

I was at the flat's front door, ready to retrieve *Anna Karenina* from the café, when the phone rang.

'Hiya. Whassup? It *was* you trying to phone me?'

I loved her to bits. I even loved her voice to bits. Its complicated sonic texture, both silk and light grit.

'Yeah,' I said. 'It's nothing serious, Mill. Just wanted to talk.'

'You're having fun, though?'

'Well, I'm working.'

'You sound pissed off,' she laughed.

'What? Pissed off?'

'You see?'

'Mill, I'm not pissed off. I'm only pissed off by you saying I am, because I'm not.'

'I'm fine, by the way.' A beat of silence, while I was working this one out. 'Thanks for asking.'

'I didn't have a chance,' I all but cried. 'Why do you think I tried phoning you up?'

'Because you were lonely.'

'Not really. Well, I haven't talked to anyone for about five days, almost.'

'How's Estonia? Snazzy enough?'

'I'm blown away. No, seriously, it's good.'

I sighed again, then realised how the sigh must have sounded like frustration.

'I wasn't going to tell you until you got back,' she said, 'but my period's three days late.'

'Three days? Wow!' I came over more astonished than I'd meant to.

'Well, it's not *that* long, but you know I'm a stickler for punctuality.'

'Sounds hopeful.'

'Keep your fingers crossed.'

'They're, um, casually crossed, so as not to attract the gods' notice.'

'How're the birds, Jack?'

'What?'

'Well,' she insisted, 'you know what everyone said before you went. The most beautiful girls in Europe.'

'Don't see it, myself. They probably meant the Ukraine. Or maybe the Balkans. Look, I'm here to work. I'm being really monkish. I've expanded to three sopranos and the theme's going haywire. I'm into static pitch-fields and all that crazy stuff.'

'Jack, don't make it painful to listen to. It's your mega break.'

'It won't be,' I assured her, modulating my annoyance with a chuckle. 'It's going to be all serene, unless otherwise stated.'

'Heard that one before. Love you. Gotta go. I'm majorly busy with a bloody great Heal's contract.'

'Big kiss.'

'Ditto,' she said.

All compositions are echoes of other works, sometimes your own. They recycle, quote, beg, borrow and steal. And yet they end up personal, and sometimes they end up memorable. I sat humped at the thick table, too hot in my coat, staring at the phone.

My wife was pregnant, at last. Very early days, but still.

And it should have been glorious news, it should have appeared somewhere in the piece as an ode of joy, solo oboe, a single sustained syllable from the second voice.

I got up and stood by the open window; the cold air was a relief. Over the six years we'd been together, we'd got to know each other better, physically and mentally, than anyone else had ever known us, including our parents. I couldn't imagine life without Milly. Without her confidence, her support, her dazzling smile, her zeal to do good in the world. The du Cranes were part of my life. Their gobsmacking wealth was in my veins: the huge Hall in Hampshire and the whopping privacy of its grounds, the wildness of its woods bordered only by a tiny winding lane hardly anyone took, bar the odd teenage maniac. It was all transfused into me.

So what was up? What was the game?

Yesterday I'd seen her walking ahead near the Dominican Monastery: skintight jeans, wasp waist, a dark-gold cascade of hair. Turned out to be a false alarm. An inner wolf whistle, that was all. Dozens similar, here. So I lost myself in work.

I'd studied Pärt's scores but had so far avoided playing the CDs: I preferred what I heard in my head.

Pärt is a Russian Orthodox believer. What does Jack Middleton believe?

I dunno what I believe.

Is your piece therefore a metaphysical challenge to the master?

I guess so. Pärt's simplicity is very sophisticated. I like the photos of Pärt on the covers of the CDs I have with me here. He's got this great Tolstoyan beard. You feel he's the symbolic Estonian, bearing his country's anguish and suffering. This makes his music far from serene.

Your own music generally lulls the audience into contemplative bliss, only to savage it with dissonance and atonal disorder.

Yeah, like a mob bursting into a cathedral. Once, when Pärt was asked a question in an interview, he poured a glass of water over his head.

Warning: removing a wedding ring can be dangerous. You can pull your finger off at the same time. Which means the ring is still on your finger. Mine – my ring, that is – only slipped off after a lot of soap, water and yanking, leaving a fleshly indent all round, like something turned in wood.

I placed the ring carefully in my bumbag. This is only a very temporary separation, I told myself.

And crossing the windy old Raekoja Plats with my head thrust forward, dodging the craft-market stalls and their floating customers, I heard myself say to myself: *You're nuts. You're having a breakdown.*

Milly and I had been trying for a kid for well over a year and a half. Now it was hallelujah time. Mill would grow plumper, her breasts would expand, she would slow down. In the end she would waddle. After the birth I would feel life-changed and compose works that even my mother would listen to without gritting her teeth. Our tall house in Richmond (too tall, I always felt, but Daddy du Crane had insisted, and it was brilliantly quiet bar the planes) would look down with horror upon bright plastic scattered on the rugs and up the original mahogany stairs, and the sweet whiff of baby lotion would permeate every room like bleach in a hospital. There would be screaming, wails, interruptions. I knew all this from my sister and from friends who had embarked on the same odyssey a little earlier. And Milly wanted six. We would (this was her plan) move to the country and have six of them, their little legs scampering over the soft lawns, squealing with happiness. Six opportunities for fatal interruption, every day.

'Uxbridge,' I teased Milly, once – keeping straight-faced. 'I fancy bringing them up in Uxbridge. Very convenient for London.'

We were having a swift one in the Plough and Horses, mulling over the future at the beginning of the year, before the real anxiety about our childless state had set in. She looked at me in horror.

'You are joking.'

'I wouldn't mind giving them, you know, what *I* had,' I said, as if meaning it. 'Similar surroundings. Very nice for kids.'

'You were brought up there. You hated it.'

'Uxbridge borders. People in Uxbridge were better off. Laughed at people in Hayes. Wouldn't ever want to go back to Hayes itself, you see. Stank of Nescaff from the factory.'

'You are quite genuinely weird, you know. Uxbridge is completely naff. So is Hayes. You said so yourself. When I first met you you said you were from Hayes, and I asked where's that, and you said it's a growth on Uxbridge's brown pipe.'

'The A4020. I was showing off.'

'Gosh, Jack, that's not like you.'

I sipped my beer, hurt, as she played with her new toy – a mobile phone. It was work again. Afterwards I asked her if she'd ever *been* to Uxbridge.

'No, but . . .'

I nodded slowly, smiling my contempt.

'Oh, everyone *knows*,' she said, twisting her face and wobbling her head.

'Ugh,' I teased. 'Uxbridge. Yuk. Nasty, sticky place.'

'Shuddup.'

'But Daddy, you should *see* them. They don't even have horses!'

'They probably do. Or certainly those disgusting four-by-fours. It's probably full of wannabe Amandas, these days.'

'Hang 'em high, bruvvers,' I intoned, giving a bunched fist salute.

Underneath, though, I felt pretty cross. I'd felt the same sensation when my best friend Howard Davenport, the viola player, had leaned over to me in an Arvo Pärt recital and said, 'Mystic chewing gum, mate.'

Why should it be five oboes and three sopranos, anyway? Why not one oboe, one voice, a cymbal and a bass drum? A tiny bell? Complete simplicity. As spare and clean as a piece of driftwood on a Baltic strand. Long pauses of nothing. The millennium welcomed on calm.

I approached the café slowly, as if walking with care over the cobbles; as if it was already winter and there was ice.

Breathtimers.

The punctuations of silence.

There were three incredibly giggly girls in their mid-teens at the central table, drinking Pepsis and finding depths of interest in a mobile phone. Even here.

The door squealed shut behind me and they looked up. I hoped they wouldn't find me naff. In my duffel, and slightly on the short side, well stocky (never fat, never fat), with messy hair that was still black, I was either very naff or very cool. They glanced at each other and burst into giggles again. I scanned the room as if I hadn't noticed, discreetly checking my hair. Sometimes my hair lets me down. It has a dollop over the forehead I have to keep pushing away. My Hitler wave, schoolmates'd call it. I've never let it go.

She wasn't in sight. My heart was nevertheless hammering, despite myself. The shaven-headed barman was wiping glasses;

he caught my eye and smiled in the faint, serious way of Estonians – if they smiled at all.

'Um, hi, I left a book here, a book, three days ago? *Anna Karenina*? Tolstoy? Left? A book?'

'Yeah, OK. Wait.'

So people left books here all the time. No sweat.

There were other customers in the Majolica: a couple of middle-aged tourists in orange parkas studying a map as if they'd walked here from the Lake District; a man in a Sartre raincoat reading *Le Monde*; a mournful woman with dyed red hair and a bibber's eye bags. The music was off. The barman had gone into the kitchen, but was still in earshot. He was talking to a girl, but the girl's voice was not the same. I tried to look relaxed, realising everything was pretty relaxed except my mouth, which could have blown a trumpet, no problem.

There was a warning behind the bar about the Millennium Bug, in English. The thought of what might happen in under three months frightened me. The giggly girls were probably only about thirteen, in fact. She'd left the job, obviously. She had vanished into the big noisy world for ever. The cheery threesome erupted into laughter at something one of them had said, or maybe at something on their mobile phone – certainly not at me – and I leaned my elbows on the bar in an attempt to look cool and mature. One day, maybe when I hit forty-six, I would feel mature, I reckoned – it must happen to you eventually. I would wear a long dark coat and look like the head of an opera house.

The barman came out with the girl who wasn't the right girl and together, without looking at me, they searched behind the bar. The girl shook her head, pulling a face. She had a sharp chin and nose and her dark hair was dyed bright green at the top, like the way they mark a spot in the road destined to be hammer-drilled.

'Sorry,' the barman said, 'no book.'

'Don't worry. My fault. Good to know someone's appreciating it.'

'Pardon me?'

'That's OK,' I said, waving my hands. 'I'll have a coffee, anyway.'

'A coffee?'

'A latte, please.'

'OK. Siddown, if you want.'

I stayed at the bar. I felt more in command, there. I was finding my breath again. I didn't mind the pretentious decor, this time. Ten or so years ago there'd have been no hip café-bars in Tallinn. Russians everywhere and a sense of grey and brown inside the head and outside the head. No ugliness because no beauty, no dissonance because no tonality.

It was probably her day off. I could pass again tomorrow. Or I could ask the barman. I could summon up the courage and ask him, outright. I practised it in my head: *Maybe your other waitress found it, put it somewhere. The other girl, you know? Coppery-blonde hair? Her day off, is it?* And I knew I would flush from either ear to the tip of my nose, the teeny-boppers watching like hungry cats.

Milly was possibly pregnant. My wife! My missus at home! One of the du Cranes, of deep Norman lineage. The woman I had sworn to stay with till death us do part. Not that I'd *wanted* a church service, and not with that vicar of several unshaven chins.

'OK?' The barman was looking at me, concerned.

'Yeah, I'm great. Thanks.'

'Y'know, sorries about the book.'

'It doesn't matter at all. Only the two of you serving, then? Short of staff today, then?'

'What?'

There'd only been two of them before, I remembered.

'No, it's great. Thanks.'

'OK. You like music?'

'I like silence. Really quiet is fine.'

The girls exploded into giggles again, as if I was triggering them. The barman was putting on some more music. It wasn't lounge, it was house – even more minimal. I'd try to keep up with the electronic scene, and this was definitely familiar. The way the bass and the drum snaked and coiled around each other, the use of effects, the hypnotic repetition and glacially slow development.

'You like?'

'Yeah, I know it. Don't tell me. It's that group from Berlin with a French name.'

The barman looked impressed. 'Hey, that's correct. Isolée,' he said, nodding. 'This is the new one. Real good, huh?' He was bobbing about a bit.

'Great. Just great. Excellent. Do you like that French band with the Scottish singer and a terrible name? Telepopmusic, they're called.'

The barman leaned on the zinc and frowned. 'Not St Germain?'

'No, not St Germain. Telepopmusic. Check them out.'

The phone went and he had to answer it, chatting in Estonian with the receiver tucked under his ear, wiping glasses. The guy's pretty cool, I thought. And in some ways I felt I had not done too badly myself.

Someone had scribbled on the wall – perhaps the interior designer – *Qui êtes-vous? Personne. Moi non plus*. A line from one of the poets etched into the chairs, perhaps. I momentarily played with the idea of being in a film, a French film – acting as a barfly in one of those intense, brooding French efforts in which nothing much happens except that it's all about desire. I'd wanted to go out in the evenings after my restaurant meals, to hit the clubs, but instead I'd walked myself around each night to exhaustion. It wasn't easy going into a place on your own, unless you were out to clock someone. There'd been a club that was all white, like an operating theatre, with acres of white leather to sit on and empty but for two black guys in the middle, drinking cocktails the colour of diluted blood. It was a new sensation, after England, wandering around a city on a Friday night without the fear of getting beaten to a pulp.

The barman dropped a couple of paper sugar-twists in front of me.

'I forgets that. Pardon me. You can't really on me.'

'Eh?'

'You can't *really* on me,' the barman insisted, as if my English was poor.

I nodded as if my ears had just cleared. 'Who can rely on anyone? Thanks.'

In fact, I'd finished my coffee. The Isolée track was beginning to swamp my mind. The words and groans were remixed to snap in two and reappear – highly sexual. It was meant to be taken with drugs.

'That's good,' said the barman. 'Sugar bad.'

'Yeah, I guess so. No, it is. Welcome to Europe,' I added, half ironically.

'Huh?'

'It's good to see your country in free Europe. One day you'll be part of the European Union.'

'We wait to see,' said the barman, sucking on a tooth as he wiped the zinc. He was about twenty-six coming on seven hundred. He was wiser than wise, because he had the history of Estonia at his back. All his childhood under the shadow.

'*I* say that to *you*,' said the barman, suddenly, pointing a finger at me. 'Welcome to free Europe! You know?'

'I like that,' I grinned, a little ashamed. 'That's true. Yeah.'

I generally notice posters the day *after* the performance it is advertising. This one on the newsagent's, which I had passed all week, was caught just in time: a concert performance that evening of Handel's opera *Acis and Galatea*. Rarely performed, though a number-one hit in Handel's time. I guessed the group was amateur, which is sometimes an advantage.

The concert was to be held in the big white church a couple of minutes' walk away, in an area that had been bombed stupid in the war: the rubble and the foundations of houses had been left ever since, surrounded by a flimsy fence, were now an example of Soviet wickedness. Grass and weeds grew thick in ground plans of lost homes. The church, called St Nicholas, had been restored, playing host to exhibitions and concerts: I wasn't sure whether or not it was deconsecrated.

I arrived later than I'd meant to and was forced to sit at the front – the only row with free places. Some of the performers were still milling about, fiddling with their instruments or chatting. Apart from the flutes, the instruments were modern. A soprano was testing her high notes beyond the back screen. Definitely amateur, but not cruelly so.

And then a man with a grey ponytail – amazingly like the customer on the café terrace nearly a week ago – arrived out of breath, carrying what looked like a theorbo case. Five minutes to go, but a theorbo could take at least ten minutes to tune up. Red in the face from running, he sat immediately opposite me, setting the huge and ridiculous instrument between his knees, tightening the strings on the long neck. It *was* the customer on the terrace. This reminder embarrassed me. My behaviour had been adolescent. Pre-adolescent, even. Since my failed attempt to retrieve the book (and to see the girl again) three days back, I had grown up. I was determined to take a hold on myself from now on.

Acis and Galatea might have been put on especially for me, as it happened: all about hopeless love. The photocopied programme had the English libretto, with a part of the Estonian introduction helpfully translated:

The nymph Galatea, daughter of Nerea, is loved of
Polyphemus, a Cyclops of monstrous body. But Galatea
loves the young shepherd Acis, son of God Pan. One
day, while Galatea was reposing to the edge of the sea on
Acis breasts, Polyphemus surprised these and, in an access
of fury, killed Acis in crushing him under a enormous
rocks. Galatea, using some magic powers, immortalised
her defunct lover in a fountain stream unfinishing.

Everyone retired and there was an expectant pause.

A man in a blue suit and cravat, with hair like Beethoven's, emerged from behind the screens. The only words I recognised in his speech were names: *Handel*, *Acis*, *Polyphemus*, *Galatea*, *Ovid* and *KP Peanut Butter* – although the last must have been a phonetic coincidence. The man bowed to a discreet clapping which went on longer than it would have done in England but not as long as it would have done in Germany. When the performers emerged, the clapping picked up from near extinction in an exaggerated crescendo that suggested the presence of friends and family.

But I was not clapping. My hands were frozen in the act, as if I was holding a ball; my mouth was open and sweat had broken out on my upper lip. Right next to the theorbo player, directly in front, a mere six feet away knee to knee, settling in her chair with her violin, was the waitress from the Café Majolica.

In the end, it was the theorbo player's fault. Up to that point, my eyes and her eyes hadn't met. I'd kept mine mostly fixed on the other players and on the singers at the back – a good dozen of each. When my gaze did wander onto her face, she was concentrating on the score in front of her. The notes were fairly straightforward, had perhaps been rendered down to something simple enough for her level, which I judged as a competent Grade 6. The violin players were named on the programme as Kaja and Riina. She had to be one or the other. She looked more like a Riina, somehow. Kaja made me think of a cage. She was wearing a black dress with floppy cuffs. It reminded me, unfortunately, of a witch's gown.

Emotion flickered and passed over her face as if she was missing a layer. It made me think of rain on water, rippling and spotting and dimpling. Anxiety, pleasure, shyness: nothing escaped the surface of her face. She sat slightly hunched, the spotlights – only softened by one or two yellow filters – polishing her high cheekbones, which again made me think of something I couldn't quite place, although a sighing or sort of soughing noise came into my head – a very pleasant and faraway sound under the Handel.

Her violin was a tad tatty, like a school instrument. No sign of recognition. Why should there be? She must serve hundreds of customers every day. I felt about fourteen. No, I felt old. About thirty-seven.

I studied her fellow musicians, to distract myself. The cellist was a Hoffnung figure, very tall and thin and chinless with a quiff of bushy hair, his jacket too big for his shoulders. One of the viola players went pop-eyed whenever she played, looking incredibly like Kenneth Williams. The theorbo player jerked his head in time to the beat, the neck of the instrument like a ship's long prow in a swell, moving up and down, up and down, over the waitress's head. The harpsichordist kept chewing his lips with anxiety. The singers were good, for amateurs, and of all shapes and sizes. The tenor playing the lover Acis was short and tubby, while the bass playing Polyphemus was tall and blond. He had rubbery lips; the passage that begins '*I rage – I melt – I burn! The feeble god has stabb'd me to the heart!*' was accompanied by a fine spray caught by the lights. Galatea was toothy and fairly plump, but her voice was like a treble's.

Until then, I'd never realised how like a woman's back a violin is: the light was playing off the soft muscular curves of the varnished alder wood, sliding past its wasp waist in lozenges of white. I have no idea why violin-makers favour alder wood: one told me, once, how they're wet-loving trees, and how he always thought of the curve of oxbows or the current's soft bulge and swell when he was turning the wood. All I could think of now was the subtle camber of bare flesh.

The choir sounded a little barbershop at times, and the English pronunciation was haywire, but the music was swirling me into an even giddier state. Everything was golden, beautiful, shifting with the shadows and shapes of the pre-industrial world. Why wasn't the girl noticing me? Passion had not altered an inch since 1718. Or since the Golden Age, when Mount Etna harboured the Cyclops.

> *Whither, fairest, are thou running,*
> *Still my warm embraces shunning?*

She was, I reckoned, in her early twenties. I hoped she wasn't a teenager. It suddenly occurred to me that I wasn't Acis, but the Cyclops. She was still avoiding the audience, avoiding me with her eyes. I saw they were coloured a very deep green. No, blue. Or even grey. Could she have turquoise eyes? She wasn't a waitress any more, she was a violinist, an amateur violinist. As if that was more legitimate.

> *O! didst thou know the pains of absent love,*
> *Acis would ne'er from Galatea rove.*

I felt this weird anxiety, which I recognised as adrenalin pumping right down to my feet and back to where it was busy crumpling my heart like it was about to go into the waste-paper basket. Everyone must be gazing on her in the rows behind me – two hundred or so people, maybe more, gazing on her in wonder. Or was I the only one? I envied the men in the group, the conductor, the theorbo player whose instrument's neck was still pitching in a deep swell just three or four inches over her head.

The theorbo player was, in fact, plucking his solo. Deep in concentration, his grey ponytail bouncing behind him, he failed to realise that his ship's long prow had descended an inch or two and was rocking about even closer to the girl's head. Dangerously close. It might knock her out.

Aware of it, she looked above her with only her eyes, hunching a little lower but still in danger of being struck, the corner of her mouth playfully tucked in with that ghost or beginning of a smile I remembered from the café.

I was smiling too, and she must have noticed because it was

at this point that she looked straight at me and we clocked each other.

Her eyes went away and came back as if from a long voyage and I smiled some more, and so did she, and we were sharing this joke about the theorbo's neck nearly braining her. We shared it as if we had known each other for years. My face flushed and then – miracle! – so did hers (a coppery red, she went) and her eyes swept off and away from mine. And then the theorbo player, his solo not yet finished, spotted the danger at a glance and the prow rose up as if on a big wave, well clear of her head, as he was pressing and plucking the strings.

Oh, I felt very good. But I couldn't bear to meet her eyes again for fear of burning up. Damon sang rather warblingly of love leading to problems all your life, and sure enough Acis was crushed, Acis was no more, and in the quietness of that lovely passage before the last act, you could hear the scrape of the bow hair on the strings.

And all she retrieves of Acis is his soul.

She didn't look at me again. After the concert she was next to a young, intense type with an afterthought of a goatee beard. I was hanging about alone among the remnants of the audience, and became convinced she was complaining about me – about the man in the front row who'd kept giving her the eye.

Nevertheless, she glanced at me and I nodded. I went up to her as if on rails.

'Great concert,' I said. 'Nice violin playing.'

'Yeah? My violin is real shit. Real cheap. From a school.'

I gabbled on, despite the shock of hearing her talk like someone at the end of the twentieth century: 'Well, I know this professional viola player in England who has a few decent violins for sale, extremely good value. He's friendly and you can trust him. Earls Court,' I added, pointlessly.

'OK,' she said, as if faintly amused. The goatee beard was studying me with apparent distaste. Of course she wouldn't be able to afford a proper violin. The whole thing sounded like an opening gambit.

I scribbled Howard's name and number on the edge of the programme and gave it to her, nevertheless. She took it with a shy chuckle that swamped my heart.

'You didn't find my book,' I said, swallowing in the middle by mistake. '*Anna Karenina?*'

She frowned at me, clearly lost. She had not a notion who I was. Two people in long scarves came up and she turned and greeted them with wild affection in Estonian.

I slipped away, feeling idiotic and foreign, and ate Chinese on my own by a tank full of mournful goldfish.

'Get a hold of yourself. This is not a film. This is real life. You only have one real life.'

The goldfish pouted at me through the glass, the waterweed swayed, a plastic shark snarled, all red mouth and white teeth as the tank gurgled and hummed. Gurgled and hummed and sighed.

I'd studied her glossy cheekbones and heard the Sounds, that was the trouble.

I had listened to the Sounds as a little boy, in Hayes, in Middlesex, circa 1966. I was playing on my parents' handker-chief of grass they'd call a garden, with its plastic chairs and ornamental shrubs, framed by washed gravel the cat stubbornly reckoned was its litter. The Sounds had come into my head. They were not the rasps of the neighbour's hand lawnmower, or the twitters of my mother's transistor radio, or the moans of the jets from Heathrow low overhead, or the big words of the big kids swearing at each other as they swerved up and down the estate on their big bikes, but came from far away, so very far away that the little kid that was me looked up into the clouds and marvelled.

The clouds rolled their piled whiteness over Hayes – over Dunstan's the greengrocer's, over Dagley's hardware store, over Hepworth's the tailor's and the humming, gurgling factories – and

34

I was hearing them. But I was stuck on that lawn, stuck to that spanking new, exemplary council estate with its thousand eyes called Ashley Park.

It was the clouds that had made the Sounds, of course. At a very private frequency. Nothing to do with a girl's cheek-bones.

Later, after I'd learned how to read music (in just a few weeks, but I was a dud at most other school subjects), I'd hear other sounds. At the end of the road that led to Ashley Park Estate, there was an old-fashioned set of telephone wires and when birds alighted on them – starlings, for instance – I'd read their little black bodies as scribbled notes, as music. And it kept changing. That was the origin of 'Not For Brass Birds' (1972), probably my favourite work, written when I was about ten.

I moped for a few days. I couldn't put my wedding ring back on my finger: something to do with the formation of the knuckle. I tried for ages to work it over the bone, just as I worked over the piece, slowly and methodically getting nowhere.

I took a couple of short trips out of the city centre – one to the zoo, the other to the massive open oyster of the Song Festival Grounds where the Singing Revolution had started. The Singing Revolution! The regime was mined by songs, and then they were blown. Hundreds and thousands of people, simultaneously singing. Boom.

The trolleybus was exciting. I thought of gritty northern cities in England a hundred years ago as it swayed and clattered past the grim blocks of the suburbs. I didn't have a ticket, because I couldn't work out how to buy one. I'd read that everyone has to speak a certain number of words each day or go mad. Now I realised why I was talking to myself. I was fulfilling my quota.

Zoos always give me the feeling that humankind is a really bad mistake. I wandered past weird-named animals I'd never heard of, that no one celebrates, ranged as if on a shelf in an

All-Must-Go sale. Standing in front of the snow leopard's cage (I didn't think any zoos had snow leopards, but there it was, very large behind a clump of withered bamboo), I imagined kissing her throat, on this very spot. Kissing her soft pale throat, on our day out.

A young couple were having a full-blown snog in front of the spotted hyenas a couple of cages down. I felt unsteady in the knees; no doubt the old Cyclops had felt just the same on the slopes of Etna. The snow leopard rose and padded up to the front. The icy wastes of drift and gneiss and mountain plain were gone, and its eyes looked as if they couldn't focus so close. Rats were tugging at a hunk of fresh meat at the back of the cage. I would test myself by going again to the café. They weren't tugging, they were eating. As I watched, the rats tore off and ate half the snow leopard's lunch. The sharp, urine-filled pong of the cage was saying: life is so futile it's almost funny.

You can't cheat the fact that things have gone very wrong in the world. But at the same time it's this very fact that you can stand above it all and say that things have gone very wrong which brings consolation; I picture it as a polyphonic chant streaked with white lightning.

I bought Milly a postcard of an armadillo, even though the cage had been empty, and wrote her a silly-billy message in the zoo's café.

The trolleybus grew packed on the way back. There was a father in – yes – a leather jacket, holding two little girls by the hand. They had thick, very fair hair. One of the girls was clutching a floppy dog, the other was old enough to do without anything but her father's hand. The future of Estonia, of the world! I was standing close enough to smell the drink off the man's skin. He had that slightly swollen, bruised look of the real boozer, but he was still young enough – about my age – not to look ugly with it. He was very attentive to his daughters, and they were full of the zoo (or so I guessed).

They never stopped chattering during the half-hour it took

36

for the trolleybus to sway its way back on its thick, childish tyres, and the father was nodding at their every word. They'd gone way past their daily quota.

I had tried to buy a ticket off the driver through a small window between the driver's cabin and the carriage, but the driver was negotiating the six-lane boulevards and their heavy traffic, the options limited by the leash of the cable. I had to keep my equilibrium while my ears were pressed against the glass to hear what the driver – in this case, a woman with hula-hoop copper earrings – was shouting at me over her shoulder, then scrabble for change in the voluminous currency. It was designed to be difficult – maybe by the Soviets.

Maybe my own music is designed to be difficult, too. Maybe all contemporary music of any worth entails keeping your balance while pressing your ear against the glass, picking up signals in another language.

I had given up my seat to a tough old bird with a checked scarf tied around her face, who had not smiled as she sat, even when I'd looked her straight in the eye and grinned. What was there to smile about? Life and history had kicked it out of her, whatever it was. The younger kid was staring up at me, her floppy dog at her mouth.

This could be my life, I thought. To be thrown back on one's own resources. Poor as a church mouse. I would have to compose to eat. I would be risen again.

That is, if I left Milly.

I winked at the kid, gave her a big smile. Her eyes widened, but she didn't smile back. When the trolleybus swayed violently, she found my leg instead of the rail. She held onto my trousers for a few minutes, until she realised. The little hand of love. The tiny pressure. It must be amazing to be her father, I thought.

Their real, boozer father would have other things on his mind, however: how to earn enough money to take his daughters to the zoo, for instance. How to afford his drinking. And where was the mum? I was sure, I didn't know why, that the wife was out of the picture. I felt compassion warm me through, looking at these people in the trolleybus. I'd never felt this on public transport in London.

There was still time to remake my life.

I bought a box of cigarillos and a tourist lighter from a kiosk by a tram stop and sat by the narrow lake in Toompark, in the shadow of the castle. The lighter had *Tallinn, City of Delights* on one side and Tallinn's coat of arms on the other. I smoked three cigarillos, one after the other, hunched in my coat on the bench. Although the wind had dropped and there was a milky sun, the autumn chill remained. The leaves dropped steadily, as if hidden elves were releasing them. I reckoned the grey-barked trees I wasn't sure of at first were aspens. Very faintly came the sound of drumming, perhaps from the group of what my father would have called 'druggies' at the other end of the park, near the kiosk and the tram stop. They wore singlets and looked haggard in their spiky goth gear, as if abandoned by their mates fifteen, twenty years ago – except that they were young, maybe even teenagers. I was slightly afraid of them, that they might follow me; I was entirely alone in the park.

Milly hated me smoking, so I'd given up a few days after we were together. Now I was smoking again. I felt good, sitting in my coat alone and smoking, surrounded by golden leaves in a park in Estonia. In some ways I'd have preferred to have been here before the Wall came down, when it was still difficult and dangerous and the West was far away. To have met composers clandestinely, in grubby cellars or in their parents' attics; KGB aerials on the tops of spires, the invisible reel-to-reels turning and turning. The bricked-up windows of torture cells. Arvo Pärt having to change the name of *Sarah was Ninety Years Old* to *Modus*, because of the anti-religious regulations. Russian soldiers instead of Finnish drunks: the whole country turned into Aldershot crossed with Watford – without the shops.

I sucked on my third cigarillo and watched a duck dip its head again and again, shaking it dry each time, ignorant of the change of regimes, of the cruelty of men. One was master of one's own destiny. I ran another little film through my head, like a trailer. I order a coffee, I remark on her English, we get chatting. Then what? Invite her for a drink? A meal? Talk music? Violins? Tell her all about Handel?

I shook my head clear of it all. This type of fantasy had to be a way of keeping going.

This particular fantasy would nourish my work. I'd keep my life stable and smooth, loving Milly and however many children we were destined to have. I picked a shred of tobacco off my tongue. I felt good. Well, better.

Jesus, we *had* to have children. I was playing with my knob through my pocket, without meaning to. I'd go back from here brimming with spunk. It was all psychology and not being anxious. We'd romp home.

On the way back to my apartment, I smelt burning. The air was misted where the sun fell between the buildings. I felt it in my throat, overriding the tobacco-burn, nastily chemical.

I turned the corner and there, in the middle of the street, stood a large filing cabinet. It was on fire. It was pouring out thick, brown smoke from its half-open drawers. The top half of the cabinet was already burned black and charred files dangled from the drawers or lay scattered on the cobbles. A man was spraying water at it through a shower-head on the end of a tube that snaked back through a window into a small office. He was chatting to interested passers-by, who seemed unaffected by the smoke, as if this happened every day.

It was a mystery, but I didn't feel like asking questions: my throat was already vulnerable from the cigarillos and the nip in the air.

So I chose a different route back.

I swung wide up Rataskaevu and then decided to stretch my legs further to clean out my lungs. I found myself taking a narrow alley I didn't know, by the eastern side of the old wall. It twisted a little, smelling of cats, and finally emerged into a cobbled street that looked strange for a few moments until I saw the sign that said *Café Majolica*. Then the street's elements fell into familiarity like the crystals in my toy kaleidoscope.

This did not hold together. I'd wanted to avoid this. I'd thought I was higher up, nearer St Olav's Church. I did not have the Knowledge for this city. In fact, the old centre of Tallinn was very small, and it was shrinking further as I became familiar with it.

My heart thumped in my ears, but not from the exercise. I knew, somehow, as I pushed the café's loose handle down (it was a nicely old-fashioned French-style door), that I was doing the wrong thing, taking the wrong turn. But it excited me too because at some level it was a recognition that I was freer than I'd ever realised.

Not that I'd ever thought I *wasn't* free. Being married hadn't changed much, in that sense, even though I'd tied the knot in one of the oldest churches in England, with a Saxon nave and a Roman yew in the graveyard. The wedding, being a du Crane wedding, was – what's the word – *embalmed* in wealth: there were five hundred guests, among them the cream of the music world, the cream of the English landed gentry, and the cream of the City. One man there, pointed out to me by the bride's mother (dear old Marjorie), had broken through the £3-million-a-year barrier, minus bonus. He looked very happy on it in his morning suit.

'His nose is ill-judged,' said Marjorie, already woozy.

My parents seemed to crouch through the whole thing, dazzled and dismayed at the sound of their own voices. Then my mum got sozzled and started to enjoy herself, much to the embarrassment of the groom; because my mum was blind (really blind, not blind drunk), I had to make sure she was chaperoned, especially around the ponds.

If it had been sunny, the day would have outshone any previous known wedding ever (in everyone's opinion), but it was a sultry, wall-to-wall grey under a blank sky; this kept a lid on things, filling the air with little flies that got into everything, including the guests. The grounds, with their sweeping lawns and copper beeches leading up to the grey-stoned Hall itself, made everyone look like spivs. The rain held off, at least – although one hysterical woman in a hat like a flying saucer was sure she felt a big drop on her cheek on emerging from the main marquee, and the sky was scanned by everyone nearby.

'Junkers 88 at five o'clock!' someone shouted. It was not me.

Because the lawns sloped, several pot-bellied invitees fell over and actually rolled, although they picked themselves up and laughed each time. I saw this myself. I was not drunk.

To my surprise, only one of the five hundred died that day: this was a twenty-year-old relative who followed the wedding in Hampshire with a night's clubbing in London and suffocated on his own vomit at dawn halfway up Primrose Hill.

As Marjorie, my fun-loving bibber of a new mother-in-law, commented afterwards: 'He was a very *distant* cousin, thank God.'

She was standing this side of the bar, talking to an elderly guy with a crooked back. My face turned into a steamed flannel, although my reflection in the mirror hardly showed it.

She hadn't noticed me. Her hair was controlled at the crown by a pink elastic band, and looked from the side like an upside-down poplar in autumn, swaying slightly as she talked.

I made for the same table in the window. Same music, same table, different light, different chair: *Rimbaud*. That felt good. And now I knew she played violin and was called either Riina or Kaja.

'Hi there.'

'Hi!' I said. I was nodding already. 'Hey, really, that was great violin.'

She looked at me more carefully, as if focusing. Recognition flickered. Customers are blurred faces giving orders in the machine of the day.

'Thanks,' she said. 'You don't know much, then.'

'Why?'

'I'm playing *really* badly the violin.'

'Then? Or generally?'

'Eh?'

'It was a great concert,' I repeated, lamely.

She was frowning at me, as if trying to work me out. 'Coffee?'

I nodded. 'Yeah. Same again.'

She looked blank.

'A latte,' I said, embarrassed.

She went away, leaving me confused, all my crazy feelings pooped. It didn't take much, did it? Inevitably, my mind cast back to the first time I met Milly, noting the contrast.

It was outside the Purcell Room, during the interval of a contemporary music concert featuring a piece by me called 'Concourse 2'. This girl was sitting behind a table with a splat of programmes in front of her. She had the nicest smile I had ever seen, and a long, springlike curl of dark hair in front of each ear. She was glamorous. I can appreciate glamour in others. I was not glamorous: I'm not tall and I've never carried off smart clothes and my hair is untidy but not interestingly so: there has always been something unfinished about me. Milly was finished, in the sense that a fine violin is finished when – and only when – the last coat of varnish has been applied. She had been born like that, with all the coats of varnish already applied. When our bodies rubbed together, the varnish lay between them, and this excited me even more.

The waitress called either Kaja or Riina brought my coffee. 'You don't want cake? Or a savoury snack? Herring with rye bread? Beef-and-onion roll?'

'OK, yeah, a cake,' I said. 'Sounds good.'

She took a menu off the neighbouring table.

I said I didn't mind which cake. 'Whatever's your favourite.'

'I like them all.'

'You can choose, then.'

She sighed, as if this was a real pain.

'Curd cake OK? With whipped cream? Or almond and bilberry cheesecake?'

'Either sounds brilliant. Especially if it's traditional Estonian. I like everything in Estonia, so far.'

She nodded, retrieving my bill from under the saucer and scribbling on it. I felt annihilated in some way. She must be used to this: older foreign blokes trying to pick her up. Her counter-strategy was impeccable.

When she returned with the curd cake topped by a heap of cream like washing, I had decided to drop the whole game.

'Looks good, thanks,' I said, hoping I sounded indifferent enough.

'It *is* good,' she said. 'Do you want your book?'

'My book?'

'You left your book. That's why you came back.'

'But they couldn't find it.'

'That's because I'd took it home.'

'Oh,' I said, waving my hand to cover my embarrassment, 'you can keep it.'

'I took it home to try mending. A lot of pages fell out.'

'To mend it?'

'Glue. My boyfriend has good glue. He's a sculptor.'

I smiled appreciatively as I fell down a trapdoor set in my own heart. She had a bloke, and he was interesting, probably with huge shoulders in a sweaty singlet, hacking at granite. Or maybe even the one with the failed goatee.

'He's good?'

'I dunno,' she shrugged. 'What's good? He's pretty good, I guess. You better eat the cake before me.'

I chuckled and said yes, I'd better, wondering if I should add: *I'd rather eat you first*. No, it was never a good idea to mock a foreigner's English, they never understood the joke. I didn't want to eat the cake in front of her, though – it was an object that would be difficult to tackle without making a mess. I asked, as my spoon sank in through the cream on the thinner edge of the wedge, 'What does he sculpt?'

'Sharks,' she sighed. 'He makes sharks out of marbles.'

'Marbles? Or marble?'

'Marble, OK. Only sharks. He . . . ah, you know, with a stone . . .'

'Polishes? Pumice stone?'

'No, rough to touch, on a little wheel . . .'

'Grinds . . .'

'Yeah, he *grinds* them, polishes them so they shine like crazy and they're beautiful but he's really miserable in doing this, he's just all lonesome in his studio and he sees not one point. In anything at all. Sharks, or anything. Very black.'

'Maybe he should change from sharks,' I suggested, cheering up.

In fact, I was enjoying this conversation very much, perhaps more than any conversation I'd ever had in my life. Someone had come in and was consulting the menu. The barman called out in Estonian. She coolly raised her hand. She was evidently tired of being a waitress. Or liked talking to this customer too much. Practising her English.

'That's what I told him. It's not sharks, the problem. He's took years to get the sharks perfect, anyway. He is just a normal depressant.'

'But he has good glue.'

'Yeah, I mended your book. I knew you left it to mean to.'

'Eh?'

The barman was serving the new customer, darting fierce looks in our direction.

'He's really lazy, this guy,' she said, under her breath.

'Are you Riina or Kaja?'

She paused, surprised by the question. Then she smiled and told me. I'd pronounced her name wrong: my version rhymed with raja, as in Indian prince; hers with Gaia, or all but. It disconcerted me, made me think of a cayak. 'Riina plays better violin,' she added.

'You Estonian, in fact?'

'Yeah, I'm from Haaremaa,' she said. 'You know Haaremaa?'

'Er, no.'

She folded her arms and looked through the window. The sun made the cobbles look like gingerbread buns.

'It's an island. You have to be going there.' She turned back to look at me.

Yes, I knew I was going to be going there, if that's what she'd meant. As I knew when I first saw Milly that she was to be my wife. Within five seconds I had known that.

'If it's worth going to,' I said.

'It's really neat,' Kaja as in Gaia assured me. She had learned her English, it seemed, from an American. 'A Soviet military's zone until 1994, you know? Closed off. Forbidden. It was forbidden to leave, for us, without a visa stamp.'

She pulled out a cigarette from her back pocket and placed it between her lips as a film actress would, enhancing the pout. I was both pleased and disappointed that she smoked. I felt I'd been chatting to her for years. Her T-shirt had the words *Planet Earth Closed For Restoration* switchbacking over her chest. My eyes kept automatically returning to read the slogan, I couldn't help it. It was Milly's kind of slogan, that was the trouble. Kaja was looking for a light, tapping her pockets, making the words on her chest swell and squash up: *Pln Eart Closd For Restratn*. I pulled out the souvenir lighter I'd bought that morning and thumbed it to life.

'Hoor?' I smiled. 'Hoor?'

'Eh?'

'Ho-or?' I repeated, with more care, making it rhyme with a Geordie 'poor'. I was smiling knowingly at her – an attempt at self-denigration, conscious (against the glistening wall of her Americanised English) of the absurdity of my pathetic attempt to speak her language. She was staring at me, open-mouthed, the cigarette in her hand. Then I saw the other hand coming down on my face in slow motion. It was only slow motion on a subjective level. The shock of the impact, which seemed to disintegrate in the marrow of my jaw, was mingled with the strange notion that this was a playful joke, even though the joke had propelled me half out of my chair, sending my coffee spinning away and onto the floor, along with the curd cake. The cup smashed against the metal leg of the neighbouring table and the cake splurged whitely on the floorboards.

I was dimly aware of a silence beyond the ringing in my ears and my pounding heart as I righted myself, nursing my cheek. The barman started on at Kaja, who had apparently run into the kitchen. Words, very loud and curt words, in Estonian. Kaja shouting back. I felt sick, suddenly, beyond the shock. I eased myself out of the chair, making for the door as best I could on legs moulded from blancmange. My nose was dripping blood: I saw it literally plopping onto the back of my hand. A girl in dungarees had sprayed me twenty years ago with a soda syphon in a student bar in Durham for speaking 'posh' (despite my council upringing), but she was a middle-class SWP member. It was explicable. This was not. Unless the girl called Kaja was mentally disturbed.

All eyes were on me: I could see this without looking. I was still holding the lighter. I hadn't paid for the coffee and the cake. I was not about to. The barman was at the door, opening it for me.

'We are not have sex business here,' the barman muttered.

'Eh?'

'You wan some hot, you go to sauna twenty-four-hour,' he said, in the same low growl.

'Ah jus offered her a lighd,' I pointed out.

'Huh?'

'Jus offered to lighd her cigaredde. Hodest.'

'You a good guy?' said the barman, with a sardonic twist to his mouth.

I sniffed and the blood tasted oddly blank. 'I'm a travel-guide writer, checking out where to go,' I improvised, equally sardonically. 'For several newspapers with huge circulations in the UK. And a very big glossy book.'

The door was open. The cool air rushed in and gave me a headache. I moved my jaw wide. It wasn't broken, although my cheek felt fractured. I'd never been hit in the face in my life, even by a bloke. A cricket ball, a football, a teddy bear whose glass eye had caught me on the nose, but never the hand of man or woman. We were out in the street, now. The door swung shut behind us, along with the furtive stares of the other customers. I dabbed my nose with a tissue. I wanted to go back to London.

'We get a lotta shit, sorry,' said the barman, out of the corner of his mouth; he was lighting his own cigarette now, shielding the match expertly. 'Shit people. Every girl a hoor. Every girl *not* hoor, in Estonia. More educationed than you. Don't put in your book this thing. My name, Andres.'

He flicked the match away and held his hand out, but I didn't shake it because a very large penny had dropped from a great height into the cavernous and stony spaces of my mind, and the echo was still going. My whole face was burning: a great rush of blood to join the shifting aches and pains.

'Oh Jesus,' I said. 'I don't believe it. My mind is bollocks. I thought *hoor* meant this.'

I thumbed the lighter in my hand. The breeze blew the flame out. 'It was the taxi driver. Olev. I make a very big mis-take,' I went on, adopting an Estonian accent for purposes of clarity. 'Error. Like computer error. You know? Stupid jerk, me.'

Andres at last let his hand drop and frowned, the studs in his nose winking in the pale sun. A real praying mantis, his nose was. He probably wasn't very bright, despite his hip look. He'd even believed the travel-guide thing. My teeth ached. I was gesticulating as I explained. I couldn't believe that I hadn't heard the other familiar word behind the Estonian word. Something to do with mental recognition: it's quite normal, apparently.

Then Andres started to grin. 'OK,' he said, 'I unnerstan', yeah. *Tulemasin*. Not *hoor*, shit no! You know what *hoor* mean?'

His *hoor* sounded like something whooshing up into the sky, or something getting caught in a fan. It had lost all semblance of being a word. It was all like a joke going on too long.

'I do now,' I said. 'Same word in English.'

Andres shook his box of matches. '*Tuletikk*.' Then he pointed to my lighter. '*Tulemasin*.'

I repeated the words. 'Yeah, I'll remember that. Thank you.'

'Estonian girl, they hit hard. Only Lithuania girl they hit more harder.'

'I definitely wouldn't like to be hit by a Lithuanian girl, in that case,' I said, mournfully – and the barman burst out laughing and put his arm round me. I laughed, too.

I felt better, standing there in the street with Andres; we were like two old mates, laughing away as passers-by glanced at us nervously and moved on.

'You know, she great with sport,' said Andres, sucking on his cigarette. He'd offered me one but I'd refused, pointing to my jaw. 'Gymnastic. Champion gymnastic.'

'Really?'

'Yah. Why she so tough, you know? Bam!'

Andres laughed, his scalp corrugating under his shaven head.

'If only I'd known,' I said. 'Wow. A champion gymnast.'

The door opened behind us but it was only a customer – a lean-looking, wind-burned guy in his twenties with thin wrists and neck and a sophisticated yellow cagoule with zip pockets all over it. He came up to the barman and said, 'Excuse me, mate, I need to pay. There's no one serving. I had a Coke and a beef-and-onion bap thing.' He was Australian, or maybe New Zealand. A cyclist, I guessed. Crossing Europe from Spain to Siberia and back.

The barman said, 'For free,' glancing at me, and took a deep drag on his cigarette. 'OK? I don' care.'

'OK, mate, that's fine by me,' said the Australian, disappointingly. He turned to me and said, 'Well, I'd better not go looking for tricks in Estonia, then.'

'Mind your own frigging business,' I muttered, looking away.

'Don't care a bloody toss,' said the cyclist. 'Actually.'

He went off on springy legs, leaving me feeling very unpleasant. My eye was watering. I wondered if you could have your eyeball dislodged slightly. My arm was being squeezed. The drill started whining from the building opposite.

'Hey,' said Andres, 'I tells her now, you know? What you say at me. Next time, knife in the heart. Yow. Nobody coming, after that. In your book, finished.'

'Unless they like blood sports.' In fact, my nose had run out of blood.

Andres squeezed my arm again and told me to take a seat, indicating the terrace. 'Please.'

He disappeared back into the café while I settled myself at the same table as the theorbo player had sat at a few days before. It wasn't too chilly out here, now. I felt my cheek, which was stiff but less painful. It was no more than the impact of a football, I told myself. But I was in really deep yogurt. I wanted to run off, run away up the pretty little cobbled street. She'd been a champion gymnast, so she was competitive and aggressive. Hit first, ask questions later. Now I was going to have to apologise, I knew it, and this irritated me. I didn't want to face her. And the barman had believed me about the travel-guide thing. Humour didn't travel, not when it was all in the tone. The drill had stopped.

When she came out with Andres, I saw she was carrying a book. It was the tatty copy of *Anna Karenina*. She had an open denim jacket over the T-shirt. Andres was guiding her by the elbow.

I stood up. 'He's explained?'

She nodded. She looked either deeply ashamed or deeply resentful, I couldn't quite make out which.

'Look, I don't blame you, I'm really, really sorry,' I began, charitably. 'A complete misunderstanding, stupid mistake on my part, language problem. Oh, thank you.'

I took the book from her. No thirty-page segment dropped out, or even protruded slightly. No notes, either. This would go down in our history, I thought; the two of us.

'Wow, it's mended,' I went on, my face in sudden agony. 'Don't worry about my cheek. It's fine. I've got hit by loads of iron weights in my life. No problem.'

Andres turned to Kaja and said, 'OK? A few minute. Be

friend.' Then he whispered something fierce – something no doubt about my travel guide – and went back inside like a headmaster leaving his charges. The said charges sat down opposite each other in silence and studied the table's rusted ironwork.

'I guess I'm not very good at Estonian,' I said, the pain settling to a nauseous ache. A whole toffee apple was stuck inside my cheek, and I had a cucumber for a right-hand jaw.

She was looking at me straight in the eyes, now, her mouth tucked in at the corner – but not in that smiling way. She hadn't yet said anything, I realised. She was judging me, maybe, judging whether I was just another visiting liar. Her eyes were the colour of the bay at twilight.

Then, miraculously, the pucker at the corner of her mouth spread its smile over the rest of her face, settling brilliantly in her eyes. My own glanced away under the strain of the intimacy, and then returned. Hers hadn't flinched, meanwhile. It was as if she was considering something right at the back of my mind.

'Well,' she said, 'I better get starting to teach you, I guess.'

One evolves. One resolves problems by taking this route or that route, each minuscule decision building like cells into a different creature.

My decision was to let this thing roll.

I knew very early on where it was going to end. But I let it roll. I was scared, in a way, my chest full of silky little wings trapped in a cage, so I took the position of least resistance.

Kaja was like no one I had ever met before. Admittedly, I'd had a sheltered life, from Hayes on – spent entirely in the portable geodesic dome of music. But still.

She had been brought up in almost total isolation from the rest of the world on a strategic island where the main business was tending rockets that could end the world. Otherwise it was farming, she explained, mostly of the collective type or on home allotments. Her father was a builder, then a supervisor in an office with responsibility for building materials. Until independence, he was one of the state's tiny, bureaucratic cogs. Now he was nothing; free, but with nothing.

'Do you know what it's like to have nothing?'

'Um, no, not really.'

'Are you married?' she asked. 'Kids?'

I still wonder at how coolly I lied, then, shaking my head, this bulky lock of hair that passed for a fringe slipping over my eyebrows. I pushed it back. I might have been answering the kids part of the question, not the marriage part. I was glad I had been unable to put my ring back on, although its trace still showed.

'I better go do my job,' she said. 'Andres is pretty angry with me from beating you up.'

'So was I.'

She laughed, for the first time. The tarp on the other side of the street billowed out in a gust and cracked back: the restorer's sign shivered – the gold-starred, blue EU badge in the corner making it look like a giant stamped letter. The building next door was caked with a furry pelt of Soviet-provided dirt.

She put her hand on *Anna Karenina* to stop the gust lifting the cover.

'How are you liking Karenin, the poor husband?'

I'd never got beyond thirty-odd pages on my previous attempts, so I shrugged. 'Pretty annoying,' I guessed.

She frowned. 'And Vronsky?'

'You've read it, then?' I ventured, battling to remember who precisely Vronsky was. A student? I knew I would come a cropper one day from not reading the world's best novel. From not really reading many novels at all.

But I do have perfect pitch.

She nodded. 'Three times, I've read it.'

'Three!'

'You?'

'Just once, when I was eighteen.' Nothing I was saying, I realised, was true. It was easy once you started. Travel-guide writer, Tolstoy reader, bachelor. 'I need to read it again, which is why I brought it along.'

'Vronsky is like a shark. Very white, very straight teeth. You like poetry, also?'

'I do. I don't read enough of it, though.'

She reached into the top pocket of her jacket and pulled out a folded sheet of paper.

'I forgot that,' she said. 'Looks important. Like plans of a big bomb.'

It was the page of my extemporised notes about the melismata. I realised how redundant they were, now.

I thanked her with gusto. 'Now I can blow up the Houses of Parliament. Phew.'

Andres popped his head round the door. 'Friend? OK?'

I said we were very good friends indeed and Andres gave a low, suggestive chuckle. Kaja said something in Estonian and Andres replied briefly, flapping his hand towards her, and left.

'He says take my time.'

'Nice guy.'

'Stoned from his head. All the time. Hashish.'

'Cool.'

'You here for business or pleasure?'

My eyes flinched at the word 'pleasure'. Wiping imaginary sweat off my brow, I said: 'For inspiration. I'm a composer.'

'Composer?'

'Contemporary music. Not pop or rock. Yeah.'

'Travel guide?'

'No. Andres got the wrong end of the stick, I think. English irony.'

'Or French,' she said. 'Voltaire. You like Voltaire?'

'Yeah. Anyway, I'm only a writer of music. But don't tell him.'

She nodded slowly, her face an open book, showing how intrigued she was. I knew I had ratcheted up the game with this one confession, never mind her evident intelligence and culture. It couldn't have been better if I'd said 'poet': this wasn't

England, this was Estonia. What was I up to? My wife was in the earliest stages of pregnancy.

'*Why* our little country?'

'It's this British millennial project to compose a big collective piece for the New Europe,' I explained, thinking how boring, even patronising, it sounded. 'One British composer per country. I got Estonia.'

'You like that?'

'I think Estonia and Estonians are wonderful,' I assured her. I was still to visit the proper countryside here, the ancient peat bogs and the wild forests. 'Even when they beat you up.'

'That's making for a change,' said Kaja. 'Normally Estonians are being beaten up, for seven hundred years.'

'Yeah, I know. But no more.'

'For the moment,' she said. 'Are you playing it here?'

'The piece? No. It's for something called the Dome.'

She hadn't heard of the Dome, to my surprise.

'The Dome,' I explained, trying not to sound like a national sales pitch, 'is this very exciting project for the millennium. It's this massive geodesic structure on a run-down bit of the Thames in London in which there are going to be all kinds of interactive things, like this giant body you can walk through, amazing trapeze artists, and so on. Our piece is going to be for a fairly major opening concert in the presence of bigwigs – the Queen, Tony Blair, you name it. *Winds for the New Europe.* I have to have one wind instrument at least, because of that title. I didn't choose the title, it's already got us into trouble, for obvious reasons.'

She frowned, puzzled.

'Anyway, it'll be cool,' I went on, hurriedly. 'In fact, the whole Dome project's in trouble, but it'll be great in the end. Fantastic, in fact. A huge honour. This is a big opportunity for me to reach a much bigger audience. Usually, I get about ten people, five of them fellow composers and the other five music academics, plus a few nasty critics.'

'That is over ten,' she pointed out.

I realised I'd said more in the last minute than in the last nine days put together. It was something about the way she listened, with a quiet intent and something amused dancing on her lips. But I also realised I'd said too much, too much about myself. She had not even asked my name, like others would have done – an excited question usually followed by a look of disappointment.

'And you, Kaja?'

The next morning, the phone rang suddenly (particularly suddenly) in the apartment. It was on the little table and made me jump. I reached for it without getting out of the sofa.

'Hi there!' I said, overenthusiastically. 'Wow. Whassup?'

'I'd have thought you'd have phoned.'

'We agreed not to.'

'That was before. Before the good news.'

'I didn't realise,' I said, vaguely.

Kaja was sitting next to me on the sofa, naked except for her slip, which had little targets dotted all over it. I rose gingerly and walked over with the cordless to the other end of the room. I was crouched, scratching my temple like a professor or someone in pain. I wanted my wife to go away, to vanish. I couldn't believe I could be so evil.

'Anyway, sweetheart,' Milly was saying; 'the good news is confirmed.'

'Oh, amazing.'

'Are you there?'

'Right here,' I said.

'Congratulations?'

'Completely. It's fantastic.'

'You're being a bit cold.'

'Yeah?'

'You in the middle of work?'

'Yup. But don't worry. It's going great.'

I looked up. Kaja had her head on one side, leafing through the TV magazine provided by the flat, with a Baltic celebrity in a thong on the cover. She was trying not to listen, obviously. She had just showered. Her skin, in the low light, was precisely the same colour as the cut apple's browning flesh on the table. I was in love with her. Her small breasts were shaped like bells. I had squeezed seed into her like pulp through a cheese cloth, the way Milly made jams. It had felt like squeezing rather than spurting, it had gone on so deliciously long. Three more times, each one a variation on the first. I was already almost game for a fifth.

Milly's voice broke in, very close. 'I won't disturb you again,' she was saying. 'I'm just sharing it. I thought you'd want to.'

'It's early days.' I was making a huge effort, and this provided its own fuel. I think I sounded genuine, now. 'That's all I'm thinking.'

'Just that?'

'I'm holding myself back, I think. Not tempting fate.'

'What are you doing?'

'Doing?'

'When you're not working? Seeing lots of snazzy girls? Lap dancing?'

I began to laugh but my glottis acted of its own accord and cut it off with a gulp. I could see Milly's dazzling smile as she'd made the joke. She loved me. I heard faint bumps and crackles as she walked about and did weekendy things in the house, the receiver tucked into her shoulder, her head at the same angle as Kaja's.

'OK, I'd better get back to the piece. I'm really into it. It's sort of flowing. Your work OK?'

'Not really.'

'Oh dear,' I sympathised, rubbing the nylon lace curtains between my finger and thumb. There was the hull of a tiny fly caught in them.

'I shouldn't be disturbing you,' said Milly, clearly having believed me. 'I do care. Best of British. Big kiss on the lips and everywhere else. Especially down there. I'm thinking about you in bed.'

'Yeah, same here. Byeee.'

I actually crooked my fingers in a little wave. I put the phone down. I shrugged.

Kaja said, the wet tips of her hair like thorns tattooed on her upper arms, 'I hope that wasn't your girlfriend in England.'

'Jesus, no,' I said, grinning like an idiot. 'That was my mum.'

TWO

Nine years earlier, back in 1990, Milly (seated behind her splat of programmes outside the Purcell Room) hadn't heard of Jack Middleton. This amused me at the time, especially as I was featuring in the concert. She was in the process of having her heart broken by her boyfriend, a quiet, severely intellectual Iranian refugee called Firuz, still slightly bowed from torture. Although Milly and I became friends she would not let it go any further, not until she had recovered.

She was in her year off, bound for Oxford to read PPE. I felt there was no other girl in the world for me and became almost completely chaste. I left England to study computer-aided composition at the Royal Conservatory in The Hague, where I failed to complete my doctorate on the works of Cornelius Cardew. I developed a brief taste for hashish and cocaine in all-night dives where serious jazz was played, until I was found waiting one night by a canal in Amsterdam for the law of the Lord to rise from the waters out of the psychedelic lozenges of light and embrace me purely and cleanly, weeping. It was a close shave.

Milly and I met again at a post-concert garden party several months after my return, three years later: I was, by now (according to one review), 'England's most promising young composer'.

Milly had left Oxford, having narrowly missed a second, and was working for the Palestinian cause from a shared house in Kilburn. Despite this, she wore a long, glittery dress and pharaonic earrings and had around her throat a thick gold collar in the form of an asp. She was Cleopatric, as (somewhat blissed out on Pimm's) I remarked. Milly seemed relieved to see me again, treating me with what felt like nostalgia, as if I'd been away in the wars. Her current man, a flamboyant Palestinian film-maker in his forties called Saleem, had just two-timed her, and she was adrift.

I had meanwhile given up any hope of being her bloke, so it was with intense surprise that I found myself shivering on my bed that same night, in my squalid room in Arsenal, entirely naked at her express command. She only followed suit, drunkenly unclothing herself down to (but not including) her jewellery, after subjecting me to a humorous lecture on the need for male sexual abstinence. She was impressed by the fact that my jism's reach (not inside her that first time, as there was no protection to hand) got as far as her chin, despite the Pimm's. I was more impressed to find myself still intact, as her honey-yellow nakedness, her spry fingers, had made me feel as if I was stuffed with pleasure's most expensive fireworks, going off at last like the Guy Fawkes all those years ago on Hayes Common.

As an eleven- or twelve-year-old, reading a novel by Nicholas Monsarrat I'd got out of Hayes Town Library and which – behind its sticky plastic cover – took place in eighteenth-century India and featured a spirited, long-limbed princess of an unearthly loveliness, I had imagined my first kiss. It was nothing like my actual first kiss a little later, in which I managed to indent a girl's cheek with my teeth in the darkness of a party game, or even my first proper French kiss in the shadows of an end-of-term grope, which was a mess of spittle, or even the first successful kiss tutored by a flat-chested thirty-two-year-old clarinettist called Marie-France on a young person's orchestral tour in Belgium, who also deflowered me in the hotel (though without success on my part, due to nerves). Neither was it anything like the first time I kissed Milly, partly because I was conscious of representing (to Milly, at least) the white working-class-boy-made-good – an example of which she hadn't yet scored with, apparently. I didn't tell her that I neither thought of myself as being working class nor as living on a council estate, although both were technically true, until I was eighteen.

Then there was Kaja.

The first kiss with Kaja was the closest I'd ever got to the kiss I'd imagined, reading that novel all those years back in my bedroom in Hayes with its bright Scalextric wallpaper (the nearest I ever got to having my own Scalextric, it has to be said).

It happened about five hours after she had whacked me on the face, which is often the way. Having told her about the Millennium Dome commission, on the café terrace, I listened gravely and with a trampolining heart as she told me in turn about her plans to study English and Russian at Tartu University once she'd earned enough money as a waitress to rent a room. Then she'd gone back in for the two hours remaining of her shift.

I had said, not unnervously, as she stood up to go, 'Let's talk some more. Um, look, I'd like to buy you dinner as an apology.'

And she had nodded and said, 'As an apology?'

'For my mistake.'

'And mine. Look at your eye. It's going yellow and blue like a bird.' She said something in Estonian, which turned out to be Russian – some lines from Anna Akhmatova which she rendered into English there and then: 'The slabs are heavy that press on your sleepless eyes.'

'Oh, I'm sleeping OK,' I said, just for something to say. No girl had ever quoted poetry at me before, or not as if she was throwing a crystal ball to see if I would catch it.

'Then it's not sleep is the trouble.'

'Probably not. Look, this dinner idea, I'm on for it. It's a peace dinner. Old and New Europe.'

'You're not so old,' she said. 'Are you?'

'Thirties. Say no more. And you?'

'Twenty-six.'

My eyebrows shot up in surprise. She leaned against the wooden rail around the café terrace.

'Yeah, I look eighteen. That's the sports.'

'The gymnastics?'

'Yeah. They gave us pills to keep us from development. East German trainer. A lot of my friends are sick, now. Swimmers especially. They took pills to make their muscles huge. Cancer, they have. Children with handicaps. Or dead babies. Or no darn babies at all.'

I nodded, trying not to think of Milly and *our* no darn babies. 'Yup, I remember. Soviet weightlifters and swimmers. Women built like houses, mammoth biceps. Won all the medals. Did *you* win any?'

She laughed.

'I was never a champion,' she said. 'But I was second best at vaulting in all the Baltic republics, age twelve. You know? Vaulting over the horse with your legs out, right wide out like scissors?'

'The Olga Korbut of Estonia,' I said, admiringly, thinking how people opened up to weirdly wonderful depths once you probed.

'No, never,' she said, shaking her head. 'How to be that? I was from Haaremaa.'

I pictured her vaulting the horse in slow motion, with legs out, doing the splits. It explained the ease and grace of her movements, the litheness, the way she twisted her wrists like an Indian dancer. Though I'd have been just as happy if she'd said she was a clog-dance champion, to be honest.

We met as planned in an African restaurant in the shadow of the old city wall. The place was brand new and very hip, with low tables and benches and good West African music. She knew one of the cooks, a large Nigerian who winked at me and made me feel good.

I gazed at Kaja across a lit candle (she had changed into a long and appetising dress and smelt of ambergris), and reckoned this was paradise.

We had not yet touched, apart from the café incident. My cheek was still slightly numb, as if I'd been to the dentist, but

60

Kaja assured me it hardly showed. My black eye had settled for even more interesting colours, like a beautiful stormy sky. That was her simile. Then, while she was in the loo, my glance strayed over the restaurant and I saw a speckled cowrie shell on a carved cupboard nearby and knew immediately what her cheekbones reminded me of. The soft polish, the thick curve, the foreign wonder of it. I knew exactly how they would feel if I were to run my finger along them, lay my lips upon them. A couple of warmed-up cowrie shells.

After the meal, during which our words seemed to have been designed by Swiss engineers to interlock perfectly, we walked out on to the grassy area below the wall. It was dark, finally, but not too cold. The lights of the suburbs below were cut by swathes of darkness, which were either water or forest. We stood side by side with a couple of inches of air between us. It wasn't really air, though: it was a scrum of electrical colours, pheromones, tiny mischievous angels. I had to take the moment by the scruff.

The final, most creative step is always a lunge, blind and momentous.

My arm seemed to twitch up and its hand came to rest on her shoulder on the far side. One thing leads to another, there is no actual beginning. I am committing adultery, I thought. My arm started to ache. Without me doing anything with my arm, she settled her side against my side. Flank on flank. Her body seemed very warm and comfortable through her thin coat. Her head rested against my neck, gently.

'I'm very happy,' I admitted.

'How is your eye?'

'Also happy.'

'My grandmother tried to kill me when I was seven,' she said, quietly.

'Really?' This slotted into the whole: it was OK.

'Yeah. She was drunk. Life was always being hard for her. She punched me on the eye then she picked this really heavy pan. My father stopped her breaking it on my little head. She died in the asylum. My eye was like yours.'

I could feel the vibrations on my neck as she spoke.

'That's terrible. Why you?'

'Maybe because I was reminding her of what she had lost.'

She turned her head and I lowered my face and that was it: the kiss I'd imagined as a twelve-year-old. A rich, smooth, slightly sticky kiss (we had finished the meal with a complimentary honey biscuit in the shape of a finger), in which my thin lips complemented the voluptuous tubbiness of hers.

We hung in there quite a long time. I felt the breath through her nose blowing hard on my sore cheek, making it tingle. I'm eleven years older than her, came the thought through the rich silken folds of my happiness. That's not so bad. She couldn't be my daughter, at least.

Then I kissed her cheekbones, one after the other.

'They're like cowrie shells,' I said, just as I'd rehearsed it.

'Like what? Carrying shelves?'

'Cowrie shells. A really beautiful shell. There was one in the restaurant.'

She didn't reply. I felt I'd better shut up.

We kept to the quieter, darker streets, slowly because her head was on my shoulder. We reached the park under the castle. The ducks were swishing about on the black water, catching the night lights on their glossy backs.

'I think this has never happened to me,' she said, as we walked.

'Your boyfriend?'

'I left him now. Right *now*.'

'OK.'

I experienced, I have to say, a momentary panic. This was serious and some.

'I think we knew each other in a past life,' she said. 'I would never hit a stranger, you know? Like that. Or feel what now I am feeling.'

'Maybe. Or maybe not.'

'You believe of past lives?'

'Not really,' I fibbed (because part of me did and still does).

'An awful weight to carry around with you, all that suffering. Over and over again. Birth, pain, death.'

'Kisses. Falling in love. Chocolate.'

I buried my nose in her hair, which smelt slightly of onions, coffee and cigarettes from her café shift and maybe from the restaurant. I was surprised she hadn't washed it. It was silkily supple against the hard bone of her skull. We were somewhere underneath the castle, possibly near where I'd smoked my cigarillos in a former life. 'Yeah, that would be nice, repeated endlessly.'

A duller part of me was worrying slightly about the gang of goths, but they seemed to have vanished. The trees whispered in the darkness. The stone tower high above us was subtly floodlit. The bubble of my happiness was swelling my ribcage. This is all for the music, I said to myself. This is what's *supposed* to happen. A lone, bearded drunk passed us, singing in what sounded like Russian but could have been, at one point, Geordie.

'You know,' I said, 'we don't even know each other's name?'

'Kaja. Jack.'

'Surname, I mean. Family name.'

'We'll keep it like that,' she said. 'Family can be difficult.'

We laughed. It was sexier, too, I realised, with some surprise.

'OK, that's cool. How about, um, a drink at my place, Kaja?'

She didn't reply, only snuggling closer as we walked on until I wanted to be teletransported instantly into the flat; the closeness of her and my simple, animal anticipation had made ordinary legwork awkward, to be honest.

In fact, we didn't go straight back to the flat, but sat in an underground bar for half an hour, listening to a withered guy with long bleached hair and a Scotch-taped Fender singing cover versions of Led Zeppelin, Procol Harum and Lynyrd Skynyrd over a drum machine. We were, incredibly, the only ones. We'd passed the place – called Rock Cavern – and Kaja had said, 'Live music, here. Let's go.' I held her hand and descended the narrow flight of stairs papered in rock posters as if burrowing down into my own past.

I didn't mind; she was clearly nervous about going straight to my place. And so was I; I was still not quite convinced that the African peanut stew hadn't been spiked with some seriously subtle hallucinogen.

Thick pillars had hidden the bulk of the room and the concomitant fact that it was entirely empty, despite night lights burning on each table. The singer waved to us in the middle of the song and looked so relieved that we felt we had to stay. It was funny. It was fun. A thin, ill-looking waiter served us beers. I hummed the best-known tunes, but she could not – she had been on her Soviet island, doubly walled off.

We snuggled up close on the bench and I thought: He's singing for us. This is the life. Um, yup and some. This is it.

I thought of Milly not liking this place, and then unthought her. It was very easy. It was like zipping up a body bag over a face.

We'd known each other three days. We were lying in bed together by the second, snug as two bugs. I'd bought a packet of condoms called Sure.

For the last year, Milly and I had been trying for a baby with all the spontaneous passion of animatronic puppets, though naturally I didn't mention this to Kaja, who still thought I was a bachelor. Kaja told me that before Heino, her shark sculptor (who had apparently not yet noticed she hadn't called), she had made love – she lifted her hands and spread her fingers – *that* many times with – showing one hand only – *that* many boys. I wasn't sure whether she meant ten times or fifty times, and didn't ask.

On a Party camp run by a drunken Lithuanian in the last days of the Soviet Empire, a fellow fifteen-year-old, while they were fetching water, had requested her quietly and politely to give him a blow job by a chicken-wire fence. They were hidden by a stand of trees. He was the grandson of someone on the committee of the Estonian Supreme Soviet. She did not enjoy it. The other times were better, but only with Heino did she ever look forward to it. Then Heino got depressed and couldn't be bothered to make any sort of love at all.

'I thought it was the pills they gave me for gymnastics,' she said. 'Maybe I was backward. Not enough hormones. I dunno.'

I shook my head in amazement. We were lying in bed, and I was on top of her. It was eleven o'clock in the morning. I was still inside her, albeit shrivelled to a soft walnut. Her chin rested on my hair. Her own hair came down to the small of her back and, in front, hid her breasts entirely if she wanted it to. Whenever she ran, her untied hair moved from side to side like a painter's brush.

She had run – from sheer joy – in the park the day after she had whacked me in the café. It was not a particularly sunny day – there were fitful attempts at rain, and only the odd dazzling October interlude – but watching her, I felt as if I had swallowed whatever sunlight was going and that it was shining in my heart. It was, quite possibly, shining out of my ears and my mouth too, like a depiction of Apollo I'd once seen in a museum in Greece. Not out of my arse, I hoped. Guilt saw to that, the old-fashioned word 'adultery' appearing in dayglo letters from time to time. Adultery was termed 'gallantry', I seemed to recall, a couple of hundred years ago.

If Milly had suddenly appeared from behind a tree, 'gallantry' would not have worked for a single minute on her. Not for a second. I saw her emerging with a cricket bat, its willow studded with nails.

Did you resolve your guilt?

To a certain extent.

How?

By thinking of these three weeks as work, as work in progress, as a framed experience towards a work of art that would free it from whatever had been nailing it down to dullness, repetition, boredom.

This was soon after the failure of 'CO2 Emissions from the Family Car', wasn't it?

Failure's too strong a word for such a tentative work. It was designed as an activist piece for a two-hundred-strong choir of Danes, to be sung at this green conference on the island of Bornholm, and the idea completely hobbled me. The commission came through my wife. It bored the pants off everyone, and the words were dreadful. Thankfully they were inaudible. There was also a freak snowstorm.

So, this framed experience . . .

Yes. Into this frame had come Kaja, the Muse. It was inevitable, somehow. I thought I might be in love with her. She seemed to be in love with me. In the back of my mind, however, was the absolute certainty that Kaja was temporary. Here, in the front of my mind, I was living in the present. In that part of my mind, the word 'temporary' didn't exist because it simply described time, which by its very nature is only real in the moment. It's like describing Beethoven's Fifth (just because it only has existence through the movement, the breath, of time) as 'temporary'. 'Temporary' and 'temporal' were the same thing, in other words.

And this satisfied you?

It did. And so I watched Kaja run in her athletic, ex-gymnast's way and felt full of sunlight. It was as if I'd never really known what it was to live, until now.

We went to Haaremaa at the end of that week. Although I wanted to see more of the countryside than the outskirts of Tallinn, I wasn't too keen to go to the island. I felt it was going in too far.

'Your parents?'

'I think it's OK. I'm your official guide to Estonia, not your girl. They left the island once only. They're open, but not *very* open. They've heard the stories. Nasty rich men looking for Estonian girls to enjoy. OK? This time, it's the best way.'

This time. Of course she'd expect there to be another. And

another. Until the island wedding. I pictured everyone smiling and shaking my hand. Simple folk. No money. I even saw her mother in a peasant's headscarf, like the women in places like Kosovo. I would be the answer, in the end, to their wildest dreams.

For about ten minutes on the Friday, while Kaja was cleaning herself up in the flat's bathroom, I did consider packing my bags and slipping away. My eyes clocked where everything was. I could do it in ten minutes, just stuff everything in and scarper, leaving my toothbrush and razor to Kaja. All so easy. Just off and away. I felt quite thrilled by the idea. But Koit the landlord had my English address. Kaja would plead with Koit to give her the English bastard's address. He was a soft man in a crumpled sweater, and would give it to her. She would pursue me to London and ruin my life. She would definitely do that, not out of spite, but out of pain.

Instead of running away, I went into the bathroom where she had decided to have a shower. The curved perspex door of the cubicle showed her as a pink blur, an impression, an ideal not yet come to focus in the real world. I tried to open the door but like shower doors the world over it would not slide easily and I had to jolt it and tug it until it juddered on its runners. She protested jokily under the pelt of steamy water, lifting one leg up and soaping the arch of her foot without toppling. A gymnast's equilibrium.

The water was finding its natural course over her body, following the curves and the gulleys, polishing her up. Pearl necklaces formed between her breasts and then broke, descending over her belly, the sudded water frothing against the snag of her bush – a little waterspout from it – only to creep down each inner thigh to her hard shins and arched feet. The nicest fingers I had ever seen. I'd noticed this when Kaja was playing her violin: really slim, tapering fingers. I wanted to have her right now. She had amazingly beautiful knees, as well.

'What exactly did you do to that nasty boy on camp?' I asked, standing stark naked by the open shower door, watching her as she smiled at me and got on with tending to herself, the luxury of the shower that Milly would have condemned as wastefully long.

'By the chicken wire?'

'By the chicken wire.'

She hesitated. 'Anything goes, huh?'

'What?'

'You might say he took advantage for me.' She turned the shower off and stepped out in a wreath of steam to take the towel I was offering, avoiding my other hand. The water pipes thumped and trembled. 'Or rape. You don't want to do that again to me, do you?'

'I didn't do it the first time. I just wanted us to be even closer. You do it to me, then I do it to you. But forget it, it doesn't matter.'

I was embarrassed by my stiffening, now. I saw the animal in it, the farmyard bull. Pigs and apes, all that. I crossed my hands to hide it, casually keeping it against my belly. My feet were cold on the tiles. The steam wrapped me in a damp warmth in which it was harder to breathe.

Then the phone rang. I let it ring on and on, my heart beating against my ribs. It stopped. The shower's heat off her body was amazing: the shower knob was further into the red than usual, I noticed.

'Your mum?'

'Bound to be,' I said, shivering from the tiles. 'I speak to her every day.'

She nodded. Then she folded the towel carefully at my feet and knelt down in front of me.

'This,' she said, uncrossing my arms and placing my hands behind her head. I slid my fingers together and rested them on the back of her skull, on her wet hair. 'I did this to him. Otherwise he'd have report me to his grandfather, high up in our Supreme Soviet, for singing Estonian songs. Welcome to Siberia, Kaja.'

'I won't report you,' I said, stroking the warm wet hair as

she began, my breath breaking against my own words. 'Although I'm really high up in the Supreme Soviet.'

I widened my feet and watched her carefully and she in turn watched me with intent, upturned eyes. 'I would really *like* you to sing some Estonian songs,' I added.

And she started humming at the same time, right at the back of her throat, so that I could feel it as a vibration in my slicked knob. And I vowed, in the delirium of my pleasure, that I would insert these songs into the piece for the Millennium Dome.

We took the coach together, four hours cross-country to the coast, the western coast of Estonia, and then the coach bumped onto the ferry, and in under an hour we were on the island of Haaremaa. Sometimes the impossible is merely imaginary, and what actually happens is easy.

Kaja had a brother; he was off studying German in Berlin. She was going home anyway, it was her holiday, she'd worked right through the summer and now the summer was over.

On the coach I told her more about the piece I was writing, about my interest in Arvo Pärt's music. She knew a bit about her compatriot's work, but not very much. She knew the album *Alina*, for instance, and *Summa*, and had gone to a performance of *Kanon Pokajanen* in the spring.

We'd visited all the main churches in Tallinn together, and taken a trip out to the Kadriorg Palace and the Tallinn TV tower. We'd held hands in the tram and hugged tight in the palace's huge park, where we'd imagined the Tsarina's summers, the elegant retinues in top hats and stays, the abundant muslin dresses. Between the bouncing red squirrels and the blustering leaves, we were completely wrapped up in ourselves.

I phoned home when Kaja was packing in her hostel. (Her hostel – clean and friendly, she said, but as basic as it was cheap – was in the grim suburbs, and she refused to let me visit her there.) I picked a time when I knew Milly would be working, and left a message on the machine. I was travelling around the countryside, I said, picking up Estonian folk songs in this land of singers, and would make contact on my return to Tallinn. Remember what Cardew had said, Mill? How there were no real folk songs any more? Well, I was hoping to find them.

I felt weirdly cool about it all. About the fact that I was treating Milly, not as my missus, but as an obstruction.

Haaremaa was an island of near-pristine bogs and forest and marshy edges, with the occasional white, empty beach stretching as far as the eye could see, and limestone barenesses known as alvars, struggled on by lichens. Cranes and seabirds flew in the northern sky, wintering over on the warmer westerly side. Kaja explained again that, being where it was, facing Sweden, sentinel in the Bay of Finland, the island had been a strictly controlled military zone under the Soviets. It was opened up only five years ago, in 1994, when the soldiers left. It had been the site of terrible battles in the Second World War, with tens of thousands of deaths and entire villages vanishing under shells, flame-throwers, the treads of tanks.

In fact, I had picked up this much already from my Baltic States' guidebook, although there had been very little about Haaremaa. But I nodded, as if fascinated. The way she told it, I *was* fascinated. The movement of her lips made it fascinating, for a start-off.

Kaja, in the coach, went on to tell me more interesting details, in fact, the kind of details no guidebook ever gets to. Her mother's uncles had both been killed – on opposite sides: one in the German Army, his brother in the Red Army. They had almost fought each other. That's why their sister, her grandmother, had drunk a lot and gone crazy. Then there were terrible purges after the war, she said: thousands of islanders either fled to Sweden in little boats or were sent to Siberia by Stalin. The civilian population was reduced by a third.

I shook my head, running flickering images of horror inside

it. It reminded me of my mum recounting the Blitz: the majestic scale of it, history as a god, the massive hairy knuckles making contact.

Her grandfather fled in a little boat, and wanted to come back for the others but couldn't, staying for good on Gotland where he married a Swedish slut. 'A slut to the rest of his family, anyway.' I'd provided the word 'slut'. Kaja remembered the island of her youth as being full of Russian soldiers with clipped hair and large ears, of no-go zones behind link fences and barbed wire where camouflaged silos hid huge rockets, ready to bring about the end of the world.

The coach rumbled on through what seemed to be empty countryside on an empty, potholed road that ran straight across the north-west mainland of Estonia. I loved the shifting of Kaja's face as she talked. She was eleven years younger than me – I had all but forgotten that inconvenient and ultimately un-important fact. She had 'trodden water' for a while after school, the newly independent country still sorting itself out, still chaotic. She had worked in a biscuit factory, one of the last factories still operating on Haaremaa. Her mother was a supervisor in the same factory. I told her that my mother had also been a supervisor in a factory, but that her English factory made sausages and ice cream.

'And your father, Jack?'

'My father also worked in a factory. He was a skilled elec-trician, working for EMI. There was a big EMI factory in Hayes. He's now retired. My mother,' I added, as I never usually did, 'is blind. There was an accident in her factory. Something dropped on her head, it wasn't an explosion or a spill. It blinded her.'

'That's sad,' said Kaja, a little too easily.

I thought she wasn't going to pursue it, but after a bit she said, turning back from the window, 'How old were you?'

'About five? It's weird, I don't really remember it. The acci-dent, I mean. I don't remember her ever not being blind. But that's because there wasn't much difference between when she was and when she wasn't, probably, because she hid it. Still does. And it's not something we ever mentioned in the family. Still don't. I've never heard the word "blind" at home.'

Kaja nodded, looking thoughtful. 'So that's why you became a composer,' she said. 'The blind people have better ears. For music, you don't need to see.'

I was shocked. I'd never made the connection. I pretended that I had.

'Yeah, probably. I dunno. I think maybe I'd shown interest before her accident, though.'

'By the way, did she have your big brown eyes?'

'I suppose she did,' I said. 'I mean, she still does. It's just they've kind of gone sort of blank. Sometimes she hardly opens her eyelids.'

This whole subject was painful to me, and I wondered why I'd brought it up. My mum had never come to terms with not being able to see. Neither had I ever come to terms with it, which is why I hardly ever brought it up. And when I did, I was usually disappointed by the reaction.

'What's that?' I asked, pointing out of the window at a couple of grey, barrack-like buildings next to a cluster of threadbare barns.

'A collectivised farm,' said Kaja.

'I've heard all about them,' I said. 'Looks pretty dire.'

'Dire?'

'Horrible.'

'Yeah, it was a bad idea. But at least there were people in the farms. Now there's no one.'

I pulled Kaja's hand out from under her thigh, then brought her hand to my lips and kissed it on the knuckles. It was warm from being pressed on by her thigh, and smelt of cloth and sweat.

The coach was carrying us both in a straight line to some- where as misty as guesswork. My alternative future! Don't you ever wish you could live two parallel lives at once? I knew I would not be leaving Milly. And yet I also knew that I would spend all of the time left to me with Kaja. The two times were at different levels of my being, two performances conducted at either end of the same room, independent but not clashing tonally – cooperating in some mysterious, apparently haphazard way. I wanted to open her button flies and let my fingers skip about in there. I wondered what Milly was doing right now: pushing photovoltaic panels on some poor planet-caring geezer, I guessed.

'And *your* dad, Kaja?'

I'd forgotten she'd already told me. He'd been an inspector of construction sites under the Russians, she said; now he was unemployed. He did building work here and there. When the Russians went, so did most of the jobs. And health security, pensions, all that. They had to start all over again.

'But we will do it, we will do it.'

She was looking out of the window, as if the rolling land-scape was part of the doing. If I was to say that I wanted to marry her, I couldn't really mean it. But a part of me did mean it. I touched the corner of her mouth with my lips. The amber-gris scent was not subtle, she must have splashed it on or maybe it was cheap, but I didn't mind. Her lips were naturally flushed, as if not yet quite used to being exposed to air. She didn't pout them, or change them in any way, as I pecked at the tuck of the corner five or six times. She knew they were perfect just as they were. It lit a little ring of flames in my groin.

'I'm sure you will,' I murmured, into her ear, finding it like a fruit through leaves and closing my teeth gently on the lobe, which made her giggle. The ambergris gave the skin a chem-ical garnish.

'You know what Haaremaa means?' she said, pulling away as the coach rocked.

'It's a very beautiful word.'

'It means the island of enfolding, *haarama*. Some say it's the island of gripping, because it doesn't let you go. In Estonian, *haare* means grip. But it's probably the island of the aspens, *haa*, from the Danish times, and we've forgotten. Do you have aspens in England?'

I nodded. For the life of me, I couldn't remember what an aspen looked like. Maybe like the ones I thought were aspens in the park below the castle. Or were they alders?

'Their leaves tremble,' she said, as if she knew I didn't know. 'They don't live too long.'

The Estonian words had made her both alien to me and even more familiar, with their extended softnesses.

'I like the island of enfolding best,' I said, stealing an arm around her and pressing her to me on the seat. 'My aspen.'

She gripped my free hand tight, as a joke, unconsciously hurting my knuckles. She still had a gymnast's strength, where she'd had to grip the bar and swing and maybe go right over and round again.

When Kaja introduced me to her parents, I recognised the words for 'English', the name 'Jack', and possibly the words for 'guide' and 'composer'.

'Hello!' I said, with a hearty grin, shaking my girl's parents' hands. I felt weirdly carefree.

They seemed very glad to meet me. The mother had eaten too many biscuits and was jowly, but had probably also been a beauty once. The father was handsome, still well built, and had given his daughter the blue-green eyes. He smelt slightly of drink and sweat and plaster.

'Hello, you are welcome,' the mother said, surprising me. 'Welcome to Haaremaa, a *very* good place.'

She didn't know how she had learned her English. Perhaps from her children. She really didn't know, she admitted. It just happened. I soon realised that it was very limited, but I was still impressed.

I was relieved by their ordinariness, in fact. They couldn't have been more different from Milly's parents. The thought struck me as I sat in the modest kitchen with its old, noisy fridge and battered gas cooker, its view through midge-speckled net curtains onto a bare dirt area where a lone kid was cycling in circles. Wadhampton Hall seemed like a joke, here. Actually,

England seemed like a joke, here, with its flabby Friday-night drunks and *Gardeners' Question Time*, its candlelit yak about nannies and house prices and air-conditioned Land Rovers. As if material prosperity was all that mattered, while the world's poor could go fuck. Sitting there in that simple kitchen, I felt I would like to scald my country free of all that, with a boiling bucket of indignation. Yet how could I? I was also a fat cat, annexed to the du Cranes' ancient and self-expanding universe of English wealth by dint of a marriage ring. Even though I'd taken it off, temporarily.

There was one framed photo of the family taken a few years back, when Kaja was about fourteen. It was the only picture in the kitchen, apart from a wildlife calendar and a prize certificate with Kaja's name written in above a discreet red Soviet star and a flying red gymnast. The photograph was black and white, fogged over as if the chemicals were unstable. Kaja was dressed in school uniform.

Later, when her parents were out of the kitchen, chatting with a neighbour, Kaja told me that a friend of the family – a military photographer – had developed the picture unofficially in his lab housed in the main rocket station. No film for sale, in Soviet days! Taking pictures was dangerous. It was very easy to be called a spy.

All this seemed so strange to me. I might as well have been looking at some exotic marvel in Peru. I thought: My life has been that dull? Well, up until now, yes. Now it's gonna change.

We had walked from the nearby bus stop where the coach had dropped us. Her parents lived on the fringe of the main town, which was on the sea, if somewhat reedily so. The town was pretty and on the sleepy side, to say the least. It had low, Nordic-looking old houses and dazzling-white churches and not many people. We'd passed a patch of wasteland where a sign announced an imminent hypermarket – Finnish, Kaja said – and come to a haphazard estate of about ten rectangular blocks, built in crumbly Soviet concrete. Each block had six floors and a main porch of uneven, clumsily grouted bricks.

The buildings were set down with a wistful disregard for order or design, while the lack of pavement, proper tarmac or floral tubs was a surprising plus: the estate was bleak but airy, with plenty of space between the buildings – not nearly as depressing as the equivalent place in Britain would have been.

There was absolutely no graffiti, nothing highly strung about the atmosphere, and no soiled kebab or KFC wrappers. There were no louts toughing it out with helpless old folk, either. Not as far as I could see. You were unlikely to be started on, here.

It was very quiet, too, because there weren't many cars: most of the cars were beaten-up, rusty Soviet models – Trabant, Moskvich, ZAZ – although there was a Renault Espace and a Ford Granada and a couple of VW Beetles among them: some people were getting rich, I surmised, but Kaja said that these were hire vehicles all owned by one man who called himself Elvis and wore dark blue shades.

I felt immediately at home, here. I had no idea why.

Kaja's parents owned an ex-KGB GAZ-13 Chaika – a black Chevy-style sedan with big chrome bumpers. You could see the ground go by next to the passenger seat, Kaja said – or would have done, if the vehicle hadn't temporarily given up the ghost. It was up on blocks in front of the ground-floor apartment. Its leather seats were torn, as if with a knife.

Kaja's parents also had a dacha, about ten minutes' drive away, a short sandy path from the sea. In the old days they would all cycle to the dacha. It was built by Kaja's father over ten summers, on land loaned to them by the Soviets in lieu of a full wage. They would go to it this evening, Kaja said, by bicycle. It would take about half an hour. I very much looked forward to the dacha. I drank tea in the kitchen and listened properly for the first time to the strange, attractive language, modulated so differently from English. Then Kaja translated a question from her mother, who was grinning at me expectantly.

'I hope you don't mind, but she says to me, "Ask him, is he a widow man?" I don't know why she thinks this, sorry.'

I pulled a face. 'A widower, you mean. Not that I know of.'

They laughed at my English humour and so I added, stoking it further, 'I think you have to be married first.'

I felt terrible, in fact, but sipped my tea and nibbled the factory's biscuits with an innocent's appreciative smile. The indent where the ring had been was still visible. Perhaps Kaja's mother was highly observant – more observant than her daughter. But didn't widowers keep their rings on?

'We love music in Estonia,' Kaja translated, after a long speech from her mother.

'Is that all she said?'

'Basically, yes,' Kaja said. 'You know about the Singing Revolution already. I told her you are an important young composer.'

'I like the young bit,' I grinned, seeing a range of faces, all fellow composers, bobbing madly up and down like tin ducks in a fairground.

'More than the important?'

'Well, most composers are only important when they're dead.'

Kaja translated the exchange for her mother, who laughed merrily, but with a glance at me that held just a shadow of suspicion in the sad eyes. Kaja's father had left us to mend a light in the bedroom. I wished this had all happened ten years ago. You're never allowed a second chance, not really. I calculated that ten years ago I was still a year older than Kaja was now, but full of dreams. In twelve years' time I'd be nearly fifty. No dreams.

'She asks if you like the biscuits?'

'I love them. I'm very happy. Thank you. Your daughter is an excellent official guide,' I added, trying to hide any trace of innuendo.

Kaja's mum chuckled appreciatively. She was called Maarje, which was quite a coincidence – pronounced like Marjorie drunk or with a stroke. In ten days' time I would be leaving Estonia, leaving Kaja, leaving my heart behind. It was like a very gamey song. Maybe, for the Dome, I should write a very gamey song. That's what most people, from Tony Blair and the Queen down, would most appreciate. In the context, it would be seen as ironic. Or maybe not. Maybe it would be the end of my career. Or the start of another.

As Kaja and her mum caught up with news in their own language, I glanced at the photo on the wall and felt this sort of dark water of sorrow rise up in my chest. I knew what it was: it was the sense that I was drifting without purpose, cut off from my past and seeing no point in the future.

The dad, Mikhel, came in and announced something in his loud, deep voice.

'He's mended the other bicycle,' Kaja explained. 'Now we can go to the dacha on the power of pedals.'

'You know you weren't allowed bicycles in Soviet time?'

'Really? Wow!'

I wasn't used to bicycling; while she pedalled painlessly ahead, I got out of breath. I'm stocky, but not overweight. The lanes were bumpy and the vegetation trailed onto them at the sides – my hair was caught by a bramble, at one point.

The dacha had a huge vegetable garden behind, like a London allotment, mainly filled with potato plants that kept the parents going now they had freedom but no money. The house itself was made from surplus-to-requirements breeze blocks and strictly conformed to Soviet limits on size, with two bedrooms tucked up in the sharply angled roof. There was a simple sauna next to the bathroom. The place was entirely pine-cladded on the inside; against one wall there was a greenhouse full of tomato plants. Water was piped from a well; the lavatory was a very deep pit with a conventional toilet seat over it, in an attached shed. The inside of the dacha smelt of pine sap and mossiness and mice. Very like a home I must have dreamed of long before. Reading *Coral Island*, probably.

Halfway down the garden there was a chicken coop and a large run with about twenty chickens and a pompous-looking cockerel. We collected three eggs from the coop and found four more in various corners of the run, embedded in hay or under dead leaves.

'They leave them in really crazy places,' said Kaja.

There were three other neighbouring dachas, but the nearest was an abandoned, shed-like construction with a huge wild plot full of overgrown raspberry and sloe bushes and broken canes. Kaja told me it had belonged to an old couple who were dead now, and their son was a businessman on the mainland.

At the very end of the vegetable garden, before the forest and next to the woodshed, was a cage that smelt like a zoo. It had a scraggy fox inside, pacing up and down, up and down, brushing against the chicken wire with a very cross look on its thin face.

'That's my father's . . . er, *reynard*,' said Kaja.

'Fox,' I said. 'Why?'

'Why what?'

'Why keep a fox in a cage?'

Kaja shrugged. 'It's been there a few years. My father catched it, I don't know how.'

'It's a bit disturbed, I think.' I found the idea of a fox in this small cage really unpleasant.

'Yeah, it's disturbed. And my father likes to call it names.'

'Really? You mean rude ones?'

'Maybe.'

I wasn't getting very far. Sometimes I wondered if the slightly surreal quality of life around Kaja was due to her English. 'What's its real name?'

'Doesn't have one. It's just Rebane, which means fox in Estonian.'

'Fox. Hi, Fox. Hi, Foxy.'

Foxy looked at us, as he paced up and down, up and down, with a malignant, yellow-eyed glare that I could quite under-stand. Part of Foxy's reddish coat was coming away like old carpet. Milly would have thrown a real wobbly seeing this, I thought. A caged fox must also be in my piece for the Dome. Seven minutes of dense experience. A poem of Estonia. Not a gamey song. Multilayered and troubling, more vertical than horizontal. Dense and full of needles, like that tall fir tree.

We stoked up the sauna with wood from the shed, splitting it next to the stove with a small axe. The temperature took an hour to climb to the right level, during which we played strip poker at the table over a glass of local vodka. I got down to my pants and one sock. Kaja was wrapped in her hair, which I thought was cheating. She could all but sit on it. We worried someone might come, like in the old Soviet days. But who?

Then we perched naked together on the sauna's little bench, watching our skin dry and, quite suddenly, come out all over in tiny clear berries of sweat. It was too hot to hold ourselves tight, although each time we were in the sauna I ran my hand over her supple, slippery form, kissing her salty lips and glistening breasts and bending down to muzzle the wet muff below.

My own sweat tickled me: it amazed me how much I could produce.

We swatched each other with fresh birch twigs soaked in a bucket. This was an entirely new sensation for me. I felt it connected me to the proper green root of things: the pain slight enough to be pleasant, the sweet scent of the shattered leaves emerging through the sweat like something very tender in a distant past that, if it wasn't mine, ought to have been. Kaja was more enthusiastic with her swatching, at first, but I soon got the hang.

It was all delicious. Her back was very red. Mine was smarting. I found Olev's card on the floor next to the sauna, dropped out of my trousers, and we laughed at it. *Disko, Baar, Saun – 24 hr.*

'So. Where's the disco, babe?'

'Instead of the disco, I will sing a song. An old song of Estonia. We used to sing here in secret, with someone to watch by the door for a spy or anyone coming. Or we might be arrested and put in the camps for provoking nationalism.'

'Promoting. That was brave.'

'No. What do you think? That we did not *have* to?'

And she sang, quietly, in the sitting room, wrapped in her towel. It was scary, really, to recognise how far I had forgotten what music could really mean.

I stayed overnight while Kaja returned to the house. I understood this. I started on *Anna Karenina*. I also worked on the score, scribbling a few more bars inspired by Kaja's traditional song, then rubbing them out. An owl hooted for half the night, quite close.

The next morning, early, I went off for a long walk on my own, watching cranes fly over the twilit reeds of the wild little bay with its tiny wavelets lapping and lapping, very black between the reed stems. I got some ideas, chromatic stuff to be folded in like yogurt. When I got back, Kaja had still not come. I waited an hour, trying not to worry, and then heard the crunch of her bicycle on the track outside. She had brought milk and bread and Finnish muesli in the pannier. I wanted to pay for them, but she refused.

After lunch we sat reading for a while – in separate easy chairs as the sofa bed was broken. This was strange, sitting in the easy chairs in silence and reading together: it was more intimate and strange than anything we had done so far. At first Kaja read a thick linguistics tome that looked like a scientific treatise. Then she turned to a volume of poems by Akhmatova, in a Russian–Estonian edition. Fortunately, I had read some of Akhmatova's poems years ago, for a vocal piece about glasnost that never happened. The chair I sat in was old and tatty and awkward. It was hard to concentrate on Tolstoy. Kaja was as beautiful as Anna, for sure.

In the late afternoon I helped lever up the potatoes, laughing with her and crushing the dried heads of dill plants between my fingers. Ever since, the sweet, spicy scent of dill always takes me straight back to that moment, that place. I straightened up and looked about me, as if to fix it all in my memory. The garden's length beyond the raspberry canes ended in a row of poplars dropping bright yellow leaves in the sea winds.

I was not too fit and thought I'd cricked my back at one point. Kaja dug heartily, stronger in her shoulders than I was, probably. She shook the earth off the creamy, fat potatoes and I realised she had been doing this all her life.

She spent most of the day with me, and we bicycled back for supper. I wanted this to go on and on for good. There again, its very temporary nature was what gave it its sweetness. Its poignancy. Although she didn't know this. It was around then I decided to call my piece 'Echo', in honour of her name and of her.

I liked her parents' flat.

I told them, without too much untruthfulness, that it reminded me of my own parents' place – also on an estate of 'social housing'. What I didn't add was 'back when I was a child in the sixties', because the flat here was full of furniture with fake brass handles and vinyl mahogany overlay. There'd be a certain chic to it all in a flat in Richmond, I considered, because it'd be deliberate, bought from a retro shop in somewhere like Brighton. Here it was jaded. The whole island was in a time warp. It felt undecided, stuck between two worlds, emptied of purpose when the troops went. The cranes and the owls had all the purpose. There were no tourists, although before the First World War it was a hydropathic health resort. Kaja explained that people would come from all over Europe, in those days – especially Prussians. The Prussians were haughty, brutal over-lords for more than two centuries, beating their Estonian serfs for nothing.

We were walking, at that point in the conversation, past the sanatorium's successor – a modernist concrete pile built in the thirties, its paint peeling off in white flakes like the kind of disease people hoped to be treated for here. There was a project to renovate the place, she said. Lots of pine beams, very Finnish. She knew the project's carpenter, he was an old school friend called Toomas. A few bent old folk shuffled about in the drive.

'Most of the young people have left the island,' Kaja said.

'Hardly a person in the fields. There were hundreds in my child-hood. It is like: OK, what do we do now? Build a hypermarket? But what for?'

'And you? Are you ever going to come back? For good, I mean?'

'I love my island,' she said, simply. 'Maybe you will, too.'

And she took my hand and pressed it to her cheek. I'd felt this very tiny beat of revulsion, at that instant. But I showed no sign of it on my face.

The family apartment was always hot, which also reminded me of Hayes and my childhood; the collective heating was on full and could not be individually adjusted, so the windows were kept open to the cold air – Milly would have disapproved of that. That waste. Thermal hole, she'd have called it.

Kaja's father was still broad in the shoulder and very fit for a man approaching sixty. He pulled out three tatty black-and-white photos from his overalls.

'Dacha,' he said.

In the first photo, the kids were small, laughing in the long grass in front of a rectangle of mud marked by poles. In the second photo, Kaja and her brother were holding a bucket between them, like something on a cuckoo clock; a roofless structure of breeze blocks behind them had the dacha's shape. Their dad was bearded and youthful, dressed in a checked lumberjack's shirt: he could have been a back-to-the-woods dude, almost. The third photo showed Kaja and her brother as spotty teenagers, shy and kind of angular, standing by an ancient-looking tractor with the vegetable garden just a maze of ruts behind. The photo was badly developed and creased.

Mikhel pointed to the photo and said something in Estonian.

Kaja smiled, translating her father's words: '"I built it for my children, and finish it just when my children were leaving!"'

I pulled a sympathetic face. The photographs were precious, Mikhel explained: a friend had developed them for him in a lab at the rocket station. You couldn't even buy film, let alone

83

find a photo shop. There was nothing in those days but the certainty of having a job and a roof – for life. I nodded as if Kaja hadn't already told me all this.

Mikhel stared at the photos for a long time, and then put them away in his pocket.

Kaja's brother, after studying German in Berlin, would go to Paris and study French. He was clever and received a European scholarship. There was a gulf between the two generations. This was not a problem, Kaja told me: love bridged the distance. I understood this. There was something about the country's historical suffering that had made this bridge firm. Firmer than my own family's bridge, which probably didn't exist except in the Middletons' wishful thinking.

Whenever I went home to Hayes, I had the impression we were hallooing each other from either side of a canyon – and especially when my parents stood sheepishly in the Richmond house, my mother admiring what she couldn't see. Once we showed her a little antique oil that Milly had bought me for my birthday, at auction. As usual, I gave subtle hints as to its appearance. It was of a woman bathing: she was modestly wrapped in a fluttering Turkish robe and was testing the water with her foot. Milly was very pleased with the present, although it had cost well into the four Os.

My mother pretended to study it, and then she said: 'Very nice, but nudes have never been my thing, dear.'

She both despised and worshipped Milly's wealth. Milly's and her son's wealth. Our wealth.

Kaja made a traditional kind of Estonian porridge she called a soup; it tasted like liquid dough, flavoured with nutmeg and cinnamon, and we drank it out of cups. We ate a lot of the soft little cakes and biscuits from her mother's factory, which a Finnish biscuit company had bought a few months back: the Finns were buying up firms and properties all over Estonia, apparently. I wondered if the heavy porridge pan was the same pan that Kaja's grandmother had tried to kill her with. I didn't like to ask. There were no photos of this grandmother. The bad times were so dark.

The family car remained on the blocks, so we cycled everywhere. All the roads bar the one to the ferry harbour were unmetalled; because it had been a military island, they were very wide and ran in straight lines through the forests: I recognised birch and spruce and Scots pine, on and on without a break. Bombers would have used the roads as runways, Kaja told me, in the event of war. That would have meant the end of forests, and of us, and of everything.

'Except for a few politicians in their bunkers,' I pointed out. 'Nice thought.'

'You've a problem with that, or something?'

'Oh no. I *lurve* politicians.'

We walked one day on a vast bareness of limestone, with the odd stunted juniper bush and dryish lichens and mosses. There were the rusted, mangled remains of military vehicles among the pebbles. It was barer than a heath: it was as if something had hoovered up all the soil, and yet it attracted me. The sea was a thin silvery line in the distance. A wind buffeted us in gusts, dropping to nothing now and again.

'This is a very, very delicate area,' she said. 'It is called an alvar. It is so rare the word is not even in your dictionaries. Swedish word, I think. A Baltic word.'

'I like it,' I said. 'It makes you think you have to tread carefully.'

'You do. And they brought tanks on here, the Soviets brought tanks. I remember that.'

'Nobody treads carefully enough,' I said, thinking how agreeable I was being, how even Milly would have been impressed. 'The whole planet is an alvar, really.'

'Our *lives* are alvars,' said Kaja, taking my hand in hers as we walked over the grey waste of pebbles and bared rock. 'Don't you think?'

We visited a lot of wooden windmills and large white empty churches and a reconstructed old farm – encouraged as an

example of harmless and obsolete folk traditions by the collec-
tivising Russians back in the fifties. I stood next to a wooden
sheep with a thick fleece and a pair of antique clippers hanging
from its rump and Kaja took a photo as I tried to look handsome and mysterious.

We went back to the farm for a folk festival. I was the only
non-Estonian there.

We sat on a bench in the cold barn and watched mostly
elderly ladies in brightly coloured traditional Estonian costume
dancing heavily in complicated patterns. Almost everyone else
in the audience was a participant, and at one point I was dragged
off my seat to dance a traditional round. I bobbed about as
Kaja watched, smiling and clapping. The hands that kept taking
mine were dry and chapped. It was a gas, although I was
conscious of my English awkwardness. My recent earth-
labouring ancestors would have known how to do it.

Kaja translated the explanations given by the festival organiser, who was a shaggy, grey-bearded man in a thick knitted
sweater. He went on too long through a faulty microphone that
turned his plosives into gunfire. There was some impassioned
but very amateur choral work by the same elderly ladies. I
listened carefully, but could spot nothing of Arvo Pärt's origins.

However, the singing of the Estonian national anthem as the
flag was raised in the muddy farmyard brought a lump to my
throat.

'This one is called "Eesti Vabaks",' Kaja told me, as the singers
began the next song, one massive soprano so perfectly out of
tune it might have been deliberate, a modernist thing. 'It was
forbidden before. To sing this song meant the camps – straight
away, you know?'

I pulled a face, embarrassed to find my eyes moistening. 'Eesti
Vabaks' sounded like a hymn, it was not intrinsically moving.
I was surprised by my reaction – it seemed out of my control,
emanating from the damp air, the muddled farmyard modesty
of it all.

Kaja leaned against me and I placed my hand around her

narrow waist. The elderly women under their quaint cloth caps were watching us without much expression but with obvious interest. I said I was worried that one of them might spill the beans to her parents.

'So? Who cares?' she whispered back. 'We're not kids. It's not the Soviet Union any more. Anyway, you think they haven't guessed?'

The festival went on for three or four hours but there was nothing to eat or drink. I started to flag. I was watching a curio, the last shreds of a life mode that both capitalism and communism had smashed and that could never be put back together again. The elderly women in their spectacles and their bright, felty costumes gave way, after two hours, to an all-woman jazz trio in bright yellow dungarees and baseball caps who played souped-up Cajun.

'I think I have to leave,' I said. 'This is too hip.'

'Hip? What's that?'

We made love in the dacha, the forest, the woodshed, on the empty beach (screened by reeds, even so), and once in the apartment, in Kaja's room, while her mother was talking on the telephone next door.

'It's OK,' Kaja said, peeling off her dress. 'It's Kadri, my aunt. She always goes chatting for really long.'

She was very slim in her white underthings, which she thought she'd better keep on.

She sat on one side of the bed, her feet on the floor, and I kneeled down and went into her hurriedly as she held me, guiding me past the seamed cotton edge of her slip. The window was open and the cold air gusted in over my back. Through the thin walls we heard Kaja's mother put the phone down and move about. There was no lock on the door. A little china squirrel on the windowsill held up its paws, as if begging us to stop. Kaja had me gripped and her breath was roaring straight into my ear and I was very close. I did, in fact, love her! I really really loved her!

If Maarje were to barge in and see us there – my underpants straddling the bottom of my thighs, Kaja's feet planted wide apart and up on their toes, her bra's cups dark and wet from my mouth (the dull taste of cotton on my tongue, with a chemical hint of fabric softener), she would have to approve, because I loved her daughter so much. And her daughter loved *me* so very, very much, especially (she was whispering, now) when I was filling her up inside with my lovely warm release.

But Maarje didn't come in. Kaja bit her lip to stop herself shrieking, although her breath in my ear was the crash of enormous breakers, running their white knuckles over the sand very fast. Then she lay back on the bed with me against her, and she said she was so glad that we had each other and knew each other, and I wasn't sure whether she meant this in a colloquial, sexual way or was completely innocent of the two verbs' other meanings, and I was very keen to break away from her and get dressed before we were discovered.

And if we were discovered – who knows? Maybe the father would kill me . . . although Mikhel didn't seem a violent man.

She wouldn't let me break away. She held me tight against her and she was smiling mischievously. The last leaves had been clinging to the tall birch in front of the dacha, that blowy morning, and I had pointed this out – and she had said, quoting a famous Estonian poet she had wanted to translate: 'Or the birch is holding onto its leaves.'

I felt my knob slip out of her and shrivel up, resting in the dense, licheny muff of hairs: it was caught slightly painfully by the edge of her pants, so I adjusted myself by wiggling my hips a little. She thought I was trying to escape and gripped me tighter around the waist, locking her hands on her own forearms either side.

'*Haare*,' I said.

'Yes.'

Her belly was very hot, and I wondered about her claim that she took the Pill, and about the madness, this time, of not protecting myself. It was the only time I had not protected myself. She might have been infected with HIV by a drunken sailor in Tallinn; she might have slept around a lot before I came along. She might bring men home all the time, although I very much doubted it. But then, a very prim-looking flautist called Marilyn Prindle once had seven one-night stands in a week, a few years back. I know because she told Howard and he told me.

I lay there, thinking really contemptible thoughts with my cheek squashed against her breast, against the broad, dark brown nipple that reminded me of bruised windfalls under the allotment's apple tree. I was shrivelled to very little by now, and it was too late. I would have liked to have gone to sleep like this, as we would have done in my bed in the low-eaved dacha. I would have liked to have slept and then woken up again and padded with her to the shower in the dacha, with its shuddering and its groaning from the pump or the pipes. I would have liked to have soaped her very intimately as she laughed, holding the cake of soap in her hand and laughing; or fired the sauna and sat her down on my lap – pulling her to me from behind on the hot bench, so my cheek could rest against her straight spine, my fingers spreading wide on her thighs, on the solid roundness of each thigh, and squeezing gently.

But I was in the family apartment with its small rooms and wafer-thin walls, and her mum was audible in the kitchen, now, maybe about to come in and offer us a cup of black tea.

THREE

'Look at Jack, for example,' said Milly's mother. 'He's put on a bit, hasn't he? He used to be an ectomorph of the first order. Or is it endomorph?'

'He? Who's he?' said Jack.

'Haven't you, come on – confess!' glared Milly's mother, who had drunk too much gin before the meal.

'It's all those wine gums,' laughed Milly, touching Jack's hand.

'Wine gums?'

'Yes, Mummy. He can't compose unless he has a packet of wine gums open in front of him.'

'How very tame of you,' said Milly's mother.

'Better that than a bottle of Scotch,' said Milly's father from the far end of the table, beyond the candlelight, in his deep bass growl.

Jack smiled. 'Who said I don't have a bottle of Scotch as well?'

'Oh, you wicked boy,' shrieked Milly's mother, who started flirting with her son-in-law only when she was sufficiently tanked up.

'The question is,' said Milly's father, snorting through his nose before the joke was made, 'are the wine gums necessary to the composition, or the composition necessary to the wine gums?'

Nobody took any notice. He was regarded, even by his own family, as an adorable bore. He made no secret of his baffled amusement in the face of his son-in-law's music.

'What's your favourite composition?' Milly's mother asked, staring at Jack over the table in earnest. 'Of yours, I mean?'

'Well, you know what they say,' said Jack. 'The next one to be written.'

'That's evading the issue,' said Milly's mother, helping herself to the burgundy.

'Don't slop it in, Mummy.'

'I'm not slopping it in. It's liquid. Of course it goes in like that.'

'Can't take her anywhere,' said Milly's father.

Milly's mother had been very ill with cancer a year or so ago but had made a miraculous recovery. No one had expected her to live more than another two or three years. Her drinking had worsened as a result. She put her mouth to her glass and sipped, gazing at Jack as she did so. Jack was very fond of his mother-in-law because he always saw in her the young, bright, wasted deb of the immediate post-war years.

'Come on, confess.'

'Confess what, Marjorie?'

'Which one you prefer? You must have *one*, out of all that noise, that lies closest to your heart.'

'You are rude, Mummy.'

'Does Jack good,' said Milly's mother. 'You're far too nice to him, like everyone else.'

'Well, he's nice to me, most of the time,' said Milly, a little too sing-song.

'What about that weird thing you wrote in Somalia?'

Jack frowned. The wine had settled pleasantly in his head. He was fond of his in-laws and it saddened him to see how old they were getting, manfully keeping decrepitude at bay. 'Somalia?'

'Ethiopia,' Marjorie corrected herself. 'Wherever. Something like that. *You* know. Something that sounds like estragon.'

'That's French for sage,' said Milly.

'And a character in *Waiting for Godot*,' said Jack.

'Saw that when it first came out,' said Milly's dad, which surprised them all. He returned their surprised stares with a nod. 'Extremely impressive.'

Jack felt a warmth of affection creep through him. There were these sides to people you never suspected, hidden from the daylight.

'You lucky beggar,' he said.

'I'm sure you didn't,' said Milly's mother.

'I did,' said Milly's father. 'I was a young man in town with nothing to do.' He looked noble, suddenly, beyond the candle-light. 'A long time ago now.'

'Latvia,' said Milly's mother. 'Nothing to do with Ethiopia. When Milly first knew she was preggers.'

There was a general intake of breath and then a silence that sang of dread, of half-hidden or obscured things in bogs.

'Estonia,' Milly said, smiling gamely.

'Well, that's what I meant,' said Marjorie, apparently oblivious of the pain she had thrilled. 'That piece called something very long and daft.'

'*A Filing Cabinet on Fire in the Middle of the Street, with Caged Fox,*' said Jack.

'That's showing off.'

'I know,' Jack smiled.

'I suppose you dreamt it.'

Jack hesitated. 'Yes, I suppose I did.'

'You don't seem very sure.'

'I probably dreamt it. Or dreamed it up.' He realised he was blushing. Milly was looking at him, he thought, with curiosity. 'It was this very vivid picture. Maybe I saw a picture of it, burning.'

'And the poor old fox in a cage?' asked Milly's father.

'And the fox in a cage. Dreamt that too.'

'It's all so *casual*,' said Marjorie, with sudden venom. 'That's what art is, these days. *Casual*. In my day it was *about* some-thing. Love or war or nature or . . . death.'

'I agree, Marjorie,' murmured Jack, who was in no position to explain the truth.

'Who's for pudding?' Milly called out, bird-like, as if there were other tables full of people. But it was only them.

'We're still on the red,' said Milly's father.

'We can take it up again for the cheese,' said Jack.

'But I brought you the '88 Fitou for the cheese,' said Milly's father.

'You mean that as a three-line whip?' grinned Jack, feeling irritated by this.

'I'll bet *that's* your favourite piece, anyway,' said Milly's mother, jabbing a finger at him on which a fat, deep blue sapphire winked.

'Not really,' said Jack, beginning to stack the plates from a half-seated position. Milly's mother raised her hands each side of her face to let him take her plate. In the low, uncertain light she looked as if she was horrified.

'Let's finish off the wine before that, then,' said Milly.

'Whatever,' said Jack.

'Don't sound cheesed off,' said Milly, whose eyes were else-where, deeply into their own realm of pain and hurt. They kept doing this, but no one other than her husband ever seemed to notice.

'I'm not in the slightest bit cheesed off,' said Jack, who certainly was.

'Why don't you let the maidservant do this?' Milly's mother called out, as Jack was taking the plates into the kitchen.

'We haven't got a maidservant,' he heard Milly explain. 'She's just a home help over here from Venezuela to learn English.'

'That's what they all say,' said Milly's father. 'Then they blow you up.'

Through the hatch and into the kitchen came the sound of laughter. Jack rinsed the plates before stacking them in the dish-washer. It was dark outside, but beyond his own reflection he could see the trees of the Heath shifting in strong gusts of wind against a paler night sky. He loved Milly so deeply it was an ache, but he knew this love was made up to strength, as cement is by sand, with pity.

With a pinch of guilt, too. Milly's mother was right, as she usually was in her messy, instinctive, cruel way: his favourite piece was the piece he wrote in Estonia, six years back. Six years! The Dome was a disaster, the *Winds for the New Europe* project replaced by a celebrity crooner – not quite Elton John – and his piece eventually premiered at the Aldeburgh Festival a year and a half later. He'd changed the name from *Echo* to the long 'daft' one and rejigged it into something more challenging, but it was essentially the same.

The piece had initially moved him, on hearing it being played in public for the first time. A smoke pellet in a burned-out filing cabinet centre stage had made playing a little trickier for the oboists, while the balalaika players right at the back of the auditorium had irritated, apparently, the highest rows by drowning out the music on the stage. It had been performed in the great barn at Snape Maltings, of course. The only place to sit was in the middle, where he and Milly and the in-laws and his parents and a few friends were positioned. He had started crying when the oboes and the voices had begun to merge with the balalaikas. He hid his tears with discreet movements of his fingers. Milly had given him one of her dazzling smiles in support.

Arvo Pärt, who was present only because his own work was being premiered the following day, sat in the row in front, dressed in a long, brown raincoat like a seedy French detective. He'd leaned forwards, a thumb buried in his huge dark beard, his bald head shining above the long hair, hunched and concentrated. He was all elbows, a lot thinner than Jack had expected, and kept nibbling the ends of his long fingers, too restless for an Old Testament prophet. His wife sat next to him, looking owl-like behind huge spectacles. She often spoke for him in interviews, and Jack was more nervous about what she might say than of Pärt himself. When the smoke started settling over the audience in a thin blur and she began to cough tubercularly, Jack knew he'd got what he deserved; Pärt and his wife slipped out with the help of an attendant – a far more interesting sound event, apparently, than anything on stage. Milly squeezed his hand as if comforting a relative at a funeral.

Jack took a bow afterwards and then, once the clapping had subsided and the house lights had gone up, surveyed members of the audience from the side. Among the silvery, distinguished heads there was a lot of winking, a lot of confiding of patient fortitude with thin-lipped smirks, provoking a subtle mirth in the others.

In other words, they were laughing at it. At him. He preferred the old, limping dowager he overheard in the bar: 'The usual awful tripe. Not nearly up to Messiaen. But one has to keep *abreast* of things, doesn't one?'

No sign of Pärt.

Milly's parents were staying two nights in Hampstead, this time.

There was the Kenwood concert on the second evening for which, as usual, they had packed a huge hamper at the Hall, strapping it to the back of the Bentley. This had become, over the last ten years, an annual excursion for the du Cranes. Nothing would dissuade Milly's father from bringing the vintage Bentley into London and parking it on Willow Road as close as possible to the house. Fortunately, many of the residents were away in their Continental second homes and so there was usually plenty of space near the house, which was up at the Well Walk end of the road. But this did not mean that the Bentley was not a potential target for thieves or vandals or even the casual, drunken groups piling out of one of the pubs lower down: Jack fussed about this, and felt petit bourgeois doing so, because the du Cranes' deep-rooted confidence in their own luck was always well founded. No one touched the Bentley. Their arrival was always announced with an elephant-like blast on its horn.

The Kenwood concerts on the Heath were convivial occasions, filling the lawns below the great wedding cake of a manor with chattering music lovers arriving with their cushions and their picnics and their booze. For those coming over the Heath from the south, there were neon strips tied to the trees along the dark, wooded paths. Progress was slow because of Marjorie du Crane's operation, which she was still getting over. The Hall back in Hampshire had been taken over by a film unit, which consisted of hundreds of people. They were filming a Jane Austen novel, which Richard du Crane insisted was *Mansfield Park* and his wife denied.

'It's *Persuasion*,' she insisted. 'And *such* a kerfuffle.'

'You must have asked them,' Jack laughed.

'They're so enormous and there are so many of them that one end probably thinks it's doing one book and the other end think they're doing another,' said Marjorie.

One of the neons was flickering, which made the path look rather sinister. People were overtaking them, talking in very loud, happy voices. Australian, Indian, American, Japanese, German. It was as if the world – the well-off world – was gathering for a powwow. Milly and Jack were carrying the hamper between them. It had a trunk lid and leather straps and had seen service in Khartoum, where Milly's uncle had been stationed in the war. It was also heavy. When the du Cranes had first started this hamper business some years back, Marjorie had taken the path in great, healthy, big-boned strides.

'Oh, I'm so slow.'

'You're fine, Mummy. We can't go faster with the hamper, anyway. It's getting heavier and heavier.'

'Growing old is much, much worse than you ever think it's going to be.'

'The film manager, producer or whatever it's called, he told me,' said Milly's father.

'We'll know when it's on the box,' said Marjorie, a little snappily. 'Are there any nettles? Last time I got stung.'

'We've hired deckchairs and we've got an enormous blanket,' said Milly.

'I'm talking about the path.'

'Then don't stray from the path,' laughed Milly's father, as if he'd made a wisecrack.

'Oh do shut up,' said his wife, stepping carefully in her long silken dress.

Because each year's concert was always on the second day of the visit, Jack's in-laws would generally be showing the strain by then. Jack dreaded it, especially since the event had been taken over by English Heritage and the classical content all but replaced by pop hits and corporate hospitality packages. It never seemed to clash with any of his commitments.

The fact is, his commitments were dwindling. He was part of the furniture of the contemporary music world . . . a spare chair, he would see himself as, in his low moments: the type produced when there were too many guests, the type that folded up and no one could quite recall where it could be found. Milly was sympathetic but too busy with her work to say any more than the truth: that he was exaggerating and should regard himself as extremely lucky.

'Most people would kill for what you've got,' she'd say.

It was a sultry, overwarm evening with a suggestion of thunder and rain. The original choice had been for Hayley Westenra, an ex-*Neighbours* singing star from New Zealand whom Jack had never heard of, but when he had seen her programme he had flatly refused to go. Because Jack was allergic to Cuban music, Ibrahim Ferrer had also been out of the question, as were both Bootleg Beatles and *Grease – the Musical, in Concert*.

'It doesn't really matter,' Milly had said. 'She just loves to hear the music wafting over the lake. It might be her last year.'

'You call it music? It's just a way for English Heritage to fill the marquees with fat business cats.'

'People love it,' Milly said. 'They love a good tune. It's always seething.'

'There are good tunes in Satie and Sibelius and Mahler and Janáček and Schumann and Britten and Bartók. Off the top of my head. Why do we have to endure crap, Mill?'

There'd been no choice but to opt for the *Classic FM Live Opera Gala*, which consisted of the usual suspects: Verdi's 'Chorus of the Hebrew Slaves', Puccini's 'Nessun dorma' and Wagner's 'Ride of the Valkyries'. It did not surprise Jack one bit that local residents complained about the noise.

He led Marjorie to her deckchair close to the water and warned her about the fireworks.

'I love fireworks,' she said.

'She *is* fireworks,' Milly's father cried, to Jack's embarrassment. In fact, everyone was shouting, he realised. Braying, was the word, as they opened their cool boxes and popped their tarry New World wine.

'I certainly used to be, didn't I?'

'You did! My God, you did!'

'Our hamper's being admired by the proles,' Milly whispered into Jack's ear, only half ironically.

She lifted the lid and pulled out the champagne, chilled from the fridge but already too warm, and Jack opened it, spraying his groin by mistake. It was always the same menu: expired English delicacies out of a picnic in some forgotten Edwardian novel, complete with gingham napkins and a soft plaid blanket. The game pie had shot in it, as usual, which his father-in-law only warned him about too late, after it had crunched against a back filling. The garden gooseberries had somehow got squashed yet again. The music was rousingly painful, the Open Bowl disgorging its sounds over the lake and lawns like a cartoon mouth with its tonsils wobbling, although Jack had discreetly inserted his custom-made, moulded ear protectors. Everyone else was happy, very happy.

Last year Jack had gone back at midnight to search for his jacket, which he'd left hanging on a tree, and was amazed to see the lawns covered in a sea of bottles, paper napkins and plastic cups. With the concert still ringing in his ears, it was (at least symbolically, because his parents were very neat) like everything he had left behind in Hayes: now it was catching up with him again, and instead of meeting it halfway, like certain other composers, he was retreating into a corner where a tiny number of people spoke among themselves.

'They *are* bashing it out, aren't they?' shouted Milly's mother.

'I think it's damn marvellous,' shouted Milly's father.

'I didn't say it wasn't!'

Milly's mother had ridden to hounds until right up to her operation. Now, of course, hunting was banned, or supposedly so: no one would take a blind bit of notice, he'd been told. Jack had watched the red-coated riders set off from the Hall and found it surprisingly beautiful and stirring, although he had never ridden a horse in his life. But when the hunters had come back with a great clatter for a cup of tea, he had found them both vain and dull. One of them, a local farmer, believed that the movement against hunting was led by 'Jews' and 'darkies'.

'He was just talking for effect,' Milly informed Jack, afterwards. 'He's really very sweet. He was terribly hit by foot-and-mouth.'

'Didn't show.'

The fireworks flashed, thumped and fizzed after the strains of the Wagner had died. It had started to rain very slightly. Jack had a childish admiration for fireworks, although a Catherine wheel had spun off its nail when he was four and singed his hair.

'Victory for the people,' he murmured, watching a green, intense light bloom into fiery explosions that turned a deep blue, dying in long weeping streaks like a psychotic's willow.

As they were packing up, Howard Davenport appeared, dressed all in black with a pink nosegay. Howard adored the Kenwood concerts, even though he was a cultural snob. Jack wondered whether it was another gay fixture, like screenings of *Lawrence of Arabia* or royal outings by the Queen.

'Fancy seeing you here,' Howard beamed.

'I'm surprised to see myself here, too,' said Jack.

'Isn't it gorgeously, outrageously naff?'

'Simply tons of people,' Milly said, folding up the plaid blanket. 'This is damp, Mummy.'

'Why are you in black?' Marjorie querulously demanded.

'Shows up the grease less,' Howard replied. He showed the big round helmet in his bag.

Jack introduced his in-laws properly and they set off back to the house together along the wooded paths; although Howard had another pressing engagement, his motorbike was parked in Tanza Road.

'I'm madly in love again,' he said to Jack, opening his arms wide.

'Who's the lucky gal?' Milly's father asked, having drunk too much champagne.

'Marcus,' Howard replied. 'He's twenty-six and is writing a biography of Cecil Stephenson.'

Milly's father said, 'I don't mind a damn, actually, as long as you keep it to yourself.'

He stumbled slightly on a tree root and Marjorie held his arm and tutted and urged him on, holding up her long dress with her other hand.

'I've known plenty of poofs in my day,' she said. 'Don't you worry about us.'

'I'll try not to, Lady du Crane,' said Howard.

Jack winced. Howard loved titles. No one admitted they had never heard of Cecil Stephenson. Jack steered him off love by asking him about his work.

'The quartet's drowning in work. Off to Japan next week.'

'That's good.'

'Exhausting, but one can't exactly skive from a quartet. I'm teaching, too, you know.'

'I thought you hated teaching.'

'Very few of us are wedded to a living and breathing cash machine.'

'Thanks, Howard,' said Milly.

'Does he mean you, poppet?' asked Milly's father.

'No, Daddy,' said Milly. 'He means a hole in the wall.'

Jack was annoyed that his in-laws were listening in, it didn't seem right. Marjorie was wheezing and they slowed down for her on the main path, to her surprise.

'You are slow, you lot,' she cried into the darkness.

'By the way,' said Howard, as they were parting in front of the house. 'I've got a prodigy.'

'Is it painful?' asked Jack, who was too tired to make better repartee.

'Astonishing. He's five years old.'

'Violin?'

'Viola, would you believe. Learns piano, too. But viola's his first love. His mother's broke, some sort of refugee, but sacrifices everything for her son. Aren't I lucky?'

'Poor little mite, ending up with you as a teacher.'

'Just what I say. She came to one of my concerts and then found me on the web. She's a hotel cleaner and rents this grotty little cupboard with cockroaches on the North Circular. I charge half price.'

The others had already disappeared into the house. The rain was pleasant, clearing the night air. Jack could smell the Heath's vegetation on the other side of the road, sweet and luxuriant.

'The thing is,' said Howard, '*you* were a prodigy, weren't you? And rather poor.'

'We weren't exactly poor, Howard.'

'Working class, then.'

'We lived on a brand-new housing estate with a garden front and back in Hayes. Dad worked in the EMI factory. Electronics. Skilled job. If we were working class, no one told me.'

'Were you otherwise completely normal?'

'Look at me. Aren't I normal?'

'Too normal.'

'Exactly.'

'This little fellow, he's called Jaan. From, hang on, Estonia. I always want to say Eritrea.'

'I spent three weeks in Estonia,' said Jack, 'a few years ago.'

'Did you? So you did.'

'I liked it very much.'

'In three months he's done what I did in three years, almost. And I started at ten. I've never met a kid that young who specifically prefers the viola to the violin.'

'Great. Don't spoil him.'

'He's endowed. I like that word, endowed. His mother used

it. Her English is terribly good but not, thank God, perfect. It is incredible, when you see the real thing. Did I tell you Marcus is writing a biography of Cecil Stephenson?'

'You did.'

Afterwards, Jack wondered why Howard had told him about the boy. Deep down, Howard lacked self-confidence. He was almost frightened of what he was taking on with the boy, it challenged his stoical cynicism.

The conversation had made Jack think back to Estonia. He'd rather not have thought about it, not right now, because deep down he believed that what had happened to him out there was in some way responsible for Milly not being able to have children. And Milly not being able to have children was in some way connected to his own inability to concentrate on his work, to produce not much more, in the last six years, than five-finger exercises. He tacitly ignored the obvious and more dreadful reason, which was to do with a banal and silly accident.

On top of the hot blast of the Kenwood concert, it was enough to make him fairly morose over the nightcap in the sitting room. Unfortunately, their neighbour had joined them. He was a recent divorcee-to-be called Edward Cochrane, a financial consultant in his late forties who seemed to have a rebound crush on Milly. He had been to a Kenwood concert earlier in the season: Jools Holland playing R & B.

'Do cheer up, ducks,' Milly said.

'I'll bet you hated the music, Jack,' said her mother.

This was the first time anyone had mentioned the concert.

'You could be right there, Marjorie.'

'At least it communicates,' said Edward Cochrane. 'Witness all those happy faces.'

'A car horn communicates, Edward.'

'You know what I mean.'

'Alas, I do.'

Milly suggested they hit the sack.

'It's just one big corporate hospitality package,' said Jack. 'It stinks.'

'Just because they don't play your works,' Edward simpered.

'Oh fuck off.'

'Jack, stop it,' said Milly.

'We don't mind,' said Marjorie. Milly's father mumbled in his sleep as if in approval. He'd dropped off on the wicker chair and was straining it noisily with his lolling weight. 'God, you should hear the staff sometimes.'

Edward, whose powder-blue summer blazer was, as usual, powdered in turn with dandruff, scratched his thinning hair. 'I really ought to leg it. I'm up at six tomorrow. Off to Glasgow.'

'Howard seemed on good form,' said Milly.

'He's got a prodigy,' said Jack, leaning his elbows on his knees. 'Five years old.'

'Is this the Howard whom we met?' said Marjorie, yawning. 'The poof?' Her fingers looked suddenly old and brittle under the lamp at her side.

'From Estonia,' added Jack. 'He's called Jaan.'

'The man seemed terribly English,' said Marjorie.

'I mean the boy. The boy's from Estonia.'

'Terrifically go-ahead,' said Edward.

'The boy?'

'Estonia,' Edward laughed.

'Jack used to be terribly keen on Arvo Pärt,' Milly explained.

'I still am.'

'Not quite so much,' said Milly, who knew every nuance of her husband's creative development up to a certain level. It often surprised him.

'They're pretty dynamic,' Edward went on. 'The most successful of all the Baltic States.' He sipped his cognac. He had heavy eye bags that came and went. 'The whole bloody country's one big dot-com.'

'I'll bet it is,' said Marjorie, as if the fact was suspect.

'I've been there,' said Jack, looking at Edward with undisguised distaste.

'So have I,' said Edward, unexpectedly. He smiled and winked, waiting for the effect. 'Bloody finest stag night *ever* in the history of the world.'

'You got drunk,' Jack stated, wanting to throw him out of the house.

'We got very . . . very . . . *very* drunk,' Edward said, leaning forward in emphasis, his public-school drawl coming to the fore. 'I'm afraid to say we were a little bit under the influence, yes. A little bit Brahms and Liszt, yes.'

'What's Liszt got to do with it?' asked Marjorie.

'Rhyming slang, Mummy.'

'Listing to starboard,' Edward chortled, making the easy chair tip.

'I'll bet Johnny Foreigner appreciated it,' Jack said, drily.

'I'll have you know, Jack, that the Estonians make an absolute killing out of us going over there and getting utterly rat-arsed. Hard cash. Hard euros.' Edward's expression had turned oddly aggressive, his eyes glittering nastily.

'Tough way to make a living,' Jack said, turning his head away from his neighbour. He was amazed at his own internal rage. It affected the tenor of his voice. One was supposed to feel sorry for Edward Cochrane – but Jack couldn't blame Lilian (the wife) one bit for scarpering, taking the kids with her.

'By the way,' said Marjorie, 'who was your bearded friend's lover writing a book about?'

'Cecil Stephenson,' said Jack.

'Who's he when he's at home?'

'Haven't the foggiest,' said Jack.

'Many tougher ways that I can think of,' Edward said, curling his upper lip.

'Tougher but with a bit of dignity to them,' Jack rejoined, scowling at him.

'Beddy-byes,' said Milly, brightly, standing up. 'Come on, Daddy.'

'Just when it was getting interesting,' said Edward, who was watching Milly carefully as she leaned over her father. Her dress was fashionably low cut, and her breasts were clear almost to the nipple from Jack's and Edward's angle.

'Come on, Daddy-o.'

'He's hopeless, isn't he?' laughed Marjorie, white with age and exhaustion.

The Venezualan girl, Marita, came in at 1 a.m., while they were heading for bed. She brought with her a strong smell of cigarettes and perfume and drink. She slept in what would have been the au pair's room on the top floor, if they'd had kids. Jack had his study under the eaves, with a view over the Heath, and Marita's music would sometimes tremble his floorboards even though it was never very loud. Marita, despite her Latin bonhomie and sweetness and perfect teeth, could irritate Jack. Her English was reasonably fluent, but very hard to understand. Her role was not quite defined, or was too diffuse: she was a cleaner, a house-sitter, an occasional teacher of Spanish to Milly, and sometimes cooked excellent meals. She waited on table when they had more than six or seven guests. She was, finally (although only in Jack's head), a nanny to the ghosts of the children they could not have, and to the ghost of the child they had lost, lost like a cricket ball in the long grass right at the end of the innings.

It had happened like this.

Twenty-nine weeks after Jack had returned from Estonia (they no longer calculated in months), Milly was magnificently pregnant. She carried it well.

So well that they had managed to move from Richmond to Hampstead, a feat eased by the prospect of looking out on trees and fields. There'd been one house for sale by the Heath, on Willow Road, absurdly expensive, which they had spotted quite by chance while visiting friends up there. Jack and Milly had constructed for themselves a future that owed more to Kate Greenaway illustrations than gritty reality. Milly had spent an entire morning sitting on the grass verge by the side of the road, checking out the weight of traffic, the noise. It was, she said, surprisingly light. The birds were louder.

'As long as they watch the road, our kids can go straight out on to the Heath and run about and play,' she said. 'It'll be as good as the country.'

'What about nasty blokes in raincoats?'

'Oh, Jack. You always see the negative side.'

'There was that case last week, Mill. In Richmond Park.'

'I could be squashed by a bus tomorrow, sweets.'

The Richmond house sold like a shot for a bloated price they could hardly believe, but there was a paper delay and they moved in eleven weeks before she was due. The place had been owned by a very old and frail spinster with twelve cats, who told them she had been patted on the head by Sir Edward Elgar in Netherhall Gardens in 1919. She assumed from the look and from the 'feel' of them that they would leave everything intact, which is why she was relinquishing her childhood home to them and to no one else for such a reasonable price (it was, in fact, horribly overvalued).

'I don't blame you,' Milly had said, dazzling the old dear with her smile. 'It's absolutely adorable.'

'You won't touch a thing, will you? It's my life, you see. My whole life.'

She moved out and the Middletons moved in and the builders got going within a fortnight. Jack and Milly had decided to gut the place from top to toe: it was seamed with dirt and neglect and overrun by mice, with a lingering sharpness of cats. No carpet had been changed since the Great War. There was rot in some of the beams and the kitchen ceiling had collapsed in a shower of laths and plaster when a hefty builder had jumped off his stepladder in the room above. The wallpaper was stained with damp and (in the main bedroom) with mysterious, sepia-red splashes. Jack found a cat's skeleton in the attic, lying in a perfect little mound of its own decay. Milly was not yet actu-ally a director of Greenleaves Designs but she had all the contacts necessary to make the house as environmentally responsible and low toxic as was possible in London, although the projected composting toilets proved impracticable. To Jack's dismay, no baths were to be installed, and the showers were the type that piddled compared to the fierce jets in the Richmond house.

When the really heavy work got going, and the house was a pillar of dust, they took a fortnight's holiday in Umbria. After that, it was a matter of living in whichever half of the house was not being worked on, sealed off as best they could from the noise and the dirt. Marjorie du Crane thought they were mad. Jack thought he would go mad. Milly fretted about the effect of the vibrations on the baby: she was sure the hammer-drilling would be sending ripples through the womb fluid. It was a trying time.

One day you are in a trying time, the next you are in a tragic time. And the trying time seems like a lovely, innocent time compared to the sad, unimaginable time of now.

They were going out for dinner with the Nicholsons, who were old Oxford chums of Milly's. He was a wealthy and successful barrister, she was a curator at the V & A. They were chiefly notable for never asking a single question about Jack's work. They lived in Maida Vale, at the furthest end of it, which was awkward to get to by car. It wasn't really that awkward, but Jack disliked going to dinner with the Nicholsons. It was not that he wanted them to ask questions about his work, because those would be bound to be dull or even stupid questions, but he would have quite liked some sort of recognition that he existed as a professional entity. They made him feel he was a social parasite, that Milly's marriage had been disappointing, merely a reflection of her leftish political views. They said nothing overtly, of course, but it was all suggested in the silences, in what was omitted. They impressed and frightened Jack, although he was slightly older than them. The Nicholsons had three small children, who were unfortunately very sweet and gifted in all sorts of directions. He was called Oscar, for some reason, and she was called Olive. Oscar and Olive. They had a Bolivian nanny called Heaven.

Milly and Jack were late. Milly had had a scan that morning in which she imagined she'd seen the eyelids among the fish-like flashes and shadows, and had spent most of the afternoon running up curtains for the nursery with builders tramping in and out and playing their radio too loud. She was tired carrying her unborn baby about, and would have liked to have gone to bed with a book. But the Nicholsons knew the Prime Minister and were not the type you cancelled dinner with. Oscar Nicholson was an expert on wines, more expert even than Daddy. He was mad about wines from South Africa.

On the way there, Jack was very grumpy. He said he wasn't going to drink apartheid wine tasting like the kerosene that brought it over and listen to Oscar and Olive go on about their fucking great mansion in the French countryside. Milly tucked her thumb under the seat belt and eased it away from her enormous tummy and told him not to be silly, apartheid ended years ago and that he only had to put up with the Nicholsons once or twice a year.

'Time scurries along,' said Jack. It was the first year – popularly, though not technically – of the twenty-first century, which already felt tarnished.

'Your favourite phrase.'

'Yup, I recycle them. I'm ecological.'

'Please slow down. You're making me feel sick.'

Jack was sure, afterwards, that he *had* actually slowed down before it happened. He was certainly pretty much within the speed limit, which was thirty coming into Maida Vale. The long, straight road was joined by another minor one to his left on which a four-by-four appeared and he clocked it as slowing down but then, quite astonishingly, its massive five-barred gate of a snout was right in front of him and he pulled hard down on the wheel and swerved, hitting the kerb of a traffic island with a jolt and then braking to a stop several yards further on. Their little VW must have missed being splodged by the four-by-four by half an inch.

'Fucking hell,' he said. 'It didn't stop. Are you all right?'

Milly was short of breath. She was holding her stomach.

'The seat belt,' she said. 'I was sort of squashed against it.'

'Oh Jesus,' said Jack, who had a tendency to panic.

'Baby's fine,' said Milly, who had a tendency to show pluck. 'It kicked in protest.'

'Could have been a lot worse,' said Jack. 'Complete *berk* driving one of those bloody great evil Amanda tractors.'

The other vehicle had stopped. Jack got out and went over to it, red with rage. An elderly woman was peering down at him through the driver's window. She reminded Jack, with her straggly, dyed blonde hair, of a famous photograph of a stricken refugee off to the death camps in a train. She opened the door and it swung right out with its own weight. Jack glared at her.

'Were you trying to kill us, or something?'

The woman was very smartly dressed, with gold bangles on her wrists.

'I looked, and I saw nothing,' she said, in an accent that might have been Dutch. 'You were arriving like a mad man.'

Jack opened his mouth in astonishment. The woman smiled at him wanly. Milly was calling him. He held the four-by-four's heavy door in his hand and, after a little effort as the vehicle was on a slight incline and the hinge seemed to be stiff, slammed it with great force and ran back to his car.

'Whassup?'

'Nothing,' Milly said. 'We're very late, that's all.'

Milly looked chalk white, but that was the street lamp on the traffic island. Jack had never liked Maida Vale with its straight roads and its enormous Victorian houses: it struck him as sterile, despite the leafiness. They got to the Nicholsons' three-quarters of an hour late. Olive said it was just as well, she'd had time to read to the children herself and now Heaven was telling them a folk story in Spanish, which they adored because they understood it. Oscar looked disgruntled under his bonhomie.

'How's the walking cradle?' he boomed.

'I'm just great,' Jack joked, before Milly could reply. He liked to play up the working-class-boy-made-good in front of the Nicholsons, even though he never *felt* working class. It disarmed their own more subtle attempts to do it for him. 'I'm rocking on fine, man.'

'Scan this morning,' said Milly. 'Heard the heartbeat. Saw the eyelids.'

'Is it a boy . . . or a girl?' asked Oscar, frowning at them as he must do in court when cross-examining a witness.

'Maybe they don't want to know!' laughed Olive, coming up along the hallway behind and putting her hands on Oscar's back.

'Exactly,' said Milly.

'Come through, you guys,' said Olive, kissing them on the cheeks in the French way. 'Meet the neighbours.'

The neighbours turned out to be a young Indian couple from Boston who were 'frighteningly brilliant' research chemists in something called biotronics. As ever at these occasions, half an hour of mutually intense, very interesting information was shared between complete strangers before familiarity crept in and the defences went up. The Indian woman, called Moona, was remarkably thin and beautiful, with breasts like a pair of eggs jutting beneath her silk blouse; Jack imagined hugging her and breaking them. There was already an immediate kerfuffle over the pre-prandial stage, since Olive was keen for everyone to go straight into the dining room to eat, while Oscar wanted the new arrivals to sample his 1964 South African sherry. Unusual nibbles in majolica bowls lay strategically distributed around the sitting room like a reproach: it looked as if no one had touched them.

'Told you, still apartheid,' Jack murmured to Milly, as they passed into the dining room.

They sampled the sherry at the vast oak table while Olive was perfecting the opening vichyssoise in the kitchen: it had a special sauce that required some last-minute operation with a lemon. The conversation drifted into politics over the main course, a superb duck *à la provençale* 'with herbs from our garden near Les Baux'. The two hosts looked horribly tanned in the candlelight, which exaggerated Milly's pallor, as did Moona next to her. Oscar and Olive were very much against letting in lots of refugees, as they thought it was bad for the refugees. A group of Kosovars had been housed in a community hall in Maida Vale.

'They were really depressed,' said Olive. 'I took them some spare toys for the little ones and, honestly, I felt like Mary Poppins. They all hugged and kissed me. Hell of an uplift but they were rather smelly.'

'Dignity's the first to go,' said Oscar.

'I hope you had a good scrub down afterwards, Olive,' said Jack.

Jack and Milly had been against the bombing of Serbia, although they recognised that Milosevic was awful; Moona and her husband declared themselves neutral, which annoyed Jack even more. Jack had written a protest piece in 1998 called *No Arms, No Legs*, which drew on Janáček's nursery rhyme sequence, *Řikadla*, and featured a mezzo-soprano, a clarinet, a piano, and three mimes. The mimes were not very good. It received a standing ovation at Dartington, a sympathetic review in the *Guardian*, and then disappeared. He described this piece self-deprecatingly but at some length, mainly for the other guests' benefit, until Oscar broke in, wondering if Milly was all right. Milly's forehead was glimmering with sweat and she looked deathly, but she dazzled them all with her smile and said that she'd overdone it and was just a little tired.

There was an awkward silence and Jack felt foolish. Then Oscar served some more Haut-Médoc from outside Johannesburg and Olive started on about Cherie Blair and how well Cherie coped with being a mother, despite being a high-flying lawyer. Beyond her head Jack noticed an old-master painting of a cow standing in a stream with *Wenzel Hollar* on the label. Olive insisted that Tony Blair was a marvellous father and husband and a very fine and very brilliant politician who wasn't afraid of having ideals.

'He's actually a terribly nice chap,' said Oscar, in case they hadn't got the point.

'You know him personally, Oscar?' Moona asked – which was precisely the point, in fact.

'The man of teeth,' Jack interleaved, but no one noticed.

'Oh yes,' said Oscar, modestly; 'have done ever since Islington.'

'What happened in Islington?' asked Moona's husband, his heavy, existentialist's spectacles flashing the candlelight.

'Oh, we lived there,' said Oscar. 'We were virtually neighbours. Borrowed tea, that sort of thing.'

Moona frowned. 'Borrowed tea? You mean you gave it back afterwards?'

'Coffee, tools, that sort of thing,' Oscar went on, ignoring her joke. 'A piece of three-ply chipboard once, God knows what for.'

'I've always found our Tony rather camp,' tried Jack again – which was in fact an observation stolen from Howard, who was deliberately camp.

'Camp?'

There was an awkward silence, during which Jack realised how camp Oscar must look in his wig and robes.

'Don't see it myself,' said Olive.

'There'd be nothing wrong with it if he was, of course,' Jack mumbled. 'On the other hand,' he said, reviving his fortunes under the influence of the thick-tasting, over-powered Haut-Médoc, 'there *would* be something wrong if he believes he has a direct line to Our Lord, as is rumoured. Most of the rest of us have to go through to the operator.' No one laughed. He floundered on. 'Olive, now, does the present Prime Minister believe he has a private direct line to our Lord?'

Olive blinked. 'That *is* one slight drawback, yes,' she said.

'In what way? Detail, detail.'

'Well, he does listen to God every evening, on his knees.'

'Thought so,' said Jack. 'That must be very reassuring for him, knowing that he can never make the wrong decision.'

'I suspect most leaders think they have God on their side,' said Moona's husband, sounding very grown-up and sensible. 'Most Americans do. We underestimate religion, believing everybody's basically rational. This George W. Bush, son of ex-President Bush, he's about to be the Republican candidate, you know?'

'Vaguely,' said Jack.

'Now he's got the Christian Right behind him,' Moona's husband went on. 'Wait till he gets to be President. Then the shit's gonna hit the fan,' he added, to Jack's relief.

Olive pulled a face, more at the expression than at the prospect of someone she had hardly heard of becoming President of America.

'Wicked,' said Jack, lifting his glass to his nose. 'Can't wait.'

'I think I'd better go and lie on the sofa,' said Milly, in a faint voice. 'I'm incredibly sorry.'

'Sorry, Mill,' said Oscar. 'What's up?'

'Sorry, we've been ignoring you, darling,' said Olive, cocking her head to one side, having clearly not heard precisely what Milly had said.

There was a pause and then a subtle ripple of panic passed over the table. Everyone except Moona's husband stood up in a chorus of apologies – perhaps in order to ward off the awful thought that something serious might be happening. Jack led Milly to the sitting room with Oscar and Olive fluttering at her side. Moona had poured out a chilled glass of water from the jug and soaked a napkin in it. Her husband stayed put, telling Moona he was better out of the way, and carried on eating. The napkin was applied to Milly's forehead.

'Oh, I'm really, really sorry,' said Milly, 'but I think I'm bleeding.'

Jack was feeling physically sick with panic.

'Oscar, where's the bloody phone?'

'Hold on, hold on. There's no point in getting in a state.'

'I'm not in a fucking state! I just want to call a doctor, urgent.'

'I can't feel my baby. I think it's all gone wrong.' Milly was running her hands over her belly. There were spots of liquid on the massive, comfortable sofa, which Olive had covered in a hand-woven tapestry. Pointlessly large, fat tassels hung inside at each corner and were getting in the way. 'I can't feel him move.' The liquid wasn't blood, however, though it wasn't quite clear either.

'But it doesn't move all the time,' Jack cried. He had never seen Milly in such a state. It was awful. She was almost annoying him. And why had she said 'him' when they didn't know? Moona was stroking her forehead and Olive had gone off to get towels. Oscar was talking to the medical services on the phone, giving them directions in his deep, careful, barrister's voice. Now Milly was crying. Jack felt his insides turning turtle. The more stressed she got, the worse for the baby.

'Do you think a brandy's out of order?' said Oscar, putting the phone down.

'It was that bloody four-by-four,' said Jack. 'The stupid woman came straight out in front of us and Mill got a bit of a shock.'

'Seat-belt pressure?' said Olive.

'Yes,' said Jack. 'Why? Is it known about?'

'It'll be fine,' said Olive, but Jack saw something else in her eyes.

When the doctor came, fifteen stretched-out minutes later, Milly had calmed down. Her face was like lightly stained marble, with red patches under the eyes. The towel was not very wet and not at all bloody, Jack was relieved to see, though there were reddish streaks. All they needed, surely, was something to bung her up with. The main discussion during the fifteen minutes had been whether to take her straight to Casualty themselves. Oscar wasn't quite sure of the quickest way to the nearest hospital, and was trying to find an A–Z. It was probably in his chambers, he told them. When the doorbell had finally rasped (there was something wrong with it, it was an original feature), they all let out a sigh of gladness. The doctor was a small, stout woman in her fifties who looked fed up at being called out on a Saturday night, but she immediately buzzed for an ambulance when she heard about the seat-belt business.

'Why didn't you call an ambulance straight away?'

'No one thought of it,' said Oscar.

'No,' sighed the doctor, as if they'd all failed the primary test.

'I did wonder about that,' said Moona's husband, who had finally come through.

Jack was sitting on the floor, holding Milly's hand. He felt as if he'd clambered up through thick fog onto a vast and calming plain. Things were under control. The details of the sofa's tapestry, the overdone tassels, the wet hairs on Milly's forehead, the needlepoint cushion behind her head, seemed to him heroic in some way. The two of them were at the centre of everything, the centre of the world and of time and of space. He wasn't sure about the third, about the invisible baby.

The scan showed a blank screen. A black screen, blacker than a blank television. There were none of those little white fishy flashes, no shadows of limbs and head, no precious movement and no heartbeat.

'There's no heartbeat, I'm afraid,' said the woman in her white coat, a biro stain at the base of its top pocket.

The screen was so incredibly black, like outer space. It didn't even yield the dead baby. Jack felt like hitting the top of the screen, as his father would do for him during *Top of the Pops* when the TV went phut, even though his father hated *Top of the Pops*. Max, they were going to call him. Or Pippa, if it had been a girl. The nurse told them to go back home until Thursday because they only did emergency deliveries. Jack tried to get angry with her but was too busy hugging Milly, who was sobbing on a plastic bucket chair in the corridor. They called for a taxi to take them to the Hospital of St John and St Elizabeth, the reassuringly private clinic overlooking Lord's cricket ground, but even there they told them to come back the next day. He wasn't sure how they survived the interim. Milly lay on their bed and, although he was holding her, said she had never felt more alone. Jack knew why this was: she had been carrying another being, and now she was not.

The ever-sleeping baby was delivered, perfect in form, with the help of a lot of drugs, in an ordinary little hospital room – but still Milly had screamed in pain as she would have done if the baby was alive. Jack had not expected that. He felt distant, as if watching from a great height. The midwife was saintly and strong, as if created in some other realm expressly for this kind of pain and solace. It was a boy.

'Max,' said Milly, fifty years older and trembling. 'Oh, Max. My Max.'

Max was cleaned up and wrapped in a towel and they held him in turn through almost two hours. He smelt of baby lotion and powder and raw fish. His eyelids were slightly open and a slit of white was visible, as in a marble sculpture. The tiny fingers didn't grip, and they had perfect little nails. Jack felt closer to Milly than ever before, but at the same time she was locked away in her own grief, something calm and white and level he could not touch.

Milly had complications, afterwards. They went back to 'John and Lizzie's' where the 'top' obstetrician in the country (better than 'the most promising', Jack wanted to say) dealt with it all and afterwards explained to them, shiny with the considerable amount of money it had cost them, that the operation was successful but the chances of her conceiving a baby, let alone carrying it full term, were heavily reduced.

'You mean I'm sterile?' said Milly, who felt that ever since the four-by-four had pulled out in front of them she had 'switched tracks' onto a very dark line.

'I didn't say that, Mrs Middleton,' said the top obstetrician, swivelling his chair gently behind a very broad antique desk. He was in his mid-forties, with chubby fingers. The backs of his hands were as smooth and gleaming as burn-scar tissue, the black hairs on them too obvious. Jack would have liked to have liked him, but he couldn't.

'I never used the dreaded "s"-word,' the doctor added, with a faint smile.

'Well, it comes to the same thing,' Milly snapped. She was never awed by top people because she could trace her family straight back to the entourage of William Rufus, where a Henri du Crane lurked behind his nose guard, but Jack knew there was also terror in her tone.

'Not exactly,' said the doctor.

There was a pause. Milly had visibly shrunk. 'We took a year even to get that far,' she said.

The doctor's eyes swivelled onto Jack's face. 'Did you have frequent, or at least regular, penetrative sex?'

'Frequent enough,' Jack replied. His face burned with embarrassment.

'Not unusual,' said the doctor, putting on his wire-rimmed, oval glasses. 'As you know, male sperm counts have lessened over the last few years, for whatever reason.'

'Pesticides,' said Milly, staring at the floor.

'Or tight jeans,' said the doctor, looking over his glasses at Jack, like a headmaster who suspects something.

'Don't wear tight jeans,' said Jack.

'Everyone expects procreation to be easy, like purchasing a hamburger or a car. But actually, although maternal and infant mortality rates have vastly improved –'

'In the rich countries,' Milly broke in.

'Exactly,' said the doctor, some of whose clientele arrived in stretch limos. 'But even here it's the same old messy, difficult business.'

'Can we sue?' Milly asked, businesslike again. She seemed to be holding herself together remarkably well.

'Sue?'

He looked alarmed, which was gratifying.

'The driver of the vehicle that pulled out in front of us and that we only just missed. Who caused the stillbirth.'

'There was no actual contact between the vehicles?'

'No, but we hit the kerb. We were late and my husband was driving a bit fast.'

'Whatever, Mrs Middleton, there is no direct proof that the accident, such as it was, caused the death of your baby. Internal organs like the brain or the womb are not fixed by seat belts, they shift forward and speed increases their weight considerably. I believe your child suffered either a lesion or a straightforward head injury on striking the obstacle of the belly wall constrained by the seat belt, but there's no objective proof here that would hold up in a court of law.'

The phone rang and he answered it. Milly and Jack looked at each other rather blankly and then at the window, where the sky was almost clear of cloud. The room was large and airy with a good view of the pitch at Lord's. They were playing a match down there: hearty, hefty men without a care in the world. Tiny spots of sound, willow on leather. Jack was wondering whether to object aloud to Milly saying he was driving a bit fast. He was sure he hadn't been driving over thirty, but then he didn't have a very clear image of anything but the huge bonnet suddenly continuing out in front of them. The doctor came off the phone and picked up a silver ballpoint and twirled it between his fingers. A notice on his pinboard warned in blood-red capitals about the Millennium Bug, looking very foolish six months after the non-event. It was somehow re-assuring, but nothing else was. It made Jack think of the Dome, his mega-break, his failure.

'And what do *you* do, Mr Middleton?'

'I'm a composer.'

The doctor's face lit up. 'Are you really? Not of pop music, I hope.'

'No. Contemporary. Lots of squeaks and squeals.'

'How interesting. I'm a great fan of Berio. What do you reckon?'

Jack nodded slowly. He felt curiously outclassed. This man had dabbled in Milly's insides and was an expert on Berio. 'Pretty good,' said Jack.

'There's no one else in Italy, is there? I used to think Ligeti was Italian but he turns out to be Romanian.'

'Hungarian,' said Jack, effortlessly seizing on the opportunity and adding a long-suffering sigh for good measure. 'Technically.'

Disappointingly, the doctor only acknowledged his error with the tiniest of nods. 'Can't think why it's all dried up in our dear old Italy. They had Verdi and Puccini, after all. I play the tubular bells.'

Milly had covered her face in her hands, although she wasn't actually crying.

'I don't know,' she said, half to herself; 'I feel completely without hope.'

They left the hospital arm in arm, watched by swarthy men in reflective sunglasses around a woman in a full veil. Milly's things were in a small rucksack on Jack's back. They could hear the applause from Lord's the other side of the road. A mother with her newborn in a carrycot was getting into a silvery-black, open-topped Audi. An X-type Jaguar was purring in neutral behind it, its very pregnant passenger laughing happily as she levered herself out.

'I'm going to watch the cricket,' said Milly, unexpectedly.

'Are you sure? Don't you want to go straight home?'

'I just want to be with normal things.'

'Not sure cricket is normal,' Jack said, 'but if we're both free –'

'Why? What would you have booked up on the day I was leaving hospital?'

'I said, we're both free.'

As they watched the cricket, Jack wondered what he had done wrong. He felt as if their life had developed some sort of shadow in it, like a tumour on an X-ray. A curse. In the old days, or if they were Americans, they'd have prayed for support and forgiveness. Why forgiveness? Because they'd been too blasé, that's all. Not a great sin.

You were arriving like a mad man. That simply wasn't true.

He knew why Milly didn't want to go home just yet. Home would mean, not just the stink of fresh paint (the builders, plumbers and electricians had by now been transmuted into the painters and decorators), but the absence of what should have been. The absence of Max. Max in the room they'd earmarked for the nursery. They'd agreed that if Max or Pippa didn't work as names, they could change them after a few days. The name had to fit the child. Now there was no child and the name was a phantom, marked in careful script on a little plastic tub of ashes they planned to scatter on the Heath or in the grounds of Wadhampton Hall one day. They were vague about this. The tub was kept behind Milly's clothes in the wardrobe. Jack opened the wardrobe from time to time, to take the tub in his hands and look at the contents. The ash was like the ash that Graham, the Hall's gardener, scattered around the roses and the cooking plums and the peaches in the greenhouse. It wasn't sieved, it had bits in it. Tiny slivers and nobbles of bone.

They watched the cricket. The game was soporific, calming. The sun warmed the wooden seats; the white figures on the bright green turf and the trees against the blue sky were re-assuring. The faint smell of linseed oil, coconut cake and warm grass completed the reverie. It was an MCC match, still early in the season. There weren't all that many spectators, and only a handful were beerily rowdy under wide straw hats further along their stand.

Et in Arcadia Ego, thought Jack, ruefully. He'd been watching Saturday cricket one sunny day in Hayes with his older brother, a tranny between them playing Sandy Shaw, when the music had been interrupted by a newsflash: Bobby Kennedy had been shot. How old was he, then? Six? Seven? He remembered it as if it had occurred last week. His brother, Denny, who'd had long hair and was ten years his senior (which was why Jack's parents had always struck him as older than most), had started crying, to his little brother's great surprise. Only recently had he realised that his brother might have been crying about their mother's blindness, the accident having happened only a year or so earlier, and not really about Bobby Kennedy.

Whatever the reason for it, Jack sometimes reckoned that all his art was attempting to crystallise that moment, set its disparate elements in permanent and mutual suspension.

'All right?' he said, squeezing Milly's hand.

She pulled it away from him and settled it in her lap. 'Of

course I'm not,' she said. 'I can't believe something so stupid can ruin your life.'

'People are actually killed,' said Jack, floundering a little. The sun was too hot on his head, even though it was only June.

'My God, someone *was* killed,' Milly said, staring at him in astonishment. 'In case you've forgotten.'

Jack kept quiet for a while, stung. The batting had resumed and the soft *thock* of each connection and the ripples of appeal and applause started to weave musical ideas in his head. He'd forgotten his shades, and his cheek muscles ached from squinting.

Eventually he said, tearing himself from the shuttle of his ideas: 'I read somewhere that getting pregnant is a complete lottery. The main thing is that our chances are not zero. Then becoming pregnant can put it all back to normal, anyway.'

He could not get out of himself, could not reach Milly. She clapped at a four, with the others, and gave the tiniest shrug of acknowledgement. Nothing more.

'Maybe that dream of yours about the filing cabinet burning was a premonition,' she said, later, in the taxi back. She had had another cry on leaving the cricket ground, and her eyes looked as they did after her weekly swim at the fitness club near her office in Soho. 'And that caged fox thing. Were they the same dream, in fact?'

Jack shook his head. 'No, different. Different dreams.' He looked out of the taxi window at the people and the traffic.

Once you start lying, that's when the shadow appears. And he thought again: That's when it appeared.

FOUR

Five years later, a couple of days after the Kenwood concert, Jack sat in his study in Hampstead listening to Pärt's *Spiegel im Spiegel*, which, although a lesson in minimalist lyricism, was popular with the educated masses. He always found it calming, just piano and violin mirroring and returning, raindrops and wind, very simple and innocent, always returning to the A. The huge Bose speakers caught the most shadowy detail, down to the slide and knock of the pedal. It was very beautiful. He sat at his piano and sketched out some of the ideas that had been running through his head, scribbled over the bars strung like hair-thin wires between one internal ear and the other. These inward bars sometimes reminded him of a barbed-wire fence on a plain somewhere vast and grassy and wind-blown like Mongolia, snagging whatever blew through. Some of it was plastic, shredded. Even that served.

Then he sat in the window seat, set to cushions in the dormer, and looked over the Heath. He had everything, and he had nothing. He didn't need to teach, not financially speaking, but he took interesting private students just to keep up with what was happening at that level, and one of them was about to arrive. Since the bombs on the Tube a month ago, this student – a nervous Thai girl – had bought a bike, which kept breaking down. That was the term she used: 'breaking down'. How could such a simple machine ever break down? What she meant was punctures or the chain falling off. So she was generally late.

Following his lesson, he was due to attend an emergency meeting of the local community group: new people had moved in three doors up and wanted to deconsecrate the parking place in front of them that was reserved for disabled drivers. Apparently, the sign on its metal post interfered with their front outlook, but their real reason was clearly even more selfish: to have the convenience of a space directly in front of their house – for their massive Jeep, braced by what looked like chrome scaffolding and with tinted windows like a hearse. It would have been Milly's job, this meeting, but Milly was at work. Jack hated meetings of any kind. He was on the advisory board of three music colleges, including Dartington, and their get-togethers kept cropping up with frightening regularity.

At least Milly's parents had gone back home to Hampshire.

It was a leaden sky, and the Heath seemed bored with itself. The bombings had happened and now they were over, the rescue workers had finished in the sweltering depths, the rats had finished eating the dead, the words had all been said. No one had anything more to say. Nobody he knew had been involved, except for those close enough each time to hear the ambulances and fire engines amassing more densely than usual and who had immediately felt a thrill of fear. Milly had been driving to Hastings to advise on a private sheltered-housing project's grey water capture and had phoned him as soon as she'd heard, but he was taking a shower and there was Shostakovich on the bedroom stereo so he didn't catch the ring. She left a message. Because she was phoning from her mobile in the car, it was scratchy and barely decipherable, but he'd picked up the gist at one o'clock, when he'd taken a break from his ideas to listen to the news over a salad. Nobody else had phoned him in the time between, so he was possibly the last person in London to know.

On the evening of the second wave of attacks, that had not killed anyone because the bombs were faulty, Milly and he had set out on foot to the Indian restaurant on Fleet Road and had seen a woman run over by a double-decker down by the old cinema. She was black, and she was dressed in a long black dress, and was very hefty in the hips. She was stepping out with her shopping on the far side of the zebra crossing. They heard this cry (something between a yell of realisation and a scream) beyond the sudden, surprising mass of the double-decker, and then a few bright oranges rolled out from under their side of the bus as it came to a stop. Jack ran across, thinking he would be about to see something terrible, something sheared in half or torn into tripe. Just in front of the bus, with the vehicle's white plastic bumper broken off and resting against her, the woman lay on her side in the road, so fat she might have been pregnant.

'This is bad,' she shouted, trying to prop herself up on one elbow, having been pushed or maybe dragged some twenty yards by the bus. 'This is bad, I know it. It's really bad, I tell you.'

An ambulance from the Royal Free happened to be right there at the junction, on Pond Street, so Jack never got to help her. She was rolled gently onto the stretcher, and all the time she was saying, 'It's bad. I know it's really bad.' She was moving her feet, however, in their high heels.

The driver of the bus had come out with his hands on his head, like a trapped felon. 'Christ, I don't know what *happened*,' he kept saying. 'I just don't know what *happened*.' Everyone was watching in the detached way people do watch such things, and the young guy who had been waiting at the zebra crossing with the victim turned to Jack and said, 'It's such a bad day. It's just such a bad day, innit?'

And now it was over, and the bad day had sunk into all the other days and was obliterated except for fragments floating on the surface or deep in people's minds.

The piece Jack was working on right now was an attempt to catch some of these ideas. Provisionally entitled *It's Just Such a Bad Day*, it was scored for chamber choir and percussion and scheduled to be performed in the Purcell Room as part of the South Bank's Contemporary Music binge in November, for which the theme of 'Terror' had been tacitly agreed by everyone involved. But it was not going well. One little fragment was not connecting to another. It was a chain bracelet without the links. Everything must have a reason for being, and must be born out of another. The four bombs were sounded on baroque timps, as modern kettledrums had too much of a spill-over of dominant overtones and he wanted a very clear and precise tonal colour. There was also a cymbal crash, which he kept moving about but could not find a place for. And yet he saw it and heard it in front of his eyes. The worst of it was that a truly brain-worming pop song about a bad day, with almost the same refrain, was being incessantly piped the minute, it seemed, he stepped outside.

He thought of the snow leopard in the zoo in Estonia. He often thought of it, as he often thought of the fox. They were related. One was before, one was after. Both were in a cage many times too small for their being. It seemed like yesterday, the whole thing. He felt his face warming with the memory. *A Filing Cabinet on Fire in the Middle of the Street, with Caged Fox* described what had happened, but in the words of music, words that have no literal sense, only the sense of one idea or emotion or texture flowing out of another until the final hush before the applause.

Listening to his piece, in the middle of the barn at Snape Maltings in 2001, Jack had wondered why he wrote anything at all. It had sounded, at first, paper-thin and trite. Then, during the middle section, with the melodic line of the voice finding its resonance in the ecstatic major of the instruments, he had been taken there, taken to the place inside himself where he had found another, all that time waiting for him.

As if the world had been turned on its axis to face her and he was helpless before her, helpless and on his own.

Howard phoned him in the middle of the lesson with the anxious Thai, who had turned up fifteen minutes late owing to the fact that her bicycle had been stolen just before she left. Jack didn't believe her because she lived in West Hampstead and it would have taken her more than fifteen minutes to walk it. He wondered what made such a gifted musician tell lies, albeit harmless lies. She was twenty-one and still lived with her parents, who ran a restaurant in Earls Court. Where Howard lived, as it happened.

He sounded excited.

'Guess what, Jack?'

'What?'

'I've broken my bloody finger.'

'That is not good, Howard.'

He meant it, too. Howard explained that he had been shaking out a tablecloth when his finger hit the wall. Jack couldn't see it.

'Where were you shaking it?'

'A friend's house. In his very nice garden. That's immaterial. The Japanese tour is off. At least for me. I'm gutted. And my lessons. I'm going to have to give one-handed lessons.'

'Oo-er.'

'It's in a splint, it's a compound fracture of the upper flange, thanks for asking. At least a month.'

'A nice word, flange.'

Howard needed consoling. He also needed someone to accompany a student of his who was playing Schumann's *Märchenbilder* for her audition at the Royal College and this was her last lesson.

'When for, Howard?'

'Five o'clock today. *Per favore.*'

'I've a meeting on a matter of great local importance.'

'Send Milly.'

'You know Milly works. She gets back at seven every day, knackered from trying to sell composting toilets and photo-voltaic panels to people who take weekend breaks in Australia.'

'Why does she work so hard, Jack? I work hard because I need the cash. She's a living cash machine –'

'Howard, do you want me to come over or not? Right now I'm teaching.'

'You ar-re notta jest a gee-nius,' said Howard, in a cod accent meant to be Italian, 'you ar-re smelling of the r-roses.'

'Yeah, yeah. Spot on. I've noted that down in case you've forgotten it by tomorrow.'

The Thai student at the piano was staring at him on the phone with an intense, smiling, patient look. They had been working on serial technique and its use of chromatic texture, and the loose paper on the desk was covered in scribbled numbers and arrows, like a chemical formula. He wondered, as he sat down again next to her, whether her brimming enthusiasm indicated that she fancied him, or was merely how Thais were, a kind of politesse. When he and Milly were considering adoption, Thailand was one of the possibilities. They were too old now (over forty), to go through the official channels, so they'd spent a long time poring over the atlas before consulting an agency. There were so many dirt-poor or conflict-riven countries to choose from. Because of her work with responsibly harvested timber suppliers, she had a lot of contacts with Thailand. And they both felt that Thais were nice and polite and friendly, like the Vietnamese. It was like choosing curtains. A moment came, last spring, when they revolted against it.

'We'll come back to it,' said Milly. 'It doesn't have to be Thailand. Maybe we should go for somewhere with much worse problems. Burkina Faso. Mali. Niger, where they've got kids coming out of their ears.'

'A disabled mite with leprosy or something, abandoned in a sewer in Somalia,' said Jack, half jokingly.

'You said it,' said Milly.

'Or we could just get a St Bernard,' Jack went on, keeping it light.

'That's not very funny.'

'No. Actually, seriously, maybe a dog would be a good idea. The Johnsons were broken into last week.'

'Not until we move to the country,' said Milly, who knew all about dogs and their snail-trails of saliva and their stinking wet coats. Her parents' present pair of golden retrievers burrowed into your groin as though they'd lost a rubber ball in there.

And then she started crying, quite unexpectedly. It was the memory of Max and the thought that she'd be forty-two soon and the move to the country was predicated on small legs pattering over the lawns. Her best friend, Samantha Carlisle, had started the menopause at forty-three. But Sammy had five girls and a large estate in Devon, farmed organically.

The truth is, Milly felt useless, compared to her parents and – this was her and Jack's secret – almost everyone else. Her older brother, Philip, would inherit the Hall, as every older brother had done since 1105 (with the odd exception, like a kink in the rope, that the family ignored). So she threw herself into her work, trying to persuade nasty little men with goatee beards in places like Basingstoke to be environmentally responsible when they did their office makeover. She also offered feng shui as a complement, having taken a part-time course. But feng shui was already losing its allure, having signally failed to improve, in any detectable, accountant-friendly way, either office relations or profits. It was all very draining. She was increasingly left with minor nursery-school conversions and corporate executives who fancied a wooden house smelling of sap with built-in sauna. Yet she was always reading about green design being an expanding sector. She still had hopes for the world: that it could be saved. Jack, who'd given up this idea long ago, admired her for it. Truly admired her.

Yeh was waiting. Jack had thought about Milly crying that time, and many other times, and felt depressed.

'OK now, Yeh, play the Schoenberg as if it's a girl crying for her lover.'

Yeh collapsed into laughter, her hand over her mouth, her frameless spectacles almost falling off her delicate nose. Jack wondered if the touch of her shoulder on his was deliberate. She reminded him of his long-ago Chinese girlfriend. He wondered, as Yeh played the late Schoenberg as if it was his early *Verklärte Nacht*, whether his lost son would have been followed by a daughter, and whether that daughter would have liked the piano as much as Yeh liked it. He corrected Yeh a couple of times and then played it himself, trying to invert the piece so that the notes became silences and the silences became notes, at least in his head.

'That's so beautiful,' she said, touching his shoulder again with hers. She didn't seem anxious any more. Maybe her anxiety was to do with him.

'Yeh, when you get out into that nasty world of music professionals, never say that to anyone superior to you in position or talent. They'll think you're saying, "I wish I could play like that."'

'I wish I could.'

'You play the way you do, I play the way I do. But what do you want to be, a composer or an interpreter?'

'Both. To compose and play for my lover.'

She was looking straight in his eyes. He looked away, flicking his bulky lock off his eyebrows.

'OK, that's it, Yeh. Same time next week. The Chopin nocturne.'

All he'd had to think of was Milly, crying that time and many other times.

There was what sounded like a tarantella being played on a fiddle as Howard opened the door to his flat. His finger was in a splint and neatly bound.

'Hear it?'

'That's not Schumann.'

'The smallest size viola. Balkan dance exercise.'

'The prodigy?'

'It's not the stereo,' Howard laughed.

The lively fiddle-playing came to an end. They went through to the living room, where a small boy stood in a white collared shirt and corduroy shorts. He had jet-black hair that flopped across his brow and was holding a small viola that still looked too large.

'This is Jaan,' said Howard. 'My little prodigy. We're almost finished.'

'Hi, Jaan. I'm Jack. Short for John. Well, it's not really shorter, is it? I guess Jaan might mean John, too. We've probably got the same name. We seem to have the same hairstyle, at any rate.'

The boy nodded but didn't say anything. He had a very serious face. Jack knew he had a tendency to gabble, with kids.

The piano took up 60 per cent of the room. It was a Bechstein salon grand. The carpet was white and fluffy, like the coat of the Dulux dog, and the piano's paws were hidden in it. Jack liked the all-whiteness of Howard's apartment, with the pottery (that Howard claimed was Sumerian, but Jack couldn't believe that) a scriptural buff on the white shelves. The books were mostly in the hallway, which made it cramped. All Howard's money had gone into this place, which looked out on Bolton Gardens – the end furthest from Earls Court Road. The kitchen and the two small bedrooms and Howard's tiny study in the box room were immaculate. The guest bedroom had a double bed on which, Jack recalled, Howard would perch while Jack tried to read before sleep (this was when he was over in London from The Hague: Howard's flat was very convenient).

'I feel very close to you, Jack,' Howard would say, in his silken dressing gown.

'Really?'

'Yes. I think we could grow even closer.'

'Probably.'

'I don't feel we're close enough.'

'No, I think it's very special as it is, our friendship.'

'But it could be an awful lot closer. There's a missing element, Jack.'

'I think it's just fine as it is.'

Howard never tried it on in any other way; no fumbling, no overt sexual innuendo. Eventually, he gave up.

The boy had a limp, a slight one. Jack tried not to notice but Jaan's little body rolled slightly from side to side as Howard took him into the kitchen to choose scores together on the table.

Jack sat at the piano and ran his fingers over the keys. The touch was tighter than his own: it didn't quite play itself in the same way. And it was due for a tuning, from the sound of its lower register. Because Jaan, the little limping boy from Estonia, was there, he played Pärt's *Für Alina*, which was a piece that left plenty of space for improvisation as long as you obeyed the composer's instruction: *Calm, exalted, listening to one's inner self.* Jack had played this piece for hours, in the past, before it became well known. He could see the boy through the open door of the kitchen, but the boy didn't look up. He had a sweet, round face. Then he and Howard came back in and Jack came to a stop, gently muting the sustained note.

'You're from Estonia? I love Estonia,' he said to Jaan.

The boy's mouth puckered at one corner. It might have meant anything. It might have been a smile.

Howard said: 'Jaan, show my friend what you can do. Jack's a famous composer.'

'Oh, so famous I am, I am,' Jack said, his own voice tinny in his head.

'Play him the Mozart, Jaan.'

The boy immediately tucked the viola under his chin and, with a five-yard stare straight ahead at the piano leg, played a little Mozart sonata. Jack had never seen a kid playing so fiercely, as if he was fighting some counter-current, and yet somehow the notes came out with relative delicacy.

Jack clapped, pulling an impressed face. 'Pretty darn good,' he said. 'A very nice tone.'

The sound was, of course, childlike on the little viola, and the playing without subtlety, but for a five-year-old with less than a year's experience, the performance was fairly remarkable.

'What do you like about the viola?' he asked. He was thinking of Kaja in the concert in Tallinn, and how he'd never quite been able to get a bead on the whole thing, which had gone mostly shadowy except in his dreams.

The child shrugged. So far, he had not said a word to Jack. Anyway, it was a stupid question. Howard was answering his mobile, which had vibrated in his pocket at the end of the Mozart.

'Your mum's on her way,' he announced to the boy. 'She's

got held up on the bus. The traffic's awful since the . . . erm . . .'
He checked himself and turned to Jack. 'So, what do you think,
Mr Famous Composer? Pretty ace, huh?'

'Pretty impressive.' He chewed his lip a little and then he
said, 'Do you know, Jaan, one of my favourite composers is
Estonian? Arvo Pärt?'

The boy was avoiding his eyes and frowning, as if thinking
hard.

'Howard,' he said, 'I need the toilet?'

'Of course, guv'nor. Don't forget to say hello to Cliff.'

Howard kept a goldfish called Cliff in a tank in the toilet
window. He'd won Cliff in a funfair nearly ten years ago and
the tank water was an opaque green. When the boy was out
of the room, Jack asked Howard about the limp.

'Club foot. He's had the works, plaster and braces, vast
improvement, but that's as good as it'll get.'

'Oh dear. Poor kid.'

'He copes.'

'Seems to.' To change the subject, he asked Howard who was
going to stand in for him in the Dumka Quartet.

'Henninge Landaas,' Howard replied, flopping onto the sofa.

'That's OK, then.'

'I was looking forward to Japan. They say the muscle action
might not be the same. I don't even have brittle bones.'

'That's woeful. Did I tell you about the woman we saw being
run over by a bus?'

The doorbell chimed and Howard levered himself up, wrink-
ling his hawk nose.

'That'll be the neurotic mother,' he said, without lowering
his voice. 'The harassed Kaja K.'

'Kaja?'

Jack's heart stopped, then reluctantly got going again with a
kind of mammalian reluctance, a more-than-my-job's-worth
sort of lunge. He got off the piano stool, then got back on it
again, too unsteady to stand. He had to escape, but the only
way was into the box room. Howard was opening the door in

the hallway, out of sight beyond the arch and the side of the bookcase. The boy came back into the room: he was Estonian and his hair was as black as Jack's used to be (it was now a false black-with-a-hint-of-henna, having lurched into a streaky grey two years ago), with the same bulky Hitler-flop of hair. He avoided Jack's eyes again and began putting away his viola. Jack did not know what to do. The voices in the little hallway became faces. One of them was Howard's, the other a young woman's that Jack had never seen before. He felt stupid. Of course Kaja was a common name in those parts, like Sarah or Helen here. These coincidences only happened in TV dramas and trash novels. London was full of Baltic women, and Russians, and Poles. She seemed very young to be the boy's mother. She was carrying a full-size viola case.

'This is Jack Middleton,' said Howard. 'The composer.'

'Hi,' said the young woman.

'Hi, Kaja,' said Jack. The name in his mouth was oddly dulled, like a sweet turned into a pebble.

'I'm Ffiona,' said the woman, frowning. 'With two *f*s. Like in toffee.'

'Fortissimo,' said Jack, surprised.

Howard laughed. 'A muddle, Ffiona. I thought it was Kaja at the door, the mother of this little boy. But you were in fact Ffiona with two *f*s, five minutes early.'

'For once,' Ffiona said.

'Jack's going to accompany us,' said Howard. 'We're very blessed.'

'Thank you, Padre,' said Jack. 'Hymn 142.'

Ffiona seemed either very serious or secretly nervous. She was dark-haired and attractive, with a rather square jaw and firm mouth – and was not much more, Jack now realised, than eighteen or nineteen. Her black eyebrows made her look permanently quizzical. The little boy sat on the sofa next to his rather battered leather viola case, his feet dangling off the edge. Jack sat at the piano, smiling his encouragement, and shook his fingers to loosen them. The boy did not smile back. Ffiona and he were a pair, Jack thought. Maybe they were counterpointing the ever-ebullient Howard. Ffiona asked Jack if he needed the music and Jack said, rather contritely, that it might be useful to have the Schumann in front of him.

She played superbly but without a great deal of soul, more earnest than musical. She needed to smile.

'Thank you, Ffiona,' he said.

Howard said that it was faultless apart from a few minor points he ran through quickly as Ffiona nodded.

'Above all, you are *going* to loosen up for the audition. That is an order. Start with the face. If you relax your face, everything else will follow. *Compris?*'

Ffiona's firm mouth flickered a smile. Jack felt it would be an interesting mouth to kiss, little pecks to soften it up followed by a long, lingering smacker. Howard's phone went off in his pocket and he answered it impatiently.

'Oh dear,' he said. 'Keep calm. I'll tell him. He's quite safe with me.' He turned to the boy and told him that his mother was still on her way but that the bus was stuck in a traffic jam.

'The traffic's really mental since the bombs,' said Ffiona.

The boy's ears pricked up. Howard asked him if he would like a glass of guava juice. The boy said, 'Yes, please.'

Ffiona had to leave and they all wished her luck.

'She never thanked you, did she?' said Howard, in the kitchen. 'I noticed that. Whereas our little Jaan here is extremely well brought up, not being English. Shall I mash, as we say in Derbyshire? "Make tea", to the likes of you. I made a strawberry-jam sponge cake yesterday and it actually *rose*.'

'Just a swift one, thanks. Where's she coming from? The mum?'

'Bounds Green.'

'Where's that?'

'Exactly. Right on the North Circular, Enfield way. Land of the zombies. Piccadilly Line, but she won't now take the Tube.'

'What's her surname?'

'Krohn.' Howard spelt it. 'Why?'

'Nothing.' He didn't recognise the name. He felt relieved but somehow reduced. 'That's a long way, Bounds Green.'

Jaan was studying the table, where the glass of guava juice threw an interesting reflection. Howard began to pour the tea. His strawberry sponge cake was ridiculous, like a tall carnival hat sawn in two when the head was still in, but it tasted good.

'Well, I'm much sought after as a teacher, for some reason,' said Howard, catching the drops off the teapot's spout with a kitchen wipe. 'Much sought after. Like a character property with a view, orig feats and FCH.'

Jack felt a twinge of jealousy, even though he had no intention of teaching beyond the minimum. Howard worked hard, he needed the money. Jack would have liked to have needed the money. Maybe she had changed her name, married.

'Milly thriving? The ecology thing?'

'That reminds me, we're going out at seven thirty. Wedding anniversary.'

'Serious?'

'Very serious.'

'Ruby or diamond?'

'Melamine, I should think. Twelve years.'

'Oh, that's bound to be something semi-precious, like jasper. Or sapphire. Twelve years! Unbelievable. Look, you two have done darn well, in the circs,' Howard added, his eyes filming. 'I'm sure something'll happen, anyway, when you least expect it.'

'It's been quite a while now,' said Jack, vaguely.

Howard got up and served the boy more guava juice. The boy was swinging his legs on the chair, making a tapping noise. Jack felt repelled by Howard's goodwill: it made him feel like a pensioner, or crippled in some way. He finished his tea and stood.

'I'll be off, then. Thanks for the cuppa.'

'And thank *you*, really truly.'

'Bye-bye, Jaan. Go well.'

The boy seemed elsewhere, studying the guava juice.

'No, I mean it,' Howard insisted, at the door. 'Ffiona Fortissimo isn't the world's gift to the viola but she's awful earnest. Meant a lot to her. I'll owe you one.'

Jack noticed Jaan watching them from the kitchen. Jack gave him a little wave. The boy looked away.

On the way down the two cold flights of marbled stairs, Jack realised that Howard was his best friend. He realised this because, out of all their friends, he was the only one who could be moved to tears by their childlessness. Howard had once considered adopting with his late partner, Julian, but they'd both been busy men (Julian had been a music festival tsar). Then again, kids were never what you expected them to be. Berio wrote his thirty-four violin duets for his son when his son was still only a baby, Jack recalled. He wasn't sure whether Berio's son had taken up the violin, in the end. Maybe the poor little squit had had no choice. Or maybe he'd looked up at the white clouds and craved the harp.

Jack left the building and turned up Bolton Gardens. He was aware of a woman crossing the road a little behind him and he stopped and he followed her with his eyes as she went into Howard's block.

He trotted back to the porch, his heart pounding. The woman was already climbing the stairs. She was dressed in a thin skirt and a loose summer blouse; a cotton cardigan was thrown around her neck.

Then she was gone.

Jack was hidden behind a tree on the other side of the road. Only his nose showed, and as much of one eye as could be used without giving his position away. The boy was talking and half skipping as he emerged, holding hands with his mother. His mother had released some cap on his shyness. She was nodding, smiling, carrying his little viola case in one hand like a kind of gun.

Jack wanted to shout her name, but instead he stayed very still. He stayed very still until she had gone.

*   *   *

Jack sat at his piano and played Pärt's *Für Alina* over and over, free to do what he would with the tempo and the metre and his memories, until Milly came up and said he was keeping her awake. She'd thought it was Keith Jarrett. It was two o'clock in the morning and she put her hands around him because she thought he was doing it for them, the night of their wedding anniversary, externalising the sadness and the joy. He stroked her hands and nodded.

The anniversary meal had been fine, although Milly reckoned he was troubled, and she knew why he was troubled because she was also troubled. Everyone was troubled but that was different, that was macro-trouble in the background. They ordered two bottles of wine and the food was not disappointing, for once – almost matching the exorbitant price. It was a new French place a few minutes' walk away and they'd had to book a table a fortnight in advance. It was cosy and chic at the same time, with lithographs of Parisian doors under soft spotlights and authentic French waiters, although they were less discreet than at home and flashed their eyes at the women, as if playing a role expected of them. Jack had great problems getting into gear throughout the meal, talking and smiling with only the front of his face. Milly was exhausted and so drank to compensate, her eyes glittering and her cheeks flushed. She was full of a contract she had just signed and sealed, involving remanufactured systems furniture for a hotel chain Jack had never heard of.

'The whole idea,' said Milly, adjusting her beaded top, 'is that green hotels are what people want to stay in.'

'Having flown there by kerosene-burning jet.'

'These hotels are all in the UK, actually. They're pretty exclusive. We're going to use unemployed artisans to recycle the furniture and make really interesting personalised stuff.'

'Composting toilets?'

'No, not yet, but you wait. When the water runs out . . .'

'Most people don't care a toss, Mill. They're fat, greedy and selfish.'

'Stop that, Jack.'

'What?'

'That funny tense thing you're doing with your lower lip. It's really ugly. It'll give you wrinkles.'

'I'll start to be respected.'

'How did the composing go?'

'Composting. Dry.'

'Jack, cheer up. It's our twelfth. I love you.'

'I love you, Mill.'

They clipped glasses and drank. The waiter came, chuckling at nothing in particular. Someone had probably made a joke in the kitchen.

As usual they'd contemplated going on to some sort of hip club, but neither of them knew much about hip clubs and, anyway, they felt too old. The nearest really hip clubs were Camden Town way and they didn't fancy braving the dealers to get to one, even by taxi. They wound up back home, sipping Calvados in the front sitting room to George Butterworth's songs in the background, which felt suitably plangent. Jack had bought her some big, open-throated white lilies which scattered orange powder from their stamens. He told her about Howard and Ffiona but not about Jaan, let alone the boy's mother.

'I've got this feeling,' said Milly, looking at him carefully. They were seated opposite each other, Milly curled with her legs up on the sofa. The scented candles were burning. That was the only light. It was restful, although Jack couldn't find this restfulness inside him.

'What?'

'It should be tonight. It'll be tonight.'

'What will?'

'I feel really chilled out. It's partly being totally knackered, actually, but who cares? My defences are down. Because I think,' said Milly – who was saying this as if she'd never said it before – 'that I'm my own worst enemy. I think it's psychological, that I'm blocking. This is a mega-major discovery, Jack. I think my mother is too dominating.'

'What's Marjorie got to do with it?'

'I think I've been denying motherhood because of her.'

'OK. Lets me off the hook.'

'If I'd just shacked up with anyone – you know, if I'd left you and just slept around, not caring, no protection –'

'And got Aids,' he pointed out.

'That's irrelevant. I'm talking theoretically. Because actually I love you.'

'Uh-huh. And so?'

'I'd have probably got the pee word, Jack.'

'Pregnant. Let's say it.'

'Yeah. Rock on.'

'And?'

'And so,' she said, gazing at him intently.

Jack had lost the thread. His face felt unformed. He had a picture in his head of Kaja in front of the Baltic Sea, twilight turning the water an astonishing colour, metallic, neither silver nor blue but that danced in your eyes and went both brighter and darker at the same time. But he went to bed with Milly and they made love in the old position, and she gripped his knees and he stroked her spine and her desperation and did his Japanese meditation thing and it was fine, she went very calm and peaceful. He crept out from beside her and played *Für Alina* until she padded up and held him from behind.

'Still got my feeling,' she said. 'Really strong, it is. I think Max is with us on this one.'

He hesitated before replying. He really couldn't cope with Max being involved from on high, or wherever, waving with those miniature fingers.

'That's cool, Mill. Really it is.'

Kaja, he recalled at that moment, meant 'echo' in Estonian.

'Love you, mate.'

'Love you to bits, Mill.'

The next day he went out to get bread and *pâtisseries* at Louis'. It was Tuesday – Milly's early hour at the fitness club. As he was about to open the front door, the *Guardian* nosed its way through the letter box and hung there, thick as a loin of venison.

He walked a mite shakily up the High Street, post-cognac. The air was swimming around him, losing the night's freshness, ready to become a hot August day. Someone looking like Errol Flynn was checking his text messages as he crossed the road without looking. The Waterstone's window was full of books by John Irving. A huge Tesco Metro truck was turning into Heath Street, wiping out the row of shops beyond. As usual he felt the world was losing its particularity of place: he wondered if anyone else under about eighty felt this.

In Louis' Patisserie he bought two apple-filled croissants for breakfast and some sticky raisin buns for tea, breathing in the fragrance of the Continent. It reminded him of Tallinn, and he had an attack of butterflies. No, it wasn't the cognac. Only one customer in the coffee room behind: a stiff, smart woman who looked guilty about having a breakfast of sweet *pâtisseries* in Louis'. Jack tried not to stare at her, as if in wonder. He was half comatose, not responsible for his actions.

You could be in deep yogurt, pal.

He crossed the road to Tesco Metro for milk and basics. He fumbled with his change at the checkout and the pence went rolling. He let them be but customers picked them up for him, as if he was disabled or old. He thought about how you knew people and then you realised you didn't, that most of what you thought about them was what you needed to think about them. The Tesco Metro truck blocked the entire view from the cash tills and was throbbing out diesel fumes and its unloading mechanism squealed and hissed so loudly that Jack had to block his ears on coming out of the shop. He was getting more and more sensitive to everyday noise, he'd noted. No one else seemed bothered by motorbikes without silencers or the crash and roar of the bin lorry or people screaming into their mobiles. Even the acceleration of a passing car made him sweat. And walking past the boutiques and their knobbly wall of music was the aural equivalent of having a sharp stick run along his ribs, up and down, up and down, up and down. What he needed was a little reed-fringed island, the slippery expurgation of a sauna.

He tried to picture the High Street when podgy-looking cars with chrome bumpers hummed by once every ten minutes or so, leaving a whiff of leather and walnut. He bought a *Ham & High* in the paper shop, his nerves flinching slightly when he saw the word *TERROR* in all the headlines: maybe something had happened while they were drinking cognac. But it hadn't, it was just the long sustained echo of the booms, the cymbal crash, the timp's calfskin, pitched C2, struck four times and resonating to the seventh harmonic over the quiet. Or maybe it was the press, stretching it out artificially, manipulating emotions in the same way music did.

Curiously, he felt a drop of disappointment mixed in with the relief. The day after the second wave of bombings, the *Independent*'s tabloid-like headline, CITY OF FEAR, had sent a chill through his body. And then he'd realised that no one around him looked in the least bit frightened.

When the wrong person was shot point-blank by the forces of order on that very day, *then* he was scared.

Waiting in the paper shop's queue, he glanced at the *Ham & High*: a young guy on a bus had been stabbed to death in Islington for objecting to having chips thrown at his girlfriend. Jack thought: That could have been me. If someone was throwing chips at my girl, I could not have turned the other cheek. One minute you're on a bus and full of life, the next minute you're dying. When he pictured the scene, he saw the chips bouncing off Kaja's face, not Milly's. He realised that he hadn't taken a bus for years.

He was separated from most people in the world by this one shit thing: money.

A silky black Rolls with a chauffeur and a Saudi-looking guy in shades in the back was waiting at the lights as Jack came out of the paper shop. Its number plate said: *AA1 UV*. He felt better, because he had something to despise.

Gap had just opened its doors and was playing that track by

the Red Hot Chili Peppers, which wormed around in his head while he was making coffee. He laid for breakfast in the 'garden room'. This was a twenty-foot extension they'd had done, with recuperated Edwardian French windows all along one side and a forest of pot plants, so that the house melted into the garden. It was a beautiful room, with elm floorboards and a 1920s Dutch pine table. It was the room in which, if the sun shone, Jack felt most contented with his life.

It smelt a little sickly today: that was the lilies. It over-powered the scents from the garden. Jack had opened the French windows wide and was watching a bird on the unkempt lawn. Their gardener, Will, was a balding hippy survival who dressed in denim dungarees and believed that weeds were beautiful. His main tool was a daisy fork, although he left the daisies. He was very expensive. Milly's landscape consultants thought the garden was not untidy but a cottage masterpiece. It had been photographed for glossy magazines. Jack reckoned it looked a bit of a scruff.

Milly was not yet back. They'd made love and maybe this time would be the jackpot. Instead of imagining her pregnant, or cradling a living baby instead of a dead one, he pictured her coming in and saying, 'Jack, I'm off to Berlin. I've fallen in love with a woman. I need a life change. I'm no longer chasing phantoms. I don't care about having or not having kids. She's a video-installation artist called . . .'

Jack thought about a name. He was hungry. He sat down at the table and bit into the croissant but couldn't find the apple. Even in Louis' it always ended up at one end, as if they were made on a slope. Better to get the plain ones, without the filling. But he was seduced by the aromas of cinnamon and honey and crust dusted by flour. Easy to be seduced. Café Majolica had smelt good, too. Coffee, almonds, curd, a girl's sweat. England was deprived of pleasant smells, there was too much sugar and beer and frying in deep fat. There was too much fat. Too much incon-tinence. His music was very 'severe', as Jean-Luc the oboist would say, meaning something different, because in French you could say it of a landscape and mean it as a compliment. A video-installation artist called Matilda. Gabriella. Lolita. Nicole. Karen. Yeah, Karen was about right, pronounced Germanically. The bad thing was, a very dark part of him – the part that once, when he was nine, wanted to push his father into the Bonfire Night pyre in the field by their estate, for instance – was hoping Milly *would* come in and say just that, because then he could start all over again, without rancour.

He would call Kaja, who was a few miles away. He would leave the country. He would pick up where he'd left off.

Broken off.

He put his head in his hands. He was frying his brain, or what? Milly was ten minutes late.

I love you, Mill, he said to himself, but almost out loud. *I love you to bits. Please don't go off with anyone, man or woman. Please don't get blown up. Please let's carry on, just as we are, because we know each other better than anyone else ever can.*

And this room, for instance. This house. Radio 3 playing Bártok, right at this moment. This massive, beautiful house smelling of lilies, its garden murmuring through the open doors. A laughable distance from the Heath. It was almost *in* the frigging Heath. What could be better than his life?

Nice try, but no. He would not change his life, or have it changed for him. All they needed was a kid or two. Or six. Has someone got a problem with that? The cosmos, for instance? The fucking cosmos?

Eh?

He would call his new piece by that old discarded title, *Echo*.

'Kaja' in Estonian. It was a silent homage. The muse thing.

Milly would come in while he was working, sometimes, and then go straight out again. Later, Jack would ask why and Milly would say, 'I felt your Muse in there. She got jealous when I came in.' She'd always say 'muse' with a hint of a capital.

Really what this meant was that he was working well. She was usually right. There was an intensity when one little element linked with the next and gradually a landscape unfolded. An interruption spun it away, broken. Even the wine gums would remain untouched.

He felt that the muse, embodied in Kaja for the last six years, could turn into an interruption. Muses could be very dangerous.

'*You're* my muse, Milly,' he wanted to say, when Milly said this thing about the muse being jealous, but he never did. It wouldn't have been true. It would have been trite. It might have led to bad consequences. Above all, he did not want to be trite. As soon as he felt a line of music as existing in only two dimensions, he scrubbed it. Two-dimensional was surface, was triteness. Everything was tempting you away into triteness, it made up 99 per cent of human manufacture. White clouds were not trite, and they were always changing, melting into other forms and wonders.

Milly phoned from the fitness club. She'd met Deborah Willetts-Nanda – remember? – and was having brekkers there.

Jack mooched, feeling lonely. He hoped Howard would phone so he wouldn't have to make the decision to phone him. He took a walk on the Heath and met no one he knew and came back by the second-hand bookshop in Flask Walk.

Jack now studied the stacked, cramped shelves without taking any books out. He found the dark catacombs of threatened places like this a metaphor for his own mind, and strangely uplifting. Echo. Everything was echo. He'd been commissioned to write a piece for Magdalen College Choir, last year, to a short poem by John Fuller, and he went to Oxford to visit the chapel, to gauge its acoustics. They were near perfect, but he wrote something that he knew would fling the sound into echo and hang there. Fuller was very pleased, and Radio 3 broadcast it live, and for a moment Jack thought that being a composer could not be touched as a profession. He had thought the same when he'd won the Munich Ernst von Siemens Prize for Young Composers when he was still young. He didn't think it very often, these days.

The music shelf had nothing interesting. He noticed a battered copy of Noel Streatfeild's *Grass in Piccadilly*, which was dated 1947 and had once belonged to an Elsie Crowthers. Jack remembered reading Streatfeild as a thirteen-year-old, skulking in Hayes Town Library. This was for adults. He kept having to remind himself that he was an adult. Married twelve years yesterday, taking his breakfasts in a twenty-foot extension called the Garden Room that he and his wife had had built on to their very own desirable and extremely tony residence.

And here it was, his des res. He had the key to it. So it must be his.

'All right, neighbour?'

'All right, Edward.'

'I'm setting to on redecorating the master bedroom!'

'Great idea!'

He scurried into the house as Edward Cochrane unloaded shopping from the boot of his Chrysler. *The sexiest thing to carry your children since your wife*, the advert for it had run. Milly had toyed with the idea of taking Chrysler to court for defamation of women. Edward had laughed at this, rather insensitively, but now the car was only carrying himself. It was rough justice. You had to be sad, anyway, to find a car sexy. Except perhaps if it was a 1923 Bugatti, Type 31A.

Milly was home again from the club, glowing from the sauna and the swim and smelling of eucalyptus. She had heard an awful story in the gym. The giant egg-timer thingy on the wall of a sauna in some hotel in Stockholm only worked at an angle. An obedient Japanese tourist wasn't told and stayed in there for an hour; found dead of dehydration.

'That's what comes,' said Jack, making a fresh, stronger coffee whose aroma filled the house, 'of putting time before pleasure.'

'I mean, it's awful, but it's funny-awful. He was obviously told not to stay in there once the lower glass had filled up. But he must have been pretty bloody thick.'

The coffee trickled through the filter, filling the jug.

'I like the idea of being killed by an hourglass,' said Jack. 'It's like a cheesy metaphor gone literal.'

'What have you got *Anna Karenina* out for? I thought you'd already ploughed through it ages ago.'

'I have.'

'This copy's hopeless. Bits fall out.'

'I know. It's a postmodern version.'

'Dump it. I'll get a new one from Daunt's at some point.'

Jack took it off her and said, 'No, it's fine now. I mended it. Anyway, I need it.'

'What for?'

'Feeling inspired. Need it, that's all. Maybe achieve what Britten didn't.'

'I'll pop out this afternoon. Is this you? This little heap of dill? At least if you have a perversion, clean up afterwards.'

Jack laughed. 'I forgot to get more lapsang, by the way.'

'You didn't forget, you never thought about it,' said Milly. 'You were *distrait*, as usual. You're very *distrait* at the moment.'

'Should you have actually gone to the sauna if, you know, things might have worked last night?'

'Oh no,' groaned Milly.

'How are you feeling, in fact?'

'Why am I so stupid? I don't really want it, do I? See?'

Jack shrugged. 'It's probably too early to make any difference.'

They drank coffee in the garden room, and Milly ate her croissant anyway. She was always trying to find ways to keep her figure, and having a sauna before breakfast was one of them. Jack didn't point out that she'd had two breakfasts.

This is how the rich live. Nothing compels them but their own guilt, which is not very strong.

'No, she lives on the edge. Right on it. Why?'

Jack cradled the receiver, pen still poised. 'Woeful. The North Circular.'

'No address, just that I know she mentioned it's almost bang opposite Homebase and the gas works.'

'Yuk. Misery. Like a Ken Loach film.'

'Oh, much worse than that I should think. At least those films are set in the North. The North is so much better.'

'Look, do you think that surname beginning with K is her real one?'

'No idea. Why the interest?'

Jack had prepared his spiel for this question.

'His very sad eyes made me think he might need, you know, a helping hand, support-wise.'

'Money?'

'Spot on.'

He heard Howard breathing close to the mouthpiece.

'Jack, throwing cash at a problem is not always the answer. His sad eyes might come from not having his dad around. Or an awareness of his club foot.'

Jack's stomach contracted. He was sitting on the sofa in his study, with Britten's *Les Illuminations* coming through the pair of Bose speakers, quite loud. Howard had commented on this, but Jack could not tell him that it was to avoid Milly over-hearing him at the door. It was a technique used by dissidents in Estonia, according to Kaja's father; to muffle the bugging devices that might well be planted in your room somewhere hard to find. It was still Tuesday and Milly had decided to work at home. Late-August fatigue, clients away, office dull. She was downstairs preparing gazpacho soup for tonight's dinner at Burgh House, in aid of the Red Cross. The gazpacho soup had to be carried up there nice and cold in a big bowl covered in cling film. They'd have to walk very steadily, especially on the hill. He'd have to walk very steadily with this whole thing, in case it spilt over into disaster and tears. The kid was five years old. Kaja must have met the dad very soon after Jack had gone back home. The kid could be his own kid, of course, but for some reason that idea did not seem feasible. She would have come looking for him earlier. She would not have called herself by that surname beginning with K.

'Wilco, Howard, but a hole in the wall is better than a lump in the throat.'

'I think he's serious, but not sad.'

Jack remembered him bouncing along in that jerky, lame way, chattering and laughing next to his mother. Next to Kaja. Kaja, a mother!

'What did my composition teacher say, Howard, when I asked her what advice she'd give me, as I was starting out?'

'Find a rich patron.'

'OK, I've sold you that one already, but she wasn't wrong.'

'Jack, being far from rich has never hurt me.'

'I would say you *are* rich, compared to an Estonian immigrant.'

'There's rich and rich. I bought that flat in the slump with me mum's inheritance. What she left me when she popped her clogs. For a rainy day. Or, as we say up in Derbyshire: *When it's gettin a bit black ower Bill's motha's.*'

'Howard, I'm sorry.'

'Don't be. If it's owt to do wi' me I'd let it alone, our kid.'

Jack always found Howard's Derbyshire dialect irritating and overdone, but he could tell how annoyed Howard was in turn by all this talk of money. He was not getting very far. He chatted about other things, mainly music gossip, to mollify Howard, and then rang off, forgetting to ask how the finger was.

He'd had a nightmare last night in which Kaja and the limping boy were an inseparable twosome with very sharp teeth, popping up in the dark alleyways of a city (a bit like New York in the thirties) that he was desperate to escape from. Kaja must not know that he was a friend of Howard's. Howard must not mention his name. He would have to tell Howard the truth, but Howard was unpredictable. He had this irritating self-righteous streak of moral virtue. A counterbalance to all the sexual indulgence.

Jack hoped the boy hadn't described him too thoroughly. He wasn't very familiar with boys of five and their descriptive powers.

He turned off the Britten at the end of 'Being Beauteous' and went downstairs.

'Hi, how's it going?'

'Left it too late,' Milly sighed. 'It's not going to be cold.'

'Put it in the freezer.'

'Won't fit. It'll be the unpopular gazpacho instead of someone else's unpopular rice salad. Please leave the dill alone. You're always rubbing it between your fingers.'

'I like the smell.'

'It gets on my nerves.'

'Does it matter if the soup's not cold?'

'Jack, who's ever had tepid gazpacho soup? I'll be a laughing stock.'

'You can't be serious.'

'I am.'

'It's only the Red Cross, Mill. Thought that counts.'

'I should have done it instead of going to the stupid sauna that's probably killed my baby.'

'Mill, stop it.'

'Stoppit, stoppit,' she repeated, in a cruel, mocking tone that was entirely meaningless. 'Oh, fuck.'

The doorbell rang.

It was Edward Cochrane in a boiler suit splashed with white paint.

'You won't believe this, guys, but I've just heard from Lilian. She's in pissing Argentina.'

'With the kids?'

'With the kids.'

And he was breathing hard, as if he'd run all the way from the other side of Hell.

Edward looked better in a boiler suit; he claimed the paint on it was old, that he hadn't yet started on the master bedroom, and slumped onto the sofa. His round, schoolboyish face, with a plump nose and laughter lines creasing up from the eyes behind the trendy, gold-rimmed spectacles, looked less debauched than it did above a suit and tie. He was in shock.

'She walked out on me but I didn't think she'd go that far.'

'Literally,' said Milly, who could get away with remarks like that because Edward had a soft spot for her. She handed him a mug of tea.

'Argentina,' he murmured, his upper lip curled in distaste.

'It must be illegal,' said Jack. 'You've got a right to see the kids.'

'She said: *Don't even try to get us back.*'

'Was her bloke Argentinian, then?' asked Milly.

'No. He was from Chiswick.'

'So why Argentina?'

Edward shrugged. 'Buenos Aires is the new Barcelona, isn't it? It's all going to be very, very messy. I'll try not to lean on you lot.'

Jack's heart sank. This meant he would lean on them. Jack didn't like Edward, but he was their next-door neighbour. The house on the other side belonged to an Italian millionaire, a mate of Berlusconi's who came with his family for about a fortnight in July; the rest of the time it was looked after by a diminutive Albanian couple with roughly thirty words of English who kept using power tools in the house and a strimmer in the garden. Edward's children had played skateboard on the sloping pavement of the hill, making a clicking noise. They had screamed and shouted on their back lawn, always arguing in posh vowels, too young to think about changing them. The absence of Edward's children was a great relief.

'I'm not even sure what I did to deserve this,' said Edward. 'I think she's gone mad.'

Milly pulled a face. She had always wondered how Lilian had put up with Edward, who would stay on every day after work for a few ales with his workmates in the City. She asked what the bloke from Chiswick did, although she knew because Lilian had told her all about him. He was called Keith Granger or Ranger and was a top systems analyst for Dell. Age: mid-thirties.

'Steals wives and children,' said Edward. 'Poison, that's what he is. A toxic geek. Poisoned my life. I keep asking her one simple question on the phone, when she rings: *What have I done? If you tell me what I've done, I'll try to do something about it.'*

'And?'

'That's it,' said Edward, spreading his arms wide, 'can't answer, hasn't got an answer.' He kept his arms wide, like a little boy playing an angel in the nativity play. 'She can't say. Because I've done absolutely nothing. Did my bit with the kids, earned our crust, took her out to nice restaurants, put the cat out at night. Made love. Sex no problem. No problem at all, in fact.'

Jack looked away. He really did not want to hear about Edward and Lilian's sex life.

'So?' said Milly.

'So she's hit the switch on our marriage and taken up with this creep from Chiswick. That's it. Finito. Tie the knot, cut the knot. For no discernible reason aside from complete bloody selfishness. We both liked Joe Cocker, for God's sake. We sang along.'

'She fell out of love with you,' said Milly – hurriedly in case Edward tried to do his imitation of Joe Cocker.

'Maybe it was that stag night in Tallinn,' Jack suggested.

Edward looked at him, mouth open; then he looked at Milly and narrowed his eyes.

'What's he on about?'

Milly said, 'I think you should go see a solicitor, Edward. I don't think we're the ones to advise you.'

'I needed someone to talk to, that's all.' He picked up his tea and sipped it. 'Very nice tea, thanks. Darjeeling? Love it. So did Lilian. Broken orange pekoe. Earl Grey. Poof's tea, her father called it. She loved it.'

'She's not dead, Edward,' Milly pointed out.

Tears were welling up in his eyes, his voice was husky. 'We went to Paris for our honeymoon and it was the best week of my life. Bloody miracle week. Fifteen years ago. We didn't just marry, we blended. All smashed because she gets the hots on some webhead from Chiswick with a Beckham scalp and a tattoo on his arse. Well, I guess her computer won't break down now.'

'Watch those computer nerds,' said Jack. 'Especially the tattooed ones.'

'Beware the fairer sex, mate,' said Edward, rather aggressively, jabbing a finger at him. 'You don't empty the dishwasher one night, and you're out on your *neck*.'

He covered his face in his hands.

'It's the kids I miss. I was in love with my kids. They were my whole life.'

And Lilian would come round on a Saturday, when Edward was playing golf with his old schoolmates from Wellington, and say: *I wouldn't mind, if he just showed some fucking interest in the kids*.

It was a couple of days later, and they were babysitting the twins. They belonged to Milly's older brother Philip, and they were no longer babies. Far from it. They attended St Dunstan's Independent School in Knightsbridge, which had been educating the junior rich since 1928. They wore a brownish uniform, remarkably similar to the summer dress of a Deutsche Jungvolk File Leader of 1934 (on which, according to rumour, it was based). Each year St Dunstan's commissioned a composer to write an opera. Jack had decided he would refuse, if asked, but up to now he had not been asked. He suspected that was Philip's doing; Philip du Crane was on the school board and liked neither his brother-in-law nor his work. His most famous line to Jack was, 'I don't suppose you'll notice retirement, will you?'

Philip had booked some tickets for a Thursday matinee at the Globe. It was *The Winter's Tale*. He was suddenly called away to Dubai (he was a big shot in Esso and was working on the Iraqi oil-field brief, which Milly was highly suspicious of), and Arabella, Milly's busy sister-in-law, asked the Middletons to take over.

This was always happening. Milly found it both gratifying and, of course, painful. 'If you have kids,' as she put it, 'you ought to look after them.' The fact is, Jack was aware that her grief for the lost baby, for little Max, was growing instead of diminishing. This was because, at the time of the loss, there was everything still to play for. Neither of them had wanted to believe the obstetrician. And as her nephews had grown up – they were ten or twelve or something now, Jack could never keep abreast of such things – they had acted as livid reminders of what Jack and Milly were missing. So Milly was always a little tense under her jollity, when looking after the twins. And bony Arabella, who worked for Sky, had no sensitivity whatsoever on this subject: she and Philip underestimated what the stillbirth had meant emotionally speaking, and appeared impatient even with the medical after-effects, or perhaps with Jack and Milly's hesitation over adoption or IVF.

Because most of her friends were out of the country stirring their swimming pools, Milly was free of impending dinner parties to host. Although it was the first day of the fourth test in the Ashes series, with England playing well enough to be in with a chance, Jack agreed to come along.

The boys were, in fact, eleven years old and down for Eton, following a long line of du Crane males. There was a du Crane – Milly's great-uncle, Hugh – on the memorial tablets in Eton's cloisters. Jack liked the boys, who were called (Arabella's influence) Lance and Rex, but he realised they only had about four years to go before becoming junior versions of their father – by way, no doubt, of a brief sludge stage of torn tracksuit bottoms and grunts. Their father had booked the most expensive seats, but Jack insisted he and the boys stay in the yard with the groundlings.

Milly took the day off, completely; the office was still very quiet. The following week looked to be busy.

The weather was hot and dull. They walked it from Philip and Arabella's place in Islington. The twins chatted non-stop, mostly about the cricket, which they were annoyed at missing. Lance did most of the chatting, in fact; he had come out of Arabella first and was well built, ruddy-cheeked and confident, while Rex was the thin, pale, insecure runt, with odd blue veins on his cheeks. An objective observer would have presumed they were out with their parents.

The foursome cut through the little strip of garden around St Paul's; pallid white-collar workers were tucking into lunch all the way along, the odour of confined spaces hanging about them like a mist. Jack caught the furtive eye of a pretty receptionist-type biting into a fruit pie, her finger catching the blackberry goo at her chin, the awkward, comic moment shared and then gone.

Because of the bombings, the theatre was half empty – which wasn't the case with theatres during the Blitz, apparently. The groundlings consisted mainly of Italian students, signalling to friends on the far side and giggling. The twins enjoyed moving about the yard, but were quiet and reasonably concentrated. They were doing a project on Shakespeare.

'He was gay,' Lance said, with great authority.

'Bisexual,' Rex corrected, his lipless mouth opening to reveal overlarge teeth in an embarrassed grin. However, Lance did better than Rex in class. Lance did everything better than Rex. It must be hell to be Rex, Jack thought, as the actors thumped about the stage a few feet away.

He decided, as the period music played from the gallery, to take a trip up to Bounds Green the following week. Lance waved at Milly, up in her expensive seat. Jack told him not to.

In the interval they ate ice creams and looked out on the river. The boys had not been allowed to bring any computer games; they knew Auntie Milly disapproved.

Lance said: 'Did you know that Shakespeare lived above a Froggy making wigs? In a flat.'

'A French wig-maker,' Rex mumbled, losing a dollop of ice cream to his brand-new chinos.

'Really?' said Milly. 'You do learn some interesting things at school.'

'He was a workaholic,' nodded Jack, feeling the need to add to their fund of facts, although he didn't know a lot about Shakespeare. He would hive off to Bounds Green and back and

Mill would never know. 'Lived in the Barbican, and worked himself to death.'

The twins had already lost interest, watching a man mouth-drumming into a mike by the river. The river was really flat and uninteresting, today. London was incapable, Jack thought, of rising above the mercantile. *Look what you can get!* it screamed. And then the sun would come out and she would give you a dazzling smile. Hive off and what, once there? He'd work that one out in situ.

He heard a sort of squeal from Milly and he turned round and it was Andrew Beak, the young and very brilliant cellist with the ENO, kissing her on both cheeks. Andrew was with his new girl, an up-and-coming composer who, Jack knew from someone else, thought Jack Middleton was old rope.

'Are these your boys?' she asked, gauchely.

'My nephews,' said Milly.

The composer's name was Abigail Staunton, Jack remembered, beaming politely. She was wearing a denim shirt over a low-cut dayglo-pink T-shirt, and the denim's cuffs hid her hands. She might have been an assistant in Top Shop. These two were almost ten years younger than he was, devouring his heels, wanting him out of the way, revering only those old enough to be their grandfathers or great-grandfathers: Webern, Kurtág, Cage, Ligeti, Messiaen.

Jack raised his hand as if he was warding them off. 'Hi! Great to see you, Andrew! How are things? Cool. Cool. We've met, yeah. Hello, Abigail. Good stuff. Really? Wow. When's that for? Brilliant!'

Jack felt a kind of nauseous panic seize him: Abigail had received a commission from Sir Simon Rattle for a piece to be played by the Berlin Philharmonic for a concert of new music by composers under thirty, to be broadcast on international television and radio. Andrew Beak would be the guest cellist.

'What are *you* working on these days, Jack?'

'Oh, small things.' It was best to play dead dog and over-modest rather than reveal how very small his commissions really were. 'Do you know the score?'

'About what?'

'The cricket.'

'Oh, I've never been interested. I'm a rugger-bugger.'

'Ugh.'

A smart woman in her sixties, with extremely short grey hair, came up with a faint scent of the WC remaining on her. Andrew introduced her as his mother, Geraldine. 'This is Milly and this is Jack, Mummy. Jack Middleton.' He didn't bother with the twins.

Mummy?

She frowned at Jack as if from a great height, although she was smaller than him. 'Do I know you?'

'You might have heard his music.'

'Are you a composer, too?'

'On good days,' Jack smiled, the bottom knocked out of him.

'I'm very bad on names, of course. Do you know Thomas Adès? I think Tom is brilliant,' added Andrew's mother, as Jack knew she would.

She asked him who he sounded like.

'Myself.'

'Oh, come on. Everyone sounds like someone else but with a discernible difference which is what we call their *identity*.' Andrew's mother blinked at him. He recalled someone saying that she was a lecturer in something like culture studies, and a long-term widow.

'Arvo Pärt,' said Andrew Beak – which infuriated Jack. Andrew's mother's face flinched and turned away. Yes, she was definitely an academic.

'Andrew darling, do get some tea. There's less of a queue now.'

Andrew's mother revealed a plastic tub in which three slices of her home-made flan were nestled. She all but wiped Andrew's nose when he came back with the tea, but Andrew didn't seem to notice. This was what had made him one of Britain's top cellists. Abigail was talking to Milly about alternative green housing in Berlin. Then she and Andrew started talking schools, inevitably, having asked the twins where they were. Andrew had a little girl from a previous partner, which Jack hadn't known about before.

'She's done an entrance interview already,' said Andrew. 'Six years old. Good training for life, though. The uniform alone's gonna cost a *fortune*.'

'Parents need very sharp elbows when it comes to education,' said his mother.

'Education begins at home,' said Andrew. 'They're magic, kids, if you don't let them get on top.'

'What's it like having twins?' asked Andrew's mother, turning to Jack. 'Double trouble?'

Jack glanced at Milly. She looked stricken, very pale, under the smile.

'They're not ours, exactly,' Jack joked. 'My wife's nephews.'

'Oh, you don't have any of your own?'

'No,' said Milly. 'We lost one at eight months.'

Andrew's mother winced unconvincingly. 'Oh, how ghastly.' Abigail managed a soft groan of sympathy.

'We've tried like hell, since,' said Milly, on one of her steam-rolling trips now. 'We've gone the whole hog, zero result, and it's bloody awful.'

Andrew's mother looked genuinely taken aback, which was very gratifying.

'Adoption?' queried her son, masking his embarrassment with a callous-seeming coolness.

'Maybe,' said Milly, not looking at him. 'But we haven't actually given up. I don't like chemicals. IVF, you get pumped silly with drugs. My insides may not be *designed* to have triplets. It's totally unnatural.'

Andrew's mother was frowning. 'Well, if taking the drugs helps people . . .'

'So do *cars* help people, and look what they're doing!'

Mill was talking candidly because she was cross. Jack felt proud of her, but also conscious that she was not doing a thing for his professional reputation. Andrew's mother pretended to study the theatre-going fauna through the strained silence, which was broken only by Andrew digging away at his lunch. Abigail Staunton was examining the large black programme. A seagull mewed overhead, as it would have done five hundred years before. Thankfully, the bell rang. Elderly Americans called to each other like hoopoes.

The second half hooked the twins, especially the business about the statue. Its paint still wet. Jack was too busy thinking. Kaja had waited six years to creep up on him. Frozen, she'd been, like the statue. But in fact – like grandmother's footsteps – creeping up the whole time. Now he'd turned round too late and been touched. He'd lost the game. He glanced up at Milly sitting in the top rows of seats among the well-dressed tourists. She gave him a little wave, still looking pale and somehow lonely. He gave her a thumbs up. Maybe he hadn't lost the game, not yet. Maybe it *was* all coincidence, Kaja getting Howard to teach her son the viola. Maybe it was sheer chance and not calculation. In that case, he still had time to act.

Hermione stepped off her pedestal and there was wonder and tears and then some jolly period dancing and then the applause.

They waited for Milly at the door. The others had gone. She thought it was quite good. He put on his involuntarily plummy voice and pointed out how like a Greek play the first act was, with long speeches instead of the chorus (he'd recently heard this on a Radio 3 interval talk).

'Where did you get that from? Radio 3?'

'No, I did *not*.'

'Anyway, I can't believe anyone would just explode with jealousy like that, for no reason.'

'People aren't jellyfish,' said Jack.

The Thames muscled its way past its own truculent currents. A couple of armed policemen strolled past, ready to rub out another innocent Brazilian on the Tube. Milly went on about this, educating Lance and Rex, who liked guns a lot. They walked to Bank and then took the Northern Line to Hampstead.

Milly disapproved of taxis, these days, as she disapproved of planes. Jack wanted to query her candid behaviour in front of his so-called colleagues, but didn't have the heart. It bit away at him, though. He felt it would take him a notch down.

They sat on the rocking, noisy train and most of the time they forgot to be frightened, but when the fear came back it felt absurd. The train was emptier than it would have been before the bombings. The young guy opposite was reading *El Código Da Vinci* with his brain wired to an iPod, turned up loud enough to hear its hissing, maddening beat, like something corrosive.

It began to corrode the shining metal of Shakespeare in Jack's head. The waste of the human gift, blended into brown gunk by society's mixer. It was polluting the effect of Shakespeare. If a bomb hit, that's what he would go out on: a stressed-up sensation of gunk. He smiled at the twins, and then at Milly, as their bodies were messed about by the hurtling little shifts and sways of the train.

He thought about the absurdity of the idea of the carriage turning into a fireball, and then about the ice caps. Melting, carelessly almost, splitting and tumbling as if they couldn't be bothered to make an effort. What was the word for ice doing that? Cleaving? Calving? That seemed equally off the cards. Floods, the end of things. Mass extinction. But both happenings were as real as his own hands. He studied his hands as the train roared and clattered through the depths. These fingers had touched Kaja, intimately and everywhere. But that didn't seem real, not here, not now. Not a trace left on his fingers.

That's because it was in the past, it was finished, and even the applause had lost its last echoes to the silence.

The point, he thought, was to feel and think at the same time, at the highest pitch of value, without one cancelling out the other. But there was so much interfering and so much interrupting. There was so much destruction. Because Pärt was popular, the academics had gone off him. The universities were crippled by theory, postmodern or otherwise (Howard, for one, disagreed with this). Nobody admitted to feeling anything any more: feeling was suspect. Theoreticians, like surgeons, didn't feel.

At the same time there were respectable composers selling themselves to populist trash. By trash, Jack meant anything that was fake, that was surface glitter, that was diluted or industrialised or plain tosspot rubbish. A good rock melody could touch the depths, it wasn't to do with complexity or difficulty. His favourite music, which he would play repeatedly, was an ethnologist's tape of 'Thinking Songs' from the Nigeria–Cameroon border, made back in the early seventies. This was human music. Its humanness rolled out under the stars. Beyond the voices and the primitive plucking instrument, you could hear the crickets and the weight of the night. But between that music and the music of here and now lay a labyrinth of technique, of signs, of self-conscious history, of people like Andrew's mother, guarding the exits.

What he needed to do was to stand many times in a wood or on the top of a mountain.

What he needed to do was to help Kaja and her son. But he was very scared. He was scared to spill what he had. So it was out of the question.

What can you get? screamed everything around him, here. *What can you get?*

And he really didn't want to know.

Last night, in fact, he'd dreamed again about Kaja. She was no longer sinister. They'd gone to the Kenwood concert, alone together without the boy; there had been some kind of mistake and the Thinking Songs were being performed by a few tribal elders on the stage, naked but for loincloths. The lawns started filling with people and cool boxes and the chattering got louder and Jack rose to his feet and started screaming at everyone to be quiet. His parents were there, shaking their heads. Milly appeared on the path, with Howard and a teacher Jack remembered from his primary school in Hayes, who'd had a furry boil on her chin. Now the boil had gone. They were all arm in arm and drunk.

Kaja had disappeared. He waded into the lake and woke up thinking, just for a moment in the half-light of their bedroom, that he was on Haaremaa and hearing the pinewood tick in the sun.

It was now nearly a fortnight since he had seen the boy.

Howard didn't phone again. So the boy couldn't have mentioned him to his mother, or maybe he had but she hadn't sensed that it might be Jack Middleton.

When he wasn't working on his pieces, or teaching, or listening to the cricket and its soft, suspended silences and cries, its wood-block percussives between the genial, detached commentary, he felt bewildered. When he wasn't right in the flow of his composing, hearing the music inwardly, and playing with what he heard on paper or just leaving it as it was, he did not know what to do with himself.

Milly was suddenly busy with, among other things, an important client whose certified wood delivery turned out to be warped and who had to be appeased down in Suffolk on the summer bank holiday, despite the traffic and the last thrilling day of the fourth test. Jack's viewing was interrupted only by his lesson with Yeh.

He made her laugh, to make up for his lack of concentration on the Chopin nocturne.

'I'm your Zywny,' he said.

'Who?'

'Zywny, Chopin's first piano teacher. And the last entry in the *Encyclopaedia Britannica*.'

'Are you in the *Encyclopaedia Britannica*?'

'Not yet,' he joked, secretly hoping he would be. And Yeh laughed with her fingers in front of her mouth.

Sometimes Jack wished he could just do good in the world

in a practical way, like Milly. Pulling sounds out of the air – out of himself – to be planted on paper and to flower eventually in some half-full concert room maybe once or twice, to be revived now and again over the following years, all this seemed crazy.

Once the cricket was off, he saw no point in anything, even in breathing from one moment to another, and realised he might be clinically depressed.

He emailed a couple of composer friends along these lines, and they were extravagantly kind in their swift replies, each telling him that he must not waste his incredible gift to the world, et cetera. Needless to say, they were not English: one was Italian, the other from the Ukraine. The three had met in The Hague as graduate students, and performed together. They had felt they were going to conquer the world. He wasn't sure they had heard any of his recent pieces (available on CD – entitled *The Barbed Wire Grows* – for the last three years), but their hearts were in the right place. They both had full-time posts at prestigious universities, which he half envied and yet knew must have damaged their talent.

Milly got in latish each evening that week, stressed out, and he had a problem ratcheting himself up to her speed. On Wednesday, spent in Datchet, all she'd had was a cheese-filled baked potato in Spud-U-Like.

'Spud-U-Like? You're slipping, Mill.'

He'd gone to the Proms alone on the Tuesday, and had been disappointed. The performance of the Beethoven never stretched itself. Compared to the last hours of play the previous day, which saw England in the lead for the first time in yonks, it was pure flab.

He read in the newspaper about someone or other aged forty-three and realised with a start that he was the same vintage: he'd pictured someone bald, middle-aged and boring. He was not seriously balding, or he'd have to do as others did and shave his hair to the scalp and put up with rib-ticklers about Lawn Grow. All his hair had done was lose its glossy black; the dye he used was natural, smelt like compost. One day he knew he would let his hair go, turn as grey as that theorbo player next to Kaja. The guy had not looked that uncool. There was hope. There was hope for the Cyclops.

Kaja's son must have taken up the viola under his mother's influence, choosing the woodier sound of the viola instead of the violin because that's what he was sensitive to, that's what he liked and responded to. At five years old! This was always happening in the art world. The amateur in one generation, the genius in the next. Not in his own case, though. In his own case, it came from the sky. At eighteen he had reckoned he was the Messiah, pretty well. Most people did, at eighteen. Now he was nothing. A mortal after all.

Lying in bed with Milly, who was reading (Milly had just had to start wearing glasses to read, which had enticed him for some unknown reason to slip his hand under her nightie), he admitted he was feeling a little low. Milly was enjoying what he was doing with his hand, but not showing it. He could tell she was enjoying it because she didn't complain, even though she was deep in her book. She didn't say anything when he said he was feeling a little low, so he left it.

'You OK, Mill?'

'Ace, baby,' she said, flatly.

'I love it when you say words like *ace* and *baby*, it turns me on.'

'Why?'

'Because you went to Roedean and it sounds so bizarre.'

'Bizarre things turn you on?'

'I guess.'

His fingers were on her belly, around the belly button, at the dangerous frontier between skin and the down feather of hair. All the information was coming through his fingers, like a blind alto he knew who read scores in Braille, holding the sheets against his stomach and shifting his fingers mysteriously over the white, blank paper as the voice soared. It was amazing information he was getting, in fact, to do with the softness of skin and the silkiness of hair that no one else, as far as he knew, had the right to touch unless for medical reasons. She had put on a bit of weight in her mid-thirties and mostly lost it again. He felt the little pit of her belly button and then crept a bit further down and he started stiffening.

'No,' she said, reading.

'No?'

'Just in case.'

'I'll touch myself then.'

'If you want.'

He started touching himself.

'Good book?'

It was a book about the industrialised horrors of British food.

'Oh, really jolly,' said Milly. 'Tesco's and the rest are just evil. You'll never want to eat again unless you've grown it yourself.'

They had, in fact, grown tomatoes in their garden, until they'd read about the toxic nature of London's polluted soil. She read out loud a worrying passage about chlorine levels in bagged salads packed by Russians living in Portakabins in Hampshire. Jack loved the movement of her lips, even after twelve years.

'That might be near us,' said Milly.

'We're in Hampstead, not Hampshire.'

'You know what I mean. What are you up to down there?'

'Feeling my bagged salad. It must be Tesco's. It's gone all limp.'

'Dried apricots and a chilli pepper,' Milly smiled. But she didn't check it out.

Maybe we did hit the jackpot week before last, Jack considered, but stopped himself feeling hopeful because, whatever he thought, it was all out of his hands and all he had to do was wait.

Walking around Hampstead the next day, sitting on the Heath on a bench dedicated to *Ken, Who Loved It Here*, he sank into a real funk. I do not love it here. I do not love being alive. It would have been better to have been Ken. But I'll bet this is all you've got. I'll bet there's nowhere better. And look what we're doing to it.

The *Guardian*'s headline was about the frozen Siberian bogs melting. The *Ham & High*'s headline was HEATH SEX OUT OF CONTROL.

It was hot enough to swim in the Ponds so he did so eventually, and felt much better for the shock of the cold green water. He towelled himself vigorously among the splayed-out, naked guys sunning their butts in the wooden changing rooms by the jetty. The talk was fairly filthy, as ever; Jack was uncomfortably conscious of his own white butt as he dried his feet, felt it was being admired, then remembered that he was no longer the supple youngster. His belly was creased against his swimming trunks. There was flab. Kaja would laugh to see him here.

He took the back towpath around the ponds, forgetting about the anglers who'd generally plant themselves there, all but blocking the way. He caught his foot on a line, stepping over it, and the boy whose line it was looked anxious but said nothing. Joggers with iPods thumped and panted past him on the paths, intent in their suffering but secretly on a high. He must look a sorry sight to them, he thought. In the middle of a high-grassed meadow a tall, lanky woman was shouting to herself. Or maybe *at* herself. Or maybe at an apparition immediately in front of her.

That's precisely what I am doing, Jack thought: yelling at a ghost. It was *all over*. All he had to do was hunker down and keep out of its sight.

He'd completely forgotten that they were due at the Grove-Careys' that night. Roger Grove-Carey was a composer in his early sixties who had taught Jack at the Royal College, worked with Cardew and others, and was deeply embittered at not being recognised as the second Schoenberg. His wife was half his age and they had a little boy. Milly arrived back home at seven thirty, saying the whole London transport system was still completely fucked from the bombings.

Jack was especially glad to see her come in these days, whatever her mood, because every day she went out into the dangerous, wide world where stuff happened. But she only had half an hour to freshen up and change and she'd felt really prefab all day. She was talking to him over her shoulder as they went up the stairs. He followed her into the bedroom, only then remembering the dinner date.

'That's OK, then.'

'OK?'

'If you felt pretty fab. It's the end of the week, anyway.'

Milly snorted, already climbing out of her trim grey work skirt. '*Prefab*, I said. As in housing. There's a big difference.'

'Sounds bad, man.'

He was appreciating Milly, and felt her sense it. He had made a largish afternoon dent in the sofa, reading a biography of Handel, and was conscious of not doing much while Milly was doing a great deal, although sitting in a crowded Tube (less crowded than before the bombings, but still unpleasant), feeling stressed and that bit more anxious, might be classed as doing even less. Milly was in her knickers and bra and the evening light fell in all sorts of interesting ways on her body. She was forty-one, with no birth wrinkles, and only a slightly more rotund belly than before – a shape which Jack found an improvement on the younger model. She was naked, now, and she padded over the rugs to the en-suite bathroom for a shower.

'You're nice and smelly,' said Jack, catching whiffs of her sweat and burned-paper hints of central London. He studied her buttocks as she wrestled the awkward, curving shower door open. Women's buttocks were always, he thought, larger than they looked in clothes. He did not know of any musical piece that celebrated a woman's buttocks. He lay back on the bed like a lord.

'Jesus, that's nice!' she shouted. It was a cold shower. She claimed that cold showers prolonged one's life. He thought of the cold water running in the warm hollows, beading in her mufflike jewels, and reckoned that things could be worse, basically. Suddenly, he was almost at that stage Milly used to describe, when you couldn't imagine the unhappiness of being someone other than yourself.

He was propped on one elbow on the bed, watching Milly towel herself through the open door. Her skin was tanned-looking, even in winter, which was an interesting throwback, possibly, to her great-great-grandfather's long stint in Burma (as were her slightly slanted eyes), rather than sojourns on the beach. Milly was possibly one-eighth or one-sixteenth Burmese, as this great-great-grandfather on her mother's side married a Burmese princess – or so the family legend went.

It figured.

Jack loved to watch his wife dress and undress, posing for a painting by Degas, Bonnard, those geniuses who celebrated women. She never said anything, but he knew she liked him watching – slightly flaunting herself, pretending she hadn't noticed him studying her breasts as she strapped a new bra over them, talking the whole time about some problem with rapid renewables. As usual, he would have liked her to have given him one of her dazzling smiles as she dressed and undressed, but there was no real reason to. Her breasts were still very firm and the shadows under them were almost black. She stood there in her bra, knickerless. The bra pushed the breasts higher and nearer, giving them a voluptuous look. If only the sole cleavage in the world was the hollow he was looking at.

'Aren't you changing?'

'I guess I'd better,' he said.

He slipped into white trousers and a tropical shirt that he knew would look youthful and yet not too casual for Roger Grove-Carey, who wore out-of-date ties. The bedroom filled with Milly's perfume, apple-like. Half naked, she was fixing her earrings – pale gold barley ears. He would have liked to have given up the Grove-Careys, to have pressed himself against his wife's body, but delayed pleasures were sweeter.

He told himself, as they were driving there (the Grove-Careys lived fifteen minutes' walk away, and Milly kept voicing her guilt about taking the car because they were late, it was no excuse), that he would not drink too much and not get into a long, heated debate so that, when they got back, they would be on form for a shot at some sex. Then he remembered that there was a curfew on all that, because Milly had felt something the other night, the night of their twelfth anniversary, and wanted to keep the full bowl very steady, and this made him feel sad, which translated into grumpiness.

Roger Grove-Carey's house was one of those white-pillared palaces at the Swiss Cottage end of Belsize Park. Jack stuck to Roger out of loyalty, although the academic's bitterness had become layered over with something approaching satisfaction since he had married one of his post-grads, a diminutive Italian flautist. She had torn up a career as a very fine orchestral player to bear Roger's second generation of children, his first being (in his description) 'as useless as their mother'. The first Mrs Grove-Carey was an early hippy who became a museum-piece hippy making jewellery out of hammered-flat bottle tops and then ran off to New York with the eldest son's *girl*friend at the age of forty-five. Jack made all the right noises to his old tutor, and felt sorry for the remaining children, one of whom cracked up during her A levels, but he could not have blamed her. Roger Grove-Carey's reputation as a Lothario made waves even in the fervid world of professional music.

Roger had prepared a barbecue outside with what he called 'ready-made coals' – an aluminium tray full of fuel you simply put a match to. Jack sensed Milly's horror at yet one more example of man's ungreen perfidy, but as Roger was so pleased with the ingenuity of it, she said nothing. Also, he had admired her eyes yet again, holding her by the shoulder after the initial welcome kiss (always slobbery in Roger's case), and calling them pools of amber. 'God,' he'd added, 'you're such a young *slip* of a girl.' Milly had loved it, despite herself.

He had a squeezy bottle of barbecue fluid on hand in case of non-ignition, which he squirted now and again for the hell of it, or to horrify Milly even further. Perhaps he's a pyromaniac, Jack thought, as the flames shot up.

'You know,' he pointed out, 'I heard of someone who burned to death, doing that.'

'Serves them right,' said Milly. 'That's pure environmental degradation.'

'How?' Roger asked, ignoring Milly.

'The squirt caught alight and burned right back into the bottle he was holding. Just like you are. Every time you squirt, you're connected to the fire by a line of highly inflammable liquid.'

Roger squirted again.

'Hell's umbilical cord,' he said, with a defiant smirk.

Roger was pot-bellied these days, and was sporting an unfortunate T-shirt declaring *I've Seen Einstein the Football-Playing Octopus*. Jack had never seen Roger in anything but shirt and tie. Claudia was upstairs putting Ricco to bed. Distant screams emanated from the upper windows.

'It's not Rochberg,' said Jack, looking up.

Jack knew Roger regarded George Rochberg as a traitor to the serial cause.

'Or Middleton, more's the pity,' said Roger ambiguously, prodding the glowing heap in the tray. 'How about a drink, my lovely young ones?'

Roger had made a seriously potent punch.

'I'm game,' said Jack.

'Who's driving?'

'I've had the kind of day you'd put straight in the bin bag, holding your nose,' said Milly, sounding more Roedean than fast-track.

Which meant that Jack had to hold back. He'd been hoping to make up for the sexual disappointment by getting tiddly. Roger was peculiarly soft and docile. The conversation through the drinks (during which Claudia appeared with a tear-bruised

Ricco, who seduced the visitors with a shy one-year-old's smile) flickered over subjects ranging from Egyptian cotton sheets to the evils of Nike. It was mostly being driven by Milly, who tended to flag only when her day's injection of adrenalin ran out.

Jack found her oddly hard and unattractive, suddenly. This happened. He could stand outside his position as long-term intimate and look at her objectively. It was weird. It was also a little frightening, because it meant that no feeling was fully reliable. Roger Grove-Carey had gone from adoring his first wife, Melinda, in her print-fabric flowing dresses, to loathing her very name – overnight. The new one, Claudia, was more like an au pair than a wife, and Jack had to keep reminding himself. He could not fathom why she had given herself to Roger and his pot belly and his longish, greasy grey hair for more than a minute. This was for life, he thought. Roger had this skill with women, even after his looks had gone. It might have been as much to do with his uncompromising stance as a composer and teacher, as with his peculiar charm when sober. Roger's music was so atonal that even Jack found it hard to listen to. It was occasionally played on Radio 3 and Jack would always imagine dials being hurriedly retuned all over the country. One piece, entitled *Eat, Drink and Be Merry*, sounded like a handsaw being inched over a vast submarine, panel by panel, bolt by bolt, with the hope that somewhere there might be a thinner area on which to make some impression and sink the vessel. It lasted twenty minutes and had made Roger Grove-Carey's reputation for a while back in the early seventies.

'I hope you're not still into Arvo Fart,' said Roger, suddenly, over the sausages and ready-seasoned spare ribs. They were eating at the table in the garden, although the coolish breeze had put out the candles and their ankles were getting bitten. He had drunk just enough to start being nasty: it was almost measurable. Jack didn't mind this question, as he didn't mind similar teasing from Howard. It made him feel that someone cared. And Roger was never anything but extravagantly sweet with Milly – whom most men fell for, in fact, wanting to do nothing but bring her red rose after red rose.

'It's pronounced Pert,' said Jack. 'To rhyme with a very posh shert.'

'Or shert as in posh crap.'

'Roger,' said Claudia, who had black rings under her eyes. 'Can you take Ricco?'

'No,' said Roger. 'I'm eating. Strap him in somewhere.'

'I think Claudia wants to eat,' said Milly, taking the edge off with a smile.

'She doesn't do anything else all day,' said Roger, chewing on a spare rib.

Milly laughed. 'Oh yes, in common with all mothers of lively infants. Do you have ready-made nappies the way you have ready-made barbecues?'

Jack realised that Milly had also drunk too much. Her jibe didn't quite come off.

'Actually, yes,' said Roger, smirking. 'In my day it was non-disposable towelling cloth. Lots of washing and drying. It's a doddle, these days.'

Claudia was rocking Ricco on her knee and attempting to eat, but Ricco kept grabbing her fork.

'I'll take him,' said Milly. 'God, he's just so gorgeous.'

'You're a guest,' said Roger. 'With lovely eyes of amber. Out of the question.'

Milly had been looking at Ricco longingly for the last hour. Jack knew how she felt. They'd both periodically melt at the sight of babies and toddlers – although they had to be careful with their cooing, this being England. They could hardly believe that such delightful beings could be created by such ugly or miserable-looking or officious parents. At other times, however, they'd feel resentful, irritated by other people's children. They veered from sentimentalism to something close to spite. It wasn't healthy.

'Claudia, take him upstairs, you're so *useless* with the child.'

There was a difficult silence, during which Claudia wiped

Ricco's mouth and carried him away. Through the French windows came the sound of her solemn tread up the stairs, emphasised by the lack of fabric in the house, which was furnished in a minimalist style, with lacquered, hardwood floorboards and bone-white furniture, much of it melamine. There were no curtains: Roger believed in transparency. The houses opposite had a full view of his night-time lovemaking, he had told Jack long ago. No one had complained. The corners of the melamine were chipped. Nothing dates quicker, Jack thought, than the avant-garde. The whole house had a faint smell of gum, for some reason.

Milly was pouring herself some more wine, which had been shipped or flown from Australia.

'I hate being hurried into the wrong country,' muttered Roger.

'Sorry?'

'What?'

He looked up at them as if he wasn't quite sure why they were there. Jack felt himself flush with the disturbing thought that Roger had got some debilitating mental disease: Alzheimer's, perhaps.

'Well, it's true,' said Roger. 'Each day is a continent of possibilities and you choose the countries or they are chosen for you. Right now I don't want to change country. Here's to Arvo Fart. Here's to Estonia, sex capital of the world.'

He drank, but Jack didn't. Milly drank without responding to the toast. Jack was struggling to say something cool and deadly in reply to Roger's remark about Estonia, but he felt too cross. He felt personally insulted, which was extraordinary; it was to do with the image of Kaja, gazing on the massed horror of the North Circular – which became a foggier picture of her peeling off in front of a fat, leering, middle-aged man.

Where did you read that, Roger? The Sun?

I didn't know you read the Sun, *Roger.*

'Is it the sex capital of the world?' said Milly, as Jack was opening his mouth to deliver, his pulse beating in his ears with anger.

'Full of whores,' said Roger. 'And Belorussia or whatever it's called: fifty per cent of the women are on the game, if they're not irradiated. Or even if they are. Chernobyl, in case you've forgotten.'

His eyes under the bushy grey eyebrows were twinkling. From the upper windows came muffled screams. Milly glanced up.

Jack said: 'Roger, you're really pissing me off now.'

'What? You were there and you didn't know it?'

'I was in Estonia, yes –'

'And the girls were juicy, weren't they? Our lovely Milly's looking worried.'

'Roger, you're a *Sun* reader, are you?' said Jack, feebly because he was trembling and hot in the face.

'It was in the broadsheets, something about Aids gripping the land of Arvo Fart. It didn't mention Fart, of course, that's my addition. I immediately thought of the leader of the Fart brigade, Jack Middleton, whose music was once interesting.'

'Thanks a lot, Roger.'

Jack had a kind of spontaneous heartburn.

'I'll go and see if I can give a hand,' said Milly, already getting up.

'Go then, go,' said Roger, as she climbed the stairs. 'She's completely *useless* with that kid,' he added, vehemently. Jack had never realised that Roger Grove-Carey was an alcoholic, until this moment. 'What?'

'Didn't say anything,' said Jack.

'Dumbstruck, are you? Oh no, I know what it is, you're playing with ideas. Silence and little tinny bells and those fucking triads in A minor.' He served himself some wine, ignoring the other glasses. 'You've done nothing decent since you went off to The Hague. You might as well open the wardrobe and shake a lot of empty coat hangers. Same effect. But not as original.'

Jack felt too deflated to reply, oddly enough. Teachers were not fathers: it was harder to scream back at your teacher. And he cared more about Roger's remarks on Estonia than on music, because he knew that Roger's academicism had crippled him and made any musical insights redundant, the product of his sad station. Yet he felt deflated.

'All I need is a shaggy beard, then,' said Jack, using a sneering reference to Pärt in some Sunday broadsheet that had prompted him to write a letter which afterwards he'd regretted, although it wasn't published.

'Quite right, quite right,' said Roger, momentarily wrong-footed. 'More spare ribs? Another sausage? Salad with it? Claudia's Italian touch, this.' He fished out a tiny block of feta cheese and popped it in his large mouth. Jack patted his stomach.

'Thanks but no, Roger.'

They exchanged glances. Jack felt close to his old teacher, against all the odds, and the shared look expressed that. Roger Grove-Carey was a wreck with awful eye bags, marital resurrection or no. Yet he, like Jack, had once been 'England's most promising young composer'. He'd been a Maoist, too, like Cornelius Cardew – very briefly, but ragged shreds remained. Jack had never been a Maoist, or anything much else: his generation had been cowed by Thatcher, lured by dosh. A vivid image of the rats tearing at the snow leopard's lunch in Tallinn Zoo crossed Jack's mind. He wondered why he had thought of that, when he might have thought of Kaja in the Café Majolica or on the island with the long-necked cranes beating up from the reeds at twilight. The feel of her hand in his. The scent of her hair. Of the hot pinewood in the sauna. The slippery skin, like a seal's.

'Jack, you have to admit.'

'Admit what, Roger?'

'That you're as badly fucked as me. What? Accept it. You weren't hard enough. You were always touching the soft button. Girlish.'

Jack shook his head.

'I'm not a fundamentalist, Roger. Fundamentalists blow up trains and buses.'

'Oh God, I said to Claudia: I'll bet you a kiss on the nipple we don't get through the evening without mentioning the biggest non-event of the year.'

'Non-event?'

'In the long term it doesn't matter, Jack. A few people blown up. So what? It happens all the time. Look at history. All history is legacy.'

'All history is legacy,' Jack repeated. 'That's really good. Seriously. I'll remember that.'

'Or look at prehistory,' Roger went on, obviously flattered in a vulnerable part of him – which was probably most of him. 'Think big, think abstract. Know what I think of when I read the latest big drama-queen headline or watch the TV news? The mass extinction of the Permian. Ninety-five per cent of life wiped out. We don't know why, not for sure. Just wiped. Fossil record blank.'

'When?'

'Two or three hundred million years ago. A long time ago. Ninety-five per cent. Zapped.'

'A very long time ago. Only geniuses like you can make sense of it, Roger.'

'Exactly,' said Roger, perhaps believing him after the flattery. The wine had left a red moustache on his upper lip. 'Now where the hell's your gorgeous wife? And she *is* gorgeous. Aesthetically. Sensually. In every way.'

'Spiritually?'

'Oh fuck that,' Roger roared.

Milly came back with Claudia (Ricco settled at last), and there was an argument before dessert about embodied energy, which Milly explained as the energy required to transport a product. She pointed out that the bottles of Aussie wine they'd consumed had been incredibly costly to the environment.

'What's the point of bringing wine over from the other side of the world,' she said, 'when we've got wine lakes in Europe?'

'It's called trade,' said Roger. 'Loyalty to the Commonwealth. Anyway, the French no longer make good wine. Even their food's gone off. We've got a hell of a lot more choice and it's tastier.'

'That's complete TV-chef crap,' said Milly, who then reeled off some frightening statistics she'd culled from her book on the British food industry, her barley-like earrings flashing gold. Jack was not really taking any of it in. Roger wasn't, either, from the look of it. Claudia was in the kitchen, spooning the sorbet into bowls.

Jack got up and joined her while Milly and Roger were arguing.

'Oh my God,' said Claudia, cheerily, in her attractive Italian accent, 'what are they discussing now?'

'The wonders of British food,' said Jack. 'Can I give you a hand?'

'It's OK,' said Claudia, who was over ten years younger than Jack. This fact suddenly struck him as annoying. Roger had no right. Claudia was small, thin in an attractive way, and gave the impression that she was not quite somebody until you talked to her, that she was retiring into the vague notion of 'Italianate'. At home in Milan she would have flowered, been firmer – would have avoided the disaster of marrying Roger Grove-Carey.

Standing next to her, chatting about Italian food, Jack was surprised at how conspiratorial he felt: it was as if she knew that he knew how much she would rather have gone off with Jack Middleton. He had drunk more than he'd meant to, although Roger's Aussie wine was way over-oaked and left a chemical backwash like creosote in the mouth. Claudia had very long, very black eyelashes and a mole, perched on her lower lip like a piercing stud.

He found he was wanting to flirt with her, and his jokes made her giggle.

She spooned out mango sorbet to join the peach sorbet and said how nice it was to have adult conversation. Jack recognised the sorbet as the classiest that the Finchley Road Waitrose ran to. Claudia could make it down there with the pushchair in a few minutes. That was her life, now. And this was his. He felt very andante, as if he'd smoked dope. Somewhere deep inside him was an excitement and a fear. It had been there ever since he'd realised his Estonian fling was not glassed off in the past. The word 'fling' was deliberately, cruelly inappropriate; he could hear it being said in Edward Cochrane's drawl. 'Fling,' he repeated to himself in his head. 'Fling. Fling. Fling.'

'Ricco is extremely cute,' Jack said, wishing he knew a lot of Italian.

Roger was raising his voice outside in a cheery tenor; he was flirting with Milly. Claudia smelt of barbecue smoke and baby oil. He imagined her small, lithe body under the simple dress and felt very much chilled out, next to her. He leaned back with his elbows on the kitchen counter.

'He's pretty lively,' said Claudia.

'Do you miss the music?' Jack said, before he could stop himself.

Claudia shook her head, firmly. 'Absolutely not!' she laughed.

For some reason, this disappointed Jack.

'You have a daughter, don't you?' said Claudia, putting the sorbet tubs back in the freezer, its breath wreathing about her face.

'Er, no.'

Claudia looked at him, surprised. 'Roger said you had a girl of five.'

'Wrong on both counts. At time of press, we don't have kids. Never have had. In fact, we lost it five years ago. Stillbirth. A boy. Called Max.'

Claudia covered her mouth with her hand, blinking furiously. 'Oh my God,' she said, 'it must have been someone else.'

'He's got a lot of ex-students,' said Jack, mastering his annoyance and, somewhere deep down, his sorrow. He hunched back his shoulders, as if his manliness had been questioned. 'It's no problem. Shall I take these out so they can throw sorbet at each other?'

Claudia laughed and squeezed his bare arm above the wrist,

which was a profoundly un-English thing to do. Later that night, Jack was to picture himself pulling down her panties right there and then in the kitchen and treating her fanny like a blob of sorbet as she sighed as quietly as she could. In real life they took the bowls out. The touch of her cold hand on his arm was something he'd always remember, he thought, as he sat down. Her hand was cold because of the sorbet and the freezer. Normally it would have been very warm.

They were at the front door when Roger said, 'We're inviting you to the christening, we'll let you know.'

Jack raised his eyebrows and expressed his surprise: part of the reason for Roger Grove-Carey's loathing of composers like Pärt and Britten was his fervent atheism. One of his most notorious pieces (now entirely forgotten) was *God's Got the Hump Because No One Believes in Him Any More, Oh How Sad*, dedicated to John Cage and played on a Korg Poly-800 synth.

'It's Claudia's idea,' said Roger, rather shiftily. Claudia had said goodbye to them and was responding to curious noises on the baby alarm.

'Good for Claudia,' said Milly.

'She must be very persuasive,' said Jack.

'I'll go through the motions for her,' said Roger, whose alcoholic nastiness had now mellowed into white-faced exhaustion. 'I don't care. I simply don't care.'

'Well, it's nice for her,' said Milly. 'We'll be there.'

'One thing I don't understand,' said Roger, with a sudden intensity in his bleary eyes: 'how you can stomach all that *belief* music when you don't believe yourself. Sacred bloody take-away!'

'Ready-made barbecues,' laughed Milly, stepping out of the door. 'Come on, sweetheart. That was so lovely, Roger.' She had flagged long ago, all but tottering on the threshold, reduced to a kind of upper-class skeleton of etiquette.

'Belief leads to exclusion,' Roger went on, not letting Jack say his bit. 'I'd respect you more if you became Russian

Orthodox, Jack, like shaggy beard himself. All music is music pretending to be *music*. Everything is music, therefore nothing is music. When I fuck the daylights out of Claudia –'

'Roger,' said Milly, looking as if she'd swallowed something sour, 'please . . .'

'When I stick my dickery-dock in my lovely young wife's various orifices, that is music, my friends.' Roger's voice was loud enough to be heard up and down the street, which slumbered respectably in the lamplight. '*Saying* it is music. I am now performing my piece entitled *Bread and Milk for Bloody Bártok*. It lasts an indeterminate length of time. In fact, it lasts my whole lifetime. The applause will be terrific. It's been gorgeous having you, guys, but I'm knackered because you stayed too late. Greetings.'

Roger raised his hand in a traffic-policeman way and looked terrible, like the Ghost in *Hamlet* under a fierce white spot, or something out of a combative production of *Don Giovanni*. Milly had backed out to the little iron gate. Jack was about to follow when he felt his arm being grabbed. Roger's face was thrust towards his own, all teeth and glaring eyes.

'You were *so good* once, you *bastard*. And you've let it *all go*.' He turned his face towards the gate, where Milly was waiting, searching for the car keys in her bag. He looked as if he was about to cry. 'For *what*?'

Jack wrestled his arm out of his ex-tutor's grip, too annoyed and upset to reply. The man was a drunk. Half deranged by failure.

'It was absolutely lovely, Roger,' Milly mouthed, tugging Jack out of the gate by the wrist. She was charm on automatic pilot.

In the car, further down the street, she said: 'Some of us have to work tomorrow. Do you know that?'

'He's a bum note,' said Jack, slipping the clutch. 'He's not even funny any more.'

'What did he say to you there, at the end? When he grabbed your wrist and then threw me a really deadly look?'

'He asked if he could have a swing on your tits,' Jack said.

179

As they passed the house, they saw Roger still standing there, as if looking out for them. The window was down and Milly gave a crooked-finger wave, her smile unbeatable for dazzle factor.

'He's more than a bum note,' Milly said, leaning back and closing her eyes. 'He's Pukesville.'

FIVE

It was late Monday morning. Certain trees had begun to hint at autumn tints over the weekend; or maybe Jack had only just noticed. Howard, who was doing a stint of teaching at University College School up the road, had dropped in for a coffee.

Inevitably, Jack mentioned Roger and there was a brief innings on atonalism. Howard bowled a low, deadly reference to Handel's sixth concerto grosso, which had a sequence of notes in the fugue that used to be considered unnatural but was in fact derived from a natural harmonic sequence; Jack hit it to the boundary by pointing out how the likes of Brahms had already threatened the whole tonal harmonic system long before Schoenberg came along. He really wanted to talk about Jaan and Kaja but Howard was behaving like a crusty old fart, goading him. Jack did not mention what Roger had said to him at the front door, gripping his arm. He'd been shaken by it. He'd been shaken by the look Roger had given Milly, and how deeply he – Jack – had understood what it meant.

And then the phone went.

It was his mother. Although her origins were Irish (leaving Dublin at the age of six), Moyna sounded, as she always did, like a much quieter, female version of Bruce Forsyth. A school-friend of Jack's had once pointed this out and Jack had cut him off for good.

It was a week or so since they'd last talked. Jack felt a fierce sympathy for his mother's state, but also an impatience. She was annoying, not being able to see. She stumbled over things and broke things. She did not understand his music, although every-thing he wrote was to enable her to see, in some way. This had only recently occurred to him. His parents had stayed in the same house on the same estate partly out of inertia, partly for practical reasons. The house was not in any way adapted for someone blind, but Jack's mother knew every corner of it by touch, if not exactly by instinct. Yet she could still say, now and again, 'For the love of Mike, where's the door?'

You do not develop your inner compass, being blind: quite the opposite. It's an added cruelty.

She had burnt her hand on the cooker, again. Otherwise there was no news. He invited them up to Hampstead in three weekends' time: booked up, any earlier. His parents adored, even worshipped, Milly, because she was class and she pulled all the stops out, as you would for people out of charity – political refugees, for instance. Black victims of torture or famine. It always made Jack wince and feel at the same time that he was not good enough as a son, because Milly would put her arm around his mum and give her a loving squeeze – something he never remembered doing in his life. Jack's father, Donald, had a crush on Milly and went all soft and soppy in her presence, his mouth hanging open slightly when he was listening to her, his balding, wrinkled head cocked on one side. The fact that Milly frequently gave Donald lectures on ecology did not bother his father one bit – he who fed their square of lawn with heaps of chemical fertiliser, sprayed Scotts Rose Clear 2 (officially banned) on his floribundas and scattered metaldehyde pellets around his hostas to keep the slugs and snails down. Jack always felt that if Milly could dent his father's addiction to garden chemicals, she would be making real progress.

'Oh, we'd love to come,' said Moyna.

'I'll clear it with Milly. Sunday lunch?'

'Lovely, dear. Your very nice lasagne,' she added – although he knew she thought it strange and disappointing, not to have a roast on Sunday.

'Milly should be free,' he insisted. 'It can't be the weekend after next as we're down to the Hall and this coming one she's got some kind of eco do in Kendal starting Sunday evening. But I'm pretty sure the twenty-fifth is good.'

'September.'

'Of course, Mum.'

The last week of September: time was white water.

And the whole of Sunday would be blown, both the morning for preparation and the afternoon for recovery. They would walk slowly on the Heath after lunch, his arm through his mother's to guide her, feeling the stiffness of the non-sighted, her caution, and he would have drunk too much red wine and eaten too much vegetable lasagne made from heavy wholemeal pasta, and the Heath on a Sunday afternoon was unbearably full of groups like them, or thickset blokes in football shirts, or screaming kids. It might even be cold and raining.

Deep down, though, he wanted to do the right thing; he had some notion that in some parallel universe the event would be comforting and somehow holy. He was, after all, the only child of his parents left in England.

'My mum.'

'How is she, the poor soul?'

It touched him, Howard's concern. Howard was always popping up to Derbyshire to visit his aunt, who was in a home. He gave many free concerts in such homes.

'Much as usual.'

'I sometimes think being deaf must be a blessing. Modern life's so full of bollock-awful noises –'

'She's blind, Howard.'

'Confusing yours with Peter's,' said Howard, quickly. 'Peter Mawes, the conductor.'

Jack stayed standing. His parents' life in Hayes was very neat, very moral. Not a slug in sight. They hadn't once strayed. It was admirable. They read the *Daily Mail*, like almost everyone.

'*Who's* looking very deep in thought?' commented Howard.

'I get like that,' said Jack, 'after my mum's phoned.'

'Don't you have those bizarre things called siblings?'

'My sister's in Australia, my brother's in Michigan. So they don't count.'

'They got out.'

'They copped out, in my view,' said Jack, who was jealous of the fact. 'Someone had to stay.'

'Cost ya,' said Howard, jabbing his good finger at him.

'Maybe. Maybe I'd be different if I was abroad. You can make Hayes in an hour and a half by Hanger Lane. How's Jaan?'

'He's great.'

'And his mum? How did she get hold of your name, by the way?'

'Reputation,' said Howard, as if it was self-evident.

'You sure?'

Howard looked at him, puzzled. 'Why?'

'Why what?'

'You've a problem with that?'

'No.'

'Then vy ze interest, Herr Middleton?'

Jack blushed slightly. Howard was examining him through narrowed eyes. 'For the official biography, Howard. Every detail counts.'

'By the way,' said Howard, 'you've reminded me. I gave her your home number. Hope you don't mind.'

'Why?'

'Don't look all shocked. Accompaniment! On the old *ivoires*. The finger's crap for at least another fortnight. Jaan was full of you, apparently. You don't mind, do you? Poor Estonian immigrant. You can do it for free, you rich sod. She's not got wheels.'

Howard had opened his diary and was scribbling a number on the dayglo-pink Post-it pad by the phone, peeling it off and handing it to Jack before Jack really knew what was happening.

'Here's her mobile. Your bit for the new Europe, mate.'

'Thanks, Howard. Great. I'll see what I can do.'

He poured a whisky for Milly and a beer for himself and set to on the meal while she chilled out as usual by phoning a close friend like Perdita Knowles or Olive Nicholson. He was cooking a fish pasta dish. He had learned today from the fishmonger in Hampstead that fish had to be laid out on kitchen paper to be dried before cooking. Sure enough, the slippery white slices soaked the paper, turned it transparent. He hoped Milly would come in and admire this professional secret, but she was deep in her call. He reckoned it was Olive Nicholson, from the tone of her voice. She was speaking quite slowly and a little huskily. By the time she came off, the cod was sizzling in a film of butter. He generally overcooked everything by a crucial fraction, so had been telling himself to underdo it, to give each side not more than a couple of minutes *at the most*.

Milly came in just at the wrong time. He asked her who it was on the phone, and she told him it was Claudia.

'Claudia?'

'Claudia Grove-Carey. You know she's half-Greek?'

'Half-Italian, half-Greek?'

'Yes. Do you find her attractive?'

'Not particularly. Planning on inviting them back, oh my Gawd.'

'Eventually. Give it time.'

'Why were you phoning her?'

'Because I knew Mr Pukesville wasn't in.'

'My composition tutor. You have to show some itsy-bitsy crumb of respect.'

'No I don't.'

'Why did you call her?'

Milly snorted. She was leaning against the fridge. The cod was cooking happily, but once again he'd forgotten at what precise time he'd put the slices in. He turned them over and they started to flake, tending to mush.

'Gestapo time,' said Milly, her vowels slightly lengthened by the effects of the whisky. 'I phoned her because I feel sorry for her. I phoned her yesterday, from work, to see how she was after our visit. I get the feeling she's very alone. We had a lovely chat up in Ricco's room, when we were there. She's very keen on green issues. Italy's not very green, as we know. Mafia and stuff.'

'Whereas the *UK* . . .'

'Puts Sweden or Denmark into the shade, doesn't it just?'

Milly stamped her foot, as she did when frustrated by the inability of humanity to get its act together. Jack had always loved that little stamp of the foot. She was wearing her side-lace sneakers, which softened the effect. He stirred the white sauce, wondering if he'd put in too much milk.

'Ze secret of cooking,' he said, in a French accent, regarding the soft wreckage of the cod, 'ees to have a perfect sense of ze timing.'

'Like the secret of screwing,' said Milly, quietly and un-expectedly.

She had showered and changed before phoning, and smelt of the cake of Pears soap Mummy du Crane would ritually, even superstitiously, replenish by post. She was wearing a jeans skirt and an embroidered lacy camisole he hadn't seen before, or not noticed. Jack had also overdone the pasta, and the prawns were stubbornly unthawed. He was forcing a block of frozen petits pois into a small saucepan (whose circumference was slightly less than the block), when he felt arms around his waist. They were Milly's arms. Her hands, with their solid, no-nonsense fingers (her father had the same fingers, as no doubt the knight did under his mailed gloves back in 1087), locked in front of his belly.

'You'll burn yourself on the ring,' she said. 'I hope that's not cod. Cod's way overfished.'

'Course it's not cod.'

'I've got to go to bloody Hitchin tomorrow. And Hull on Thursday. What a turn-on.'

He backed a step away from the cooker. Her cheek pressed against his spine. She squeezed him, pressing his back against her front. He felt her breasts as a firmish resistance under the lacy camisole. The petits pois were scattering like pellets over the cooker and, as the other rings were still hot, sticking to them and burning.

'How can I cook?' he said, mock-despairingly.

'Love you, man,' said Milly, dreamily. 'I love you because you're so useless and you're so clever.'

He wasn't sure why, but a sharp burn of anger shot straight up from his belly to his head. He sighed, to blow it away. She must have felt his body stiffen, because she released him.

'I really *hate* people bothering me when I'm cooking,' she said, pouring herself another shot. 'Do you know, Hitchin was a kind of green pioneer town?'

'Are you trying to make her leave Roger?' he asked, slopping the tagliatelle strips into the glass oven dish.

'Piss off,' said Milly, laughing. 'I'm not a marriage breaker!'

'Just wondered.'

'I'm not preggers, by the way.'

He looked at her. She was rubbing her lower lip with the whisky glass, staring down at the floor, her arms half folded. He was not sure whether this was an invitation to make love to her, or just a familiar confession. He felt sorry for her, but not for himself.

'Wait,' he said.

He slipped the fish in on top of the pasta, scattered the half-thawed prawns out of the colander, and poured on the white sauce. This was all done in silence, and Milly never moved, except for the whisky glass rubbing on her lip. The petits pois could be added in a minute, he thought. He shook grated cheese from the packet over the top and slid the dish into the oven, the heat hitting him in the face. Then he went to Milly and folded her in his arms – awkwardly, because of the whisky glass. She allowed herself to be folded, her eyes closed, holding up the glass by his head. His hands were greasy with butter and with the unpleasant polish of fish, so he held them free of the back of her camisole. He felt exposed to the street and to the Heath beyond – it was twilight, and the spots in the kitchen were switched on, but he didn't care. It was a simple, loving hug.

He felt her body quiver, then shudder, then shake, and shake again, as if it was being given a mild electric shock. There were no sounds.

It was just her body and the deep inside of her. By the time they separated, though, his shoulder was as wet as the kitchen towel on the cutting board, where he'd lain the fish to dry as the fishmonger had suggested.

'Nearly ready,' he said.

That was all he could think of saying.

Bounds Green was a bit nicer than Jack had expected. Dull to the point of comatose, but not crumbling or even that grim. He'd looked at the map and found it just too far to walk comfortably, incredibly awkward to get to by Tube and the buses were complicated. Unfortunately, Milly's appointment in Hitchin meant she'd got the wheels: she was transporting samples of pure-wool loft insulation in the boot. He told her he'd be working all day, but may well emerge for a breather on the Heath. As soon as she'd left for Hitchin, he'd phoned for a taxi, but the bombings meant they were still booked clean out.

He had backache, and didn't feel like cycling all that way. He resigned himself to dropping down on the Tube to King's Cross and then up on the Piccadilly Line – a daft dog's leg, but one which gave him time to think.

On the last stretch, he imagined what might happen if a bomb did its thing and he was killed and Milly would wonder for the rest of her life where the hell he'd been off to. The girl next to him was attractive in a bony French way, deep into *The Da Vinci Code*. A bomb might blow them together in a heap and Milly might wonder for the rest of her life; he actually pictured her looking feverishly at the entwined, calcinated bodies in the morgue.

The squeaky brakes on the train reminded him of Roger. He reflected on their Friday evening together, concentrating especially on the part that had begun once they'd left. Milly had talked a little about Ricco, and how frightened she was that they would be disappointed yet again. She had already bought a pregnancy-test kit from Boots, but couldn't bring herself to use it, not yet. Anyway, it was maybe too early to tell. Jack had drunk over the limit, unintentionally, and he knew he had to be careful. Then Milly told him he was driving too fast up Belsize Avenue. It was midnight, and there was no traffic on that particular wide road. He denied he was driving too fast, and then Milly had flipped.

Thrusting her face towards his, she had shouted: 'I lost my baby! I lost my little baby! How much have you drunk?'

He slowed down, shaken. He was doing twenty, which felt absurdly slow. It felt more like a walking pace.

'Milly, chill out. There's no madwoman coming out of a side road in a four-by-four.'

'How do you know? You won't know until you're on top of her.'

'I'm doing nineteen.'

'Now you are. *Now* you are. Men are so fucking pig-headed.'

'You could be married to Roger,' he said, inwardly agonised that she could still be blaming him for the loss of their baby *five years* back.

She didn't reply, which could have meant anything. She had her arms folded and was turned away from him as they drove too slowly up Rosslyn Hill so that he all but stalled in third.

Then he said, changing down awkwardly as the car juddered: 'If you go on thinking I killed our baby, then why don't you leave me?' He didn't want to say it, but he said it. And the worst thing was, she kept silent again.

He felt, therefore, that the evening had been really negative and that he was floating towards some mental or domestic crisis which meant he had to take affirmative action. Last night, maybe because of Milly telling him that she wasn't on the way, and the sunset sadness over the fish supper, he'd had insomnia. He'd lain awake in bed, composing emails to send to Roger that would really shake him. In the end he settled on, and actually tapped out: *Hi, Roger, I've recently come to the conclusion that Vaughan*

189

Williams's 'Flos Campi' is one of the great works of the twentieth century. I mean this. Jx

That would probably mean Roger breaking off all contact. That suited Jack. He was into burning clapped-out bridges. If he could do the same with Howard, he might well solve the Kaja threat. Kaja's number was burning a dayglo-pink hole in his back pocket. He'd considered memorising it and then destroying it, like James Bond. But he was hopeless with numbers.

Anyway, he meant what he'd said in the email to Roger, although he didn't even send it. The next morning he set out, albeit blindly, perhaps instinctively, certainly bleary-eyed, for Kaja's neck of the woods. It was better to be the hunter than the hunted.

Bounds Green station might have been quite interesting in the thirties, when it was new and modernist with its big windows and brick tower and glazed tiles. Now, stranded on a main artery and edged with litter, it looked like a public convenience. Happens to all of us.

Jack was struck by the lack of trees. He didn't like the look of the main road and its roars of traffic, so took a parallel route which, studying the A–Z, he saw would still take him up to the right spot on the North Circular with only a minor additional kink. The gas works was marked on the map as an unnamed circle. He passed sad-looking shops and agencies and then turned up a tree-lined residential street which was surprisingly quiet after the main road.

He felt oddly at home, here; Hampstead was vaguely unreal, even after six years. Here there were no cobbles, no boutiques, no one who looked as though you should know them by reputation or from a recent film you couldn't quite place. Bounds Green must have been built around a hundred years ago for minor clerks in one great late-Victorian orgasm and then given up the fight somewhere around 1936 on a grey, drizzly day smelling of coal. Hayes had felt like that, even on their spanking new council estate. Much of London felt like that, when it wasn't on the razzle. But Hampstead didn't.

Real life went on here, he thought, if it went on anywhere. Which meant that stuff happened without anyone noticing, or suddenly and shockingly, or very secretly. Someone had chalked *CUNT* in huge letters on the bucking pavement slabs. He somehow felt he understood why. It was the land where you visited your great-aunt and then scurried home. He thought of something Howard had said about his own family back in Derby: he hoped they were insured against death by dowdiness. And then, as if to rebuke his shallow first impressions, a girl with a sharp, cheeky smile passed him carrying a cello in its case.

He came out on the North Circular five minutes after he had heard it at the end of the long, straight street. A multi-lane nightmare, with cars moving fast and much closer to each other than on any motorway. He had never seen it except from behind the wheel, corroded by frustration. It was even worse from a pedestrian's viewpoint. The day was stuffy and lidded with grey, and the fumes were already making his eyes smart.

The houses on either side were set back a pavement's width from the road. It was crazy: ribbon development gone mad. Yet the houses were respectable semi-detached jobs with bay windows and tile-lapped frontages. In the twenties, this road must have been like a quiet, calm river, set in pale concrete. Modernist, like the Tube station. You could have driven out of your garage and shot off anywhere, like a message in a suction tube. It must have been thrilling, even, living on the North Circular seventy or eighty years back. The future.

He walked towards the gasholder, which was the other side of the road and the size of the *Titanic* in dry dock. It was a throwback. It didn't fit with the postmodern times of big-box stores and their convenience car parks put to shrubbery and flags. Slap bang next to the towering gasholder was the entrance to Homebase. From where he was standing, if what Howard had said was true, he might well be looking at Kaja's house.

He leaned against the tubular rail that lightly separated the pavement from the road and felt its grime on his palms. There were no houses immediately opposite the gasholder, only a no-man's-land with dirty-leaved trees and a litter of what looked like condoms, so he walked east again. Cars coming the other way were close enough to touch and he was conscious of their occupants staring at him, strangers and more strangers, over and over again.

Some of the houses were boarded up, their front gardens filled with rubbish, while others were clinging by their nails to respectability, their bedroom windows put to lace, their plots neatly mown or cemented over for a car. There were shops, too, if you could call them shops, but he didn't think Kaja would be living above a shop: Howard would have mentioned it. He'd have said, 'The poor girl rents above a Chinese and is *suffocated* by the smell.' Or: 'She's woken horrifically early by the delivery men, of course.' Or perhaps not.

The more houses he passed, still in view of the gasholder, buffeted by the noise of the North Circular's traffic, the more he realised how hopeless his mission was. Howard always exaggerated for effect. She might well live down the street he'd come up, or the one next to it. Immediately 'opposite' the gasholder there was nothing residential. So there was already a discrepancy. Did Kaja exaggerate? She might have done; she might have said to Howard, 'I'm very close to an enormous gas tank next to a big store called Homebase.' It was strange, imagining her voice, her decent English with its Estonian lilt, putting words into her mouth. He felt he was creating her in some way.

He suddenly wondered what the hell he was up to. He was sweating from the heat, because it was hotter here than in Hampstead – artificially hot. It was cooking in fumes. He was getting poisoned by the filth. Milly would know which poisons, what filth.

The last words Kaja had said to him were: 'I think you will come back before you forget me.' Six years ago, that was. With a view of the Bay of Finland.

A lorry the size of a house belched black diesel smoke over him as it set off from the lights. He could no longer see the gasholder. He had gone much too far. He could make enquiries, but that might get back to her and she would grow suspicious. He didn't know what she felt about him. Whatever she felt, she would interfere in some way with his marriage, with his life. Blow it all up. He'd turned and was walking back, now, making not much less headway on foot than the cars and trucks and excruciating motorbikes. How the hell did you come out of one of these houses in your car? Boldly, or inch by inch?

Near a footbridge over the railway, the pavement spread out to a fence and three blokes lounging among green shards and crushed cans. They called out to Jack as he passed, and one of them, in ripped-up Belgian Army gear, caught up with him and asked him for change, walking adroitly backwards as Jack carried on shaking his head. He didn't want his head bounced off the pavement, and so kept smiling. The man, who was missing teeth between his sunken cheeks, gave up and shouted after him, 'I know what you're fucking thinking, fuckface,' and the others laughed.

Jack wasn't sure what the guy had thought he was thinking, but it wouldn't have been what he was really thinking, which was a muddle of fear and sympathy.

He got to the street he'd come up, a few blocks before the main road that ran back past the Tube. It was a massively over-used junction, the main road carrying on over the other side, past the gasholder and Homebase. He tried a few doors. This was dangerous, because it might well be Kaja answering the bell. In which case, he would accept his destiny. His heart hammered each time he knocked or rang. It was a bit like hearing the phone go off at home, since Howard's visit. From two of the houses there was no answer. A third yielded a young Asian girl in a sari, who shrugged her shoulders shyly and smiled. The door was on its chain. All he saw behind her was a thick, flocked carpet. The fourth was answered by the frenzied barking and snarling of several dogs. There was a card taped under the bell: *Hypnotherapist. Past Life Regressions. Spirit Releasement. Give Up Smoking.* He felt quite tempted.

The fifth, reached by squeezing between a supermarket trolley and sheets of warped plywood, had him chatting with a podgy, thickset bloke in a stained white T-shirt and shorts — a friendly Londoner who wanted to help as best he could and who gave Jack a long, tedious description of an accident that had taken place a few doors up last month and the inability of the powers that be to improve the safety of the local residents. He was clutching a can of White Stripe, shouting over the traffic noise. Jack could see the telly on in the front room. The guy had an almost misshapen face, and Jack wondered briefly what it must be like being this man, as he went on and on in a smell of socks and stale fries.

Jack ran out of courage. He tried no more doors.

Walking back down the quiet, residential streets of Bounds Green, keeping his head lowered in case, he wondered why no one in power had thought to knock down the ribbon of houses either side of the North Circular, and put it all to woodland. Compulsory purchase in the name of humanity. Applicable to whole swathes of the country, that was the trouble. He passed an estate agent's and saw that even here the houses were a bicycle race of noughts.

Descending into the Tube on the steps (the down escalator was out of service), he saw the young hoodie in front unwrap a chewing gum and toss away the wrapper — not even toss it, just let the paper and the foil drop fluttering on the steps. Jack wanted to say something, like an old prat.

He wondered what Kaja made of the civilised, wealthy West. He would like to know. She would be interesting about it. He very much wanted to hear what she had to say about it, but he could no more talk to her than he could ever talk to the kid who'd littered the steps and was now three yards away on the platform, happily and noisily chewing.

What right had Howard got to give her the fucking number?

Anyway, the East was as bad. A friend had just got back from a tour in provincial Russia and said that the towns and their hotels were not just dilapidated, it was as if no one saw the point of even cleaning them any more. It was a society in decomposition. Even less equal than England. The first thing he'd done was to rush into W.H. Smith's at the airport, gagging for normality. Sad.

Jack, sitting again in the Tube, wondered if Kaja, as an Estonian, as a member of a country bubbling with enthusiasm, might think that this was all Russia deserved. He very much wanted to hear her views on Russia as well as England. He very much wanted to hear her voice, the way she'd laughed with her upper lip curled back, the way when he'd told a joke or put on a funny voice she'd squeezed her face between her hands and gone, 'Oh God, you are *so* mad,' and then squeezed his. The way she'd used a CD in her bag as a mirror to brush her hair in, that day they'd walked on the empty little beach of Haaremaa's main town, hand in hand, when he'd wondered what further joy would ever be possible, feeling the warmth and weight of her against his shoulder and the brisk wind off the Baltic that made the netball posts hoot hauntingly, like ghost owls.

Did she remember it all in the same way? Or with anger, even with grief? A frenzy of loss, anyway.

Did that satisfy him, then? Serve his vanity?

Maybe she just thought he was a spoilt knobhead.

He felt trapped and afraid of dying, sitting there in the Tube carriage as it lurched through the under-darkness, recalling these moments of his life, spotlighting them, their curiously hushed quality; his life was an extraordinary gift and he didn't want it stolen from him. He might have been that ugly, thickset bloke living right on the North Circular. He might have been a leper in the thirteenth century. He might have been the obese, chalk-white teenage kid squeezed into the seat opposite, munching through a giant Wispa, in her short pink skirt, spots like bogeys on her forehead, a track top from somewhere like JJB Sports making her sweat. Pure chav, he thought. ('Chav' was a term Milly was fanatically opposed to, likening it to 'Yid' or 'darkie'.)

Then the fireball might come and it would all be over in a painful few seconds or maybe minutes, or with the true horror of a slow suffocation.

And he would have entirely wasted his gift. Fumbled and frittered it away. Those days with Kaja were the true potential of the gift; they had compelled him to be more than he had settled for. The trouble with England, he thought, was that it compelled you to be exactly that: what you had settled for, which was always less than you had originally imagined or anticipated. Or, worse: what England had settled for you. Even Roger Grove-Carey had not prevailed against that.

It was not a question of money, he corrected himself. He had once seen a huge scrawl on a railway bridge which had said: *Poverty Stops You Making Love.* At the time, before he had teamed up with Milly, when he was living hand to mouth off meagre grants as a student, that graffito had struck him as having a point. Now that he was immensely comfortable in material terms, he was not so sure it was true. Being rich also got in the way of love. In his case, however, it had granted him a reprieve by making it clear that it had limited powers: it could not make children.

Ultimately, he thought, as the station lift delivered him from the depths at Hampstead, the time with Kaja six years back was a magical interlude. No more than that. He could not mistake it for the main action.

Wednesday was nervously indifferent and Thursday was very good right up to the phone call – mainly because Jack put the Kaja problem to one side, it being the first day of the final test. England were heading for the Ashes, but it could all go wrong. It usually did go wrong. Hell's umbilical cord.

If she were to phone and Milly answered, he would double-bluff, say she was an ex-lover, ooh la la. He rehearsed it on his own in the study. It sounded incredibly unconvincing to his own ears: he was a hopeless actor. But it would fool Milly because she was not the suspicious type and, anyway, he had never otherwise cheated on her. This made him all but unique in the music world. Perhaps it explained everything, he mused.

He was still in demand, though. He had to give a talk tomorrow contrasting Stockhausen, Cardew and Pärt at a conference in Newcastle, but he would scribble it on the train going up. Since he would be in competition with the cricket, he was not expecting more than about three peculiar people. In two months' time he was due in Stockholm for a couple of nights, at a music festival whose theme was the New European Music, in which someone he felt must be out of touch had asked him to perform his twelve-minute solo piano piece, *Take Delivery of the Sumptuous* (2001). Milly had thought it indulgent to spew thousands of gallons of burnt kerosene into the atmosphere for the sake of twelve minutes on the ivories in front of thirty or forty Swedes, but Jack had accepted. Demands on his time were not that frequent, these days: he was lazy about meetings of the various committees he was on, and had been politely asked to drop himself from the RCM board. Only now was he beginning to realise that entropy had set in: the fewer of these meetings he attended, the fewer the commissions.

Out of sight, out of mind. Whenever they went off the radar for a few days down at Wadhampton Hall to chill out, Milly would come back to two hundred emails. Jack would come back to two or three. Never mind that most of Milly's were pointless, it was still an indication.

He had the feeling that, were he to write a devastatingly good major work – an opera, say, with a crazy and ironic title like (he amused himself opening a *Guardian* supplement languishing on his desk and stabbing his finger on a couple of pages, finding adverts both times) *A Reasonably Well-Adjusted Dog* or *The Peculiar Incident of the Fishmonger* – well, were he to write this work it would probably be ignored, because he was so out of the swim. It would end up being done in the smaller hall in Cirencester and then disappear. There wasn't even an avant-garde to make waves with, these days: the only way he could bring attention to himself was by composing something flagrantly anti-Islam or anti-Born-Again Christian; but it would be very unwelcome attention, and possibly fatal. It was like living in the Middle Ages. The delicate sensitivities of the fanatic must not be hurt.

Ultimately, of course, it was his own fault. He had taken the lonely path of the full-time artist, which got lonelier and lonelier by some poxy internal law. Sometimes he thought he might actually have produced more were he a fully-fledged lecturer, especially at some rich college in the States. Or a massively busy festival organiser, his shoulder permanently crooked from the phone, his brain microwaved by the mobile, his voice hoarse from use. You accreted confidence, that way. You gained status, like an ape did. He saw it in trains. Right now he was in no-man's-land, neither young nor old. When you were old with a big beard and about to die, people rediscovered you, though perhaps not for long.

Trescothick, who'd stroked ball after ball over the boundary line, was caught by Hayden at slip. Jack groaned aloud, listening. England were eighty-two after eighteen overs. No sweat.

He preferred cricket on the radio. As a kid, he'd bike about with a tranny Scotched to his handlebars, listening to the commentary. England were slogging away just beautifully. Life could quite often be fairly good. Milly had bought him, for his fortieth, an early nineteenth-century ceramic lantern, yellow and blue, with its original candle still inside; a beautiful object cheering his desk. If England won the Ashes, he would light the candle.

He looked around him at his eyrie in the eaves, sensing like something oversweet the massive dollops of cash sunk in to make it this way – casual chic, as Tim the funky designer called it, with thermal comfort and fine-grained hardwood flooring (FSC certified), and Ligeti playing through the Bose (theoretically, only now there was cricket). It was OK. But it was also killing, because he was not getting it together. But today is today and I am free until the evening to compose, he said to himself, rolling an apple over his desk, sucking on a wine gum – a green one, which was his least favourite flavour. He was supposed to be working on the piece for the Purcell Room inspired by the bus accident in Pond Street on the day of the second bombings, but *It's Just Such a Bad Day*, or maybe *Echo*, was stuck.

He switched off the radio as Strauss cut to the boundary. It was a cruel, self-lacerating act. He swept the pencilled score sheets aside and took a fresh one and bit into the apple and hunkered down and the fragments started to link and mutate and stream out through the day until at least two minutes of music had occurred that had never occurred in the world before. He didn't do lunch, or not properly: just a graze around one o'clock, catching the score, checking no more Tubes or buses had gone up while he wasn't around, rolling his shoulders, doing fifteen minutes on the treadmill in the bedroom, saying hi to Marita in the hallway and asking her please, please, to keep her music down if she was staying in, which she wasn't, she said, smiling at him with her perfect teeth and fridging the tub of cottage cheese he'd forgotten on the kitchen table. Her T-shirt said *Expecting Style since 1987*.

'Anticipating,' Jack smiled, almost prodding her chest.

She flinched and looked vaguely alarmed.

'I mean, instead of *Expecting*. On your T-shirt.' His ears were red, he knew it. 'That's English for you. It's weird. You can just miss. Right?'

She was off to the Globe, unbelievably; it was part of her English course.

'To shee Sexspeare.'

'*The Winter's Tale*?'

'Shorry?'

'About a woman who comes back after years away? As a statue? Paint still wet?'

'Oh my rally shens,' said Marita, which Jack interpreted about two hours later as 'human relations'.

The only caller was Trevor Norris, from three doors up, at about half past one. Trevor was eighty-odd, fighting fit and head of the local neighbourhood committee. He gave Jack the impression that if he had been his father he would have sorted him out, but as he was not Jack's father he would have to keep his mouth shut. It was about the new couple fighting to remove the disabled space in front of their home in Gayton Road. Jack remembered just in time, before he looked as if he was on drugs.

Jack agreed that it was a strange way of going about things, interfering with the neighbourhood before you had even moved in. He heard his voice as Trevor must hear it: Middlesex vowels, immature, failing to be a cool dude.

'I agree, Trevor, it's pretty strange.'

'This was once a community. We looked after each other. Now it's all self, self, self.'

Trevor Norris swept his pale blue eyes up and down the street like enfilade fire. 'The rot set in with the coffee shops,' he said, his eyes now fixed on Jack. 'El Serrano's. Dubious men in duffel coats ordering risottos. The rise of the bed-sitting room.'

Jack realised, after a moment's confusion, that Trevor Norris was talking about the 1950s. Trevor would have been barely thirty years old, his white shock of hair greased down and dark, a rolled umbrella under his arm. The last clatter of deliveries by horse and cart.

He had a nice new Labrador with him, like a guide dog, with an irritating bell on its bright red collar.

'It's my chief staff and comfort,' he said. 'Meet Spritzy.'

Spritzy mounted Jack's thigh on trembling back legs as Trevor gave him the brief. The relevant authorities had decided that the disabled space would go, it was all very technical, and Jack made the right scandalised noises while trying to shake off the fervid dog, its heavy, hard chest pressed against his thigh, its tiny bell ringing like a mockery of Pärt's.

'All they care about is if the place looks *clean*,' said Trevor, moving off towards the gate while Spritzy stayed put on his extendable lead, gagging for a touch more of Jack. 'And they can't even get *that* right.'

The whole day was mostly pro, therefore, right up to the phone call – the only real con being an hour of Edward's painter-decorator drilling through into a party wall, and the faint whisper of his tranny tuned to the cricket that Jack first excluded by keeping the windows shut, which made it too warm, and then by wearing his moulded ear protectors, which made it hard to hear the phone he didn't want to answer, anyway – but Milly didn't like the idea of being out of contact in these 'in case' times, so the phone was next to him as he scribbled with his fine pencil on the score sheets right up till she came back home at seven, as totally drained as he was, though for such different reasons: while he was hunched over his desk, way down on the glamour scale, she was shooting up to Hull and back.

'Hi. How'd it go?' she sighed, coming up the stairs, head and shoulders appearing beyond the beam. She gave him the dazzling smile bit.

'OK. And you?'

'Incredibly irritable,' she said. 'I think I need iron. Or magnesium. Or both.'

'I didn't listen to the cricket.'

'So?'

A pang of disappointment, like a little boy expecting praise for not eating his sweets.

'How was Hull?'

'Boots, Dixons, Primark, McDonald's, Waterstone's, Lunn Poly, Starbucks, Thomas Cook, Top Shop,' she said, moving her head from side to side like a metronome, her fish-scale earrings swinging. 'Nice views from the train, though. Nice light on the water.'

'That's something,' he said, feeling envious of what she had seen, of the unimaginable complexity of her day. She had dark rings under her eyes. She helped herself to a wine gum, one of the black ones he'd saved up for himself.

'You stopping? I need a drink.'

'Lemme get you a drink, Mill,' he said, as if he hadn't heard.

'Trouble is,' she said, as she led down the stairs in her bare feet, leaving faint prints of perspiration on the steps, 'you feel a loon, talking about captured rainwater in the middle of Hull. It's all like, *so* ordinary and you're just the weirdo, imagining the end of the world. Like those smelly guys who used to go round with placards saying *The End is Nigh*.'

'Yeah, that's how I feel,' said Jack, the reasonable glow of his day shrivelling. 'A complete weirdo.'

While she changed into her usual combats and sloppy shirt, he splashed a couple of Johnnie Walker Blacks in the front sitting room, one small, one large, and opened a beer for himself: his nip was a chaser. He suddenly felt a need to listen to Ravel. Any Ravel. This happened, sometimes. Or Janáček. Janáček would fire him. But he resisted. Milly would want something else. Something easier.

Sitting on the sofa with her Scotch, Milly asked him how his work had gone. Jack still found her saying 'work' with inverted commas around it where he was concerned, even after all these years.

'Oh, two minutes of pretty good stuff. Non-orchestrated, of course. Out of the blue. Maybe that's a good title. I've dropped the timps, the bombs going off. It was holding up the whole thing. What Roger would call *your little darlings*. *Get rid of your little darlings*,' Jack added, imitating Roger Grove-Carey's teacherly growl.

'*Wallace and Gromit*,' said Milly, 'is even slower. I think about five seconds a day.'

'Slight difference,' said Jack, rather stung. He sat down next to her with a grunt, but not touching. 'I mean, I don't work in plasticine.'

'Watch it.'

'Watch what?'

'You grunted as you sat.'

'So?'

'That's what our dads do. Sign of age.'

'Oh, it's been quite a while now,' said Jack, not wanting to hear this.

They took a sip accidentally in unison, so Jack let his glass hover at his lips for a bit or it would look comic. The Scotch bayed in his throat and buzzed in his head. Perfect pitch. Mélophone. He was wondering when he could check the final score. He'd watch the highlights tonight.

'I wasn't judging,' Milly said. 'About your productivity. It's even better, two minutes.'

'Yeah, and after all that pain and effort it'll be played to about thirty people, four of whom will be listening enough to pick up all the subtleties. Two of those four will be academics and hate it and the third will think it's fairly darn good.'

'What about the fourth?'

'That's me, and I'll have my head in my hands and I'll be thinking: God, did I actually *write* this junk?'

Milly sighed, instead of smiling. 'Well, at least one person'll appreciate it.'

'Great.'

Neither of them said anything for a few moments. Jack thought he could sense the movement of Milly's journey – the trains, the taxis – in the air around her, in the heat of her form next to his.

She asked if Marita was in.

'Marita's gone to the Globe, can you believe,' Jack said. '*Sexspeare, I go to shee Sexspeare.*'

'You make her sound like Manuel, poor thing.'

'*Don't mind him, he's from Barcelona,*' said Jack, in a feebler imitation of Basil Fawlty than usual. 'It's weird, she's almost fluent but barely comprehensible. No ear. Anyway, it's drizzling, so she'll probably hate it. But at least she's not clubbing. Or shopping.'

'Put on Noir Désir,' she said. 'I'm so sick of England. Really gets on my tits.'

They had discovered Noir Désir on a trip to France, and liked the band very much. Then the singer had ended up languishing in a Latvian jail, having bashed his actress girlfriend to death while filming there – all very French. Despite her politics, Milly fancied the singer's voice because it was dark and dangerous. Jack found the whole deal a bit dodgy.

'Let's live in France,' said Milly, as the heavy bass sounded and the French words over it took them elsewhere. 'Or at least buy a house there. Like everyone else who's normal. A mill with a meadow, a stream, horses. Oh let's, oh let's!' she added, half mockingly, a faint echo of the dorm in Roedean. 'Milly's Mill! Lots of *terrain*. The locals can do all the looking after,' she added, more serious again. 'They're desperate for work, French unemployment's about eighty per cent or something.'

'That's Somalia you're thinking of,' Jack said.

'I mean in the *countryside*, not Paris obviously.'

'It'd kill my career,' he pointed out, settling back in the sofa.

'What career?'

'Thanks.'

'Only imitating you,' Milly growled, removing a cushion and snuggling up to him.

'And we are in fact correct.'

'Oh shut up,' said Milly. 'Don't start that one again. Anyway, it's not a career. It's art.'

'I'm OK,' Jack murmured, then kissed her hair, which smelt of other people's cigarettes, trains, the offices of Hull. The faint golden sheen of organic henna hid most of the grey hairs. He was glad to be with her, day in, day out.

'I think maybe the whole ecosystem is going to find some way of rejecting us,' she said, into his shoulder. 'Like antibodies with a killer virus. We're just so invasive.'

'Oh.'

'We're just too problematic. It's scary. We undo the whole delicate thing even when we don't know it because we're just so clever-boots. It makes me think that I've wasted my hour on this earth.'

Jack quite enjoyed hearing this: unlike himself, Milly was not one to regret things, usually, and this was a truly mega regret. Regret was not the same as grief. He saw the blank screen of the hospital scan, its absolute stillness and blackness. Five years, it had stayed blank! In a deliberately high, unconvincing voice, he intoned: 'I'm sure you haven't wasted it, Mill.'

'I'm worrying about dry toilet systems while the fu-ucking Siberian permafrost is melting,' she said, unsnuggling herself and leaning back. 'I might as well deal in classic handbags.'

'Best Italian leather and decent zips.'

'Live on nothing but carrots,' she went on. 'Give all my money to War on Want. Torch those bloody awful four-by-fours with the bastards still inside.'

Jack regarded his beer can closely, ignoring the 'my' of 'my money', although it made him twitch. 'It's weird how the world isn't the way you think it's going to be,' he said, 'and then you're all right anyway because you work out how to be joyless.'

He'd let the words come out of him before he could filter them; he was actually surprised by the word 'joyless'. He sipped his beer and wondered if he'd ever used that word in his life before.

Milly ruffled his hair so that the generous lock fell over his eyes. 'When did you last get it cut? No, sorry – when did you last *comb* it? Hey, you look incredibly cool like that.'

He cleared his eyes with a toss of his head. 'I thought, if I *looked* like Beethoven, hey, I might *sound* like him too,' Jack said.

'There's still time,' Milly declared, staring towards the window and its view of the Heath. It was drizzling outside, and the room was muggy. 'Actually, there probably isn't.'

'It's hard,' said Jack, rather lamely.

'We need to give the people a true democratic voice,' Milly said, 'instead of *manipulating* them.'

'Are these the same people you say shouldn't trespass on your parents' estate? Or are there several peoples?'

Milly ignored this, and Jack felt mean. Then she said: 'Roger took Claudia's car out and wrote it off on Primrose Hill. All he's got is a headache. He was pissed.'

'Roger's smashed her car?'

'Yup. Claudia told me.'

'Told you when?'

'On the train. She phoned.'

'Nobody phoned me today,' said Jack. 'Except someone trying to sell me timber treatment. They know I'm dead wood,' he added, surprised at the quality of his joke. He was really desperate to know the score, which was probably why he couldn't relax.

'You didn't go out at all?'

'I was about to, onto the Heath, but some bloke was playing Scott Joplin on a flute behind that tree. I dived, literally *dived*, back in here before *too* much damage was done.'

'So you didn't get the stuff for supper,' she said, wearily, closing her eyes. 'Or ask Marita to.'

'Nah,' said Jack, confidently, having entirely forgotten; 'I thought we'd get in a curry. Marita wasn't around.'

'We had curry on Friday.'

'Indians have curry every day,' said Jack, finding it hard to locate the comfort zone on the unwieldy extent of the sofa.

'Keep still, you're jogging me,' Milly said. Then, after a moment's silence: 'You forgot, didn't you?'

'Not really,' he said. 'I just lost sense of time. I mean, *the* time.'

He got up and changed the CD, Noir Désir having turned out too heavy for now. He felt like playing Pärt's *Fratres*, but Milly saw the CD in his hand and asked for *Atom Heart Mother*, because it took her right back. Jack conceded because he always appreciated Pink Floyd's use of the bass line as their harmonic front.

'Swan & Edgar,' Milly said, closing her eyes. 'We used to go shopping when we still had the flats in Bayswater for ourselves. They don't even *need* to rent them off, that's what so silly. They'd come up much more if they had a pied-à-terre. Mummy thinks we should plant a quince tree, by the way.'

'Don't think so,' said Jack. 'We've got loads of room.'

'Yer wha'?'

'I mean they wouldn't come up much more, having their own place.'

'Well, they don't like to disturb you, because you're at home all the time.'

Bollocks, was what Jack wanted to say, but he didn't. The whisky was lengthening her vowels, poshing her up. The same thing happened whenever she phoned Hampshire. She'd lose the London voice, as her face would lose its London sallowness after a weekend there, and go all apple-cheeked. He felt like an invalid, sometimes. Pink Floyd's epic chromatic sweeps went pianissimo and then somebody in the road made an ululating sound that wrote itself out in his head as a sort of embroidered hem. People didn't realise they had a voice except those that didn't, usually.

If Kaja was after him, like a stalker, like a hunter closing in, moving in via Howard, closer and closer, then he had to figure out a way of telling Milly before Kaja struck. It's what the girl from the timber treatment place had said on the phone, who was probably working for an organised crime syndicate. *Preventative treatment.*

'Seriously,' he said, suddenly needing to move. 'Why don't we go out for a curry? That nice place on Fleet Road.'

'Thursday?'

'So what, Thursday?'

'Let me check my emails,' she said, without stirring.

'Again?'

'I haven't since Hull. Lunchtime.'

'I'll book a table,' he suggested, looking around for the cordless.

It rang, suddenly, and they laughed. Milly answered it, as it was next to her on the sofa, hidden under a gardening supplement. She started off smiling and then she said, in an anxious voice, 'Oh, yes, God, here he is, Donald.'

'Something's happened to your mum, Jack,' she said, pulling an anxious face.

Jack frowned and took the phone, his heart stopping and then hammering at his chest as if a leopard had walked into the room. It was his father. Milly lowered the volume of *Atom*

Heart Mother just as it was shifting towards the major sixth. It left him stranded.

'Hello? Dad?'

At first Jack could only hear the sound of breathing. Then his father's voice came on and announced, breathless, as if it was jogging along, 'John, she's had, a bad, accident. Mum.'

'A bad one?'

'Had a turn, myself but, I'm OK now. In Hillingdon, Emergency. We shot here, straight away in, the ambulance. Yes.'

There was a lot of noise behind him: Jack pictured a crowd of doctors and nurses and machines. Pink Floyd was scouring the air beyond in great swoops.

'She's OK, then? Mill, get rid of the music.'

'Get rid of what?' asked his father.

'No, I'm just asking Milly to turn the music *right off*.'

She did so, in a rush, spilling her whisky.

'Well, at least, she's still, breathing,' his father said, as if Jack had asked the question.

'Still *breathing*? Oh God. Shit.'

'Look, I've got, to sit down.'

'Then sit down then, quickly, then,' said Jack, strange heat flushes racing over his face.

'It's, so stupid,' said his father, still sounding as if he was jogging up a hill, 'it's all so, stupid. Her neck's not, broken, they don't think.'

'Her *neck* might be? Oh my God.'

Jack felt he was in the dark, observing through a window a scene of very white, brightly lit figures, one of whom was his mother.

'She can move, her legs,' said his father, panting hard. 'She's conscious, talking, you know, gibberish. *I* can't, understand any of it, anyway. It's all, what d'you call it, under her breath. And there's, the cat to feed.'

Jack felt that this was all sounding a bit better than a few seconds back. This was his mother's second accident in six months – she was too bold with her blindness and kept falling

208

down stairs or tripping over onto shop windows: it was going to be fine, it was initial panic, that's all. Milly was standing by the stereo with her hand over her mouth. He covered the receiver and said to her, 'My mum's had another accident.'

She nodded. His father was sounding as if he was breaking down.

'I had, a turn, in the ambulance,' he panted, 'but I'm OK now.'

Jack thought: I could lose both of them in one night. My parents.

'John?'

'Yeah, I'm here. I'd better come down.'

'That'd be nice, John.'

'How did it happen, Dad?'

'She fell out, of the window.'

'The *window*? Oh no. Which one?'

'The one above the, lean-to. She was taking, the curtains down to, clean them, I told her not to. She was standing, on this chair.'

'Oh blimey, that's bad,' said Jack, running his hand through his hair, thinking of the black girl lying in front of the bus.

'The phone went and, she must have wobbled, you see. She fell out onto, the lean-to's roof and, slid off from, there onto the patio. I heard her fall, John. I thought she was dead, honestly. Big pool, of blood. I feel awful, myself.'

'Who'd called her?'

'What?'

'On the phone? Making her wobble?'

'Why?'

Then Jack heard another voice, a rustle, his father saying, 'All right, yes.' He wondered if the person who'd called her on the phone knew what they'd brought about.

'I have to go, John. I'll keep you, informed.'

'I'll be right over, Dad. And, hey, Dad.'

'Yes?'

'You don't happen to know the final score, do you?'

'Three hundred and nineteen for seven.'

'Ace. Thanks, Dad. Ta-ra.'

When Jack came off the phone, Milly was coming back from the kitchen, her glass refilled.

'So?' she said.

It irritated him to see that she'd topped up. 'Yeah, it's a bad one. She fell out of the window. She's still breathing, but that's about it.'

'Oh dear,' said Milly, pulling a face above the glass, the ice jingling. 'That does sound bad.'

The sitting-room door opened and Marita appeared in a joyful, spirited burst of perfect white teeth and low-slung jeans and a scent of fruit bubble gum. She was half hidden behind huge square boutique bags that rustled like white noise.

'Hi! You OK?'

'Not really. Jack's mother's had a bad accident.'

'Oh, sho *shorry*,' Marita said, dropping her shopping bags. 'She is shteell lee*v*ing?'

'Yeah,' said Jack, standing up and only now beginning to feel his legs tremble; 'she could well be leaving, I reckon.'

What with his daily visits to the big hospital in Hillingdon – where his mother was confined to the High-Dependency Unit with a fractured upper vertebra, her neck and head scaffolded by a metal brace like something out of *Dr Who*, her broken wrists in plaster, her arm attached to a drip, a bleeping machine recording her pulse rate along with something else that was not brainwaves but just as important, her bruised face swollen around the unseeing eyes like a peach forgotten in the bowl – and the need to catch the cricket in what slots were left, Jack did nothing about the Kaja question. It was over two weeks since he'd spotted her coming out of Howard's, and now he had her number, and he'd been totally inert. And so had she.

His mother was mostly conscious and surprisingly bright. The nurses appeared confident of her recovery, although more through their jolly manner than anything concrete. His mother's skull had cracked like an egg and brain fluid had leaked out of her nose. It amazed Jack that anybody, let alone a woman of seventy-five, could have survived all this. The bed opposite was occupied by an elderly woman who appeared to have enormous difficulty in fetching each breath, as if out of a deep well, and was never visited. Although she was half comatose, the nurses addressed her loudly and cheerily: 'How are we today, Eileen?'

Jack found the silence between each breath extraordinary, but only once did a nurse stare down at Eileen, a little worried, until the breath was drawn.

'Eileen seems in a bad way over there,' said Jack.

'She's a bit poorly,' said the nurse, who was a Liverpudlian in her early thirties, and openly flirtatious with him: *Sue*, it said, on her badge. Jack told Sue that he'd been supposed to be going up to Newcastle today for a lecture, but didn't think he'd be that missed. He pronounced 'castle' in a self-consciously northern way, as you were supposed to do.

'Oh, I'm sure they will miss you, gorgeous,' beamed Sue.

Jack liked being called 'gorgeous'. In fact, his daily two hours or so in High Dependency were oddly cheering. His mother was not, after all, dying, and the ward's action was weirdly exciting. Nobody actually died in his presence, but there were several emergencies when the doctors rushed in, curtains were drawn, and an orderly manhandled an oxygen tank on squeaky wheels over the yellow-and-black cable-cover across the doorway, *Trip Hazard* emblazoned as a warning on the door. He liked the term *Trip Hazard*. He could use it as a title.

And then he thought: Kaja's my trip hazard. Better than *Echo*.

'John?'

'I'm here, Mum.'

He kept forgetting, even after thirty-odd years, that his mother couldn't see him, or only as a memory of what he had looked like aged five. Apart from that memory, he only had existence as a voice and as touch – this touch of his hand on the fingers protruding from the plaster, their skin dry as husks. It was good, holding her hand, pumping in support; it gave him purpose. It put off everything else, which was less important. He didn't even mind her calling him John, something he'd tried and failed to wean his parents off twenty years ago.

The Temple of Healing, he called this place. It was a bit dirty in the corners and smelt of chemical swabs and bedpans and bleach, and there were signs that in less dependent wards the patients were correspondingly less attended, but he had a kind of affection for it after a few days, mixed in with the dread and the anxiety – not to mention the fatigue from the travelling. It was overwarm in High Dependency, as there was no air conditioning; the big windows, although they swung open a few inches, merely let in more hot air. His mother had to wear a thick sheepskin cover over her shoulders to stop the head brace from chafing them, and because the brace was screwed directly into her skull, Frankenstein-like, she was very uncomfortable.

An old fan was brought in after the weekend, its grille thick with congealed dirt and dust, and it rattled away on the bedside table.

'That's better,' said his mother. 'That's much more comfortable.'

He went down to get a coffee and a chocolate bar from the lugubrious visitors' café, and saw a middle-aged woman weeping in front of the lifts, the man with her – her husband, perhaps, or her brother – resting a hand on her back, waiting for her to stop. God knows who she'd lost or was fearful for. The café was playing Stevie Wonder, which was a nice try, although 'You are the Sunshine of my Life' made wormholes in his brain for the rest of the day.

That Monday night he was alone in Hampstead. Milly was on a three-day consultancy somewhere near Kendal. The weekend in Hampshire had been postponed. Donald had offered a bed in Hayes, but Jack couldn't face it, pleading work. They'd watched the cricket together, at least, but Donald kept nodding off, exhausted.

He didn't phone Kaja; in fact, he'd mislaid the number on its little Post-it. Apart from anything else, Monday was the last nail-biting day of the whole test series. He got in takeaways and left half. The victory was peculiar: the umpires dragged out play through fading light until it whimpered and paused and the moment was lost. But Jack still punched the air, all alone, as Michael Vaughan received the tiny urn. Then everything else flooded in. The bad stuff. The stuff that sport kept at bay, most of the time. And music.

Fishing in a drawer, he found his Tallinn souvenir lighter, which had proved so fateful in his life. It still worked. He used it to light the original candle in his antique ceramic lantern, as he'd vowed in the unlikely event of an England win. He watched the early nineteenth-century wax swell and drip as the flame bobbed on the wick, as if about to take off. Was it an early nineteenth-century flame? The smoke was surprisingly thick and black, presumably because of the dust, the two centuries of grime. He closed his eyes and smelt burnt tallow, which was not all that pleasant, and imagined a shadowy, Dickensian room down some soiled backstreet. The smoke seemed to be blackening the ceramic as it rose through the holes in the lantern's top, so he blew out the flame.

He put on an old vinyl recording of Haydn's Symphony Number 49 in F minor, *La Passione*, even though the needle jumped. The work was both tense and sombre enough, that's why: hammering on in its delicate way, little taps on the heart, mostly very dark. A kind of homeopathy.

He had bad, period dreams in which he was wielding a ceramic bat against all-comers in a tangle of mulberry and quince.

The following day he was in the hospital shop and taking out change for a paper, when someone behind tapped him on the shoulder. It was a man with the liverish, blotched face and sickly smell of the serious cancer sufferer. 'You've dropped this, mate,' he said. 'Bound to be the one you want. Always like that with me. Innit? Always the one you want. Eh? The vital bit of paper. Yeah,' he went on, as Jack was mumbling his thanks, 'it's got me in the liver. Ten days, they said. That was six months ago. Blimey. Never say die, eh?'

It was the pink Post-it with Kaja's number, marked by the imprint of a heel.

Jack was back holding his mother's hand, her breathing heavy but regular in her sleep, the heart rate pulsing undramatically on the machine, the vital numbers flickering as less vital numbers flickered on screens in the City, when it occurred to him that Moyna might be Jaan's grandmother.

'Hiya, gorgeous, you're looking upset. She's doing fine, luv! Y'want some cheering up, then just take me out on the town, duck.'

'I'm fine, thanks, Sue.'

'Any time, OK?' she said, winking. It was all a delicious, harmless game, like a rerun of *The Liver Birds*. 'You're luverly. I don't like 'em tall.'

'Thanks.'

'What d'you do, if it's not a rude question?'

'I write music.'

Sue's eyes widened in her friendly, slightly podgy face. 'What, you're a rock star, are you? Or just write it down?'

'Just write it down.'

'I've always wondered about that. Do you hear it first, then, all in one go?'

'Well, I sort of hear little bits and then glue them together until they make a bigger piece of music.'

'Just songs, is it? What's your name again?'

'Jack Middleton. John to my parents.'

Sue shook her head. 'No, doesn't ring a bell. Gimme someone you sound like. Ricky Martin?'

'It's not pop or rock, it's sort of classical. Really hard, modern stuff that no one likes listening to.'

She laughed. 'I'll bet it's really good, anyway. I'm a Liverbird, y'know. A Scouser.'

'Next door to John Lennon?'

'No, no idea where they lived, actually. I don't even bloody like 'em! You make y'living from that, do you? I'll bet y'mam's proud of yuz an' all.'

He shrugged, feeling about fourteen. He wasn't sure whether she *was* proud of him. His mother was always saying to him: 'I don't care what you do, as long as you're happy.' He felt a great love and a great sorrow, watching her sleeping inside her brutal crown.

His father came in to take over. He looked ill with worry and fatigue.

'How are things?' he said, blinking at his wife with rheumy eyes. 'All in order?'

'Your son's luverly,' said Sue. 'Can I borrow him?'

The line on the machine, panning up and down like a readout of the Himalayas, suddenly looked like Norfolk. The machine's sympathetic bleep, semiquavers in four-four time, turned into a long sustained note that had Sue glancing up at it. Jack's heart started to thump as, presumably, his mother's was not. This is what happened, he thought, in TV soaps. Except that no one was rushing towards his mother and his father was dealing with the stuff he'd brought along in a big Asda bag – a *Daily Mail* for him to read to her, sucky sweets, a cardboard nail file. Jack did not want to overreact. His mother had opened her eyes – although it made no difference, the darkness was always there.

'Is it OK?' Jack asked, his voice tiny and hoarse.

The Himalayas reeled into view again, the bleep returned, the world sang.

'Funny,' said Sue, 'it does that from time to time. I think it needs a good thump.'

He did go back with his father on the Wednesday, to keep him company overnight: Donald was looking very pale. Jack's sister and brother were planning on flying over the moment things got worse. The critical few days had passed and Jack's mum was still among them, in better spirits, the heart rate settling down. The doctor announced that she was very pleased.

Each time he went back to the house in Hayes, where he'd been brought up, another layer was added to the layers that separated him from his childhood, because the present house was like a distortion of the place he had known as a boy. The spanking new council estate was now as old as he was, and because a lot of the tenants had bought their houses over the years and added porches or conservatories or long extensions, or in several cases stuck stone cladding on the front, it was a slightly bewildering mishmash.

A sprinkling of takeaway tubs, giant polystyrene cups and several one-litre Smirnoff bottles were tucked into the leylandii hedges bordering the fresh, red-top tarmac; the THIS IS A NEIGHBOURHOOD WATCH sign was already faded, with what looked like gunshot holes in it but were probably kids being adept with a sharp instrument. The overall effect was even less consoling than the stark estate of concrete blocks on Haaremaa where Kaja had been brought up. Bloated-looking kids with shaven heads trailed around on their bikes, just as he had done once, although he wasn't sure he'd made that much noise or yelled '*Wa-ank-er!*' at a friend over the road just as a frail old lady was passing.

Some things in his old home hadn't changed, however: the scuffed fake-leather folder with a very faint, once gilded, *Radio Times* on its cover, that now held the *TV Times*; the dented Hovis biscuit tin full of digestives; the smell of peach air-freshener and fatty, toasted things; the hyperrealistic painting of the Alps in the sitting room that he'd once believed was an original, printed as it was on a textured surface.

His little bedroom was now a guest room, although the only guests were his sister or his brother on very occasional visits (about once every three or four years). The room had been newly wallpapered since he'd last seen it, removing the last traces of his boyhood – Blu-Tack scars from posters or quotes from John Cage and Jim Morrison, mainly. The wallpaper was pinstripe pink, rather tasteful, although the overall effect of the revamp still made it feel like a single in a Premier Lodge.

He stood for a moment at the window, which looked down on the little square of lawn and then the rest of the estate, now expanded onto what had been tussocky fields beyond, where he used to play and that had seemed so large and wild. The other gardens were all but hidden by fences, these days, and the silver birch in the corner had grown big enough to block out the entire right-hand side of the view. It made him feel dark and obscure, as if he was being cheated of his right to see a long way.

His mother had fallen – or thrown herself – out of the room next to this one, which was his parents' bedroom. He sneaked a look in, as if at something historic. The lace curtains she'd been taking down were still up. He opened the window and looked out. There was a dark stain on the patio. It seemed a very long way down.

His father had been repainting the kitchen cabinets when the accident happened. 'Crinkly Tan,' he said, 'your mum chose it. And the handles.' He showed Jack a set of porcelain-like knobs decorated with tiny sprigs of flowers, still to be screwed on. Jack offered to do it in the morning. His father looked out of the kitchen window and remarked, 'It's quite nice today,' as if he hadn't just come in. He must be in a state of shock, Jack thought. His father had always been small and self-effacing, the spit of that actor who'd played the attendant in the stuck lift in that famous Hancock sketch, but now he was even smaller, all but disappearing into the background. When Jack was a boy he'd been confused by the fact that his father was a member of an Airfix Club, making models and meticulously painting them with the more expensive Humbrol range. He spent three years, once, on a balsa-wood model glider which crashed into a cowpat on its maiden flight. Perhaps in reaction, Jack had never made a model in his life.

They sat down to an early dinner of fishcakes, frozen peas and packet mash. Jack had offered to phone for a Chinese takeaway, but his father insisted on cooking. It kept him sane, he said. Despite his mother's Irish origins (or perhaps because of them),

Jack's parents were lapsed Baptists, and still avoided alcohol except for a few doses of sweet sherry over Christmas. Jack thought it would do him good, not drinking for one day. The portions were small, as neither of his parents had a large appetite. He felt huge in the kitchen, getting the food down too quickly and then surreptitiously scraping at the plate. The newish cat, a tortoise-shell called Minx, sat at his feet and purred, not realising.

'There's pudding,' said his father, whose plate appeared untouched. 'A bit like Angel Delight. Remember? I know you always liked it. Mango and guano flavour. Or lime and Victoria plum.'

'Guava. I hope not guano.'

'That's it. A new one. Can't keep up. They're always changing them round. And I'd got your mother those mints for our anniversary,' he said, indicating a box on the mantelpiece. 'She's hardly touched them.'

'She'll have them when she gets out,' said Jack.

He was sweating, suddenly. The neon light was on, although it was still daylight outside. The kitchen faced north and was always dark. Its wall tiles had been changed when his parents had bought the house from the council; they showed a blow-up of the opened, dented cap of a Schweppes bottle over and over again. They were quite daring, he thought; Warhol-like, you could say. There was not a single indication that the house was inhabited by a blind person.

'I think Mum's doing really well, Dad.'

'In the circs,' replied his father, his mouth receiving a forkful of mash. Jack tried to remember how old he was. Seventy-five or seven or something. The framed Grade Eight certificate with Jack's name already faded was still slightly askew behind his head. They were still planning to frame the others, presumably. *We can't keep up*, his mother would joke.

'We can but wait,' said Jack, trying to shake the image of his mother flying out of the window and bouncing off the roof.

'Nothing else for it.'

A phone went. His father, who was fond of new gadgets,

had a cordless that he tended (like his son) to leave lying about in strange places. Now they both tracked it down to the sitting room, under the *Radio Times* folder, just before the answer-phone broke in. Every call was a potential peal of doom and they were nervous. It was Milly.

'Hello, my dear!' said Jack's father. Jack could hear the faint registers of Milly's voice, saying all the right things. The sitting room was the width of a pair of outflung arms, fingers bunched: about the size of the stall Richard du Crane's hunter shuffled in. The whole house, for that matter, would have easily fitted into one of Wadhampton Hall's Tudor food cupboards. They were due there at the weekend: Jack fancied that idea – fancied a break, a gust of greenness. His father gave him the phone after a few minutes.

'Hi, Jack,' Milly said, businesslike after Kendal. 'I've got the latest on Moyna. That's good news. You've got this weird message on the phone.'

'*I* have?'

'Yup. I was listening to the messages and it just came up. It's this woman who seems to know you. Hang on, I wrote it down. Shit. Can't find the paper. Something snazzy like Karen or Kristina or maybe Xanthea, even. Sorry. I'm mega knackered. Really awful trains.'

'OK. I don't know.'

'Well, she knows you. She says you've got to ring her back as soon as possible. Here it is. Kai-yah. I've no bloody memory. Nothing like Xanthea. That's age. Kai-yah. God knows if I've spelt it right.'

'OK.' He tried to make his voice sound dull and uninterested, like Dustin Hoffman's in *The Graduate*, but his throat had physically constricted. 'And that's it? Sorry, the hospital's got into my throat. Stuffy.'

'Do you know a Kaiyah?'

He looked up at the ceiling, as if pondering. Polystyrene tiles, like an office. Very inflammable. Toxic. Banned, these days, apparently.

'I'm trying to think,' he said. His double bluff faded into extinction like a bad sketch.

'Estonia?'

'Estonia?'

'She said Kaiyah from Estonia. Sounds very romantic.'

'Ah, they're *all* called Kaja,' Jack said, although he had no idea whether this was true – Kaja was the only Kaja he'd met out there.

'That's well pronounced. You mean all the lovely girls Edward keeps going on about?'

'Does he?'

'You must be selectively deaf. Do you want her mobile?'

'Yup.' He faffed around a bit with a *Daily Mail* on the coffee table, making paper sound effects, the big inky *TERROR* chiming with something inside him. 'OK, found a pen. Go ahead.'

His father was looking at him, puzzled.

'Do you want a pen?'

'It's OK, Dad. Carry on with your pudding. No, just talking to Dad. Go ahead.'

Milly gave him Kaja's mobile number. He'd really screwed things up, not making contact first. Not going into the attack. Waiting like a pillock. He was blushing, and sweat was tickling the sides of his body, under his shirt. He vaguely mimed writing the digits down with his finger.

'That's great,' he said. 'God knows what she wants.'

There was a silence. All his creative instincts had vanished. He was left with a bare, hard nub that refused to be embroidered.

'Maybe she wants you again,' said Milly, sounding very sad.

'Mill! Puh-lease! I spent my free time in Estonia, as I told you back then, walking around churches and stuff or visiting bogs. I was not about to have –' he dropped his voice – 'an affair.'

He caught himself in the mirror above the electric fire: he looked agonised, almost misshapen.

'I hope you're right and not hiding anything from me, Jack.'

'It's six years ago. It's probably some student I chatted to in a museum or something. I mean, I did *talk* to people.'

'No need to be aggressive.'

'I'm not aggressive, I'm just thinking how silly this is.'

Silly: he was using his mum's words. He was going back in time. He'd be sucking his thumb, next, after the pseudo-Angel Delight.

'Take care,' said Milly, after a moment.

'Yeah, take care, Mill.'

He replaced the upright receiver in its stand, struggling a bit to make it bleep, then stood there for a few moments before taking on the kitchen and his father and the normal eddying of life.

'I do like Milly,' said his father. 'She's very thoughtful. It's not everyone who fits that bill, not by a long chalk.'

'I agree,' Jack sighed, not meaning it to be a sigh.

'Which one?' his father smiled, displaying the two opened desserts. One was mauve, one was pink, like an interior designer's mood board. Behind the toaster was a pinned-up leaflet that said: *Incontact, Action on Incontinence. Enter the Bladder Zone.*

'I'll go for either,' said Jack.

It was dry enough to sit outside, afterwards: the plastic chairs had been tipped against the rain, as they always were, and they sat on the twilit patio with its square of lawn and corner rockery. His father sat with his legs crossed, his flannels riding up to show his bony ankles above the grey socks. Jack and Milly would give them trendy designer stuff for Christmas – steel letter holders from Habitat, suede throws from Prêt à Vivre, white feather lights from Heal's – but it was never on display, and it was rude to ask. Jack was desperate for a drink, something sharp and strong. The Milly call had made him very nervy, and he kept biting his lip. Someone was operating what sounded like a petrol-driven hedge trimmer.

'That's antisocial,' said Jack. 'On nice evenings.'

His father nodded. An invisible jet rumbled overhead, the noise fanning out into an intermittent roar that seemed to billow and continue for ages. Minx the cat was sniffing about in the washed-gravel edging.

'She knows perfectly well it's not for doings,' said Donald.

Jack had always found it hard to think of things to say to his father; Donald had almost no small talk, and locked his memories (of the war, say) behind an apparent shyness. He could no longer make Airfix models, he was too trembly, and those he had made with such care over the years had disappeared, too awkward to dust. His life was rolling up and there was little to show for it except those he had helped bring into the world, which was why Jack felt a responsibility in his presence and a corresponding, keener sense of diminishing success. His father said very little, either good or bad, about his son's music. Now Jack wondered again, as he usually did in Hayes (even when his chattier mother was there), why anyone believed in a future at all.

'Her horoscope in the paper said that her needs had to come first this week,' said his father, as if reading his son's mind.

'Really? Well, how perceptive.'

'Load of rubbish,' said his father. 'In my opinion. It also said last week that things would be taking an upward turn from Thursday.'

Jack smiled. 'A literally downward turn,' he said.

His father eyed the window she had jumped from. The bloodstain on the patio slabs was huge and tea-coloured. Maybe no one had tried to scrub it off. 'Yes,' he said, 'she didn't realise the lean-to was underneath, you see.'

'Eh?'

His father looked at him. 'Or else she'd have done herself in straight away, like she wanted.'

'Dad, are you serious? I thought someone phoned, she was taking the curtains down –'

'She can't fool me,' said his father. 'You imagine not being able to see all those years. You get to the point when you . . .'

His lower lip was puckering. His legs were still crossed, showing the white flesh, and he bent down and scratched his ankle, hiding his face.

'I guess so,' said Jack, feeling this was possibly one of the most important moments of his life, but that he was passing it by on the far side. He studied the top of his father's head, covered in wispy hairs, and the moment folded into its own silence, like a complicated flower.

The idea that his mother might have tried to top herself floated about like grease in a sinkful of water. It could not be absorbed. On the one hand, he quite admired her action, given the despair of her situation. On the other hand, he could not quite believe it. His father was voicing a worry, that was all. It was still virtual. It was not yet meatspace. Her own attitude right now, sweating under a massive brace screwed into her skull, her broken wrists hurting, stuck sightless in the bleeps and groans and voices, was weirdly cheery – it was pure Beckett, really. It was pure existential heroism. Spitting at the dark. She hadn't once complained, except to say that it was a little hot. Maybe people in Purgatory didn't complain. Her cracked skull was healing, amazingly. She wasn't Humpty-Dumpty, after all.

She looked like something out of an experimental German opera. He smiled to himself. Why not a British opera? He could write it. The masterwork. Bleak and enduring, set in a hospital. Early Pärt crossed with late Schoenberg. Everyone would hate it.

He picked up the phone and dialled the number on the Post-it sitting on his thigh.

It was the moment to do it. He'd not watched the time: it was already eleven in the evening, and his father had gone to bed. Jack had prowled around the house and found some Gilbey's he and Milly'd brought along about five Christmases ago, on their way to the Hall. Joy of joys, there was a carton of orange juice in the fridge. He didn't ever drink gin and orange, but he added half a tray's worth of ice and it was good, very good, but not quite strong enough. Another lash of the gin, and it wavered in his chest like the Northern Lights and he thought about the times in the dacha he and Kaja, stark naked in the tiny bedroom under the eaves, had knocked back the local vodka, neat in little glasses – and he wanted to cry with regret that he had not *stayed* on Haaremaa. Some centrifugal force was forever whirling him back into the same patterns, he thought – so that for one moment he felt he'd never left this house at all; had never left, at eighteen years old, Ashley Park at all (the name 'Ashley Park' etched into his infant brain as *ashlypar*, a sort of ganglion of his own body), but had dreamed everything since.

Ear to the receiver, he heard a tune he knew: Mendelssohn's 'Spring Song'. Over it came Kaja's voice, first speaking in English, then in Estonian. The words were fast and rather automatic, clearly being read. His heart was thumping again, he had to take in air deeply and exhale slowly, settle back into the sofa. He started to leave a message, trying to sound cool but concerned, when a real voice broke in before the beep.

'He-llo,' it said, like someone pretending to be foreign.

'Kaja?'

'Hi. It's you.'

'It's me.' He felt completely in control, suddenly. He felt strong. He'd ride this one out.

'I know.'

There was a silence. She'd sounded oddly far away, not the other side of London.

'I'm in Hayes,' he said, assuming she'd remember what he'd told her about his parents. 'My mother's had an accident.'

'Oh. A bad one?'

He explained what had happened, without reference to any suicide attempt. It was sheer excess, talking to her like this as if they'd left each other the day before. He sounded fake, though, to his own ears: as if the very important event concerning his mother had not touched him, and he was playing the role of an anxious, upset son putting on a brave face, light-heartedly obscuring his own feelings of shock and, perhaps, grief. It was complicated. He did not know at what point to mention Jaan. It was like a very burning point, he'd have to touch it quickly and then withdraw his finger.

'That's too bad,' she said, sounding even more American. Maybe she'd made it to Tartu University and met an American lecturer called Krohn. A cool dude with a doctorate. Her voice didn't thrill him, but maybe that was the fact that he was phoning from a room in which he felt like a boy, the hyperreal picture of the Alps and the varnished red-brick surround of the electric fire locking him into his old self.

'Yeah, that's too bad,' she repeated. 'That's sad.'

'So how did you get to find Howard Davenport?'

'You gave me the name and number, remember? On the Handel programme.'

'Oh yeah.'

He laughed. He had entirely forgotten giving her the contact, though now he could picture it clearly: his fumbling advance, goatee'd boyfriend looking on, her shy chuckle.

'How are *your* parents, Kaja?'

He was playing *very* concerned, now, he realised. Mr Compassionate Bloke 2005.

'My father died last year,' she said. 'My mother's OK, she has my brother back for now until two weeks more.'

She sounded tired, or as if she didn't care what he thought – although he said how sorry he was to hear Mikhel had died. He *was* sorry: it didn't seem fair, somehow, and he told her that. Her father hadn't even been that old, not old at all. He didn't like to ask *how* Mikhel had died, although he vaguely remembered some heart weakness stemming from an impoverished childhood.

'I have to say they were angry with you.'

'Uh-huh. And with you?'

'Yeah, a bit. They loved Jaan, though. They helped me out.'

'You must have been pretty angry, too. With me.'

'I was lots of things.'

'I'd have gone spare,' he said, unconsciously using a Milly expression. 'I mean, hey. You *ought* to've been angry. Look. About Jaan. Here's a straight question. Um . . .'

'Maybe.'

'Maybe?' he said, feeling his eyes go white.

'*Maybe* he's your son.'

'OK. That's cool. Maybe. Yup.'

'You have a problem with that?'

'Nope. Well, actually, I'd quite like to know either way.'

There was no reply. He was jealous, that's what he was. He felt it as an ache in his teeth. She had gone out and slept with someone else straight away. Probably not her ex-boyfriend of the marble sharks, either. Fuck. The gin was finished. Fuck. He forced himself on through this fog of jealousy.

'And are *you* OK, here in Blighty?'

'In what?'

'In England.'

'So, what d'you think?'

'It's probably hard.'

His hand holding the receiver was trembling. He took another deep breath. 'I think I was a bit . . . I think I was a bit, um, a bit of a coward.'

She didn't reply, again. He felt waves of contempt in the silence. There was an irritating buzz way behind, and he wished he was talking face to face. His hand still smelt of the dollops of alcohol gel he'd had to squeeze out of the dry handwash dispenser, going in and out of the ward. He saw Sue's cheery grin and heard her calling him 'gorgeous'. Maybe Sue's life was very straightforward.

'OK, Kaja,' he said, 'I think we should meet up. Talk face to face.'

'No problem. I would appreciate this,' she added, softly. It surprised him. Then he realised that she was crying. And *he* wanted to cry. He was having to blink wells of moisture from his eyes. His eyes stung. It was wholly unexpected. He felt his mother's hand, dry as bone in his. He saw Mikhel grinning at the caged fox next to the woodshed. He saw the black silhouette of a little boy.

'I'd like to see my maybe son,' he said, rather too hoarsely and loud. He looked up at the ceiling: his father was sleeping – or not sleeping – directly above, and the houses were cheaply built by the council. 'I'd like to see Jaan,' he repeated, in a stage whisper. 'Meet him.'

'Of course you do,' she replied, in a firm and even mocking voice, as if she hadn't been crying at all. 'But there's no hurry for you, is there?'

'You took five years.'

'That's a problem?'

'Why now, I'm wondering.'

'Which is your contact number during your stay in your parents?'

'There's only one,' he said, realising as he said it that he'd taken her imperfect English too literally, that he wasn't being sensitive enough. 'It's this one.' He gave her the number. She was being very efficient, like a secretary. I guess you have to be to survive that kind of precariousness, he thought.

'We'll arrange something soon,' she said. 'There's no hurry. You invite us when you want.'

He was a little aghast. He hadn't expected this. 'Well, in fact, I'm married now, in fact.'

'You were already married back then,' she said, so quietly he almost lost it.

He struggled to find something to say, but failed.

'Oh, by the way,' she went on, 'you confused him concerning your name. In Estonian, Jaak is a diminutive of Jacob. Not John. I didn't name him from you, if that's what you think.'

After his father had gone to bed, around ten, an hour before the call, Jack had considered what Kaja had done, and why she'd done it. He felt cross, but knew this cross feeling was unjustifiable. He wondered whether there was some kind of emergency, some problem maybe with the immigration authorities or with her flat or even with Jaan. He studied the cordless phone on its stand as if it was some kind of door to somewhere he didn't really want to go, but that he had no choice about opening. Kaja must have known that leaving a message might lead to trouble. He'd kept seeing, in his mind's eye, a Kaja who probably didn't look like that any more: and now he at least knew that her voice wasn't quite the same – it had lost some of its easy lilt, had grown up a bit along, presumably, with the rest of her. She'd been buffeted, maybe. He liked that word, *buffeted*. And that was partly his fault. Or very much his fault.

The odd thing was, sitting there in that very familiar sitting room, made simultaneously strange by the newish chintz covers on the suite (newish meant well over ten years old, he worked out!), he couldn't feel remorse, or not as a real emotion.

Actually, he'd probably screwed up her life, her hopes, certainly her studies and her inner freedom, but he had maybe given her something irreplaceable and joyous, at least: a child. Maybe. Maybe. He didn't like this maybe. He wanted to clear it up. It snagged. Maybe it was that word that was stopping him feeling much remorse. Or had he always been like this – even in the early days before he'd stumbled into Milly's life, when he was almost completely broke, ekeing out his scholarship grant in Scotch eggs and the cheapest instant coffee, holes in his shoes, his underpants fraying at the loose elastic? Had he always been able to distance himself? He couldn't say.

Basically, if he wrote five bars that he was later conscious in performance were slack, or sheer crap – marring the whole – he felt more remorse than he did now. And that was not good.

He stayed two nights in Hayes, in the end. Donald asked him to. So he only got back around three on Friday. Milly was away again until the late evening, contributing to a one-day environmental symbiosis course at Dartington. They'd be getting up fairly early Saturday to beat the crush and arrive in Hampshire in time for a morning walk.

He'd slept very badly after the call to Kaja, and now felt

lousy. The three hours in the hospital in the morning had floated past him as if he was a virtual entity in them, a ghost. The place ran on completely different rules from the world outside: the woman called Eileen had apparently died in the night, because her bed was empty. The fresh pillow was like her erased face, although he had never properly seen her face – just a shock of hair and a mask. Yet no one commented on this dramatic fact. People came in here and they died or they didn't and left. Either way, they left. But the whole thing was rendered down into a kind of grey mass of uneventfulness, in which people crying in lifts or groaning in their death agony gradually lost their contours, became part of the swirl.

The doctors were 'happy' with his mother's progress, and she'd had a 'good' night, even though she was being helped along with an oxygen mask. Even 'happy' and 'good' had changed their meaning, in here. You had to take on the hospital when feeling strong, not tired, or its smell soaked into your skin, poisoned your blood. Coming out onto the main road in a taxi at lunchtime (too tired to walk to the station), excusing himself with the invite to Wadhampton Hall, the need for a break and to be with Milly (his father was quite understanding about this), he saw fire engines and two ambulances parked and flashing on the main road by the exit next to the wreckage of two cars, their roofs sheared away by cutters.

'Young doctor leaving after his night shift,' the taxi driver explained. 'Crazy, this exit. People drive down that road like maniacs, especially on the way to work. Not the first time.'

'Dead?'

'Back in the hospital, a right mess. You don't think of doctors being in a hospital bed, do you? Other bloke what went into him, I dunno about him. Crazy, innit?'

'Yeah. Mad.'

'At least he was close to help, eh?' grinned the taxi driver, glancing back. 'You visiting, or out after a spell?'

'Visiting. My mother had an accident.'

'Sorry to hear it, mate. Sorry to hear it. I lost my mum last year. Still haven't got over it. Great girl, she was. It's never fair, is it? But at least we won the Ashes.'

If he had managed, years ago, to have catapulted himself out of England, he might have discovered who he really was. A composer friend who had moved to France five years ago said that he had simply taken his hang-ups with him to somewhere it was very hard to find Fry's Turkish Delight (wine gums, in Jack's case), so maybe no great change would have happened.

He looked around him in the Tube carriage and thought: *Hey, guys, I'm a dad.* They must see the difference in his eyes. Then sudden, scary waves hit him: the idea that it might be true.

Coming up the hundreds of stairs at Hampstead Tube rather than taking the lift, a feat which reminded him of climbing the tower of St Olav's Church in Tallinn six years earlier – a tower which had, hundreds of years ago, been the tallest structure on earth, and on which the KGB had installed their listening antennae, according to Kaja – Jack wondered whether it was a bigger deal, in an existential way, to do harm to someone, or to do good to them.

He had, in fact, done more harm to Milly than to Kaja, because of the children thing. A child could not be harmful to someone, just maybe inconvenient. He had perhaps been going a tad too fast that evening in Maida Vale, although the elderly woman in the four-by-four was the principal, devastating and extremely brief cause-and-effect that had so damaged their lives. But he had also done good, where Milly was concerned: their marriage of mind and body was strong and loving. He loved her. He loved her to bits.

With Kaja, if you discounted Jaan for a moment, because that was too complicated, too heavy to take in, and not even certain, he had not done all that much good, he didn't suppose. She knew he had lied to her, and that must be nasty to know when you've invested your heart in someone. On the other hand, she'd got screwed by someone else pretty well immediately. Even before she knew he'd bolted under cover of a false name. This had only just occurred to him! So they were equally false.

'You can't make an omelette without breaking eggs,' as his mum would have said.

He was nervous about Milly getting back that evening and the two of them having to have this thing out about Kaja. He had elaborated a whole symphony of untruths, but he feared her feminine acuity. She wouldn't let it rest. Not Mill. It was like that moment she'd asked him about the wedding ring. He'd taken it off in Estonia and put it in his bumbag. Incredibly, he'd forgotten to try to put it back on again after his initial struggle. They were eating out the second evening of his return and he'd felt both shifty and triumphant but managed to disguise it. They were still in Richmond back then, of course, and were eating in a new flash Thai place.

All of a sudden she'd said: 'I thought they cut your finger off as well?'

'Eh?'

'When they nick one's ring in these poorer countries?'

Out of the shock and humiliation of it – of not remembering that he'd not got it on – he couldn't improvise an answer. Instead, he stared at the finger, and the ring's slightly faded indent, as if he'd only just noticed.

'Um, yeah. Really embarrassing.'

'What, you lost your heart as well as your ring?'

'Blimey, how did you guess?' He felt physically sick. The Thai soup's spicy, fishy smell seemed to be wrapped around his neck. 'No, in fact I had to take it off. Can't get it back on again.'

'Why did you have to take it off?'

'This bloody grand in Tallinn. An antique, amazing forgotten sound. The guy reckoned I'd damage it, the delicate ivories. With the ring. I said to him, I don't play the keys like I'm a three-year-old standing on the stool. But he wouldn't budge.'

'Did you say that? He must have good English.'

'No, I'd made huge advances with my Estonian. *Tuletikk. Rebane.*'

'What's that mean?'

'Matches. Fox. The really embarrassing thing, Mill, is I completely forgot about it, after not being able to get it back on. It's OK, it's in my bumbag,' he hastily added, because Milly was looking very anxious. The ring was incredibly expensive, he knew that, although it looked like any other gold ring. 'I'll ask at a jeweller's or something.'

'You just need to heat it up,' she said. 'And use some Vaseline.'

'Sounds fun,' he said, grinning.

Six years on, he was up in his study, stretched out on the sofa, turning the ring around and around on its finger, noting the minuscule scratches on its lustre. It was as if nothing had developed since that meal. That moment. As if life was just a whole load of parallel times, running a marathon with each other.

He looked through what he'd composed a week before. At first glance he winced, but by the end of the two minutes of scribbled score it was singing to him, he was on its level. He'd reconceived this whole piece – maybe half an hour long – as something for a lot of woodwind, perhaps mostly saxophones and intermittent percussion and, quietly above it all (their playing would be generally pianissimo, the poor sods!), a baroque violin. Now he was hearing it again as voices, and he added a line for a mechanical bleeper. He scrawled a title on the first sheet: *Life is a Trip Hazard*, then pulled a face and put a line through *Life is a* and wrote *Waters of the*. That was more in keeping with his general style, although Howard claimed all Jack Middleton's titles sounded like something off a King Crimson album (this was confusing, because Howard was nuts about King Crimson).

Waters of the Trip Hazard evolved back into a choral work during what remained of the afternoon, half of which Jack spent slumbering under his papers.

Each time he woke up he saw the quote from John Cage he'd stuck up on the wall above the photo of himself receiving the Ernst von Siemens Prize over twenty years ago: '*Pay attention, but stop short of explanation.*' The paper was yellowing and the ink faded, because he'd written it out when he was still a student.

He had not heeded its advice one little bit.

Yes. The easiest thing, aside from going to the Estonian Embassy and finding out, possibly, that she wasn't even registered and therefore an illegal immigrant, was to give her money. That was obviously what she wanted; why, otherwise, take over five years to get hold of him? She hadn't answered that question. He was maybe the father. He'd prefer a DNA test before committing himself: he'd met his maybe son – unknowingly, the best test of all – and felt no paternal impulse whatever. He'd read about these things, these scams. Even now, he felt abstracted from the possibility that he was, at long last, a dad. He'd throw money at her, maybe on a regular basis, in return for leaving him be. Whether Jaan was his blood or not.

The only snag was that Milly and he had a shared bank account and that she, being that sort of person, kept a close eye on it. He had looked up rents for rooms on the North Circular and reckoned they averaged around £60 a week. One would have to add £30 or £40 to that for anything halfway decent for two people. Assuming Kaja was earning money somehow (waitressing, he supposed), but having only the vaguest idea of what that might be from his enquiries in a couple of local bars (he realised there was a lot of underpaying in this country), he calculated on giving a boost to her income of around £50 a week – if it were to make any difference. That, he reckoned, was about what she'd be happy with.

Milly would notice that, he was sure. This annoyed him. The more he thought about it, the more he realised how dependent on her he was, financially speaking. He earned peanuts from his commissions and odd bouts of conducting or performance, and had not really bothered with snuffling for awards. The one impressive prize he'd got – the Simonetti Prize for Contributions to New Music – was mainly thanks to Milly's City brother, the awful Philip, who'd been owed a favour by the most influential member of the three-person prize panel.

This had never troubled him much before: it was good not to be constrained by the idea that one lived by one's art. Now the idea of living by one's art, counting the pennies gained from the most meagre commission, like a jazz artist in a bedsit, struck him as rather noble and even effective. Which German composer had noted his monthly earnings down to the last schilling? He couldn't remember, but it was a big one. Nothing concentrates the mind better than the thought of imminent poverty. Which is why (quite unjustifiably, given his own position) he had no respect for composers with weighty professorial posts. It seemed to him cheating in some way. Yet they were the ones who dictated everything, like the career-culture middlemen, the consultants and glorified accountants, fat on lottery cash.

Milly had at least saved him from the humiliation of music-in-education, of touting himself around grot schools outside Huddersfield or Bradford or somewhere he was equally ignorant of, banging on a triangle as part of some whizzo arts-for-everyone scheme. The very thought made him shudder. Let them see the white clouds for themselves, as he had done. Let them make their own way out of the grot.

Milly arrived back in the middle of the news, in the middle of another car bomb in Iraq, in the middle of scattered clothes and shoes and people running about shouting in dust or smoke. She was exhausted after a day in Dartington. 'Oh please switch that stuff off,' she said, so he did so on a shot of a hysterical man cradling his small son spattered in blood, the two of them ghosting his brain as he got her one of the Afghan pouffes. She put her feet up on it in the garden room with Telemann playing on the stereo. After a few minutes she asked for something calm and modern but not Arvo Pärt. He put on Castledown's latest album. She seemed to approve at first, until its folkish side gave way to something darker.

'It's called slow-core,' said Jack. 'Or lo-fi. Or nu-folk, even. Not this bit so much.'

'Let's try nothing at all,' she said. 'I'm feeling like a very fragile habitat.'

'An alvar,' said Jack, without thinking.

'A what?'

'What? Oh, just this kind of really rare habitat, pebbly, bare rock, very thin soil. Very interesting little plants, moss and lichens and stuff.'

Milly was staring at him. Her drink was making gurgling noises in her chest. This and her expression made her seem very middle-aged, suddenly.

'Yer wha'?'

'An alvar. It's not in the dictionary.'

'Never heard of it.'

'Not in the dictionary, I said. It's practically only in . . . in the Baltic area.'

'Estonia?'

'Um, yeah. Probably Latvia, too.'

'Alvar.'

'Yeah.'

'You saw one for yourself?'

'Oh, yeah,' he said, as if surprised she should ask, as if he was one of their dinner-party friends just back from a fortnight in Kenya and asked the same question about elephants or lions.

Her eyes left his face and she drank her Pernod thoughtfully. Alvars were probably only found on Haaremaa, he realised. It was a gaffe. She'd find out. Or maybe she wouldn't bother. No, of course she wouldn't trace it back to Haaremaa. There was bound to be an alvar or two on the mainland.

They chatted amiably enough, after a bit. Then the neighbour's strimmer started up, yet again. Milly, to Jack's embarrassment, said *Fuck* and got up and ran out into the garden and yelled at the top of her voice, like someone having a major row, her arms akimbo, spilling her drink.

'Please, please stop it! Just stop it! Please!'

And the strimmer did, even though they were Albanian. Milly had this way.

A little later she said, just when he wasn't expecting it, 'Talking of Estonia, did you phone your bit?'

He laughed, feeling his ears torch and moistness slapped onto his brow like a flannel: 'Yeah, she wants to sing duets.'

'Seriously?'

'No, she's doing her PhD on Pärt's influences. I mean, people influenced by Pärt. I must have met her at a concert in Tallinn. Terrible, the way you forget people.'

'Why have you gone all hot and bothered?'

'Because you're teasing me, maybe?'

'Thank God for the weekend,' she sighed, after looking at him for a moment with anxious eyes. 'I really feel I've done the mileage, this week.'

SIX

They took the train to Basingstoke, where Graham picked them
up in the Humber. Graham was a mystery: some thought he was
from the Isle of Wight, others (encouraged by Graham himself)
from Arizona. He was aged anywhere from thirty-five to sixty,
with a wispy ponytail and lined cheeks and a perpetual smell of
leathery, slightly manury things overlaid with patchouli. He had
a mournful voice and his nickname was Eeyore. Marjorie had
found him in a drug-rehab unit, apparently. Without him, it was
generally acknowledged that life at Wadhampton Hall would
disintegrate.

Daddy du Crane collected vintage cars, apart from the Bentley,
and liked to give them an airing; the 1935 Humber had become
something of a runabout, despite Milly's complaints about its
fuel consumption. There were no seat belts. The leather seats
were scuffed and sagging from seventy years of use and the very
heavy doors opened the wrong way.

'Train OK?'

'Fine, thanks, Graham. How's everybody?'

'I think everybody's cool, as far as I can figure.'

'Great. And you?'

'I'm still trying to figure that one out, yeah.'

Wadhampton Hall was set on a slight rise in the middle of
a beech wood, with lawns and paddocks and a large meadow
immediately around the house, keeping the trees at bay on three
sides. It would normally take five minutes to get from the main
gate to the front door by the rather ill-kempt driveway; today
it took them fifteen, as the Humber coughed into silence halfway
along. They left Graham buried in the engine.

'We're *coming*,' said Milly, into her mobile. Marjorie was already worried. Jack and Milly loved the walk to the house: the sun was vaguely out and the air was astonishingly fresh, wholesome, and full of foliage.

'The Heath never *smells* like this,' said Jack.

After a while they were too hot, walking, even though it was mid-September. Jack was always inspired by this first contact with the real countryside. The infinite beech wood either side looked as if it had been waiting for them, but it was like a hotel with jammed revolving doors: London took hours to wear off. He'd been playing in his head with an idea that had probably emerged on the train, a semitonal oscillation crossing into something fugue-like in D minor. The trill of the mobile had interrupted it.

'Squirrel,' said Milly, pointing. 'Horrid grey one.'

The Humber purred past as they were about to hit the gravel sweep, the size of three football pitches, in front of the house. They waved, but Graham ignored them. Drum and Bass, the two young slobbery golden retrievers (named by Jack one weekend a couple of years ago), lolloped out to greet them.

'How odd,' called out Marjorie, blinking furiously on the top of the steps. 'Why were you not in the car?'

'I told you on the mobile, Mummy,' said Milly.

'If you think I listen to mobiles,' Marjorie replied.

But it was worrying, her lapse.

Dinner was just them. Jack was relieved. Even when, instead of the usual clutch of fat-arsed local dignitaries banging on about horses or Romanian fieldworkers, it was a faith-troubled vicar or a bearded leper specialist from India, he found the whole ritual exhausting. For a start, the table was too broad and shiny for comfortable chit-chat; he was never quite sure which fork or glass to start with; and there was always the dreaded question of what he actually *did*, when he would feel the paltriness of his life's achievements reflected in the puzzled, even bewildered and often suspicious look on his interlocutor's face. He generally drank too much of the very good, heady old wine (served by Keith, the jejune young family butler) and ended up saying something a little overenthusiastically. Also, the fresh air of the countryside would always hit him for six at about nine o'clock: he had an overwhelming desire to retire to the large bedroom with the ancient rocking horse and the pop-eyed china dolls on the mantelpiece and slip profoundly into sleep.

He would always sleep well in the Hall, despite its ghosts. Graham, in particular, was in frequent communication with these – being especially close to Lady Felicity du Crane, who tripped and fell against a stone mantelpiece at the age of twenty-five in 1787 and was usually manifested by an abrupt, over-powering smell of lilies in the Orange Room.

'She's a very nice woman,' Graham would say, in his mournful way. 'A really gentle dude. We get on very well. Call me Felicity, she says, and don't mind the lilies, it's what they put in my tomb. OK?'

Jack had sat in an easy chair for three or four hours one night in the Orange Room, ghost-hunting, his attention continually drawn by the unmoving, unchanging stone mantelpiece and its porcelain figurines, but nothing had come of it. He'd scared himself stupid, though. Since then, he was pretty sure that Graham was crazy, and worried about him. He suspected him of having slept with Marjorie, but that was their business. What he didn't want Graham to do was to take a gun and kill everyone, as a long-ago butler had tried to do before the war. If that felt like a long time ago, it was sometime last week in Wadhampton Hall: although most of the medieval structure had burned to its flagstones in 1606, to be entirely rebuilt by 1627 (only to be bashed about a bit in the Civil War), it still felt very old. Well, it *was* old. Because it hadn't changed hands, it was silted up with generational possessions that dramatically tele-scoped Jack's sense of history. His toothglass was a George III silver strainer; the chunky bedside tables were late fifteenth century (carried out onto the lawns in 1606); Milly dropped her earrings onto a chipped delftware plate from the 1690s;

their bed was a wormholed and lumpily mattressed four-poster apparently graced for one night by the considerable bulk of another King George – *which* one Milly could never quite remember. And it was uncomfortable, like almost everything in the house. The Victorian cabinets and art deco glass lamps scattered about (there was an arty Lady du Crane two generations back, an intimate friend of Bertrand Russell and Augustus John) were parvenus. Daddy du Crane's study had an articulated standard lamp like something out of Jules Verne, of whom it was a contemporary. Even the frayed and moth-eaten umbrellas in the hallway stand, with their carved walnut handles, had been operating there for at least a century. The massive valve wireless in the airy breakfast room looked cheekily modern, while what was actually contemporary – the flatscreen television, the smart stereo, the glossy magazines spilling from the day's *Times* – lurched into the consciousness like something nightmarish, skulking from history's daylight.

'We don't *want* to adopt, Mummy. At least not yet.'

They were taking coffee and a succulent old brandy in the morning room, although it was ten o'clock at night: the morning room was used on balmy evenings as it had the nicest 'give' onto the garden, as Marjorie put it – in the shape of a large windowed bay. It also had an upright walnut-burred piano, which Jack had been asked to play. He had moved from French *variété* numbers from the fifties (Marjorie's favourite, redolent of her wild year in Paris) to Keith Jarrett-style impro. The piano needed tuning but he had drunk enough vintage wines not to care. It had been good enough for Augustus John, apparently. One of the staff had left a bolt spanner on the bass strings and Jack had made a joke about a prepared piano that no one got.

'Do you go along with this non-adoption thing, Jack?'

'Yeah, I do.'

He was pressing some great harmonies out of the ivories, letting his fingers enjoy themselves. He could feel the whole room turning into an ECM album cover – a frozen Scandinavian bog with gaunt trees and a leaden sky. The blowing reeds of Haaremaa, silvered by sunlight, long-necked cranes lifting –

'Well I think it's *such* a shame,' said Marjorie. 'All those orphans in awful places like China. I can understand not wanting *Africa*, but China's relatively clean, I believe. Don't think Aids has hit China, has it?'

'Mummy, will you please shut up about this subject? I'm here to relax.'

'What do you think, Richard?'

'What?'

'He never listens,' complained Marjorie. 'You're going deaf. I could call you a boring old tosspot and you wouldn't even react.'

Richard du Crane laughed. 'That's because I know I'm a boring old tosspot!'

'How weak,' said his wife, whose inability to hold her drink was probably due to age, her physical withering after the cancer. For some reason she got nervous about her daughter's visits and then overcompensated. 'You've always been terribly weak. Philip's weak, too. I think it's interbreeding.'

'What do you mean by weak, Mummy? Not going off to fight the Crusades?'

Marjorie scowled at her daughter, who knew that her mother had been forbidden to become a bohemian painter at twenty-one and therefore forgave her everything.

'What are you talking about? Unless you mean this awful bloody Iran business.'

'Iraq,' said Richard.

Marjorie ignored him. 'Very boring, life without children.'

'There's still this medical bit of a chance,' said Milly, staring at the patterns in the threadbare Persian carpet, 'that something will happen. It's not at zero. It'll probably happen when I've completely given up hope. But I can't give up hope.'

Jack coaxed something very gentle, very poignant, from the middle register, working with fourths in A minor, his whole body turning into it because he felt very cool, very relaxed.

The garden was puffing scents into the room on the warm night air: mainly jasmine from the gazebo, with hints of beech mast. It was at times like this that he reckoned he'd married well, but also that he missed his unmade children more, and Max most of all.

'That's what you say each time,' said Marjorie. 'Time goes by awfully fast, you know. Look at me. Philip is about to be fifty, for God's sake.'

'In three years,' said Milly, who sounded far away. Jack glanced at her out of the corner of his eye, keeping his head in that twisted position like a jazz player, crouched low over the keyboard. When he let the silence come through under *la résonance*, it was filled by all the clocks in the house and their antique movements, from the grandfathers to the little ormolus, keeping Wadhampton Hall time, which was the time of woods and dynasties stretching back to a mailed glove around the throat of a Saxon serf.

'He's been nearly fifty for as long as I can remember,' said Marjorie, who disapproved of Philip and was disapproved of back. 'Right from birth, probably. Awfully large baby.'

Jack was desperate to avoid a bad atmosphere, and pumped the room with his ambient chilling-out sound as discreetly as he could.

'This your latest reading?' asked Milly, picking up a book on the little Indian table next to her chair. It was a hardback book called *Politics*, by Adam Thirlwell. Marjorie's eyes twinkled.

'Richard thinks it's all about Westminster, don't you, darling?'

'Talking of which,' said Richard, 'somebody on the wireless had a most interesting anecdote. Did you hear it, Jack?'

'Which one?' said Jack, slightly annoyed that a subtle shift from D minor to G could go so unnoticed, trampled under Daddy du Crane's strong tenor voice. One of his eyebrows was wonky after a riding accident; it made him look permanently quizzical.

'Some judge condemned a whole load of Luddites to hang for some minor misdemeanour, and he was asked if it was right to hang so many chaps from one beam.'

'Does this go on and on?' asked Marjorie, helping herself to the brandy.

'And the judge thought about it for a while, you see, and then he said – hang on, let me get this right –'

'Here we go,' said Marjorie. 'You talk about me! How's your friend Sally, Milly?'

'Sammy, you mean? Sammy Carlisle? Let Daddy finish. She's *fine*,' Milly added, all but mouthing it and tucking her legs up under her on the creaking rattan wing chair.

'The judge said, "You're right. Maybe they'd be more comfortable on two!" Isn't that marvellous? Two beams.'

'They were awful in those days,' said Milly, vaguely.

'I thought it was marvellous!'

'You always do,' said Marjorie, drawing a hand over her eyes as if there was some phantom lock of hair there from her wild youth.

'I hope you don't think what he *said* was marvellous,' said Milly, frowning gently at her father. 'That's really off-piste, if so.'

'What I think is neither here nor there,' said her father. 'It's history.'

Jack was pressing the chords out and looking forward to going to bed with Milly. He found her sexier in Wadhampton Hall, whose lawns she ran about on as a little girl, whose tennis court (a lumpy grass one from the twenties) she bounced about on through summers on holiday from Roedean, dressed in a fetching Chris Evert-type skirt (he'd seen the snaps). He was looking forward to her climbing on top and grinding away with her usual passion and intensity, massaging her own breasts.

Because now, a fortnight after disappointment, it was the green light for tricks, she'd said.

'Mummy, what *is* this?' Milly was reading the hardback novel in her lap. She sounded shocked.

'Some like it hot, as we used to say,' said Marjorie, taking a large sip of her brandy and winking over it. 'Pink woolly handcuffs.'

Jack had heard of the novel ages ago and was embarrassed

that Milly hadn't. He hardly ever read novels, aside from Kafka and so on – he preferred books about history and myth – but at least he tried to keep up with names. Milly was too busy to read reviews, let alone novels; she had so much green save-the-world stuff to wade through.

'Do you know,' said Milly, turning the pages, 'despite computers, or because of computers, we use twice the amount of paper compared to ten years ago?'

'Romans wrote on birch bark,' said Richard, expanding his chest and sighing. His face was very red in the low light.

'How many does Sally have now?' asked Marjorie.

'Can't keep count,' said Milly. 'Five, actually.'

'There's so much they can do these days,' said Marjorie.

'Mother-in-law,' said Jack, in a laid-back American way that went with the vibes he was coaxing out, 'let's give that subject a break, huh?'

'I'll say it one more time, Mummy,' said Milly, in her clipped, office tone that Jack didn't like. 'We are not fiddling about with unnatural procedures and pumping me with chemicals just in order to please ourselves and, by the way, increase the burden of the planet with yet another human being to support. OK?'

'I'm glad I don't look at life like you do, my darling,' said Marjorie, gazing through the French windows into the night's murmuring blackness.

'I'm getting bitten,' said Richard, scratching his ankles.

'We don't have to have lights on,' said Marjorie. 'It's not really dark out there at all. It's only the lights in here that make it look dark. I think,' she continued, after a tiny pause, 'that I'd have painted like early Picasso. What a funny thought.'

'And now?' asked Jack, quoting subtly from Orlando Gibbons, the chords ebbing and flowing under his hands in F sharp minor.

'Frank Auerbach,' she said, without hesitation, then wiped her lips with her arthritic forefinger.

'Wow,' said Jack.

'Frank who?' asked Milly.

'Oh, you must know Auerbach. I thought you went to Oxford.'

'You *know* I haven't the faintest how I got in,' said Milly, pulling a face.

'We're all like that,' Richard commented, ambiguously, his voice hollowed out by the big brandy balloon as he tipped it, nestling in the fumes.

'Milly's always *saying* she's thick,' said Jack, without quite knowing why.

'She was keen on dancing as a little girl,' said Marjorie. 'Danced away on the lawn. By the way, Richard, Tony went on and on about the gooseberries. Something about pruning the new shoots in summer. We're summer now, aren't we? How's your poor mother, Jack? How awful not to see.'

'When?' asked Richard.

'She's bearing up,' said Jack.

'Now, you big oaf.'

'I know nothing about gooseberries except that I like them in fool. Can't he just do whatever he thinks right?'

'No one ever does,' said Marjorie, laying her head back against the cushion and closing her eyes. 'No one seems to have heard of foam flowers, these days. That's because they're small and not showy. Yet they were all the rage when I was a child.'

Jack allowed the last chords to purr to an end.

'Oh, thank goodness,' sighed Marjorie. 'It did go on and on.'

In bed that night, the rocking horse's one good eye catching the moonlight from the thinly curtained window, Jack was finding it hard to sleep, worked up not by Milly's body (which she had kept him from touching in any meaningful way, being too stressed out), but by her mind. She had gone on and on about her parents in a fierce whisper (the house was too complicated, with too many hidden passages and ducts, to trust one's privacy to): they were, she reckoned, incredibly annoying and selfish. Particularly her mother. Milly had hardly ever talked about her parents like this; Jack was afraid she might cut herself off from them, like her younger and never-mentioned brother Benedict who had last been spotted on a beach somewhere in

Goa more than a year ago, with a limp from a motorcycle crash in Sydney two years earlier.

Jack liked coming to Wadhampton Hall, it inspired him and amused him in some way, it made him feel *placed*. In fact, he couldn't bear the thought of Philip taking over: Philip du Crane was a tall, tight-arsed City bastard who drove a four-by-four as big as a snowplough and regarded Jack as one might a smear of dogshit on one's very expensive shoe, and had frequently expressed his desire to get Wadhampton Hall *earning*. There were dark rumours of turning it into a business conference centre, but his father dismissed these as Milly's paranoia: Richard admired his son for being the first du Crane since Edmund du Crane, a Tory minister in the 1830s, to actually live a real, wage-earning existence. Milly, apparently, didn't count.

Whatever, Jack very much doubted that life at Wadhampton Hall under the reign of Philip would be anything but unpleasant for the Middletons, and so wished as long a life as possible for Richard and Marjorie. No one had considered which twin might inherit from Philip, although technically it was Lance by about ten minutes. Poor Rex, again.

Milly was annoyed with her mother, mostly, for going on about children, and with her father for not getting involved. Underneath it all, of course, was Milly's abiding grief and sense of failure. She sat up against the pillows and complained, her new silk nightie falling away from her breasts just enough in the moonlight to entice. He put on his most compassionate tone, a kind of vocal soft jazz, while very much wanting to bury his nose in her.

'They won't even agree to putting up a bloody yurt in the grounds,' said Milly. 'They think it'll attract hippy travellers. They're so *Tory*.'

'Well, I guess it's their grounds,' said Jack, unhelpfully.

'Philip's soon,' she said. 'To escape death duties.'

'Oh, then they'd better get the yurt for themselves.'

'He can't chuck them out,' she pointed out. 'Only once they're dead.'

Jack laughed at Milly's accidental joke and the high bed-end wobbled. Its wood was thick, dark, wormholed and carved with late fifteenth-century flower and fish motifs. Men, women and children must have died in this bed — pestilence, pox, whatever. It creaked every time they moved. One TV crew had used it for a murder scene in an Edgar Allan Poe adaptation. Milly got born in it — a fact which Jack liked to dwell on only in the abstract — with Richard du Crane pacing up and down in the main bedroom, a tall young man who had in turn been born in the same bed three decades earlier. It was, Jack thought, like flicking through the leaves of a book. He wished he could think up a more arresting image, but his mind converted it into musical fragments scored for (he frowned, trying to focus on the sounds and the shapes and the scribbles) clarinet, percussion, violin, double bass and girls' choir. Weird. Mental. Because somewhere in there was the squawk of a lorry's brakes advancing bit by bit in a traffic jam.

Milly was breathing softly in her sleep and the old rocking horse was eyeing him with a glint, but not moving. If it started to move he would be seriously worried. The faint chimes of midnight hustled through the house over a period of some ten minutes, because (he smiled to himself) the house was so big it had different time zones.

Being that time of night, his situation fell away into three distinct parts: Kaja had turned up in his life again, maybe staking his maybe son; she undoubtedly thought of the maybe father as a lying bastard (though not in so many words); but she was not going to destroy what she had again turned up in, or she'd lose the winnings. The whole thing was framed fine. All he had to keep was his cool. Dialogue, not war.

Echo. Kaja meant echo in Estonian. She was an echo in his life, and he was an echo in hers. But echoes were still solid sound. Her hotel work was probably carried out during antisocial hours. He wondered what she did with Jaan. Maybe a child-minding neighbour took him to and from school. He wondered if she'd ever completed her studies in the end. He could ask her these things when they met. His stomach lurched with apprehension. He hoped it wasn't anticipation.

The bed-end smelt of countless applications of beeswax and of something deeper and darker, something like smoke, a sootiness: he had rested his hands on it, behind his head, and his skin now had that smell. Maybe the countless fires that had burned in the fireplace since 1627 had been absorbed by the wood of the bed-end. The musical fragments were not cohering, but twisting and turning between his ears. The bed was hurtling along through time – he and Milly were a momentary flicker, soon they'd be dead. No doubt he would be forgotten, an extremely minor composer whose pieces would now and again be revived – assuming the whole culture binge was still in place, or recognisable. No guarantee: eco-disaster would bring about the rule of tyrants, of police states, of religious maniacs. Music would be banned, or military, or purely sacred. Or (even more depressing, because so nearly there already) easy-listening jingle-tingle crap chosen by corporate executives – the greatest, tenderest, most astonishing human gift just squandered, chewed up and compressed into pure product, piped incessantly into every public space. No more thinking songs in the forest, let alone Schubert. Who in fact wrote a lot of crap stuff amid the genius.

Jack was getting himself seriously miserable. The human future looked very, very dark. As Milly had pointed out on the train down, the most powerful men in the world with the most powerful army ever in world history were *anti-evolution*. That was, like, *so* insane. Like being anti-tree, she'd said. And everybody else in the carriage was younger than they were – mostly men in suits with thick necks and loud voices bound for Basingstoke and beyond, hooked up to their iPods or mobiles, who really did not look as if they cared a toss either way.

He didn't think he'd fallen asleep, because he wasn't conscious of having woken up, but there was a woman standing by the window.

Milly? No, Milly was right there beside him, mouth open.

The woman seemed to have a wind-billowing tent for a dress and something on her head, but she was in silhouette and the moonlight behind her was dimmer, now. She was crying. He couldn't hear her crying, but he knew she was because the whole dark room thrilled with it: the walls were − to put it in the way he was feeling it (almost as a visual thing) − running with her tears. There was nothing he could do: he knew it was a ghost, a spectral presence left over from some far-off time, like a means to an end that never came. He lay there looking at her and *absorbing* her sorrow. He felt he was helping her, simply by sharing the burden.

On top of everything else, there was something sexual involved; he had been chosen by the spectral woman (he judged her, purely by inward sensation, to be in her twenties), because he was a young, sappy guy.

It was a shock when she floated over to him and revealed herself as Kaja, with slightly larger teeth. With, in fact, very large teeth that appeared to be filed sharp. She was grinning at him and her eyes were stitched on.

He only remembered after he had woken up in a sweat, heart pounding, that he was actually forty-three.

After breakfast he went immediately out to find Graham, who was watching the tiny young groom, Dean, brush Richard du Crane's chestnut hunter in the stable yard. Jack had never known Graham to do anything other than watch, he realised, yet apparently he was always busy. He almost called him Eeyore. Only Marjorie was allowed to call him that.

'Graham, can I have a word?'

'But yes.'

Jack told him about his nightmare in the early hours, in the West Wing bedroom − Milly's old room. Graham nodded.

'And so?'

'What are the vibes in that room, Graham?'

'Heavy. Lady Margaret, died 1473, is a frequent visitor.'

'In that room?'

'Yeah,' said Graham, as if he'd been asked a stupid question. 'Gave birth to stillborn triplets the size of mice and died.'

'Jesus. So that part of the house was not burnt down?'

'No idea.'

'But you just said she died in that room in 1473, way before the fire.'

'So, it's all cool.' Graham turned to Dean. 'You can have a go at *my* fucking ponytail afterwards, man.'

Dean laughed. His brush was bringing up the chestnut's flanks to a shine like a conker's, over the hip bones.

All four of them went for a walk in the grounds before lunch. It was a dog-leg that took in a very nice pub called the Hen and Chickens on the quiet B-road that bordered the estate for half a mile on the south side. Because Marjorie was slower these days, they took the quicker route, following the wide wood-land track that had once been a Roman and then a Saxon thor-oughfare, and was now used only by the local hunt, of which Richard was the titulary Master.

'We've had trouble with these Right to Roam people,' said Richard. 'They're even worse than the Ramblers' Association types with their awful hair and anoraks. I'm convinced some of them are saboteurs, like the whole bloody government.'

Richard du Crane had gone down to London and waved a placard against the Countryside Act – the only demo he'd ever attended.

'You can see their point,' said Milly.

'They've got a footpath! It was all settled years ago! In the eighties!'

'One footpath that goes through one end of a huge splodge of thousands of acres.'

'Don't call it a splodge, Milly. It's not a splodge,' said Richard, who was crusty this morning. He often was on a Sunday.

'Sorry. The olde oaken heart of England!' she cried, with an American or possibly Hampshire twang.

'They do tend to leave their clutter,' said Marjorie.

'You could put up a sign, or a litter bin,' suggested Jack, although he didn't like the idea at all. Secretly, he wanted the whole of the estate to be totally private, but he would never say that out loud.

'Think they can read?' said Richard.

'Daddy, if you could hear yourself,' said Milly. 'You're such an old fascist.'

'A tosspot, not a fascist,' said Marjorie.

'Feathers,' said Richard, pointing to a downy heap of them on the rim of a rut, as if no more need be said.

'Fox,' Jack commented, needlessly, and because no one agreed or disagreed, the word hung embarrassingly in the air. 'I once saw a fox kept in a cage for years,' he said, without thinking. 'I wish I'd let it out.'

'That was a dream, or so you told me,' said Milly.

'Kind of a waking dream,' murmured Jack, vaguely, pretending to go off on something inwardly creative.

It was a sunny day and the light under the beech trees was green, like an aquarium's, although the leaves were turning and some were fluttering down already. They'd been issued with canes, old walking canes with ivory handles and steel tips that stabbed the soft ground as they advanced at a pace suitable for Marjorie. It was like the film of a novel, Jack thought, his glance panning over the trees. He could do the music: pure neo-classical, pure postmodern pastiche. Milly came into his shot and he smiled at her – the sun was being a little cruel with her face, though, exposing lines and the faint blur of facial hair. Last night, in the candlelight of the dinner and then in the moonlight of the bedroom, she'd looked ten years younger. In her early thirties, say. Or even as she'd been when he'd first set eyes on her outside the Purcell Room.

'Philip said the boys got bored by it,' said Marjorie, as if she was continuing a subject of conversation.

'By what, Mummy?'

'The play. The Shakespeare you took them to. Sorry, weren't we talking about it?'

'Not that I know of,' said Milly.

'I do that all the time,' commented Jack, helpfully.

'Do what?' snapped Marjorie, scowling at him.

'Philip asked us a favour,' said Milly, crossly. 'It wasn't our idea. *He'd* booked the tickets. Or Arabella had.'

'And *were* they bored?' said Jack, who was as annoyed as Milly. 'That's news to me.' He pictured Philip in Dubai, swapping arms for oil or whatever, smirking under his Ray-Bans while his sons were gazing on Shakespeare.

A jay shrieked like a child being murdered and floundered through the treetops. It made Jack jump.

'Some bloody lookout!' shouted Richard. His strong tenor echoed through the woods. He was almost as tall as the trees, or gave that impression.

'Darling, you've just frightened any remaining wildlife away.'

'I'm their boss,' said Richard, twirling his cane in the air in front of him. 'I'm their executive manager.'

The jay squawked again and the others laughed. The scent of the woods and the track's chewed-up grass was mustily sweet. It was almost too hot, and Richard had come out in his 'tropical' kit – tough shirt and shorts and boots – that he'd last used on their walking tour of Madagascar in 2000. It would be embarrassing in the pub.

'I know you're going to say I'm going on about it,' said Marjorie, blinking furiously all of a sudden, 'but why don't you at least *consult* this friend of mine in Harley Street?'

'I don't believe it,' Milly exploded, keeping to the side of the rut. 'We had all this out yesterday. And last week! And last month! Shut *up* about it, Mummy! God, you keep talking to me like I'm a dog-bitch! A fucking mare!'

'Well, you know what I think,' said Marjorie, quietly, over the hum of wild things getting on with their unknown, unseen lives either side.

'Let's wait,' said Richard, in a placating voice, 'until we've got some pints in the oak.'

'Let's not,' snapped Milly, 'because I don't want to discuss it *ever again*, you two. I'm sorry, but. *Sorry,*' she added, in a fierce hiss.

Jack kept quiet in the ensuing silence. Blank. Blank as a dead screen. The nightmare hung about him in a cloud. What he had to do was see the real Kaja in order to dispel it.

'You look awfully pale, Jack,' said Marjorie.

'Do I?'

'Jolly good,' said Richard, absently, flicking last year's leaves up with his cane as he walked while this year's leaves were beginning to join them. 'Jolly good.'

'Complete tosspot,' muttered Marjorie, who was overexerted by what until recently had been a short little stroll for her.

'I think it went fairly well,' said Jack, on the way back in the train, 'all things considered.'

Richard had driven them to the station in the Bentley, as even Graham had Sunday afternoons off. It was a little hair-raising: Lord du Crane had downed two pints in the Hen and Chickens and polished off half a bottle of a 1989 burgundy over the roast (overdone as usual by the new cook, Sandra, in the Rayburn), and there were at least thirty speed cameras between Wadhampton Hall and the station, the winding road striped with bright yellow markings like a helipad.

Drink, however, would have the opposite effect on Richard: it made him drive slower, and any wandering was due to the Bentley's pre-precision steering. What was hair-raising was the extra time it took. They leapt from the car and hurtled into the station and felt sick. As it was Sunday, the train arrived twenty minutes late and there was no first class and no one in a uniform to ask.

'I hope there's a train driver, at least,' said Milly.

All the carriages smelt of smoke – or worse, of smoky breath – with a subtle hint of stomach gas. It was always strange for Jack to come back to earth after Wadhampton Hall, but it was particularly unfortunate that 'earth' was, by geographical prox-imity, Basingstoke. Although it was teatime on Sunday, the new shopping mall was packed with people, and their vehicles and pushchairs had added to the panic on the way to the station.

'Everyone in England's so *ugly*,' Milly had muttered, peering from the Bentley's window. She'd had a barley wine before lunch, which was a mistake. 'So ugly and *fat*, with awful hamster eyelashes and really really *really* nasty clothes they shouldn't *ever* even *try* to put on.'

'I say, you mustn't actually *call* 'em chavs,' Jack had joked, pretending to be a posh, weak-chinned jerk.

'I'm not *labelling* them,' Milly had rejoined. 'I'm just observing a *reality*. It's because they're *manipulated*. They're *victims*.'

Men with weak shoulders and huge exposed thighs had gawped at them as they'd purred past. Hefty children in pastel sportswear had pointed. Tubby, pink-clad women in snow-white trainers had nodded, as if they recognised the celebrities within. Jack, in the snug leathery vastness of the Bentley's interior, had enjoyed feeling like a fascist dictator. You could so easily wipe out millions, if it came to it; call them chavs first and turn them into a subspecies, into ants to be crushed.

His parents would also store-cruise on Sundays, generally climaxing in IKEA.

'God, it's more and more of an effort with the parentals,' Milly was saying, folding her arms in the near-empty train carriage. 'They're not getting any younger, anyway.'

'That's true, too. I think it's good you told them where to get –'

Milly's mobile went off: its ringtone was the rainforest at dawn, rising to a horrendous pitch of parrots and monkeys if left unanswered. Jack hated it. Milly scrabbled for it in her bag. The train was stopped for engineering works between Frimley and Woking, perhaps for days, ticking calmly like a drip in a dungeon. Jack's heart always thumped when Milly's mobile went off: it must be a lot worse when you have kids, he thought.

'Hello? Hi? What? Oh Gawd. No. No. No. Brilliant,' she said, too loud and with that mad, exultant stare people on mobiles have, as if someone's secretly jacking them off. 'Brill. Yeah. No, I haven't. Gordon Bennett. *Neil?* Oh shit. Blimey. Yeah. No. Oh shit. I've – we've *told* them about the waste stream, Doug. Yup. I know. Hey, is there anyone out there, and all that. So *really* annoying.'

Jack watched her, smiling. Milly had remade herself from a Roedean upper-class deb into a right-on, save-the-world businesswoman, and he admired that.

'Grey water at eighty per cent recoverable,' she said. 'Ye-es. I bloody told him. Yeah, a real smart-arse!'

For a moment, when the mobile had rung, he'd imagined it was Kaja, that Kaja had somehow found out Milly's number. He was still afraid of her, then. Afraid of this comfortable life – underachieving, maybe, but comfortable – getting shattered as lives were, not by a train crash or an earthquake or a bomb in a rucksack, but by something connecting that shouldn't connect. Or that should, maybe, by the laws of evolutionary chance.

He looked out of the dirty carriage window and tried to work out what he should do next. He had hoped that the beechwoods would have given him an answer, but they hadn't. The hours had whipped past, mostly steeped in ale or wine, and he now felt overindulged and seedy, like the view that he was looking at: a retail park surrounded by what looked like scrub desert. Somebody had painted, in big dripping black letters, *BACK OF ARSHOLE BEYOND* on the metal fence, like something for a fashion magazine's photo shoot.

He had to get a grip on this whole thing. He was sleepy and he had to get a grip.

'On a sodding Sunday!' said Milly, snapping her mobile shut and startling Jack out of a micro-nap. 'Panic stations.'

'Everything all right, then?'

Milly had something in her eye. 'It never is, and at the same time it is,' she said. 'You know what I mean?'

'Exactly,' said Jack. 'I know exactly what you mean.'

The train squealed and shoved itself forward for a few yards, then stopped with a weirdly human groan.

'Oh no, you can't be serious,' said Milly, to the window, to the air – to the entire steely elaboration of the privatised railway network, it seemed to Jack.

And then: 'I'm supercool. I am not stressed. It's only a frigging train.'

Howard was up their way again for a lunchtime concert he'd been booked for previous to his digital accident. His replacement was Ffiona of the two fs, playing Schumann and Frank Bridge on Howard's 1625 loaned viola. It made a sound that was unearthly.

Jack sat in the pews during the rehearsal, tapping the suspended prayer cushion from side to side with his knees. The church acoustics were muddy and the piano too loud, and the pianist had to soften his game. Whenever the tenor – Jonathan Matthews, a rising, slightly conceited star – made a mistake he slapped his own cheek, playfully. Ffiona came in late with a note and apologised: it was the Bridge piece arranged by Britten and the metre was demanding. Matthews lifted his leg out to the side and laughed. He was dressed in jeans. Howard said not to mind. Jack leaned his arms on the pew, his chin on his arms, and watched. The piece came to an end.

'That's great,' Howard said, all four smiling broadly, confident of their skill and their powers. The audience was already beginning to gather outside, the programmes spread on the table in the entrance. The tenor was adjusting his position onstage.

'I don't want you further away,' said the pianist.

'All right, OK.'

'Yeah, that's right.'

And then Howard looked towards the pews and found Jack and said, 'Was that tempo OK, Jack? Not too fast?'

'A little bit fast,' replied Jack, standing up and coming forward helpfully.

Jonathan Matthews had disappeared into the back to change. Howard nodded. 'OK, Ffiona honey, take it a bit slower. OK?'

'OK,' said Ffiona, clearly a bit nervous. She looked attractive in the sombre light of the church, under the yellowish spots.

'That's good,' said the pianist, who was Norwegian.

It was all very polite and informal. Jack felt good about his world. Then he turned to the right and with an intoxicating punch, like a triple Scotch downed in one, saw two familiar profiles: Kaja and Jaan, picking up a programme, smiling at the elderly woman on the desk. Howard must have invited them. Howard hadn't told him. Why should Howard have told him? Howard didn't know anything.

Jack walked briskly up onto the stage and dived down past the piano into the vestry. The tenor was in there, his trousers off to red boxer pants. He had plump knees and looked surprised. The vestry smelt like an inn in a state of grace.

'That was lovely,' said Jack, 'sorry I can't stay. My mother's in hospital, all that. Tell him, please, tell Howard, *Howard*, to drop round as planned afterwards, but *on his own*. Solo. OK?'

'On his own. Howard. Right.'

He emerged by the vestry door into the graveyard. The air was grey and sultry. He stopped by Rex Harrison's grave and wanted to burst into tears: he might well be running away from his own child. But he kept on going.

'A pity you had to hurtle off like that. Jaan's here. My prodigy. With his mum.'

'Didn't Jonathan tell you? My *own* mum.'

'That's why you're down at the hospital, is it?'

'Howard, be understanding.'

Howard was phoning from the church on his mobile. His voice had the acoustics of a tinny god's.

'I need to talk to you about summat,' Jack said. 'On your ownsome. Walk on the Heath grab you?'

September was well over halfway through, but the Heath hadn't noticed. It was hot. Howard had long arms and they swung loosely as he walked. He had changed at the house into his *Helsinki Musica Nova* T-shirt and tropical shorts that half covered his bony knees and in which his bottom looked over-large. They had hidden his 1625 viola under the dirty washing in the utility room, in case. It only now occurred to Jack that Marita might come back and throw it into the machine along with the smalls.

Despite his pupil's success in the concert, Howard had started off in a tizz. Cliff was shimmying. Shimmying? Swimming on the spot, without advancing. Jack said he knew the feeling. The prelude to death, Howard insisted. He had looked it up on the Internet and the list of goldfish ailments was staggering.

Jack wondered how to dovetail Kaja into the conversation, coolly and calmly. He needed help. He needed to stop shimmying.

He'd decided to cut down on his own expenditure, at least. Buy fewer clothes and luxury items like these Oakley shades. Avoid the pointlessness that wealth generates. Siphon it to her. A direct sacrifice. A kind of redemption. Milly would never know.

Howard was banging on about how much more hassle everything was, these days.

'These days,' said Howard, 'if you don't have a DPhil in Goldfish Care, they die within hours.'

They walked up towards Kenwood. Jack always had high expectations of time out with Howard, but was generally disappointed. He gave the impression of being someone very open, but he was made up of layer after layer of complication, matted like fibreglass. The sun had disappeared behind a huge advancing ice cap of cloud. The clear sky at its edge was a luminous green.

He cleared his throat. 'Um, she hasn't phoned, by the way.'
'Who?'
'Jaan's mum.'
'You could have arranged something just now.'
'Blimey, I've explained.'
'Then why mention her?' asked Howard, with a sideways look.

They passed a picnic crawling with small pre-school children, their faces streaked with warpaint. A dad with a tuft of hair under his lip was constructing something interesting out of bendy wires. Mothers in glasses and flowing printed summer dresses were talking to one other as if they were at a political meeting. It was like a historical reconstruction of the seventies.

So self-satisfied, so expert. As if they hadn't ever *not* had kids.

The only jarring note was a woman in yellow dungarees doing feeble jumps off a little trampoline: perhaps the hired entertainment. She looked amazingly like Jimmy Savile. No one clapped as she landed with a wobble and spread her arms out each time.

'Aren't people *good*?' said Howard, beaming at the picnickers.

'Any idea who the father is?'

'Whose father is?'

'Jaan's.'

'Oh no. I don't pry.'

Kenwood House loomed like the big wedding cake it was always being compared to, down to the icing-like glisten of its stucco front.

'I don't suppose she can get a grant for Jaan, can she?'

Howard shook his head. 'Given she's probably an illegal, no.'

'What does that mean?'

'Not a clue.'

They flopped onto the grass bank in front of the house. Howard lay on his back. On the slope down towards the lake and the ugly white giant arch of the open-air concerts, couples in various states of passionate embrace were dotted about. One seated couple appeared to be copulating, the girl's bared legs straddling her man's waist, but it might have been an illusion.

'A great musician,' said Howard, 'now I think of it.'

'Who?'

'The father. *Gr-reat* musician. Mystery of Jaan's gifts solved, ho ho.'

Jack pulled a face, feeling his chest burn. 'Really? How do you know?'

'She told me.' Howard was chewing on a stem of grass. 'Mr

Davenport, he was a *gr-reat* musician. Just that. Nothing more. I didn't ask. She told me to keep it secret. I'm very good at keeping secrets.'

Jack stared down the slope. Two men were throwing a bright yellow Frisbee. He followed it as it sailed each time over their outstretched arms, unreachable.

'Do you feel you're in need of constant reassurance?' asked Howard, suddenly. His bony knees, covered in a light down of hair, irritated Jack, who had opened his eyes with a slight swimming giddiness. Incredibly, it appeared he had nodded off.

'Oh, know what you mean,' he said, expecting a reassuring confession from Howard.

'Thought you were.'

'Me?'

'Why your recent work, er, lacks cohesion,' said Howard.

Jack felt himself pinned to the slope by dismay.

'You're forever looking over your shoulder instead of into your soul, heart, or whatever it's called nowadays.'

'You're talking about me?'

'For once.'

Jack wanted to scream, to turn everyone's heads their way on the pleasant green lawns of Kenwood, with its slight whiffs of dog turd.

Instead, he said: 'Listen. Do you know what it says on the website where you buy tickets for the Kenwood concerts, Howard? It says that for an extra charge you can have dinner for thirty-plus in the fabulous pile behind us – *with*, I roughly quote, *its two hundred and sixty million pounds' worth of paintings*. Not which paintings or by whom – not Rembrandt or Gainsborough or Stubbs or that French one, the phallic cherries –'

'Boucher.'

'Or Boucher. No, just the value. So that the punters get the point in the only way they know how. That's one end. I try to be at the other end. That's all I'm trying to be. Hey, please don't call me commercial, Howard.'

'But you're a rich boy, Jack. You don't *need* to think about your CD sales. About chasing engagements –'

'Even if I were *not* rich, I wouldn't think about it. You can't confuse CD sales with musical *quality*. That's the road to shite.'

'E. coli capitalism,' said Howard, raising a finger. 'We're all in it. Even you. I think what you do, Jack, you do very well,' he added, in a compassionate tone. 'And *Good in Adland* is brilliant, as is *Why Are We the Same?*'

'Composed in 1992 and 2000 respectively. Great.'

'*Good in Adland* is a classic. You can roll over and spend the rest of your life having your tummy tickled.'

'It's eleven minutes long,' Jack pointed out.

'Most people,' said Howard, 'would give their left ear to have written a classic. Even two minutes long.'

Jack felt suddenly that he couldn't be bothered. About anything. About Kaja or Jaan or music or the end of the world. The lawn was too nice, too warm. He could drift off for ever. Howard was a piece of shite. He could tell him what he really thought of his viola playing. Unearthly, beautiful, but shallow.

'I watched you hide behind the tree, the other day, Jack.'

'Eh?'

'In Bolton Gardens, when Kaja K was leaving. Like a dirty old man. Then you scarper from my concert. I saw you. You spotted her, went pale, and scarpered. Every time I mention her your ears go dayglo pink.'

Jack levered himself with an effort onto his feet and brushed grass from his trousers. He refused to wear shorts and his legs were sweaty.

'It's complicated.'

He started walking away. His friend sprang up, bouncing on his toes. Howard swam three times a week and did weights in a Soho gym. One forgot that. Running in front, he turned and stood with his arms out.

People were glancing at them, wondering if it was community theatre.

'Go to hell,' said Jack, brushing past him.

'You know how she found me, Jack?'

'She went to a concert or something.'

They were walking down the slope towards the bridge over the stream and the damp, rather evil-smelling hollow where there were always nettles. Jack's feet were out on their own, just taking the rest of him with them, one at a time.

'She did,' Howard nodded. 'The Florian Rooms, last year. Lots of Haydn. But before that. How did she find me before that?'

'Perhaps she likes Haydn.'

'She already knew about me. Via your CD. *Why Are We the Same?* On which, if you recall, I make a fiendish little contribution in the second variation.'

'She told you?'

'She asked me to sign the CD. She gave nothing away, not then. I thought she was unusual, having such a recherché taste in music. I told her so.'

'Thank you, Howard.'

'Took some time to get ourselves organised. For the lessons. She was extremely persistent.'

'You mean, you're thinking she's taking her son to your lessons in order to get near me?'

'Spot on.'

'Way off-piste, Howard. She could've contacted me directly. If she's about trying to squidge money out of me, she could've called me.'

Howard was smiling at him. He'd walked straight into the trap, if trap it was.

'She's called you already, apparently.'

Jack's face flushed crimson. He turned away. Howard hammily cleared his throat.

'What actually happened in Estonia, Jack?'

'Eh?'

'Fill me in.'

Jack blew a soft raspberry. 'I met her in Tallinn, in a café. Then I saw her in this amateur concert. I gave her your name and number. We had a fling.'

'A fling. Is Jaan your kid?'

'Um, possibly.'

'Harrumph,' said Howard. 'As Pooh said. I think.'

Jack looked away and down at the stream. They were in the evil-smelling hollow. There were flies and nettles around the bridge and the stream was more black mud than water. A group of hefty Americans were trying to pass. Some of them were waddling in their shorts, misshapen with obesity. Howard and Jack had to press themselves to the bridge parapet to let them pass: very cheery and loud, they were, like a nightmare vision of the future of the human race.

'Penguins,' said Howard, loud enough for them to hear. 'Although penguins are supremely graceful underwater.'

'OK, Howard. How about you come back for a bite to eat? I've got some nice Stilton, organic celery, stuff. My complete confession for pudding.'

'Yum yum,' said Howard.

'They're probably eating fugu,' said Howard, biting his celery.

They were in the garden room, doors wide open.

'Who are?'

'The Quartet, in Nagasaki. Fugu is deadly if it's not prepared properly. They'll think they're coming down with something and then their tongues will tingle and they'll all die and I'll be the only survivor. I'll be interviewed and appear on telly. It's all meant.'

The grape juice settled sweetly in Jack's mouth, leaving a slight furriness. It didn't go with Stilton. He could not tell Howard about the magical interlude in Estonia. The two – Howard and Estonia – were incompatible. There was a strained silence, punctured at intervals by Howard's celery, its cleft filled with cottage cheese.

'I'm waiting,' said Howard. 'Assuming Milly hasn't got the place bugged.'

'Marita's downstairs.'

'I hadn't noticed her ultrasonic ears. Question one: did you meet the parents?'

'What?'

'Well, you obviously knocked her up.'

'Howard, you're gross.'

'It's an interrogator's technique,' said Howard, scratching his neat, brindled beard.

'I just don't . . .'

'You just don't.'

'No.'

They looked at each other. A strand of celery was stuck in Howard's teeth. He was negotiating it out with his tongue. His gingery eyebrows were raised. He looked very ugly.

'You'd have made a good fucking priest,' said Jack.

'Thank you. I did consider it when I was thirteen. Then my voice broke. OK, tune up with: I remember. Go on. I, remember.'

'I, remember. This café,' said Jack, surprising himself. 'The Café Majolica. In Tallinn. Back in '99 it was the Finns, not the Brits, who were the drunken oafs.'

'We're only havin' fun, guv,' said Howard, with his arms out like an Italian. 'Carry on. It's good. I, remember.'

'I, remember. Her in the café. Seeing her. In the window. As a reflection, at first. The waitress.'

'Oh, Jack.'

Howard was pitying him. He was pitiable.

'Sorry, sorry.' He waved his hands in the air, conducting a phantom orchestra of embarrassment.

'You got the most ginormous crush.'

'Probably. Probably that.'

'You git.'

The clarinet in the Barber sang swan-like through the speakers. Sometimes Howard simply pissed him off. Then the strimmer started.

He got up and closed the French windows, muting the machine's whine.

'I can't believe there's anything left to sodding strim,' he said. 'And?'

He briefly sketched what had happened, a kind of potted translation of some wild and complex and very profound happening in another language. He got up to about their third day on Haaremaa. He was pacing up and down the room. He stopped. The batteries or whatever were empty. It was like thinking about Mahler in text messages.

'I was a git, fine. Now she's obviously come back to blackmail me, it's what these girls from the ex-Communist states or Thailand or wherever do: they put the nets out, sleep with everyone, and then they hook some poor sod and then they keep on reeling in until you're out of the water, gasping. You end up either having to marry them, the whole passport angle, or pay them off. It's classic. It's obviously not my kid.'

'You've been reading those newspapers again, naughty boy.'

'I'm pissed off. Really *pissed off*.'

Jack started to tremble, suddenly. He was standing against the French windows and trembling. He ran his hand over his face.

'I really fucking am,' he said.

He walked out into the garden with long strides, right to the end where generous piles of shrubbery hid the houses beyond. The rough lawn was bare of toys, because this house had no children. The garden's calculated wildness now did nothing for Jack's peace of mind. Overgrown, summer-blown flowers were bowed over in the beds, no longer beautiful – weeds to anyone else. Right at this moment, he'd have gone for the chemical-fuelled bleakness of his parents' garden in Hayes, with its plastic chairs tipped against the rain.

Howard appeared in the distant French windows, looking down the length of the lawn to where Jack was standing, arms folded and mouth pursed. Max would have been running about with a ball, the same age as Jaan so he could picture him. Max's hair had been blond, very pale and thin. It might have turned black, though. He hadn't actually seen the eyes: they would have been a newborn's blue. Max wasn't a newborn, he was a newdead. Probably not even worth a ghost, or a soul, or whatever. That fucking four-by-four. It wasn't fair. The strimmer next door started up again, wincing on something tougher than grass.

Jack yelled. He yelled so fiercely it hurt his throat, lifting him onto the balls of his feet like a cartoon figure.

'Don't worry, carry on, don't mind me, I'll just go on taking my *fucking Valium*!'

The strimmer stopped.

'What do you say?' came a deep, silky tenor voice from over the fence. It was not the male half of the diminutive Albanian couple, it was the Italian millionaire himself.

'That noise, all the time,' shouted Jack, enunciating clearly for the foreigner. 'Sorry, but it is fairly antisocial. I'm a composer!' he added, as if this was something comic.

Jack knew what the Italian millionaire looked like: he was a scary, short, big-shouldered man in his late forties who wore the requisite black shades, but who only came for two weeks in July and left an expensive ambery scent drifting up and down the street whenever he dived in or out of his red Porsche. Jack had never talked to him before.

Howard had vanished. There was a silence. Jack could not imagine Harrison Birtwistle doing this.

'You are a – what?'

'A composer. Of music. Modern music.'

He felt his voice was audible all over Hampstead, and that everyone was listening.

'Modern music? Rock? Pop? Heep-hop?'

There was a smile in the voice. Faintly mocking. Total superiority.

'No, definitely not,' called out Jack, who wanted this to stop. He'd approached the side of the garden, but the uncropped shrubs grew out at least five feet from the fence. 'Contemporary,' he added. 'Contemporary, um, classical!'

'I like Ricky Martin!' came a shout from the other side of the garden. It was the painter-decorator with the tinny tranny.

'Great!' Jack shouted back. 'I don't!'

The painter-decorator laughed. 'I didn't think you would! You don't know what you're missing, mate!'

There was a sudden burst of Italian from beyond the shrub-bery: the millionaire was talking to, or scolding, a girl, perhaps his daughter or his mistress. Or perhaps the housekeeper. Or even his wife. He sounded annoyed, and so did she. Jack started to walk back to the house.

'What about Cream?' shouted the painter-decorator.

Jack opened his mouth to reply but the strimmer started up again like a dentist's drill for ogres.

'You're spilling the beans but keeping half of them pocketed,' said Howard, who had switched on the TV in the front sitting room and was watching cricket on Star Sports. Sri Lanka versus Bangladesh, live from Colombo. He looked as if he owned the place.

Jack had apologised for his behaviour, and Howard had waved it away like a bad smell. 'Samaraweera's at ninety-nine,' he said. 'The pitch is too small for him.'

Jack sat on the arm of the sofa. Now the cricket was on, he felt disinclined to continue. Cricket made everything outside it feel overdramatised. He wished he hadn't told Howard anything. His relief was accompanied by a sense of loss. He'd shared the treasure that he'd guarded for six years. It was no longer quite as precious.

'Y'know, I didn't feel in any way, um, paternal towards the kid, over in your place. Nothing. Sweet kid, but that was it. There'd have been some instinctual attraction, wouldn't there?'

'No idea. I've never had a kid.'

'Well, I reckon there'd have been something,' Jack said, watching Mashud miss a catch off Samaraweera, wincing at it as Howard rocked back on the sofa. 'Yup. I reckon there'd have been something.'

Howard was examining his bad finger. He had sat on it in his excitement.

'He does quite look like you, that's the funny thing. Right down to the Hitler flop of hair. Oof! Corker!'

Jayawardene's stumps had gone flying.

'Bye-bye, captain. So. How did you ride off into the sunset? Tallinn airport, was it? In front of the twin-prop? Here's looking at you, kid?'

'Aren't you watching the cricket?'

'Simultaneously, Jack. It's called multitasking. I've got half an hour. Then it's straight back home for our Jaan's lesson. Gimme the authorised, pocket version.'

'Not the revised?'

'Absolutely not,' Howard murmured with his fists in the air, as Samaraweera hit the next ball for four.

We sat on the little terrace at the back of the dacha and looked out at the vegetable garden and the raspberry canes and the golden poplars at the end, where the forest began. The fox in its cage was a dim shadow, silent as ever but moving. I wished I could release it. I ignored its psychotic-looking glare, though, not even trying to talk to it when I went down there to fetch wood. Rooting for eggs in the chicken run nearer the house, I'd be close enough to the cage to know it was watching me, and it was uncomfortable. I could feel its animosity as this kind of corrosive force, worse than the fetid smell of the cage. Kaja or Mikhel would feed it on scraps, which it ignored for a while and then wolfed up when it thought we weren't looking.

I needed to get back to Tallinn and phone Mill. She might have tried the flat. I should have left a contact number. She might have had an accident. I looked out at the dacha's long garden.

'I've got to go back to England in two days. You know I said that.'

We would be going back to Tallinn in the bus, together.

Catching it the day after tomorrow. I had hardly worked on my piece since meeting Kaja. I felt a sense of panic, suddenly.

'It's going to be hard,' I added.

'For me, or for you?'

'Both of us, obviously.'

'Oh, well, maybe,' she said.

I did not want a scene before the restaurant. I was taking the family out. It was a thank-you meal. Kaja was hunched up in her chair. She rubbed her forehead with the back of her fingers, shook the hair from her eyes. She might have been crying: the edges of the lids were red. She would stroke the trunks of trees and say, 'Hi there. How are you doing, tree?' And then, in case they wouldn't understand, she said the same thing in Estonian. It sounded like a poem in Estonian. She knew a lot of the work of a famous Estonian poet called Jaan Kaplinski off by heart:

> *The radio is still playing*
> *Schubert's unfinished symphony,*
> *the voice of the rain fills the pauses,*
> *the silence the voice of the rain.*
> *No one knows where they come from.*
> *No one knows where they go.*

She believed everyone was on earth to fulfil something unique.

This unique thing was a mystery to the one fulfilling it, and to everyone else, but it was not a mystery to God. When I asked her one time what kind of Christian she was – the island being mainly Lutheran – she laughed and said, 'Why do you think I'm a Christian?'

'You believe in God, so I thought . . .'

And she'd laughed again, putting her hand over my lips, but I was none the wiser. Her hand was slightly sticky, not with tree sap but with sugar. She had been making an egg-flip.

She explained that sometimes in special moments that weren't always on solitary walks in the forest, you could come very close to knowing why you were here on earth. This was her one belief, unconnected to any religion. This revelation was not a thought, it was not a feeling, it was something for which the human brain had no instruments to register, so your whole body received the sensation like a tide in the blood. I was spellbound, listening to this.

I told her about the white clouds and the music from them in Hayes.

This was the next day, in the rocket station. A few piss-smelling concrete huts with smashed windows; wooden poles without wires; the puddled dilapidation of something resembling a mini golf course, then a long track to four big squared-off tumuli, half covered in tufts of grass. The launch pads. One of the Cold War hot spots. Young birch sprouting already.

I had never told anyone in my life before about the music from the white clouds. Not even Milly.

'Is Hayes a magic town? Very old and English with beautiful gardens and roses?'

I laughed. 'Er, not quite,' I said.

I wanted to run it down, but didn't know where to begin. I even felt a pulse of affection for it. For Hayes! We had climbed one of the launch pads, hand in hand. I said, quite puffed, on the top: 'OK. Put it like this. If the Soviets had nuked Hayes from here, the joke goes, they'd have caused millions of pounds' worth of improvements.'

'Ah,' she said, without smiling. 'So you are even more special than I think.'

And she pressed me close against her as we looked out from the grassed-over launch pad.

I *did* feel special, just then. I did feel that I was placed on earth for a purpose, mysterious though that was and would always be.

Tallinn was very noisy after the island. We decided to walk to where you could see over the Bay of Finland. It was like an operatic backdrop. Her eyelids were swollen and red, again. She hugged me and whispered in my ear.

Is this real life? Will you take me with you?

We held each other for a very long time. My mouth was in her hair. I'll come back for you, I wanted to say.

She realised, suddenly, that we hadn't exchanged addresses. This procedure seemed to belong to another, duller world. We scribbled under a dim street lamp, we exchanged the scraps of paper.

Then she walked away without looking back. It was like a bit of me tearing off.

'I'll drop you a line!' I shouted, waving the scrap of paper.

She turned round: too far away perhaps.

'What?'

'I'll drop you a line!'

She didn't understand the phrase, I could see that. I wondered why I'd even used it. I gave the kind of wave you give from high up on the deck of a ship, and then she understood only too well.

Too far away.

SEVEN

Jack was in Howard's spare room, off the living room, and it was very small. A box room, as it would once have been called, but not shaped like a box: it was narrow, not much wider than a single bed. Howard's computer sat on the table, beyond which was the spare bed. The door could never be fully opened because of the desk and chair. Jack was sitting in the chair, his head resting against the closed door. A little inclination of his head would bring his eye or his ear to the keyhole. He felt ridiculous.

Before Jaan arrived, while Howard was making coffee to sustain the spy, Jack had pointed out how interested Kaja had been in his work.

'We talked a lot about my work. She reckoned the biggest thing in life is to be honest to your self. To your inner soul. That kind of thing. Not to block yourself. You know, the way people take a crap job so they don't *have* to write the concerto or the great novel or try to paint, or whatever. Yes, they have to earn a *wage*, but . . . maybe they don't *need* to . . .'

Howard had laughed. 'When were *you* last strapped for cash, m'boy?'

'I'm questioning myself, Howard.'

'Go ahead, then. Starve in a garret. I mean, eat vegan in your designer loft space, man.'

He'd laughed again, then stared at Jack with his serious expression, similar to a scowl. It had rained in Colombo, fortunately. A sudden squall. They hadn't missed much.

'This is no joke, Jack. We're trying to go forward with minimal damage. She's waiting for you to invite her over. *Them* over.

We don't want her to feel uninvited. Or uninviting. She might then force the pace.'

'As Schoenberg said, there are masterpieces –'

'Still to be written in C major, yes, and what a pity Schoenberg didn't write them. Hm?'

Now Jack's coffee was sitting in front of him, turned cold. He could hear fairly clearly through the door, but the keyhole offered only a very partial view. The lesson was half over. He thought of the lessons he had given and how much better Howard was at explaining things. Jack remembered a lesson with his piano teacher when he was ten or eleven and already very advanced: they had been working on Satie, on the first *Gymnopédie*. His piano teacher, Clara Knowles, who soon afterwards contracted multiple sclerosis, told him that the key to these pieces was Satie's use of *résonance* (which she said in French, because she was originally Belgian). She played the E and showed him how its echo went on for nine beats, through which the other notes played off its *résonance*, and that unless he pressed the E hard enough all the simple beauty of the effect would be lost. Too hard, however, and all Satie's gentleness and sadness and nostalgia would be lost. It was a question of getting *le juste milieu*.

Then she played the E and sure enough it continued like the string of the beads of the other notes, and Jack felt a kind of deep thrill in his belly. The music he'd heard from the white clouds above Hayes was like that *résonance* of the E just audible under the notes at that moment being pressed from the piano and vibrating with or against them and giving the experience all its beauty. But it took him the rest of the lesson to get it right, and then it was not as beautiful as when Clara played it. He was half in love with Clara, anyway, who had a mane of jet-black hair she kept tossing to one side and, if Jack was on that side, it would hit his face in a quite painful but delicious way, but she never noticed because he wanted it to happen again and so he didn't even flinch.

'It's like throwing a ball just the right distance,' she said. 'You throw balls, don't you?'

Jack nodded in the box room, as if Clara was asking him right then and there. He would have liked to have told her, now, that Pärt used the same device in *Für Alina*, but she was beyond anything, beyond silence even. Jaan was hardly speaking in the room next door, or if he was speaking he was speaking very softly. Howard's deep voice rumbled away. He was a permanently lean-forward person, all but bossy, and this could irritate Jack to the point where he would wonder why he was Howard's friend at all.

Kaja had sent Jaan up without coming up herself, and as she sometimes collected him without appearing in person, Howard had explicitly asked her to come and see him at the end of the lesson. Jack and he had worked out what questions to weave into the conversation, which would be mainly about Jaan's progress.

There was a large framed photograph of the Queen in full mink-and-diamond regalia above Howard's desk, taken many years ago. She seemed to be wondering what on earth one of her subjects was up to.

Jack closed his eyes. It had been Howard's suggestion, this. Howard's wheeze. To boil the maybe down to something hard and certain. Probably.

After a moment with his eyes closed, he thought: this is how my mother experiences life all the time. To Mum, life is always a box room with voices. A box room, because the limits of her secure space are the stretch of her hands. He stretched out his own hands and knocked something over on Howard's desk – a pencil holder, which spilt its contents with what sounded to Jack like a gunshot. He froze, but Howard's voice carried on and then Jaan played a passage of an étude on his viola to a one-handed accompaniment on the piano.

Jack found it hard to entertain the idea that he was the father to the boy playing the viola, the sound slightly muffled by the door. His feelings were not as he might have expected them to be, and therefore he supposed that Howard's subtle probing would reveal the truth – which would be that the father was another lover, possibly the man whose name Kaja now carried but whose status as a 'great musician' had been exaggerated, or who had never achieved proper recognition. Maybe he had died tragically, as Clara Knowles had done – not in an accident but slowly and horribly, hoping right up to the end for a cure.

Because hope was the *résonance* that made life possible and poignant and beautiful; especially when life – or death – was in counterpoint to it.

He looked through the keyhole, but Jaan's bobbing elbow was still the only part of him visible. He calculated that his width of vision was about five or six feet. They had experimented earlier: Howard had placed a chair in the middle of Jack's field of vision. If Kaja didn't sit there, or if she moved about, he wouldn't see her. He imagined her suddenly opening the box-room door and finding him there, crouched down with one eye squeezed tight. She would probably laugh. He hoped she would laugh.

He felt quite cool about the prospect of spying on her, but nervous about what she might say in answer to Howard's probing.

It was hot in the box room; in winter it would be even hotter, as the radiator was too large and Howard liked to go about all year with summer clothes on, inside, so he kept the heating high. Sometimes you would find him in shorts in December. Milly hated that sort of behaviour, it was American and criminally selfish. It reminded Jack of Kaja's parents' apartment on Haaremaa. Sweat was dripping down from his under-arms onto his ribs. He had put on a smart shirt, just in case, but he'd have been better off in a T-shirt. The window was closed, to keep down the noise – there was a pneumatic drill going somewhere and the usual trundle of London. He didn't want to miss a word.

Jaan's shoulder and his bow-hand came in sight, but however Jack twisted his head nothing more could be made out. Then the lesson was over and Howard's legs could be seen, close, diminishing as they walked towards the table where the vital chair was placed. Jaan came fully into view for a few moments. Yes, he looked like Mikhel, Kaja's father. His face proved nothing. Lots of people had black hair. Maybe fewer in Estonia, but . . .

'The toilet, please,' he said.

'Go ahead, buster. Put it back when you've finished with it.'

Jack watched Jaan smile uncertainly up at Howard for a moment and then limp off. That uncertain smile, the face craned up, shipped the onlooker with a warm feel. It surprised him. It was because he knew exactly what that uncertainty felt like and how terribly tall the adults were.

Howard turned and gave the box-room door a wink.

There was the buzz of a bell. After what seemed a very long time, Howard appeared again, talking, holding the chair like a waiter.

'I'm OK standing,' came Kaja's voice.

She was off to the left, out of sight. Perhaps there was just the edge of a knee. Jeans, maybe. Jack's back was uncomfortable and he found it hard to breathe easily in this position. He should have kneeled, he should have tested the whole thing better. Howard was off to the right, half of him visible lengthways.

Howard was saying: 'He's making very good progress. He's rather exceptional, we're agreed. I hope you don't mind me knowing a little more about his background.'

'People, you mean? Or the scenery?' said Kaja, as if it was a caustic joke.

Howard smiled. 'Both?'

'OK.'

He recognised something had changed about Kaja's voice, now he could hear it live and not on what had been a poor line. Then, at the same instant Jack smelt it, he knew: she was still a smoker. More of a smoker, since she'd hardly smoked more than one or two a day when he'd known her. She was smoking and, as far as he knew, she hadn't asked Howard's permission. Howard didn't like smokers, but nothing was said.

Then Jack saw the cigarette in her hand, which was thrust forward into his keyhole view. Those were the tapering fingers that had touched him intimately. Those were the knuckles he had enclosed with his lips.

'Well,' said Kaja, in her huskier voice, 'does it matter, in fact?'

'It would help me. Are you sure you won't sit?'

'I've been sitting all day. It feels like it. The traffic is bad. I sit on the lower deck because, I don't know, I feel safer.'

The hand disappeared and then reappeared, and smoke misted the space behind it. The jeans knee showed a bit more of itself: it was in a jeans skirt. It retreated again. Jack took a long breath to calm himself down.

'For instance,' said Howard, 'was his father a jazz musician? I mean, was he good at improvisation? Was he spontaneous and inventive?'

'Why?'

'Because it would help me to know in which direction –'

'My son is as he is. Do you believe in musical genes or something?'

This was a more aggressive Kaja, a more impatient Kaja. An angry Kaja, underneath. Had he made Kaja into this? Then her face suddenly came into view, dipping towards an ashtray that Howard had placed on the table; her face staying for a moment and then vanishing back. It was the same face and a different face: her full head of hair was piled up loosely on top, like something from a Greek vase, coils falling in front of her ears. It was not quite the face he'd held all these years in his memory. It was both startling and reassuring. It was still beautiful, in his opinion, if slightly thinner. He felt confused and anxious. He didn't think he was in love with her any more.

'It's more a case,' said Howard, as if he'd been reflecting deeply, 'of unconscious influences. I don't even know if Jaan knew his father. Now I don't want to probe, but for all I know he may have heard his father play the viola, for instance.'

'He heard me play the violin,' Kaja laughed. '*That's* why he chose the viola!'

'Negative attraction,' Howard grinned, clearly enjoying himself.

'I never made him play music. I never pulled him into it. He heard the viola on a CD and said he wanted to play it. I thought he would start on the violin, but he protested really a lot. On Haaremaa there was this nice viola teacher in her sixties, with a holiday house. She had to bring a junior viola from Tallinn, for us to hire. Then Jaan was so quick to learn she taught him for free, whenever she was over in the island.'

'Amazing,' said Howard. 'Must have been the genes.'

Jaan appeared between them. She folded her arms over her son's chest as he rested back against her skirt. The fag must be in her mouth, Jack thought. Sure enough, an arm disappeared and the space misted with smoke. That's not good for the kid. That's not good at all.

'He never knew him, by the way,' said Kaja.

The boy twisted his head up and said something in Estonian. Kaja replied, rubbing Jaan's chest with her hand. Jack felt alarmed at life, suddenly, and what might be about to happen. The pneumatic drill started up again, faint through the shut window. It was much too hot.

'What's he saying?' said Howard, smiling affectionately.

'He asks if we are talking about his father,' said Kaja, with an ironic lilt that Jack found attractive.

'And we are. Or trying to,' said Howard, nodding at the boy.

'My philosophy,' said Kaja, 'is that you look forward, not back. If Estonians look back they see a lot of shit. If English look back they see a lot of nice things.'

'Not all nice,' said Howard.

'They think it's nice,' said Kaja. 'We can't think it's nice because it's like barbed wire growing into a tree. The wire doesn't grow but the tree does. By the way, this is a poet who's saying this, a famous poet, not me.'

'A very striking image,' said Howard, 'but clearly it suggests that your personal memories of the crucial liaison were rather painful.'

'There's nothing I want to say without Jaan understanding it,' said Kaja.

'OK, agreed, yes,' said Howard, sounding bereft of ideas.

'I'll tell you what I've said to him,' said Kaja, after the cigarette had briefly disappeared again. 'I've said that his father went away before he was born.'

'Away?'

'Back.'

'Back?'

A silence.

'So, the father wasn't a viola player. But he might've been a rock musician.'

Kaja laughed. It was good to hear her laugh.

'You are *really* mad, Mr Davenport. Anyway, you know it already, what you're trying to find out. It's like the KGB, they would always ask what they knew already.'

Jack was resting his ear against the door. All he could think of was a technical phrase of Milly's: *life-cycle cost*.

'Why do you think I know already?' said Howard, clearly taken aback.

Kaja's hand tousled her son's hair.

'I've said too much things. It doesn't matter. Was Jaan fine today?'

Jack, while Howard was passing on his lesson notes, remembered arriving in a village with Kaja one morning – one of the tiny, rebuilt, half-deserted villages of the island – and seeing some six or seven young lads playing football on the local pitch, between a cemetery and a litter-strewn wood. The lads had politely invited them to play. Kaja was tired from cycling and watched from the touchline. The pitch had ruts in it, and the odd rusty bit of metal sticking up an inch or two, but Jack had a lot of fun, pretending to play well in front of his girl and scoring a goal.

Afterwards he'd felt desperate to have a son, but had said nothing about it to Kaja.

Jaan was leaning with his elbows on his mother's knee, his bad foot at an awkward angle – but that was probably coincidence. Jack had no memory of leaning against his mother's knee. He must have done, though.

He rested his head quietly against the door, picturing himself taking Jaan up to the Heath and kicking a football about. He experienced a sense of life's complications – a kind of abstract mesh drawn over his mind. He didn't like the blackness of Jaan's hair, or the way it fell over his ears and across his brow. But he loved the way the boy leaned awkwardly like that, his chin in his hands, moving his hips from side to side until his mother stopped him. Dreamy. Very tall adults.

Kaja was in keyhole shot again: she looked much the same as she had six years ago. A little thinner, that's all. And standing in front of her, very serious now he had broken away from her knee, was her son. Who was quite likely *his* son.

And he was spying on them.

And then, looking at a sheet of paper – maybe a score – that Howard had given her, she put on a pair of black, oval glasses.

'A cup of tea?' offered Howard, as per the script, although rather later than planned.

'No problem. I am *so* thirsty,' she said, nodding like a studious schoolgirl in her unappealing glasses.

'Do you think you can be a Christian and as well believe that the Passion is just a symbol of private suffering, a kind of poem? Just that?'

'You mean,' said Howard, 'nothing really religious, just a metaphor?'

'Yes. A metaphor. Not of God's purpose, but of our situation here on earth.'

'That's your view, is it?'

'It's you I asked the question to. So, what do you think?'

She was finally sitting in the right chair, the one with a slung canvas seat, full in Jack's view. She had on a jeans skirt and bright pink tights and black sandals. Her short-sleeved top, buttoned at the back, was a yellowy cream and kept her shoulders bare. Jack was surprised to see a violet ink-stain on her right shoulder, just above the shoulder blade: in fact, he realised, it was a tattoo, some sort of heraldic dragon or bird. She had crossed her legs. Jack could mainly see her back and her hair. There was a wooden farmyard and animals on a shelf in Howard's bedroom – a childhood souvenir – and Jaan was in there playing with it. This had also been planned. It meant that Jaan was out of earshot. She had taken her glasses off, he reckoned.

Howard cupped his chin in his hand. He was, Jack realised, being unnaturally serious.

'You know what they say about us English, that we like to keep our religion, like our sexual habits, to ourselves? You know, do it in the dark?'

Kaja giggled. She was slowly becoming the Kaja that Jack remembered.

'Well,' Howard went on, 'I tend to think that anything's possible – speaking as an Anglican – as long as it doesn't hurt anyone. Terribly wishy-washy, sorry.' He snorted through his nose, a noise Jack knew well: it was self-derisory. Howard was a supporter of the invasion of Iraq, on the basis that Saddam Hussein hurt a lot of people.

'No,' said Kaja, 'I really agree.'

'Good. Because I hate punch-ups about God.'

Kaja laughed. Howard was doing great. In fact, almost too great. Jack felt a twinge of jealousy. He was now kneeling, but his knees were sore.

'And do you think your life's a Passion, Mrs Krohn?'

'Kaja. I hate that Mrs Krohn. But it's complicated to change, right now.'

'Then call me Howard.'

'Oh yeah,' said Kaja, 'but you're a great viola player and teacher, by the way.'

'That somewhat diminishes your description of Jaan's father,' said Howard. '*Great musician.*'

'Yeah, maybe,' said Kaja. 'But I don't think so.'

There was a little silence. Jack didn't like the way Kaja said 'yeah' all the time, and that language-school 'by the way', but she had done the same six years ago and he'd found it fine. Kaja was turned away from him and that's how it must always be.

'No, this musician was *really* great.'

'Uh-huh.'

There was a pause, during which Jack's heartbeats themselves seemed to be rapt.

'He played banjo.'

Howard made a really peculiar noise, like bathwater going out.

'*Banjo?*'

'Cajun, jazz. Brilliant. And Estonian songs. He could play anything on the banjo. Then he stopped.'

'The banjo?'

'Why? Is there something wrong about it?'

Howard was staring at his splinted finger. 'Not at all. But it's not like the viola.'

She nodded, smiling and pulling on her cigarette. She blew the smoke out as if she was blowing out a candle.

'Then he stopped. Just like that. He became a sculptor. He made sharks out of marble.'

'Sharks?'

'Why? Is there something wrong about sharks, too?'

Howard laughed. 'Is this Mr Krohn?'

'Are you the KGB?'

'No, the CIA.'

Jack's eyelids were cold against the metal of the keyhole. He felt sick. Kaja's glance swept sideways and suddenly it seemed to meet his, which was impossible, but he removed himself with a lurch that wasn't all that silent. And he froze, in case. But the voices went on. Jaan wasn't his son. He did not have a son. The Queen looked down at him with regal contempt, the old faggot.

The voices had stopped. He looked through the keyhole again. Kaja was very still, looking downwards, her face mostly hidden. Then she fished out a tissue and blew her nose and wiped her eyes and held the tissue against them. Jack couldn't see her eyes but he assumed this was what she was doing. He realised his face was screwed up into a kind of ball. He let the muscles in his cheeks go, very slowly. His knees were painful on Howard's carpet. He wanted a cup of tea.

'Truth was important for us,' she said. 'It was the only light. The only one. And the nature – and nature, too. Nature never lies, does she?'

'I suppose not,' said Howard, who looked pale and tired, as he would do after a concert. 'Nature just gets on with it. Although you might call camouflage a lie. One of those moths with a fierce face in its tail. Or the other way round: a lie could be termed a camouflage.'

'How can nature lie,' said Kaja, very earnestly, with her head forward, 'when she doesn't know what the hell *is* a lie?'

That evening, as Jack was turning down the ring to the absolute minimum under the petits pois, feeling emotionally and physically spent, Milly started pulling her lacy top up carefully over her head. She wasn't wearing a bra.

It had been a long day at a thermal comfort conference in Bath; her eyes were still smarting from the city's horrendous pollution levels.

She unbuttoned her jeans skirt and stepped out of it. Then she got down on all fours, on the kitchen floor.

She was wearing a thong, which surprised him even more. It disappeared between the cheeks of her buttocks and reminded him of the cheese slicer in the delicatessen, sinking into a Dutch Gouda. She waved her rump at him, like an animal.

'Take me,' she ordered.

The blind wasn't lowered, the light was on: everyone could see in. At the moment, there was no one passing on Willow Road, but there soon would be.

'Eh?'

'Quickly, it's what the consultant said. Get the adrenalin going. Make it dangerous. Apparently the adrenalin helps. It's an incredibly animal thing. Deep in the system. You might be eaten. Leapt on by a sabretooth.'

'Which consultant?'

'The new one. Juan-Carlos. Never give up, he said. It's incredibly psycho-physical. That's why he's so expensive. And today's good. Lunar cycle.'

'Everyone can see in,' he pointed out.

'Just do it, for fuck's sake. Pretend I'm a whore. Pretend I'm your mistress. Do it with my panties on. Doggy position.'

'I haven't got a mistress.'

She lowered her top half further, sinking onto her elbows, her head on the floor, so her buttocks were even more prominent, two great globes as pale as honeydew melons. There was a swollen red spot on the right cheek.

'Please,' she said. 'Please.'

He calculated that the sight line from the street would be obscured by the kitchen units against the window, unless someone was looking from the Heath, from the twilit bushes on the rise the other side, where a bevy of giggly schoolgirls would usually gather of an evening, smoking and gossiping. Or up a tree: they'd have to be equipped with binoculars. He crouched and bent his knees and pulled his trousers and pants down, bewildered, scared, but already excited.

'Not that one!' she cried, reaching behind her, correcting him, guiding him past the cotton strip. 'We're making my baby! We're making my *baby*, for God's sake!'

A group walked past, talking and laughing, on heels that sounded as though they were in the kitchen itself. They didn't look in, thank God. Milly was groaning and moaning, not keeping the volume down, as he tried to hurry himself up, grinding away between the straits of her cervical muscles. It was, in fact, pretty exciting, pretty pleasurable. He was crouching, trying to keep his head as low as possible.

Then he saw Edward Cochrane.

Edward Cochrane was waving at him from the street, an Oddbins bag in his other hand.

'What's the matter?' gasped Milly.

'It's Edward.'

'Just ignore him. Oh, it's so good. Come, darling, come!'

'I can't. Not with bloody Edward looking.'

'Oh, it's so good, stay in, you're so good! It's the adrenalin! It's the danger! It's the sabretooth! Touch my breasts! Touch them!'

Jack nodded calmly at Edward from this awkward, crouched position, keeping his buttery, fish-smeared hands cupped over Milly's breasts, moving his groin minimally but sufficiently so it didn't show in his upper torso – the only part of him that could possibly, he reckoned, be visible to Edward. But Edward was looking puzzled. He'd probably been drinking in the Flask on the corner, his usual haunt. Jack's chief terror was that Edward would come up to the front door, peer in through the window by the porch.

'Oh, darling! Come! Come!'

Jack said, out of the corner of his mouth, 'Edward's still there. He's lifting an Oddbins bag. I think he's asking us round for a drink.'

'Oh, come as you're looking at him! He's the danger! He's the adrenalin! He's the sabretooth!'

Her hand reached between her legs and subjected his chest-nuts to little delicious arpeggios with the tips of her fingers, partly subduing his embarrassment. Jack managed to shake his head politely at Edward and mouth a 'No' as Milly gave a great gasping moan and shuddered, sinking her head onto her arms.

'Have you come yet?' she asked.

'Nearly.'

He had pain in his lower back. He was not a gymnast.

'Oh, darling!' she said, revolving her behind so much that he could barely keep his balance, let alone hold his head and shoulders still. 'Fill me up with your spunky spunk!'

He saw Edward give a mournful shrug, looking very like Tony Hancock.

'I'm nearly there. Don't move around so much.'

Then, in a sudden surprising lurch, he slipped out of her by mistake and simultaneously, as she was attempting to stuff his equipment back in, all their hopes spilt out into her hand.

EIGHT

The following morning he was staring into space in his study, feeling a great hollow in his chest, when he was interrupted by a ring on the doorbell.

It was Edward Cochrane, no longer holding an Oddbins bag. Although it was ten in the morning, his neighbour was lightly drunk.

'Did you get it open in the end?'

'Get what open?'

'The bottle! Cork stiff, was it? Wrist weak? I'll bet it was a good one. I use a vacuum pump.'

'It was not that good, Edward.'

'Nothing worse than drinking a decent bottle on your own. At first I thought you were screwing your wife, all crouched over like that.'

'Look, I'm working right now –'

'Just keep an eye on her. Or you'll end up like me. Drinking on your own. Doing everything on your own. No weak wrist here, look.' He chortled, horribly. 'You can always loan her to me, by the way. She's terribly attractive and you don't even *know* it. Sired three bonny nippers, me. No probs. No deficiencies in *that* quarter.'

He was sounding weirdly like a 1950s Etonian, suddenly.

'Hey, Edward, sorry, we don't even find you, um, funny any more. Just *fucking* rude.'

And Jack slammed the door on him, peevishly. On his own neighbour. Swearing at his own neighbour. Then he brooded on the term 'deficiencies', pacing up and down in his study.

Howard had reckoned the keyhole wheeze a resounding

287

success. Jack wasn't so sure. No, he wasn't the father – in fact, he wasn't anything much at all to Kaja. Maybe he was deficient in every way. But that didn't stop him being involved.

He was faintly scared of her, because he didn't know what she was up to. And therefore he was involved. She had come to London, to Howard, to his world, in the expectation – the sure knowledge – that she would meet him. And now they had talked. And she had said 'maybe'. Why? This 'maybe' was a fudge. Jaan was nothing to do with him. More straightforward if he had been. Very special. His son.

But Jaan was someone else's son. And not even Kaja's ex-husband's.

Jack felt himself part of a long line of men, shuffling past her. Head bowed. One of many.

'I missed a bit,' he'd said to Howard, afterwards. 'Why did she start to cry, and then go on about truth?'

'Apropros of nothing,' said Howard. 'Or maybe because I joked about being the CIA. You never know which bits are tender, with foreigners. By the way, at the door she said she was *definitely* going to phone you. About accompanying Jaan. It's all much simpler now, isn't it? No blood link. Collateral damage avoided. Thank me then, you ungrateful old sod.'

'Thank you, Howard.'

Jack slept half the afternoon away, on his sofa, without meaning to. The phone went when he was deep in a dream, of which he could remember only a sense of confused flight and horses covered in black goo. He cleared his throat and answered. It wasn't Kaja, as he'd anticipated. It was his Tuesday student, a little twelve-year-old Indian genius called Raj with perfect pitch, like his tutor. Raj lived above his parents' snazzy deli in Chalk Farm. Jack had completely forgotten. Raj was ringing from the Middletons' front door on his mobile, as no one was answering. It was after half past five.

Jack pretended he'd been in the garden, and splashed his face with cold water. They were working on phrasing, mainly, and Jack had suggested Satie's second *Gymnopédie* in honour of Clara

Knowles. The lesson went well, surprisingly. He told Raj to put more body into his little finger as it played the lowest note, and Raj found this very funny.

'Your phrases don't know where they end,' Jack continued, tapping the score. 'They have a beginning, a middle and an end, but you get to the middle at the end, or the end in the middle, so you've got nowhere to go for the next two bars. Each phrase is a story. Look, this one lasts five bars. You have to anticipate the progression of that story.'

'Then by the end I've told all these stories,' Raj said, very perky as usual. Apparently he was bullied at school because he was top in everything except sport.

'Right,' said Jack, feeling a warmth of appreciation inside him that was one of the nice things about teaching. 'The big story Satie wants you to tell has all these smaller stories inside it. Mood stories, my old teacher called them. Like all of us,' he added. 'We're each one big story with lots and lots of smaller stories.'

'Except with each person they go on at the same time, some of them,' piped Raj. 'They overlap like scales on a fish. Not like in the music.'

Jesus, no wonder he gets bullied, Jack thought.

'I think it's more confusing than scales on a fish, with us, Raj,' Jack said. 'I think it's more like a bundle of wires.'

'Not bare wires connected up to a really massive generator, I hope,' said Raj, squirming on the piano stool.

'Nah,' said Jack. 'Only if you're me.'

Which made Raj laugh so hard he nearly fell off.

And then the phone went again, and it was Kaja.

He didn't want to get electrocuted. More to the point, he didn't want anyone else to get electrocuted. He was due to meet Kaja at eleven tomorrow morning in Regent's Park. Wednesday was her day off from the hotel work, she'd said. He'd not asked her what she did in the hotel, it didn't seem the moment for possibly awkward questions. She might well be a room maid – peeling off soiled sheets and rubbing at drink rings on the bedside table, digging out stiff tissues from behind the mattress, piling up damp furry towels at the door to be washed and bleached at the expense of the planet. Once, in a four-star hotel in Madrid, he'd surprised the cleaner pilfering his bag. Big hotels were fungal, wish-fulfilment places you didn't want to scrape at too hard.

You could say that, he thought, about the music world, and smiled to himself as he fiddled in the kitchen, waiting for Milly to get back from Oxford. His main task was to orchestrate this whole deal so that no one got hurt, no one squealed. Kaja had to understand that the whole thing was over. He'd apologise for fibbing, and then it would all be fine. He'd make amends with free lessons for Jaan. Help her out with cash. Do his bit for the new Europe.

Milly need never know. Kaja would become the mother of one of his music pupils, and no one would be the wiser.

His shirt smelt of the hospital, although it had been washed. His mother had settled into a routine of suffering that was almost banal.

When Milly got back at ten thirty – the Oxford train having stopped for an hour and a half in a tunnel for no apparent reason – she was exhausted and irritable. Enter the PMT Zone, Jack thought. Tread like a fox. Now Mikhel was dead, maybe the fox had been released from the cage by the woodshed. He really must ask Kaja.

The supper he'd prepared with care was not good: his usual shepherd's pie, Milly's favourite, but languishing in a low oven for an hour longer than it should have done had killed it in some way: it was dried out, with a smell that recalled sweaty pyjamas. Milly just frowned and poured herself more wine. It wasn't his fault, he considered.

He'd been watching an obscure documentary on cable about a Romanian opera version of Racine's *Andromache*, and now felt slack and English and dull. The killing of Pyrrhus had been enacted instead of reported, gallons of pigs' blood poured into a tin bath behind the admittedly weak and screechy music. The young male composer had a stud in each ear and punkish hair and was obsessed by Stockhausen and Cage. Everything was fresh, in the end, if you wanted it to be.

Jack wished he was born somewhere painful and interesting, knowing this desire in itself to be Hampsteadthink.

He was describing the documentary to Milly, but she was grunting her responses. She was far away, glazed over. She had given a talk at a conference on yurts, and berated a planning official for the laws that made yurt-dwelling difficult. The official had smothered her in stupid, bony words and made her feel like a hippy.

This far-awayness irritated him, as if it was her duty to be fascinated – following some ideal domestic model – in a Romanian opera version of *Andromache* after a tough day with the yurts.

The bandstand in Regent's Park was occupied by a children's group from Croatia, some in jeans and T-shirts with *Hot Shot Good – Its' Croatia!* printed on the front, the rest of them in folk costume.

He was early, and there was no sign of Kaja. It was weirdly, creepily hot for late September. He tried not to feel worried about it.

He sat down in a deckchair and the attendant came up to him and charged him. The singing was fine until it veered from Croatian choral or folk works to embrace British pop classics. 'A Hard Day's Night' forced him to leave. This was all a mistake, he thought. The other people in the deckchairs, mostly elderly or tourists with cameras, smiled tolerantly and clapped along.

He felt sour and superior and damaged, and walked to the lake's edge and back, just to check she wasn't there.

As 'Yellow Submarine' began with a treble solo in unrecognisable English, he realised that this was probably the worst place in London to meet anyone, short of maybe the HMV store in

Oxford Street. A sudden fit of nerves made him want to go to the lavatory.

At which point, of course, Kaja was suddenly walking towards him.

'Hi!'

'Hi, Kaja.'

He couldn't decide, in the last few seconds, whether to kiss her lightly on each cheek or shake her hand, and there was a confusion in which their heads dipped and their hands flapped.

Kaja laughed and put her hands either side of her face.

'This is *so* mad!' she cried.

He could see her more clearly here in the sunlight than he had through the keyhole at Howard's or in the gloom of the Hampstead church or across the street from the tree. The only difference from six years back was the tiny crow's feet and an overall look of tiredness. Her hair was loose and long again and chimed precisely with the gilded necklace at her throat, which was like a circle of ancient hammered coins. Her tawny hair would turn heads all on its own: the Estonian strong point, she'd said, once. And her extraordinary blue-green eyes, tending to slate grey when the light couldn't decide. Her cheekbones were still slightly polished, curving just under the skin: he knew how they felt when they were kissed.

'Pretty crazy,' Jack agreed, not feeling like smiling, feeling instead a sudden irritation at her ease and beauty.

'*You're* a bit older,' she said, her head cocked to one side, running her eyes over his face and hair.

'You're not,' he replied, his irritation going out of him like air from a tyre.

She was dressed in low-cut denim shorts and a thin armless cream singlet under which she was not apparently wearing a bra. He thought he saw a stud in her bared navel, like a golden bead of sweat. The shorts were stonewashed and torn and reached her knees: expensive, he reckoned. He was annoyed that he was sexually excited. He'd forgotten how lithe and gymnastic she looked, with her emphasised shoulders and no-nonsense back –

so different from the cowed look of the English. He wondered if she had dressed like a diva deliberately.

'OK,' he said, rather coldly. 'Let's find our bench. Nice day, yeah?'

They walked up the side of the long, thin stretch of water in virtual silence, commenting only on the ducks. The water was low and smelt slightly rotten from the exposed mud on the edges and around the islands. The ducks were, as usual, very loud, breaking into squabbling fits or individually embarking on a solo riff that echoed up and down and made the little kids here and there pause, then point and squawk in turn. There were not many people, in fact.

They found the bench and sat with a gap of several inches between them. The wicked idea passed through Jack's mind that passers-by would think of them as a couple, the men admiring the girl. It was especially wicked because a part of him would have liked to have stolen an arm around Kaja's slim and naked waist, or pressed his lips on the tattoo above her shoulder blade, or removed her Roman-style sandals and squeezed her feet.

'Is this a crane?' he asked, almost tapping the tattoo on her bared shoulder.

'It's a phoenix,' she said. 'Rising up from the ashes.'

'OK,' he nodded, hiding his hands under his thighs.

'I don't want to be long, Jack.'

'Oh?'

She was looking straight out at the water and the reeds and the floating birdlife, which included coots and the odd cross-looking swan. The huge willow, to their left, gave partial shade from the sun. Passers-by spoke in mostly Italian or French; the English sounded posh and intellectual and too loud, like cast-offs from some arts programme. A sign indicated the way to the Zoo and to Regent's College, where Milly used to see a homeopathic doctor called Brian. Jack felt snagged on what he had always known.

'You see, this could be more serious,' she said, finally. 'There won't be any shooting or stabbing or things like that. Like in Tolstoy's *The Kreutzer Sonata*. You know that story?'

'Yeah,' said Jack, although he'd never read it. 'Heavy things happen, even so. Or they can do.'

'I was waiting six years.'

A duck was dipping its head in and out of the water. In and out. Out and shake a bit and look about and in.

This was probably the end of the long plangent phrase that had begun in the park in Tallinn, to the whiff of a cigarillo, to the dipping of a duck's sleek head the colour of the inside of a mussel shell.

'Never gave up?'

'Nope,' she said.

She took out a creased photograph and showed it to him. He was dismayed to see himself, standing in front of a wooden sheep with a pair of clippers hanging off its rump. Dismayed, because he looked such a twerp, and noticeably younger. Very pleased with himself, he looked. And awkward. A magical time. A madness time.

'Hey-ho,' he said.

She put the snap away and replaced it with a packet of Camel cigarettes; she offered him one and he said why not and took it. His eyes met hers for a second and he saw that their colour was also the inside of a mussel shell. He felt he'd got this image from somewhere, maybe a magazine or a novel or a poem he'd read as a stimulus for a piece or as a setting. She lit his and then hers with a plastic Bic lighter, the type he'd seen people use in Paris. He took a drag of his and coughed.

'At least you didn't hit me this time,' he said, slapping his chest. She laughed as he coughed again, apologising. 'Sorry. I hate cigarettes, really.'

'You mean, your wife does.'

'OK, but I agree with her.'

'She's very strong, isn't she?'

'Yeah.' He didn't like Kaja talking about Milly. He felt defensive. His mouth was full of a nasty bush of smoke.

'First I need to say,' she went on, 'that I know about the baby. That one you lost. I know it through your music.'

'You can't be serious.'

'*Cantus from the Black Screen.*'

'Wow. Bravo. Worst title in the world.'

'It's made me cry. I had to listen a lot to like it, though.'

'Haven't been able to have any others, almost certainly as a direct result of losing it. Some kind of . . . damage. Lessens the chances, anyway.'

'You believe that?'

'Medical expert's opinion, not mine.'

He didn't like the idea of her sharing in something so personal to him and Milly, and yet he'd deliberately made it public. A toddler wanting something it couldn't have was screaming at a fair distance, but it grated. It was astonishingly like someone in extreme agony. It stopped and started like a machine. It must be terrible to be next to it, he thought. He brushed a coppery leaf out of his hair.

'I'm not going to say we haven't been trying, either,' he added, feeling the tips of his ears go hot.

'No problem.'

She took a drag on her cigarette with pouted lips and blew the smoke out immediately. The sunlight, filtered by the willow, was dropping its spare cash on her hair. It was extremely long and so light, lifting in the barely perceptible breeze. Naked, she could still conceal her breasts with it, he thought.

Lathering them.

'Our son, his damage was —' she searched for the word — '*provoked.*'

The 'our' was significant. It probably meant the father was still involved.

'You're talking about his foot?'

'Yeah. A lot better now, a lot straighter. Plaster and braces and doctors, when he was tiny. It'll always be a bit short and stiff. You know? The sports drugs provoked it.'

'Sports drugs?'

'From when I was a gymnast in Soviet times. I told you this.'

'Oh, yeah.'

All she'd told him, in fact, was that she'd been forced to take performance-enhancing drugs and maybe that's why she looked like a teenager. She no longer looked like a teenager, though.

'I didn't vomit up enough, that stuff. Maybe I'll get cancer, soon.'

Jack frowned, picturing a grey labyrinth and white-coated figures with needles. 'Seriously? It was the drugs? What kind of drugs?'

'Hormonal shit. Friends have researched it, the chemicals we swallowed, and they are looking at their own death, you know? A lot of people in my team, their kids come out damaged, or even dead. We were little weapons in the Cold War. It wasn't sport. We had to be armed. We had to win, at all cost. Politics.'

She sucked deeply on her cigarette. He wished she didn't smoke, it wouldn't help the cancer thing.

'How's your mother?' she asked, which he appreciated, still trying to absorb this sports-and-drugs thing, this after-effect, this damage. Like an old abandoned factory still leaking its poisons into the ground. An interference from the past. He didn't feel he'd been sympathetic enough, but the moment was over, as moments tended to be.

'She's ill, actually,' he replied. 'Not good. Blind.'

She nodded. 'You have the music,' she said.

'Me?'

'*Your* music. Mr Davenport told me that you don't write much, but I think what you write is pretty nice.'

He was disappointed in her 'pretty nice'. As the sentence was unfolding in her soft, foreign lilt he had anticipated something more.

'Er, pretty nice.'

'Yeah. It's OK. I bought all your CDs.'

'All three of them. Surprised you could find them.'

'I hunted them right up, of course. I know all the gigs you've done, all the lectures. All the ones that popped up over the Internet. I've been following you. You gave me a false name, but I searched on the web for Jack and Hayes and Arvo Pärt. It took a few minutes to find you, because this is six years ago. But it found you. In a few *minutes*. Jack Middleton! Hey! There he is! Nice photo, leaning on the back of a plastic chair and looking cool. No problem getting your address. I cried a lot. You know what name you gave me?'

It had been off-the-cuff, scribbled down at the last moment. He shook his head.

She was looking at him and her eyes had filmed over again. The bench wasn't bolted in properly and rocked slightly.

'Stewforth,' she said. 'Jack Stewforth.'

'OK, OK,' he muttered, turning his head away and hoping she wouldn't cry outright. Part of him was relieved, though. He hadn't just been another jerk in a line of shuffling men. 'So that's why,' he said, staring hard at the willow's long tresses in the middle distance, 'you used my friend Howard as a cover. To track me. To approach me.'

'I have to know what Jaan's father is doing,' she said, firmly.

'Er, hang on,' he began, thinking she was ribbing him.

'It's like Kaplinski says, by the way – you know, that poet I kept reading to you? He says, a poem is like taking a walk within yourself. When I look you up, it's like that kind of poem.'

'Slight problem: Jaan's not my son.'

'He is.'

'Kaja, I *know* he isn't. In fact.'

'I know you *think* he isn't. But he is. And not maybe. Now I'm looking at you, I can tell you straight. Not maybe. For sure.'

'Um, sorry, but you told Howard – I mean, Howard Davenport told me – that Jaan was definitely the son of a – banjo player. Who liked Cajun. Your shark man.'

Jack felt he was looking at a disturbed, inveterate liar: straight into the untrustworthy depths of the eyes that filled up all their space.

'I said that because I was so angry.'

'With whom?'

'With you. For spying.'

'Spying?'

'For listening in like a spy. Why didn't you plant a micro-phone? Huh?' She shook her head as he tried to look as if someone was stepping hard on his toes – comically, painfully guilty. 'It's so pathetic and so primitive, looking into a keyhole. Yeah, I saw you there. I was really angry.'

'You saw me?'

'I knew it was you. When Mr Davenport mentioned the father, his eyes went like this, over towards the door. Just a flick. And then I saw the eye, in the keyhole. Of course it was you. Who else?'

Jack looked amazed. And so she snorted, contemptuously.

'You don't think I haven't grown up with this? We used to sing songs in the dacha. Estonian songs. They were forbidden. Nationalist agitation. You know?' He nodded, again not really able to imagine it. 'Folk songs, beautiful songs. Forbidden. We had to know if someone was listening, hiding. Then we sang, but in fear, and secret. But we sang. For me, a keyhole is really giant. I can see everything behind it. A change of light, a sound, a shadow in it, a movement. A lynx eye, I have. You see? An Estonian lynx. You think I'm really stupid, or what? We had to read people's eyes and faces all the time. Your own father or sister or uncle can be a spy. Your best friend. All the time we were reading faces. For lies.'

Jack couldn't reply; he was internally rolling himself into a tight, defensive, woodlouse ball.

The water and the grass and the trees darkened abruptly as the sun went in. An armed battalion of nerves rushed his chest. Really, it was because of Jaan.

He had a son. And he'd known it all along, really. And now he had to take some kind of responsibility. He took a deep breath.

'OK,' she said, before he could speak. 'So now you know.

You are his dad. For definite. Because there was no one else. I have my – dignity. I waited for you. I wrote letters –'

'We moved house,' said Jack, feebly.

He'd torn the forwarded letters up. Without opening them.

'Look,' he said, as Kaja was shaking her head again in contempt, 'I'm going to have a bash. At being a father. But I want to stay with – with my wife. Milly.'

Kaja looked at him, her eyes reconnoitring the surface of his face as if she was not sure of her ground. 'What about me?' she said.

'You?'

She laughed, pressing the sides of her face, her cigarette burning between her fingers. 'Shit, this is so *mad*.'

'What's mad?'

'You wrote me the wrong number and address when you left Tallinn. You gave me the wrong damn name. You shouted something I didn't get, then you waved like you were on a ship going a really long way away. You didn't want me to follow, Mr Stewforth, but I have followed.'

'I said I'd drop you a line. That means write to you.'

'Another low-rent lie,' she said.

He bit his lip, feeling annoyance mixed in with the remorse. He watched the smoke rise from his cigarette as it burned back. Perhaps the American lecturer had taught her that 'low rent'.

'I got in the way of your life,' he murmured. 'Your plans. Ruined things for you. Can I say I'm sorry?'

'I still *studied*,' she said, as if surprised. 'My parents helped with Jaan, after a couple of years, you know? I did Russian and French and English. I'm beginning my doctorate at the University of Westminster in October.'

'Wow,' said Jack, vaguely alarmed.

'It's on the aesthetics of Russian Futurism before the Revolution. They threw out symbolism for phonetics, by the way – the linguistics of the language. The *music* of it, the stuff poets didn't put in because it was too, you know, like grinding . . .'

'Harsh?'

'Yeah, harsh. It's real fascinating. Imagine – a native Estonian studying the Russians! That's integration. Really forgiving. Well, it just got a bit delayed, that's all. I was married for a year. This guy called Krohn, Estonian-Finnish. Building a supermarket on Haaremaa. I left him. He was into really bad stuff, I didn't know it. Money stuff, not drugs or girls or all that crap. Money laundry? He got kicked off back to Finland.'

She pulled on her cigarette again, keeping the smoke in for several moments. Jack was impressed by her history. She had somehow seen more than him. He couldn't imagine it. Mr Krohn, with wide shoulders and a loud tie and a broad Finnish face.

'You kept his name?'

'I was happy for a few months.'

'It's good about your studies, though.'

She was happy with Mr Middleton for only a few days. Ten, maybe. A thin little voice in him declared: *I'm paying for this too dearly. All I did was score with her.* But he shoved the voice aside and leaned forward, resting his elbows on his knees. The bench rocked again: it was irritating, it didn't help matters.

'Some things are always good,' she said, eventually.

'I did try to find your place in Bounds Green, on the legendary North Circular.'

'We have the back room,' said Kaja, looking down at her sandalled feet. Her toenails were painted a cheery green, like a joke. 'It only shakes when the really big trucks pass. The toilet is always full of shit. But toilets weren't too good back home, either. Jaan gets looked after by a girl from Latvia when I'm at work and there's no school.'

'You pay her?'

'I give her English lessons. Exchange. She's a waitress.'

'In the same hotel?'

'I work for an agency. I work in two or three different hotels. Big ones. The pay is really low. Under eight thousand a year.'

'Cleaner?'

She laughed. 'They call it room attendant. I did three weeks, it was shit, then they asked me to be a receptionist. I look OK, I speak English and Russian and French. *Les jardins, comme des femmes, semblent faire leur toilette pour les fêtes de l'été.*'

'Not bad. Baudelaire?'

'Flaubert. *Madame Bovary.* I had to translate the whole paragraph into Estonian one time. It's a beautiful line. It's music, you know? And Flaubert is going to be in my paper, too.'

He stroked his chin, nodding, not knowing what to do with his hands. 'What I really remember about *Madame Bovary* is bracken getting caught in the stirrups.'

'Huh?'

He tucked his hands under his thighs and the bench jolted. 'That, um, that bit before they make love in the wood, when they're riding along, she and her lover? And he has to lean over to get the bracken out of her stirrup? I was thinking of writing an opera called *Madame Bovary*. I was seventeen. Really, really ambitious. I had no idea!'

'Anyway, I'm a receptionist,' she said, and he was conscious of having upstaged her with his twaddle about bracken, his early ambition, his precociousness.

'I'm glad you're not a cleaner.'

'Except I'm sick of guys coming to the desk and trying to pick me up.'

Jack nodded, ears reddening.

'You know,' she went on, 'as a cleaner you have to check the tissue level with your finger?'

'The *tissue* level?' he snorted.

'Well, why not? If they're too low in the box you throw it out and put a new one. If a guest finds no tissues in the box, it's the worst thing, apparently. For the guest and for you.'

'Really?'

'Worse than a mark in the toilet. You get fired. I looked in the garbage bags in the corridor and what did I see? That most of the boxes we dumped had half their tissues still in. A big waste, huh? I thought of the answer. Can you think what?'

He couldn't quite work out whether this was serious or not.

Maybe it was some elaborate metaphor. He savoured the movement of her mouth as she talked.

'Nope, sorry.'

'And you think you're a genius?'

'I wish I did.'

'OK. You have a red line to say it's running out, like on the ticket roll for the cash machines in stores. This line could be printed on the last fifteen or let's say twenty tissues inside the box. Then we don't need to use the finger test and there's no waste. It's a great idea, huh? That's how I'm going to be rich.'

He nodded, feeling vague and solitary.

'Pretty good idea, Kaja. Listen, until that happens I'd like to get you out of your crap place. I mean, support you, obviously. Even if we don't do a DNA test.'

'A DNA test?'

He waved his hand about, dismissively. 'Just a formality. Check I *am* the father. A legal thing. I mean, I trust you, personally speaking, but I think there's this kind of formal process . . .' He scratched his hair, uncomfortable.

She looked at him and said: 'You haven't understood me. He's yours. Your son.'

'I know, but –'

'*Fuck* your formal test.'

He was shocked, and his face burned. He stared out at the lake, where something – maybe a large fish – had seemed to leap out of the water and back again. He didn't want to look at her as she berated him, rocking the bench.

'Do you think I'm also a liar? I didn't have any man after you, not for two years. You know what it's like, with a baby? Full time? You don't say anything? How can you do this? I've not one moment stopped loving you. I listen to your music and I look at your pictures on the Net and I love you even more. I've had your baby. He needs his daddy, doesn't he, now? You know?' His head was bowed. He gave it a tiny little nod, as if the cogs in his neck had seized up. 'I was so *nervous* of meeting you and now I'm screwing it. But Jaan *needs* his daddy.

Huh? What do you think of this?' she insisted, loud enough and intensely enough that a passing elderly couple looked over at them, faintly amused by this picturesque tiff in the park.

His head stayed bowed. The ground was intricately detailed between his feet: innocent little stones, dust and earth, a crushed bottletop, the torn Snickers wrapper like a broken flower.

'How's the fox?' he asked, very quietly, at the ground. 'That fox in the cage? Without your father?'

'The fox?' She gave a short, harsh laugh. 'Oh, still there. My mom feeds him. She calls it Mik-mik. So it's got a name, now.'

'Well, you should have called it Jack,' he said.

He spent a lot of the next few days shuttling between Hampstead and Hayes, accompanying his father to Hillingdon Hospital. They'd catch the bus opposite the Travel Inn, a few minutes' walk from home.

Jack was amazed at how Hayes, like so many other places, kept on declining despite being surrounded by wealth, by a trillion-pound consumer boom, by an England soggy with credit. The familiar Waitrose had gone, replaced by a huge Lidl the colour of waste water. Dunstan's the greengrocer's and Dagley's for hardware and Hepworth's the tailor's and the corner shop where they'd slice your butter off the main chunk and slap it into shape with wooden palettes: they'd all long gone, of course, but now it was mostly naff boutiques, fluo-bedecked cost-cutters and grimy games arcades – if there was anything at all. The Uxbridge Road walloped through with even more merciless-ness, not much better than the North Circular. The tatty pub he would go to as an underage schoolboy was now a dolled-up chain bar with a permanent gaggle of what looked like junkies outside, dressed in burberries and bright white trainers, leaning on the Happy Hour board. Unfortunately, Jack and his father had to pass it on the way to the bus stop. They kept to the far side of the street but were ritually jeered, C-words and F-words falling like hail.

'Used to it from the army,' was all his father said.

'I'd like to, but I don't think I'd better risk saying anything back.'

'That's just what the yobbos want, John. They'd break your fingers if you were *lucky*. We ought to bring back national service. Get them digging holes to sleep in under driving rain in November.'

Looking at him sideways, Jack saw a great anger well hidden, the vein at the temple thick below the cap.

'Maybe it was always like that,' he ventured. 'We've just forgotten.'

'Rubbish. This lot are subhuman. And most of them aren't even coloureds.'

His mother was out of immediate danger but, rather worryingly, had moved up to the penultimate floor, the sixth, which was Geriatric. Above Geriatric, like the afterlife right at the top, was Children. Above Children was the sky. She was thinner but perky. His father was exhausted. Nobody seemed to remember she was blind. It was never the same nurses and their grasp of English was imperfect. The sister put a big sign saying BLIND PATIENT on the bed-end but it made no difference: a nurse would hold out a glass of water for her to take, or nod instead of acknowledging her request in words.

'It's cultural,' his father said. 'They're not taught their Ps and Qs wherever they come from.'

'One or two are nice,' said his mother, leaning back and sighing against her pillows.

The wounds where the screws fixed the skull brace to her bone were infected. There were concerns about MRSA, but no action was being taken apart from the odd wipe with disinfectant. The place struck Jack as a kind of huge monument to illusion, especially up here in Geriatric. If you went beyond the surface, you hit an existential despair as hard as concrete. And there was no pause: death would wait for no man. He kept thinking, however, of that little Chinese chap with the plastic bag, standing in the way of a column of tanks in Tiananmen Square.

Jack began to smell of the hospital, even after he'd showered and changed his clothes. It had seeped beneath his skin. Even Milly detected it. The journey was a pain and he couldn't concentrate enough to read on the train. All he could think of was Kaja and Jaan. Especially Jaan. He was juggling with eggs, and they weren't either wooden or hard-boiled. He'd tried to phone since their meeting in Regent's Park, but Kaja had not been friendly. Uncompromising, she was.

The lakeside meeting had ended unsatisfactorily, to say the least:

'So? What d'you think?'

'I don't know, Kaja. I've got my life here. My wife's, um, expecting a baby,' he added, convincing himself it was half true.

They had made love again yesterday. Milly hadn't had PMT, after all. She'd drunk a lot of wine and relaxed and they'd done it on the sofa, in front of *Newsnight* and its report on Afghanistan.

'So?'

The ducks were suddenly raucous, hysterical, like an introductory drum roll.

'So. I'm keen not to . . . We can agree on some sort of . . .'

'What?'

'As I said,' Jack pressed on, conscious that he had to get down to the real McCoy or go on slipping about; 'well, I'd really like to support Jaan. Financially. I'll work it out.'

Kaja stared at the ducks on the lake. A little boy was trying to shoo them away with angry jerks of his arm. No, he was feeding them. The bread peppered the surface and the ducks pivoted about. The boy's throw was wild and some of the bread went behind his head. His mother came up, holding his arm and spoiling it. Kaja was watching them, her mouth puckered at the corner. Now it didn't look like a smile, it looked like annoyance.

'Getting you out of that crap flat and into something decent, for a start,' Jack repeated. A woman in a jacket like Milly's appeared, setting his pulse rate into woodpecker mode. Milly might happen to be in Regent's Park. She might have cancelled her Devon trip and be heading down this path right now. Easily. Or someone he knew. Andrew Beak. Abigail Staunton. Or one of Milly's friends. Olive Nicholson.

'Money,' Kaja said, nodding.

'Eh?'

'Not too painful.'

'Don't follow.'

'You'll catch up with it.'

Jack didn't mean to shrug, but he did. Kaja was foreign, he thought. Locked away on a Soviet island for most of her life. Her English irritated him; it wasn't as good as she thought it was. On the other hand, sometimes his own voice sounded awful to him. Flat and uninteresting. Too comfortable with its Englishness. Middlesex nasal. He wished he had a foreign accent.

'What I want,' Kaja said, carefully, 'is my son to have his father.'

'That's what he will have. I promise. I can see him. We'll be all Canadian and decent about this.'

She looked straight into his eyes. He was saying stupid things, or sensible things badly.

'And me?'

'Yup,' he said, looking away; 'I can see you too. To talk.'

Bevvy! someone shouted, like an alarm call.

'What does that mean?'

'Just stay friends. Just friends.' He felt he was sounding like a teenager on another bench in another park. He was forty-three. He fixed his jaw and tried to feel forty-three.

Bev-vay! Echoing over the water. Self-conscious.

She nodded. 'That's nice for you,' she said. 'Everything's real nice for you. You know he's being teased at school? His foot? And for his English? The other kids teasing him? He's unhappy. And me? Why am I here? Because of Jaan. Because of you.'

Jack spread his hands modestly, his eyes glancing off hers as she stared. He wondered why he wrote music. He wondered why he lived at all. The little boy was now screaming and being dragged off by his mother on tiny rotating legs, the ducks keeping their distance.

'The thing is, if my wife finds out about Jaan . . .' He gave a demonstrative sigh, rubbing his forehead with his fingers. It'll be worse for everyone, he wanted to say. But his voice wouldn't come. For the first time he regretted entering the Café Magnolia six years ago. Magnolia? That wasn't the name. Christ, he'd forgotten the name! Marjoram? Margarine! Majestic! He wanted to laugh. He was going mad. Who had led who on? There's the ecstatic, and there's just getting on with life. You can't build a life on the expectation of the ecstatic.

'That's real nice for you,' she said, as if she hadn't heard him.

She then got up impatiently, shaking the loose bench so that Jack thought it was tipping over backwards for a second and took evasive action and felt idiotic, thrusting half out and flinging his hands forward.

She threw her cigarette stub on the ground. He could see she was crying. She stared at the stub smoking on the path with red, glistening eyes, hands thrust in her back pockets. Her back was so straight, a real prize gymnast's back and shoulders. A passing trio of goofy, round-shouldered delinquents whistled at her. She didn't even flinch. Jack avoided meeting their gaze as they looked back, whooping, from under the back strap of their caps. A boy passed the other way, his iPod turned up so loud it was audible, like a distant aviary of parrots. Magyar. Mohammed. Café Mandible.

'What did you want, then?' he asked, leaning forward, elbows on his knees. 'Hoping for? In the way of . . . more?'

What she'd then answered kept echoing in his head for days, especially in the hospital, sitting next to his mother:

'To take the nails out of my hands and feet.'

Milly was seeing a lot of Claudia Grove-Carey. Roger, having written off her car and given himself a knock on the head, complained of dizzy spells. This meant Claudia did everything while Roger stayed most of the day in a deckchair in the garden.

By the end of the week in which Jack had met Kaja in the park, Roger was under observation – Claudia had said 'under surveillance' by mistake – in the Royal Free. Deprived of alcohol, he was giving the nurses a hard time. Work was not so frantic, it seemed, that Milly couldn't take the odd afternoon off and look after the baby while Claudia 'got out'.

Milly would come back home and burst into tears. She reckoned there was nothing lovelier in life than looking after a baby, than holding it, than kissing its head through the soft hair. She had everything, she said, and she had nothing. Jack tried to console her, but very little remained in his batteries after the hospital visits.

He thought about what they had done in the kitchen a few days back and felt bad that he'd slipped up. Maybe their kid had ended up drying in Milly's hand. Charitably, she had said it was her fault, and drunk too much over the fish pie. The petits pois had been as soft as school peas.

The first proper meeting between himself and Jaan was to take place on Monday, so Jack would have found the weekend a strain anyway. And it was spent either entertaining ('killing off', as Milly put it) those they owed meals to, or accumulating further debt. Milly felt exhausted so the killing off was done in restaurants, as was currently acceptable among their set, while the debt was incurred yet again at the indefatigable Nicholsons' after shuffling in the crush at the Matisse exhibition, where the smell of ageing bodies and stale perfume reminded Jack of the hospital.

The whole process seemed to consume the entire two days, leaving nothing to themselves. Exotic holidays in places only aid workers or film crews would ever visit a few years back were still being unrolled in tedious detail. The Hewlett-Arkwells had spent a fortnight in August walking in Nepal with their three young kids, casually referring to it as if they'd been on a weekend excursion to the Lakes. Jack felt dull and inadequate. Very small potatoes, as his mother would have put it. An older couple at the Nicholsons' had an antique wooden yacht and had just sailed to the Canaries and back. They were a coppery red all over, slicked with self-esteem.

'The trouble is,' the wife drawled, 'everyone these days is so obsessed with money, money, money. There's so much more to life than money. Well-being, for instance.'

And everyone had agreed, although Jack had said (keeping up his reputation with the Nicholsons): 'Did your boat come free, then?'

Which Milly thought was rude, informing him later that the couple had lost their only daughter through drugs.

Milly, of course, was against flying and tourism or even using the car for anything but essentials. But it wasn't just that: it was also lethargy. Jack couldn't be bothered. It was the whole organisational thing. Tickets, advance booking, the lot. The only area he vaguely hankered after was the islands of the White Sea, for reasons he'd long forgotten; maybe a book about Russia from childhood. Haaremaa had got close.

To cap it, they went to a concert at the Wigmore Hall on Sunday evening – only because Jack had faithfully promised Barnaby he'd go. Barnaby was an old friend from College days who played harpsichord and was on the edge of a nervous breakdown. Milly fell asleep. The performance was dry and below par – almost at typewriter level. Afterwards, Jack gave Barnaby a hug and said it was fantastic.

He was very nervous about the meeting with Jaan, in case it proved a let-down for both parties. Unexpectedly, this proved to be the case.

Kaja had suggested Kensington Gardens, by the Peter Pan statue, straight after the viola lesson. Jack had bought a big red plastic football which turned out to be irritatingly light: it was a blustery autumnal day and the ball kept curving up and away. Jaan's club foot meant he found the game frustrating instead of pleasurable. Kaja watched from the trees for a while then slipped away.

He'd forgotten to ask whether she'd told Jaan that Jack was his father, so he didn't quite know how to play it. In a film, he'd have given him a hug, but he didn't dare do that until *he* knew whether *Jaan* knew.

Watching Jaan struggle to kick the ball, he decided to change the game. He came up closer.

'Let's play catch!'

Jaan was hopeless at catching, too. He didn't seem to be enjoying himself. He looked round for his mother. Jack walked over to the ball and tapped it from palm to palm, fist to fist, but the ball seemed to have a life of its own in the gusts. The boy smiled briefly and then stopped himself. Jack began to scratch at the fluo-green price tag, without much success. It was too hot and the stickiness stayed. The child squinted up at him.

'Do you know cricket?' Jack said.

Jaan shrugged. 'Kaja? My mum?'

He'd already got a trace of Enfield. 'She's gone for a little walk.'

'Why?'

'Because it's sunny.'

He tried to catch Jaan's eye but the boy was deep in thought. He evidently didn't like looking people in the eye, or being looked at. It was a kind of extreme shyness. He was a sad little boy, in many ways. But then a smile would break across his face and the sadness seemed like something else: a deep interiority, perhaps. Maybe he *was* a prodigy. Maybe he'd taken after his father. Jack had never been able to kick balls or catch them properly, either.

There was a boisterous group of French schoolkids around Peter Pan, otherwise he'd have shown Jaan the statue close up. Instead, they watched the model boats on the Round Pond. Jaan wouldn't take Jack's hand, but just stood in a very absorbed way, standing in his jeans and bright red sweatshirt near the water, following a raucous little speedboat as it circled manically at the behest of a round-shouldered man in khaki fatigues.

It was weird for Jack, seeing himself as a little boy. He had a sudden vision of Jaan as fulfilling a potential that the father had not fulfilled. The father? Yes, he supposed he was the father, that Kaja wasn't fooling around. Unless she was a fantasist, disturbed in some way.

He felt a wall between himself and this boy who was meant to be his son – a gauze screen between them. A tiny element of repulsion, seeing his own offspring, seeing himself reproduced. He was reasonably sure this would not have been the case if this was his son by Milly, all above board and official. Here he was in a forced, artificial situation. He was behaving. He was defusing a potentially lethal bomb, wire by wire. But there were an awful lot of wires.

The two of them returned to the lawn by the statue and, much to both parties' relief, Kaja came walking across the grass. Jaan scampered up to hug her, burying his face in her thighs as if totally relieved. She spoke to her son in Estonian, smiling through the long vowels.

'We had fun,' said Jack. 'He's a champ.'

They arranged to meet in a week's time, same place.

'Maybe more after that,' said Kaja, her eyes unnerving in the sunlight.

'Let's see how it goes,' Jack replied, ruffling Jaan's hair.

'How it goes,' Kaja repeated, looking down at her son as he smoothed his hair back. 'Very English. Very practical.'

'Softly-softly.'

'Would you like piano lessons with Jack?' she asked Jaan. 'In his house? Piano's really useful.'

The boy nodded. Although Jack knew this would come up at some point, and had considered mentioning it himself to Jaan, he still thought: that was a very crafty move. Kaja was dressed in torn-off shorts and another cut-away top, but didn't seem to be cold. She smelt duskily of sweat, not the amber-gris perfume of six years ago. It would be good to hold her tight again. He felt himself sinking into the possibility while she said something to Jaan in Estonian. A large girl walked past with *Vacation are the Best Moment of Year* on her pink top.

Jaan nodded a second time. His mother turned to Jack and

said: 'He'd love you to teach him piano. When? He's free from three thirty.'

Whenever my wife isn't in.

'Tuesdays are good. I teach another boy at five thirty. Four o'clock? Four o'clock on Tuesday coming?'

'That's tomorrow.'

'So it is.'

She squinted at him again, with her hand on her hip and the other in Jaan's hand. Jaan was experimenting with his eyebrows, moving them up and down, and wasn't listening.

'You're not the same,' she said, softly. 'You know? Maybe that wasn't you in Estonia.'

'My identical twin,' said Jack, peculiarly hurt.

She shook her head. 'Twins are the same.'

'Which version of me do you prefer?'

She gave a snort of a laugh. 'Certainly not this English one,' she said. 'But maybe that is the *true* one. See you tomorrow,' she added.

She walked away before his crestfallen face could summon a voice, with Jaan limping next to her as if a ball and chain was attached to his little leg. Jack knew what that ball and chain was.

There was no such thing as history. Only legacy.

He hadn't quite worked out what Kaja was up to. If she was up to anything. This made any defensive strategy difficult to plot. What he did feel was completely exposed, which was why he'd not even kept Howard up to date. And Howard was off to Sicily soon, to teach on a summer course in front of a mass of bougainvillea, roughly where the Cyclops had squashed Acis.

He tended not to go to Hayes on Mondays and Tuesdays or most weekends, because of his own spots of teaching: he was in a routine, and now Kaja was part of that routine.

There was a ring on the doorbell the next day at precisely four o'clock.

'Kaja, hi! Hi, Jaan!'

He was playing hearty, English, normal. There was a taxi at the gate, a plump bloke standing by it with folded arms.

'I don't have cash,' she said. 'He won't accept my card.'

'No problem.'

He stepped out into the sun. Unfortunately, Edward Cochrane was in his porch, talking to the painter-decorator as the latter was packing up. The two men were ogling Kaja as they chatted. Jack went out of the little iron gate and paid the taxi driver, whose various bellies poked through his velvety shirt and made Jack think of the front of a hovercraft.

He waved coolly to Edward as he came back. Maybe he'd lost his job as well as his wife.

'I'll pay you,' she said.

'No you won't. So, you'll pick him up in an hour?' They were safely out of sight in the hallway.

'Or I can wait here,' she suggested, as if she found his question ridiculous. 'It looks like you have a bit of space.'

'OK. There's shade in the garden. It's really warm for the end of September. Worrying.'

Afterwards, he felt awful about this. He'd been so royally welcomed on Haaremaa. He was treating her like any mum. He spent ten minutes making her a cup of tea, spreading Milly's bland hay-tasting sugar-free biscuits on a plate, conscious of the size and wealth of his home in which he was play-acting his own life. Kaja said very little about the house, mainly making comments to keep Jaan happy. Jack felt an inch away from the notion that they were a family, this was their home, and that Milly did not exist. It was terrifying. At the same time, he felt resentful that she'd wheedled her way in so deeply. She was in charge. He couldn't think what to do about it.

Marjorie phoned while the kettle was boiling, thinking her daughter was at home. She'd gone to sleep on the upper lawn, she explained, and thought it was later than it was. The sun had come round and she'd got roasted in her sleep like a sausage. He put the phone down with a sigh. She'd called him 'Jacko'.

'Your mum?'

313

'No,' Jack replied, dodging Kaja's knowing smile. He found it intrusive. He showed her out into the garden, hoping Edward wasn't in his.

'This is a *typical* English garden, Jaan,' she said. She repeated it in Estonian. Or that's what Jack assumed. She said something else and Jaan stepped onto the lawn and solemnly performed, as best he could, a forward roll. It was all legs. Jack and Kaja clapped.

'Gymnast in the making,' Jack smiled, without perceiving the irony until he'd said it. 'By the way,' he added, in a murmur, 'have you told him yet?'

'No. Not yet. I'm waiting to see it. How it goes.'

Jaan stood up straight with his head bent down and studied the soft grass, frowning. Jack's heart gave a little fish-leap. That's what I used to do, he thought, on our little handkerchief of grass in Hayes. Because when you're five you're closer to it and you can see things going on in there without having to go on your knees. There wasn't ever much going on in our grass, he thought – not after Dad had been at it.

Kaja sat in a chair on the lawn, reading a linguistics tome in Estonian, while Jack taught Jaan up in the lair. Any minute Milly might open the door, although she wasn't due back from a meeting in Hackney until seven or eight. He found the lesson difficult – not because of Jaan, who responded well in his quiet five-year-old's way, but because of this terror that Milly might come back early from Hackney. The boy's small fingers were flat on the keys, splayed out, and Jack had to curve them for him. When he touched Jaan's fingers, showing him the curve, positioning them, they were like the stems of flowers. Clara Knowles had touched his own ten-year-old's fingers and said they were like wood anemones, because they were never still. Wood anemones are also called windflowers, she would say, stroking his fingers between the knuckles. Jack had looked this up in his *Ladybird Book of Wild Flowers* and found almost the same sentence as Clara had used. Jack wanted to stroke Jaan's fingers but was a little scared to. He'd met a piano teacher at a London school who said she wasn't allowed to touch her pupils' fingers at all, either to position them or rap them. But Jaan was his son: he had the right to hold his hand, to squeeze it. He very much wanted to squeeze the little hand, but Jaan didn't know Jack was his father. It was a silly situation.

When the lesson was over, Jaan went out to fetch his mother. Jack stayed inside, in the garden room.

'Thank you,' said Kaja. 'He liked it.'

'So did I. I'll call a taxi.'

'No. We'll take the bus.'

'I thought you didn't like to.'

'I don't, much. But I was brought up to handle these fears. How much do I pay you?'

'You must be joking.'

Kaja looked at him as if studying his expression. He felt strangely exhausted.

'OK,' she said. 'Next week, same time?'

'Why not?'

'And Kensington Gardens? Monday, after the viola lesson? He loved that with you, playing the ball.'

'Could be a bit tricky next week,' Jack lied. He wanted to assert some kind of control. He felt as if his control was ebbing away, somehow. But he was touched to hear that Jaan had enjoyed himself. Very pleased, in fact.

'I'll ring? The day before? Sunday?'

'Maybe not a good idea to ring here.'

'I'm only a pupil's mother.'

'Not quite,' said Jack, softly enough so that Jaan couldn't hear.

'Get them younger and younger, don't you?' called Edward, after Jack had seen them out. The newly painted porch was a tasteful shade of yellow, and Edward was admiring it as if he'd been standing there an hour. The painter had gone, with all his clutter. Not for the first time, Jack wished the low hedge that separated the two doors was a lot higher.

'Five's a good age to start,' he answered. He would play it straight. 'Four, even.'

'I was thinking of the mum. Or is she the nanny?'

'The mum.'

'Looked foreign. Where's she from?'

Jack shrugged.

'Latvia or somewhere,' he said.

'Doesn't want a sugar daddy, does she? I could get the show on the road again with her sort.'

'She's taken, I think.'

Edward grunted. 'They all are,' he said. 'That wasn't the prodigy, was it?'

'Prodigy?'

'The one you talked about after the Kenwood do. Remember? Howard's prodigy. Estonian, not Latvian. Made me think I ought to go back there and pick up a wife, actually, you talking about Estonia.'

'Just like that?'

He had the impression that Edward was watching him. 'Women use us, that's the trouble. We're desperate for fanny and they use us. What do you think of the colour?'

'Fine,' said Jack, already in the door.

'Lilian hated yellow!' Edward shouted after him.

Milly said, as he climbed into bed next to her – wanting her very much, wanting to have her in her new cream silk nightie with its enticing ribbony strap over the scoop of each collarbone: 'Edward says you've got a new pupil.'

'Yeah. Howard's prodigy.'

'You didn't tell me. You'd normally tell me.'

'Didn't I?'

He ran his hand like a conjuror's over her slippery silk-hidden breasts, barely making contact, then started on the thighs, taking care not to touch her groin. Milly never liked him to be abrupt with foreplay: she found it sexist. On the other hand, she didn't usually wait long either before getting down to it.

'Maybe it's because of the mother,' she said.

'Eh?'

Although his heart was thudding in his throat, he made sure he carried on faultlessly. He wondered whether she could hear his heart, or feel it.

'Edward said she's a real corker. I quote, of course.'

He gathered his hand in and settled down on his back, totally alarmed but smiling inanely and allowing their shoulders and hips to touch. He felt her fractionally shift away.

'What's Edward trying to do? Get off with you?'

'Why should he want to do that?'

'Everyone wants to get off with you,' said Jack, keeping it light. 'Don't blame them.' He wanted to say: I could kill that bastard neighbour, but held himself back. Not a good move to hate thy neighbour in front of Milly.

She sighed. 'Claudia says Roger's got to have some operation. Relieve pressure on the brain.'

'Oh dear.'

'He might even die.'

'Really?'

He was genuinely surprised.

They were lying on top of the sheets; it was a very warm night for late September. There were still mosquitoes around, a legacy of the Ponds. The mark on the ceiling above Jack's head vanished, then reappeared a few inches away. He couldn't imagine Roger Grove-Carey not being alive.

'It'd be the best thing that could happen to her,' said Milly. 'She's a prisoner, except for when she goes out on parole to Waitrose. She might as well wear a burkha. An incredibly awful thing to say. Where did you tell me your new pupil's from?'

'Eh?'

'Howard's genius? With the beautiful mum?'

'Latvia, I think.'

Milly stared up at the ceiling.

'I thought it was Estonia.'

'Probably. Why did you ask, then?'

'I only just remembered.'

'Estonia. That's right.'

'Weird. That you couldn't remember, when you've actually *been* there.'

'Weird,' said Jack, in an American twang. It came out strangled by the tension in his throat. He could feel Milly's whole body radiating suspicion.

'Do you want to read a bit?' he asked, as coolly as he could, his voice better. He looked at the little slew of books on his bedside table. Milly had given him a massive hardback critical biography of Mozart, but he found it annoying in bed. 'I've finally started on the Mozart,' he lied. 'It's brilliant. I'll take it to the hospital. Dad's buying junk provisions at Lidl. They've knocked down the Waitrose and put up a Lidl. The stuff's dirt cheap but complete junk. The frozen lasagne was a joke. I'll keep myself going with Mozart.'

'Is she the one who phoned up here when you were in Hayes?'

'When I was in Hayes . . .' he repeated, like the beginning of a joke. 'Yeah, I think it was.' He couldn't remember what Kaja had told her, that was the trouble.

'Then she's the Kaja from Estonia,' Milly said. 'That's how she put it on the answerphone.'

'That was to organise the lessons,' said Jack.

'Kaja from Estonia,' Milly repeated. 'Of *course* you knew where she was from. The one doing her thing on Arvo Pärt.'

'Pärt?'

He suddenly remembered: the Pärt thing was his cover. He couldn't even keep track of his own dissemblings. She rolled over and switched her bedside light off. Jack began to rub her back but she twitched it away. He wasn't certain, but he thought he could hear her snuffling.

He switched his own bedside light off and said into the darkness, 'I think I was confused because she's half-Latvian or something. Or Russian. It's like all these Baltic countries, they sort of merge into one. People get them confused with the Balkans, even.' He had no real idea how to play against woman's intu-ition, which always had a spin on it, but he was trying. And since Milly didn't reply, didn't even perform the ritual good-night kiss, he rolled over and waited for sleep, his mouth open in a kind of slow-motion panic. Then he heard Milly murmur, 'Do what you *want* with me.'

'Eh?'

'Pretend I'm a prostitute. Do what you want. Rape me.'

'Mill . . .'

'I mean it. Fuck me stupid. From behind.'

'Really?'

He rolled over to lie against her. She lifted her arm and rested it on her face.

'Have me,' she said, into her arm, as if tearful. 'Rough trade. Eastern European. Your private Estonian ditzy-head. I'll just lie here while you do whatever you *want* with me. Please please please.'

He hoped this wasn't a trap. He hoped – no, guessed – this was another of her strategies, probably suggested by her wacky fertility counsellor with the pseudo-Spanish name. But he didn't mind. It excited him. He lifted her silk nightie clear of her buttocks and pulled down her knickers all the way over her feet and threw them on the floor. She lay there on her side on the top of the sheet as if she was in the tropics. Her body was heavy, sleep-heavy. Her skin was damp and warm as he stroked the hip and the long cooler thigh, then up again to the edge of her breast, the skin taut at the ribs where the breast obeyed gravity, like a stocking with an orange in it. He pressed himself hard against her rump, wiggling to be comfortable, and pushed her nightie higher, fingers lightly playing her nipples on the far side, in the way she liked. Her nipples were squashed close together, so he could palm them both at the same time, a couple of tangerines. Still she didn't move. She was on her side, foetal, head lowered, and he was her twin, knees in the backs of hers. His left elbow hurt, caught under his ribs. He shifted it, unable to find a comfortable spot. Her armpit smelt, not of her swanky natural deodorant, but of London-induced sweat that he breathed in the way you'd breathe in mountain air.

'Do what you *want*,' she insisted, as if through her teeth. 'I'm your *slave*. I'm not in con*trol*. Buttfuck me, you bloody awful *ape*.'

Sometimes he would marvel that, in the privacy of their bed, they actually had the sanctioned right to do this, to do what they did do to each other, to give each other pleasure in pleasuring themselves, turning the heat up mutually, completely spoiling themselves. The very fact of her pleasure, her little shudderings and moanings, would excite him in turn; seeing her edging slowly up to ecstasy through his own little contributions, even in the most animatronic of their baby-making exercises, would in itself work him up. There was something generous in it, almost selfless (or that was the illusion, when in fact it was something evolutionary, probably).

Now, faced with Milly acting dead mutton, he had to try that much harder. A mosquito bit him on the haunch, he slapped it and carried on, his arm stretched over her hip, his fingers working away at the front – on her breasts and on her forehead and on her belly, where the navel had a little frown of lazy flesh over it, these days. He forced her leg lower so he could stroke the fur, the feral heat of it, slipping his hand between the pressed thighs as into a foxhole. It was awkward, and his arm ached. His other arm had gone dead under his weight. He thought she might have made a sound. An ambulance wailed past, leaving its ripples as he poked about. A small night freshness had started to waft over his bare thighbone. Maybe they needed the sheets, after all, but he'd leave it.

He was ready to pitch in and guzzle, now. The wacky fertility counsellor referred to penetration as 'the moment of integration'. Tonight this crucial moment was more self-conscious than usual, because of her inertness – he pictured the mating of beasts and thought of pig farms, then of something Milly had said over supper, about the global grocery business, about Asda being part of Wal-Mart, their immigrant workers washing Asda salads for peanuts, living in crowded squalor, Milly wanting to take snaps, to risk her neck in a big field near King's Lynn or somewhere. Asda Asda Asda. Asdafuck. Walfuckmartfuckwaaal. He kissed her spine, the knobbly vertebrae, as he pitched forward and back, feeling that familiar, blissful frenzy as something faint trying to get through from a long way away, a kind of distant fizz – but nothing stronger, none of that overwhelming force which swept everything else aside, including stray thoughts of Wal-Mart and the pins and needles in his awakening arm and the cooling night air over his skin.

He was relieved when she moved her head upwards on the pillow and began to sigh, to make little grunting noises in her throat, to say 'Oh' as his movements on her made her distinctive, lovely, fine-boned du Crane profile shift up and down, her thin-nish shoulders bared enticingly from the silk, exposing the dot of tiny black mole by the BCG jab, the scoop of the clavicle where water would always pool in the shower. He loved his wife. He loved the fact that she was forty-one. He loved having sex with her. He loved her heritage blood. He loved the way her poshness showed through and the fact that she was so rich and yet he could be doing this with her, the whiff like stables thickening from under her arm, the lemony homeopathic toothpaste on her breath.

'Do it, do it,' she said, her eyes still closed, her face thrust up on the pillow, her fingers scratching her exposed neck. 'But don't *talk*.'

He hadn't said a word, in fact. Unless they were so close, these days, she could read his thoughts.

He failed to deliver, in the end. He had to stop, it was no good. Milly, however, had yelped and screeched as if being murdered, and for longer than usual. Jack thought this was followed by a muffled thump on the wall, Edward's side, but it might have been his thumb next to his ear on the pillow.

'Sorry,' he said.

'Sustainable yield,' she murmured, smiling faintly. 'Rapid renewables. Life-cycle cost.'

'I'm really sorry. Maybe it doesn't work when I rape you.'

'It does for the Grove-Careys.'

'I don't think that's rape,' said Jack, rather shocked at her flippancy. He was exhausted. He felt he'd been squeezed dry in some way.

'*Think* whatever you like,' Milly said, so quietly it was almost a breath. 'Men always have done. But don't think you can *do* whatever you like.'

She settled again, without a goodnight kiss, under the sheet. Jack left it. He thought it best not to query what she meant, not aloud. He didn't get to sleep for a long time, and it wasn't only the sudden coolness of the night air on his shoulders.

'It's going to be very tricky. My wife's very suspicious. The neighbours. This mustn't all blow up in our faces. For Jaan's sake.'

'For yours?'

'For yours, too.'

'You care about *me*, do you?'

'Kaja, of course I do.'

The connection wavered under static. Her voice came back, stronger.

'Same time in the park, with Jaan? Monday?'

'Sure. That's no problem. But not coming to the house.'

'So it's just once a week?'

'To begin with.'

'He loved his lesson with you. He doesn't stop talking about it.'

'Let's start with just the park and footie and stuff, OK?'

'That's not enough for Jaan.'

'It's better than nothing, Kaja. I can take him to the Toy Museum and the London Eye and things. We'll work out the money this week.'

'Pay me away, you mean?'

'Eh? Say that again.'

'Nice for you. See you in the park. By Peter Pan.'

She put the phone down before he had time to reply. He was nettled. He was definitely beginning to find life a bit of an egg-juggling act, something he wasn't used to.

He pressed his tongue on the rubbery soapishness of a wine gum. Lime. His least favourite. He was sure they were putting more sugar in.

He wasn't used to it at all, no.

Somehow, grey Hayes had blended into the sweeping lawns and beeswaxed floors of the Royal College, and from then on in – it was all fairly easy. Scaffolded by the music world, by Milly and everything she came with, he'd never looked back, or down. He'd spent four or five hours a day practising the piano up to his early twenties. That didn't leave much time to be a wild boy, to roam, to knock up against the hardness. Now it was too late to learn.

He was quite glad of the hospital, it took his mind off things. He still liked being called 'gorgeous' by Nurse Susan. He read the *Daily Mail* to his mother, avoiding the nasty or the distressing or the right-wing rants (which didn't leave much else), and spooned Actimel into her as once she'd spooned baby food into him. Her wrists were still in plaster, she was sweating under the skull brace, her life was being lived on the fifth circle of hell. 'Lovely weather, but a bit uncomfortable,' she'd say. The wizened old man in the other single room next door cried out like clockwork every two minutes. That was all he did. Raise himself up, shudder, and cry out with unbelievable force and volume as if someone was stabbing him. No one ever closed his door.

'Poor man,' said his mother. 'I do feel sorry for him.'

At home, Jack fiddled about with *Waters of the Trip Hazard* or walked on the Heath, trying to elucidate the score in his head. His lower back ached, he sat badly in his special chiropractic chair, he went on eating too many wine gums and felt sick, anxious and depressed. He reinstated the timp bombs, but as an inner headache. No way could you not have them thumping at some point. The trees were shedding their leaves in warm air, the squirrels looked confused. He heard a cello, in a velvety second position in C, and rewrote the beginning entirely.

Edward Cochrane came round with a bottle of Bollinger's just as Milly got back from work on Friday evening. She invited him through. Jack was reading the Mozart biography at the table under the plum tree at the other end of the garden. Marita was cooking a typical Venezuelan dish, so he had nothing to do. He closed his book as Edward approached over the lawn, but didn't get up. He had shifted, unsurprisingly, from disliking Edward Cochrane to thinking he was of less value than a stepped-in dogpile.

It was the last day of September, but summer hadn't noticed. The falling leaves were an irrelevance.

'What's this in aid of?'

'I only drink champagne these days,' said Edward.

Milly pulled up two chairs. She believed in loving thy neighbour, whatever.

'We need glasses, Jack.'

'Couldn't you have got them on the way?'

'You want me to get them.'

'No no. I'll get them.'

'I'll wait to open it,' said Edward. 'Gagging for it though I am.'

Marita was singing to herself in the kitchen, in Spanish. Things smelt good through the hatch. The extractor fan wheezed away – he was supposed to have seen to cleaning its filter a year ago. He fished out the glasses from the dresser in a little threnody of clear crystal notes. On his way back, stepping onto the long lawn, Jack heard someone hammering. It was his own blood, doing something funny in his ears.

Edward popped the bottle and slopped the coruscating foam into the glass with practised ease. A car alarm was whining over the sluggish air, calling its master.

'Here's to wine, women and song,' said Edward.

'Here's to incredibly sexist men who bring bubbly,' said Milly.

'Cheers,' said Jack. 'Here's to climate change. Allowing us this.'

'Puh-lease,' Milly said.

'And to absent loved ones,' added Edward, with a sniff.

They drank.

'Heard from her?' asked Milly.

Edward shook his head. 'Me wants the address of your corker, Jack,' he said. 'Pronto.'

'My corker?'

'The Estonienne. Bound to be skint. Even if she's not on the game.'

'On the game?'

'Don't be drippy. By the way, did you read about her compatriot, this Estonian prossy who thought she was marrying a seventy-two-year-old squillionaire in Surrey, who turned out not to be? Lived in a loathsome little rented flat. Way below the poverty line, probably. She stabbed him when the cash ran out. Spent it on furs and jewellery. Claims it was an accident. Rather amusing.'

'I hadn't,' said Jack.

Milly was studying her glass.

Edward sniffed and said: 'Run this past the focus group, lads. I'm barely forty, I'm rolling around in my house like a dried pea in a tin, I'm about to be a divorcee, I earn a truly disgusting amount of money, not even counting the bonuses. What do you think? The wee lad just has to pop next door for a tinkle on the ivories. Oh go on, give the nod. Say it's charity. Old Europe meets New Europe. All that.'

Jack said, trying to ease his neck, 'She's already got someone. A French-Canadian banker.'

'Bugger,' said Edward. 'I was honestly quite gone on her. Love at first sight. Plonk.'

'A French-Canadian banker?' repeated Milly.

Jack had no idea where he'd plucked that one from.

'By the name of Raoul,' he nodded. '*French* Canadian. He was a guest at the hotel where she works. There was this conference a few months ago and she was working on the buffet and met him over the pineapple slices. He's trilingual and loves Arvo Pärt.'

Edward and Milly were staring at him.

'And Flaubert,' he added. With every extra embroidering he felt powerful, avenged. 'That bit about bracken in the stirrups. *Madame Bovary*.'

'You seem to know a lot about him,' said Milly.

'Oh piss,' said Edward. 'I really thought it was anything goes, the way she looked in the porch.'

'The way she looked?' Jack felt he might leap on his neighbour and tear his throat out like the zombies in *Shaun of the Dead*, a film he'd seen five times.

'Hungry for love,' said Edward, 'as long as it comes with a big fat nest egg.'

'You're certainly big and fat,' sighed Milly, who'd had a bad day with photovoltaic panels.

'I don't think she'd appreciate your observation, somehow, Edward. It's maybe something to do with self-respect and dignity.'

'Come on, Jack. She's an utter fucking bomb. He drools over her, in secret,' he said, leaning towards Milly rather drunkenly.

Milly said, staring into the shrubbery next to her, 'Edward, grow up.'

'Can't. My father committed suicide when I was fourteen.'

'What?'

Edward looked at each of them in turn with an air of conceited triumph. 'Didn't I ever let on? Hanged himself from a hook in the garage. Careless with money. I was away at school. Wellington. The Master himself told me – it was fine, he was terribly sensitive and all that. Frightful bore because it meant I missed the fives selection. The bloody funeral!'

Milly was aghast. 'Edward, that's so really, *really* awful. *Really* sad.'

Jack was annoyed. It meant he couldn't hate him any more, or not cleanly. 'So you can't grow up,' he said.

'No. Never cried about it. I'm screwy. Sicko. Lilian kept

telling me this over and over and over. In psychological Shit Street, me.'

'Did you *love* your father?' asked Milly, head on one side in the concerned position, apparently much more animated now.

'Away all the time, didn't really know him,' said Edward, raising his eyebrows like a clown. 'That's the pain. That's why I'm stuck. Didn't really *know* him, did I?'

NINE

When he saw Kaja and Jaan next to the Peter Pan statue, waiting for him, he felt like running away.

'Hiya! Been waiting long?'

'It's no matter,' said Kaja. 'How are you?'

'I'm fine,' said Jack. 'OK, Jaan, is it catch or footie?'

'Cricket,' said the little boy, very serious but trembling with excitement, his head bent right back to look up at the adult he didn't yet know was his father.

'Cricket? Of course. Stupid me, I forgot to bring a set along. I'll bring one next time. Meanwhile, we'll practise fielding and bowling.'

Jack had been useless at cricket at school, and hadn't touched it since. His enjoyment of it was purely as a spectator – or rather, as a listener. Fortunately, he'd brought along a tennis ball instead of the big red airy one that was too light. The weather was grey and sultry, this time, without a breath of wind.

'He watched the Ashes competition,' said Kaja. 'There's a Bulgarian with a TV in the house. We could never work out any of the rules.'

Kaja was sporting a long T-shirt with a neatly printed slogan: *Not All That It Seems*. Her gymnast's straight back and firm shoulders stretched it tight over her breasts.

'A Bulgarian?'

'Yeah. Why?'

'Dunno. He's a nice guy, is he?'

'A woman, actually. She's a friend, now.'

A Japanese couple came up and asked Jack to take a photo of them in front of Peter Pan. Jack had trouble including them and the statue, being too close inside the railings, and had to crouch down like a war photographer, angling up. The couple laughed. He'd been about Jaan's age when he'd first seen the statue. A much higher statue, then.

Once Kaja had left them, Jack showed Jaan the fairies and rabbits and squirrels forged into the tree stump, their bodies polished to a shiny bronze by ninety years of touching fingers, the fairies' wings beautifully corroded by verdigris.

'Peter Pan never grew up,' he said. 'He was a fairy who took a girl called Wendy to Never-Never Land. This is where he first landed.'

The corner of Jaan's mouth puckered, producing a large dimple.

The trouble with Kensington Gardens was that everyone looked vaguely familiar. It made Jack nervous as he threw and caught the tennis ball. People – generally the foreigners – smiled as they passed. He realised Jaan was rather cute, enthusiastically failing to catch the ball most times, his dark tousled hair giving him a bit of a scamp look, until you saw the seriousness of his expression.

This is my son, he was thinking.

They walked along the wide path by the Serpentine to buy an ice cream, kicking at newly fallen leaves, trying to catch the ones that were still so briefly in the air. Jack had an old post-card up in his study, showing the same view in 1911. Nannies with perambulators and boys in knickerbockers or dressed as girls, girls in lacy bonnets. He bought Jaan a double cornet, which looked enormous in Jaan's miniature hand and reduced his face to something out of an old shaving-cream advert. Jack had no tissues on him and didn't know what to do.

'Lick it all off with your tongue,' he suggested.

The tongue couldn't reach more than a little circle around the lips. Taking a corner of his soft cotton shirt and kneeling down to Jaan's level, he held the boy's shoulder and wiped his face clean, avoiding the actual mouth. The smell and stickiness of the melted ice cream was unpleasant, but the passive gratefulness of the little face touched Jack profoundly. He wiped his shirt-flap on the warm, dense grass of the lawn. He wanted to return Jaan as he'd found him.

He winked at him. 'What a kerfuffle, eh?'

Jaan produced a dimple again, this time looking him in the eye.

When Kaja got back, Jack told her he'd like a word in private. She said something in Estonian to Jaan, who kneeled on the grass with the tennis ball while his parents sat together on a bench a few yards away, out of earshot.

'He still doesn't know who I am, does he?'

'No. Just my friend. I'll tell him soon.'

'I like being with him. It's working. I'll give him a piano lesson at Howard's or hire somewhere. Not at home. I've got this horrible neighbour and my wife might come in. She'll ask you questions.'

'He wants to see you more.'

'Well, he can see me a couple of times a week.'

Kaja snorted. 'Two hours a week?'

'To begin with, Kaja. We've got to go carefully on this one. I really like seeing him, don't get me wrong. I like seeing you, too,' he added, heart hammering suddenly.

She folded her arms. 'He's your son. He's not a piano pupil. He's not your little hobby or your club.'

'I didn't say he was my hobby!'

'You're his dad. You can't do this. It's easy as pie, isn't it? You just take that little bit you want. Fine. That's not being a dad.'

They sat on the bench in the warm sun and Jack felt it was all very unfair. Jaan was rolling the ball from hand to hand, on his own on the grass.

'Your wife is called Milly, yeah?'

Jack nodded.

'She sounded nice and understanding, on the answerphone.'

'That's pie in the sky.'

'It's what?'

'She'll explode if I tell her. We've been trying for a kid for years. I can't risk it. It'll be gloves right off.'

'Then I'll go back to Estonia with Jaan. I'll tell him about you when he's eighteen. Are you surprised?'

'Well, a bit.'

'There's a guy I know, on Haaremaa. I was at school with him. He went away to university and now he's returned. He's a carpenter, works hard because he's really a good carpenter. He'd be a good father to Jaan. Jaan likes him a lot.'

Jack felt a sudden stiffening in his stomach. 'Your boyfriend, is he?'

'I think if I go back he'll be my husband. That's what he wants. Up to now he's just my old friend. He's called Toomas. It means a rock.'

'You can trust him. Because you've known him since childhood.'

She nodded. 'I shall work for the island radio. They've got some money, I'll be paid a little. They want me to. It's a community radio. I have a lot of ideas. I can study by correspondence, I know professors in Tartu.'

'Not quite London.'

'London's all money,' she said. 'I miss the island.'

'Like I'll miss you and Jaan really, really badly. Unless I can visit?'

She shook her head. 'That's not the right deal,' she said. 'My life's not a website. Either you're a dad, or you are not one.'

He leaned forward, trying not to tremble, and rested his elbows on his knees.

'I don't want *not* to see Jaan *ever again*,' he said, with a conviction that surprised him.

'Tell you what, exactly, Mill?'

'About Estonia.'

Milly and he were in Hayes, in the garden, sitting on the plastic chairs, noting the number of cat's doings in the gravel and wondering whether the shiny little B&Q barbecue set on wheels was ever used. They'd been to the hospital. Because it was a Sunday, there were a lot of visitors and no medical staff apart from a couple of harassed nurses and a sister with a migraine. Milly was shocked by her mum-in-law's state, and immediately felt bad that she'd been too caught up in work to see her earlier. They'd handed over to his dad mid-afternoon and come back to sort out the house a bit. Milly didn't tend to vacuum herself at all, these days, and took to it with gusto, although she was wearing the type of dress that zipped up the side but looked as if it had been slid into like a glasses case. The house was pretty dirty. They'd brought along a Fortnum's hamper to cheer Donald up, and a cooked free-range chicken for a late lunch.

She was flushed with virtue and vacuuming. It was a real sacrifice, losing her Sunday to Hayes. She did not like Hayes, except as a reminder of where her husband had come from, which always made her feel better – about him, particularly: she tended to forget he was a working-class boy. A gifted working-class boy. Knowing this Hayes effect, even though he found it ludicrous, Jack had calculated that this was the best environment in which to make his confession. He had no option.

Milly wanted a kid, right? Jaan could be her stepson! Weekends, high days, holidays. Whenever. Fun. Milly was a generous, right-on person who thought about the planet and the poor, about asylum seekers and child labourers. She'd spent six months in a revolutionary Berlin commune while he was in The Hague behaving himself. She'd worked in the kitchens in Action Space. In a village in Zimbabwe, even, while he was analysing 12-tone rows in Luigi Dallapiccola. She'd keep reminding him, apropros of nothing, that one in four kids in the UK lived below the poverty line – or perhaps reminding herself because it was very easy to forget, nobody mentioned it except the leaflets through the door that tended to go binward. She had an open and honest mind.

The trouble is, she'd got there first. By a few minutes, probably.

'About Estonia,' Milly repeated. 'Tell me all about Estonia.'

'Yup. Actually, um –'

Lees was being screamed for somewhere nearby on the estate. Jack wished Lees would reply. Lees was like himself, perhaps, unable to find the words. A plane from Heathrow went over, almost low enough to identify the airline. Pushing its shadow of noise.

'I've had my heart broken twice,' Milly said. 'Once by the boy I knew before you –'

'Firuz,' he nodded. 'No, Saleem.'

'And once when I lost my baby that I loved so much even though I hadn't ever seen him alive.'

'Right,' said Jack. 'In fact, funny you should ask.'

The air glared, suddenly, as the sun bit through the thin sheet of cloud and bounced off the white table, and they simultaneously donned their shades. He didn't know how to begin.

'I feel,' continued Milly, 'I'm going to have it broken a third time.'

'Why?'

'I think you've lied to me.'

Her face under the sunglasses was not friendly. She didn't suit sunglasses, in fact. Jack could see his own tiny head in each lens, crossed by a black stripe like a blindfold.

'Not exactly,' he countered, in the same way he'd once denied having eaten his mother's Dairy Milk some thirty-five years ago on this very spot. 'Let me say my bit, then you can judge.'

She muttered something that was drowned by a passing car with woofers designed to perturb the deepest rhythms of the body. It accelerated with a whine, belted round the cul-de-sac and left on a squeal of tyres. Lees had been located, though.

There was relative silence, aside from the murmur of Middlesex. He felt out of breath.

'About Estonia,' she said, again.

'Yup. You reckon I didn't just walk round a lot of museums and churches and bogs. Six years ago.'

He could still retract. He could still pretend he wanted to

thrash this thing out in order to clear his name. He could compose something detailed enough to persuade her for good. He was stroking the plastic table as he'd do as a boy – not the same plastic table, but its facsimile. The estate houses were crouched around them, brown-brick listening boxes, their upper windows jammed against the guttering, the roofs pulled down like caps as far as the eye could see, polka-dotted by satellite dishes. This was all a mistake.

'You tell me,' she said.

The silent space between them was a racket, in fact – drums, trombones, piccolos.

'Well, OK, I've had this *feeling* for a while now,' he said, eventually, 'that all this . . . it would all be better . . . in the open.'

'This is so incredibly scary.'

'Look, give me a chance, Mill.'

She stared down at the table. Or seemed to be doing so, through her black aviator shades. He couldn't be quite sure; her eyes might be swivelled up, staring at him.

'You'll get it off your chest. Feel better about it. And what about me.'

'We ought to go inside,' he suggested, hearing the neighbour – a wiry old bird called Daphne – coughing beyond the fence.

'I'm going to have to leave you.'

'Right. I haven't even said anything and you're going to leave me. Try to keep your voice down.'

'Sorry, put that in another way,' she said. '*You're* going to have to leave *me*.'

Daphne coughed again, as if she was actually in the garden.

'OK,' he said.

'That's all?'

'No. Yes: I wish I could see your eyes.'

'Ditto.'

She took off her sunglasses and her eyes were wet and slightly red around the lids. He kept his on, because his eyes refused to be wet. A head popped up above the fence on the road side, shocking him. A girl, her hair scraped back tight in what was

334

known locally as a Harlington facelift, grinned and called out, 'Oi, there's two of 'em!' Then she disappeared, squealing with hysterics along with her hidden friends.

'Let's go inside.'

Perched on the arm of the sitting room's leatherette sofa, he felt his face pucker like a little boy's – but there were no tears. Milly was hugging her knees on the thick carpet in front of the fireplace. She had vacuumed its artificial coals, stuck like giant boiled sweets in exactly the same position for as long as Jack could remember. Her side-lace sneakers were laid in front of it, like prim twins. She was waggling her toes.

'I think you should, y'know, hear the defence,' he said.

'What? That you shagged this bimbo Katia or Kayak or what-ever her name is and then – oh bugger,' said Milly, putting her hands up to her face, turning white before his very eyes. 'Oh my God oh my God.'

'What?'

'The prodigy. Howard's prodigy. Who came to the house with her, Edward said. He *is*, isn't he? Oh my God.'

Milly looked straight at him, her mouth open. He nodded his head slightly, unable to articulate words. His mother had thrown herself out of the window. His wife was going to throw him out of the house. It was *so weird*, the way life could turn turtle from one moment to the next.

'A child,' said Milly, in a high voice. 'Well done. Ten out of ten.'

'Mill, Mill, Mill. Please.'

'Oh fuck.'

'A complete accident. That's what I was trying . . . you know . . .'

'I'm sure it was,' said Milly, her brow pitted with anguish. 'I'm sure she's not the *only* one. Oh fuck.'

He insisted there weren't any others, but now the *truth* didn't even convince him.

Milly said, 'I've hoovered your parents' pissing place from top to pissing bottom.'

'It's not very big,' he pointed out.

She laughed. No, she was crying, into her hands. He explained everything over the moaning noises, setting it out clearly just as he'd rehearsed it over and over in his study, like a recitative. The trouble is, it still sounded like a rehearsal: how he'd been lonely and done a stupid thing all those years ago, how it was finished the next day, how he knew what Milly felt, how he loved her to bits, how he felt nothing for Kaja. But he had to do his duty and be a dad to Jaan. On weekends, say, like loads of other people did. Loads of their friends. Diego, Rupert, Barnaby, Nick. There were others but he couldn't bring their names to mind. Her moaning stopped after he stopped. She was breathing hard.

Then she said: 'I feel like pinching you with my nails until you die. I feel like drawing your teeth out one by one with a pair of metal – those big pincer things. I really do.'

'Pliers,' he said, helpfully.

Lees was lost again, or still not located, or still fast asleep. The voice was screaming it, now, surprisingly clear through the open windows. Then it stopped. His skin and his teeth felt tender and vulnerable.

She turned her face to him. Her eyes were very red, very swollen, and she hadn't got a tissue. He went off to search for one in the kitchen and in the bathroom. He felt really narked with his dad for not having any tissues. He tore off a length of pink loo paper, folding it carefully, carrying it to her like a cup of the finest porcelain.

'Thanks,' she whispered.

There was a small silence that he felt he could roll in his hand, this time, like a ball bearing, as Milly dealt with her nose and eyes.

'I feel bricked up,' she said, at last, examining the sodden ball of paper. 'Like one of those nuns.'

'Honestly, Mill, it was just this one little . . . this tiny fling thing . . . can hardly even remember it . . . Got completely drunk, in fact. That was the problem. Blitzed. Stupid local vodka. Tallinn vodka. You know? Naive. Quick fix,' he added, with a rueful grimace, pretending to be ruefully honest.

She said nothing. His words hung out into space. Thankfully, because they were rotten, they eventually snapped and fell into the depths for ever.

There had been brief times before in their marriage when, after a row, Jack would sleep in his study and they'd behave like polite strangers for a few days, bar the occasional burst over something trivial like leaving the loo seat up or propping a jam-stained knife against one of the cooker rings.

Even now, Jack had not been thrown out onto the pavement, his bag flying after him, with Edward Cochrane looking on bemused and pigeons flapping up from the road in alarm and disappearing into the sky. Jack played out this scene in his mind many times, half wishing it would happen. Instead, there were three days of the old polite avoidance. Everything buttoned tight: most of all Milly's expression.

She spent a lot of the time at Claudia's, when she wasn't at work. Work could do without her, it seemed. Clients blithering about grey water recovery and composting toilets went silent. Yurts folded themselves up in quiet fields. Entire projects – even the teetering Oxford one – were put on hold. This struck Jack as mysterious. Milly's work was like a great mansion, suddenly deserted. He drank too much coffee and had nightmares, if he slept at all.

He phoned Kaja, to check that Monday in Kensington Gardens was still on. He didn't say anything more. He didn't phone anyone else. His only students were Yeh and Raj, for the moment. He answered emails curtly, 'in haste', giving the impression he had loads of work. Then he worked out how to use the *Out of the Office* option. It amused him, using this.

On Tuesday evening Milly walked a long time on the Heath, by herself. She'd already made arrangements with her parents to stay down at Wadhampton Hall for at least a week, not telling them the reason. Jack set off half an hour later and, across a meadow of plumey grasses shedding seed like smoke, recognised Milly's dark hair and the way she strode purposefully along, swinging her arms. Then he really did feel a sense of the unbelievable complexity of what he still could not quite accept he might be losing. She had phoned her old girlfriend Sammy in Devon, a very long call in which he feared that any lingering doubts about her action in Milly's mind would have been dispersed, because Samantha Carlisle and Jack Middleton had never got on. More worryingly, he'd overheard her equally long conversation with Claudia, after which Milly had let him know that Roger was in a serious condition. Jack didn't fancy visiting, since he felt lightly concussed himself.

He might never cross the threshold of Wadhampton Hall again, might never even see Marjorie and Richard again, who would be very cross with him. Milly might go for a divorce and he might lose the lot. He dug himself into his own drama as far as he could go, but it didn't yield him the comfort of more than a very shallow self-pity that mutated at times into a pitiable, sustained note of remorse. The trees and shrubs on the Heath went on being trees and shrubs. The trees had enough to do just keeping alive, but this is not how he had thought when he was eighteen or nineteen. Then, he had thought the trees were at one with him, like the white clouds.

Milly didn't get back till well after dark. He was not listening to Schubert or Chopin or Britten or Berio but watching junk TV on cable. She refused to speak with him and went straight upstairs, leaving a whiff of spirits and expensive cigarettes. The game-show host, in his glittery jacket, waved at him personally with a mocking smile.

Things were complicated by a phone call from his father, who made out that Mum wasn't doing that well, although there was no need to panic, and since he would rather have Jack's brother and sister fly over when or if the situation worsened, he would appreciate it if Jack could stay over one or two nights in the week.

'You can always do your work here, John,' his father added, who had no idea what composing involved.

He sounded a little desperate, and was surprised when Jack seized on the possibility of escaping Willow Road on the back of a perfectly valid and even admirable excuse. 'Six nights, tops, Dad.' Maybe things would resolve themselves – battered and seasoned, perhaps, but not used up. It reminded him of the lovely chunk of pale timber he and Kaja had found on the long white beach at the northern edge of Haaremaa, where the only other living creatures were a pair of sandpipers on spindly legs.

The next day – the day before Milly was due to leave for Hampshire – Jack went down to Hamleys and bought a child's cricket set in a clear plastic case. The ball was an imitation in rubber, the bat made of some pale wood that was probably pine rather than willow, with *County Cricket* printed in blue on the back. There were four stumps and one double bail. It was the most junior set he could find.

This purchase cheered him up. He came back into the house knowing it would be empty: Milly had been out till late on previous days. They had said about ten words to each other since Hayes. Milly had gone into a kind of autism, had taken a vow of silence like the nun she'd compared herself to. It was a strain. He'd been rebuffed a couple of times, when he'd tried to make an approach. The first time she'd said, 'Right now, I think I might be incredibly close to a nervous breakdown. Give me time.'

The second attempt was met with: 'Get some help.'

It was already the hottest recorded autumn ever, they were saying. The lawn was sprinkled all over with bright yellow leaves, which was normal. Will the gardener was not due till the end of the week, but the leaves kept on descending. Sweeping them made no difference. He whistled Janáček's *Říkadla – the beetroot got married, the carrot danced, tidli tidli tidli* – as he screwed the stumps in.

It was not easy, the ground was still dry and quite hard: the wicket stayed a bit drunk. He practised his bowling. He tried overarm at first, beamers every time, but the ball went nowhere near the stumps. He hadn't bowled in about twenty-five years. Underarm was more successful, although the wicket was junior size and he mostly missed it. He wished he had a fielder, it was tiring retrieving the ball each time and walking back to where he'd placed the extra stump. But he had to practise: he didn't want to make himself look stupid in front of Jaan, or the numerous visitors to Kensington Gardens.

To take the nails out of my hands and feet.

He tried overarm again and a perfect leg-cutter jumped towards the slips and rolled into the black shade of a wooden trellis that 'Eeyore' Graham at the Hall had knocked up for them out of antique beams. It was overgrown with passion flower, piled and coiling down. In the summer, the open flowers were dotted about like happy white stars on the deep green; now it was a golden-yellow mess with dark dangling withered bits like dried cat's doings.

To his surprise, the ball flew out again with great force, as if it had bounced off something elastic.

He removed his sunglasses and the blackness under the passion flower lightened, revealing what he thought at first was an upright wheelbarrow. Will liked using the wheelbarrow, as he liked to make bonfires, and was always leaving it about. With a jolt to his blood supply Jack realised the wheelbarrow was, in fact, a human form, crouched or perhaps seated on the bench under the trellis. He picked up the little bat, just in case.

'Will?'

The human form rose and melted into Milly as it strode out into the sunlight. She was holding a tall glass of either lemon barley water or Pernod. He could just hear the ice.

Shielding her eyes, she shouted, 'What do you think this *does* to me?'

Jack thought he heard laughter from a couple of gardens away.

'I dunno,' he said, feebly.

'It *kills* me. You're *killing* me.'

'Better call the police,' came a falsetto voice. It was probably the rented place two doors down, full of braying trainee City lawyers a couple of years off from their first million.

'Shuddup!' Jack shouted, into the air. 'Or I'll come straight round and clobber you!'

He'd surprised himself. He was a yob, after all. But he was really livid. He shook his little bat. It was hot in the sun in the middle of the lawn. Oddly, there was no response. Perhaps he hadn't shouted loud enough: a high jet was moaning overhead, drawing every other sound into its own shadow.

'Bravo,' said Milly.

'And don't you start,' said Jack, without meaning to.

He stood helplessly, the bat dangling from his hand. Milly came nearer and stopped and took a swig of her drink. He smelt aniseed – it was definitely Pernod. It looked by the colour to be mixed strong. She glared at him and then she said, very quietly, 'I'm phoning the bank. Just in case she has a taste for schlock skirts and flash jewellery.'

'What are you talking about?'

'You know what I'm talking about.'

'I don't.'

'Get a haircut, first. Then go fuck the hell out of her, maybe even for free. Have five more half-Estonian kids.'

Jack sighed. He was slightly frightened of her, like this. 'You know she's got this . . . French-Canadian banker guy. It's over, me and her. It was just that one . . . you know . . . just that one single . . .'

'Lovely and productive and totally mental night of sex,' said Milly. 'Righto. I'm obviously *le problème*. Or is it *la problème*?'

She shook her head as if shaking off a fly. Her fish earrings leapt about on the end of their line. She was staring fixedly at one point near her on the lawn.

'Go catch something painful and lingering,' she said, and took a gulp of her drink. Then, once again: 'I'm incredibly close to a complete nervous collapse.'

She was definitely fairly drunk. That was unusual. She was still staring.

'Milly,' said Jack, dropping his voice right down, imagining Edward's ear taking grain-prints off the fence, 'I'm still in love with you. I'm not in love with her. I love you to bits, in fact. I don't love her. I forgot all about her once I'd left Estonia, until she popped up again. We have to get on top of this one, right? She and I had a very civilised chat in Regent's Park, by the Boating Lake –'

'Good setting,' said Milly, sourly. 'Lots of quacking. *I love you, I love you*,' she squawked, very loudly so that it bounced off the house. She'd been at the Pernod more than he'd realised.

He smiled, keeping it cool and reasonable and low. 'There was a bit of quacking from the ducks, yeah. Look, we had this nice chat and she told me about her . . . about René from Quebec . . .'

'Raoul.'

'Yeah, I meant Raoul. About Raoul from Quebec . . . and it's like this. As follows. I'm going to help Jaan with his music and with his cricket skills, take him out on the Heath, that kind of stuff. Extremely civilised. I'm really naff at cricket, as you can see, but –'

'And me? What do I do? Play bridge?'

'You've never played bridge.'

'Keep hens? I've always wanted to keep hens.'

'I'm gutted, Mill, I really am . . .'

'Snort cocaine? Shack up with Edward Cochrane?'

'I'd kill him first,' Jack chuckled. 'You do what you think is right to do.'

'I'm planning to.' She gave a shrill peal of what might have been laughter. 'The story of my life. Trying not to screw up the environment.'

'And that's incredibly admirable, Mill.'

'Oh, *fuck off*!' she screamed. 'You conceited little lying *prick*!'

She hurled the glass down on the lawn, where it broke and jaggedly rolled, looking dangerous.

'Hear! hear!' came the same voice as before, its nasally youthful bray pinpointing its origin.

Jack turned, gripping his junior bat in both hands like a club.

'*Come here and say that, you bastard!*' he screamed, in the trainee City lawyer's general direction. And then sank to his knees, exhausted, as if something vital had snapped in him.

There was no response except a few high-pitched snorts, presumably of helpless laughter. Milly was already storming off towards the house. His own voice was peculiar to him, as if all he'd heard was an echo of it in a vast cathedral. His soul felt like a peasant in old-fashioned costume, walking away from him down a country lane overshadowed by thick trees. He had never considered himself as having a soul in the conventional sense, or not since he was a boy, but now he felt it very strongly. The grass by his knees was so interesting. He really didn't want never to know grass again – its intricacies, its faint hint of incense and golden things, its summery warmth after a day absorbing the sun. Its apparent passivity.

Eventually, he recovered enough to go inside, sensing the house as empty; that Milly had left – vanished, perhaps, into the fog of unknowing for ever.

As he walked up the three flights to his eyrie, he thought of Kaja quoting Flaubert in French, his remark about the bracken caught in the stirrup. He was a complete pseud: he knew sod all about literature, French or otherwise. Or about much else.

All he knew about was music. In a sort of swollen, over-developed way. Parallel to life. Its own world. Like maths.

But birds made music, didn't they?

As he lay on the study couch, Debussy's *First Arabesque* uncoiling on the stereo, Milly's invective ran through his mind over and over again. She had called him conceited – which was quite untrue – and a liar. He could not deny having lied. Didn't everyone lie, more or less, just to get by, as a form of necessary negotiation? He tried to think how Milly or Kaja had lied, failing to find a single example. He resolved never to lie again. Or even to fib.

He lay on the couch and tried to force his tears to the surface, squeezing his heart, but failed. The strange point about making music was that lies were impossible. No words or pictures meant no lies. And no honesty either, maybe. It seemed to him the height of honesty, that detail of the bracken getting caught in the stirrup. He really would like to write a piece of music expressing that detail, that honesty. He could smell the bracken. He could hear it tear from the stirrup as the lover, what's-his-name, pulled on it. He would like to tell Kaja about this inspiration, because she would understand its impulse. Milly wouldn't. She had never understood him, in fact – or not this part of him. Milly had called him a conceited little lying prick.

That was it, then. His marriage was over.

He tasted his tears, as people did in books. He was lying there, quite still on the couch, and tears were welling up in his eyes and making their way erratically over his cheeks to nestle in his lips. He let them, along with the mucus from his nose. He recalled doing this as a small boy, surprised at how much kept coming out. He felt an abject failure. About ten years ago he had felt the opposite: that he was altogether to be envied – admired as the most promising English composer; married to a wealthy heiress of ancient stock; bound for the glories already bubbling in the cauldron of his gift; anticipating children. The years had slipped by from snowdrop to snowdrop ten times and no one had noticed. There was nothing you could do about it: he was well past forty, he was greying above the ears, he was no longer young and promising, his mother was probably dying. He was not even fermenting in the bottle of this house, whose value rose and accumulated wealth faster than either of them could earn through their work, their art. It was crippling, this knowledge of their wealth, suppurating second by second from the brick, the new stucco, the strip of garden, even the simple grass. All over London and further afield it was the same: wealth like a smell, like the air itself, ebbing and flowing and leaving the unfortunate millions who did not breathe it stranded further on their dry rock, grappling with badly fitting masks. To them, wealth was a gas, a poison. He had never realised this before. He would like to have smashed the City lawyer over the head with the bat, seen his teeth mix with his clear brain fluid. It was amazing, that he could feel so violent, so dangerous. He was touching something in him that was as hidden and deep as coal.

He went to the piano, sitting bowed, not making a sound. He saw his hands turn dark as he spread his fingers as wide as they would go – dark with the coaly violence in him, and blurred from his tears – and brought them down in one great massed chord that was the beginning of something more.

The next day, he sat in his bare-walled childhood bedroom in Hayes and thought about what the doctor had said a couple of hours ago in his clipped and careful Indian English.

'I'm not sure your dad quite understands, but your mum is a very ill lady, Mr Middleton. Unless we believe in miracles, she is not going to pull through. I feel so sorry for her. Moyna has been so brave. Being blind, too. It's jolly difficult.'

The doctor's room in the hospital was gloomy but generous, its big desk awash with papers. His mother had an infection, it had got into a heart valve, she was refusing to eat, she was thin and desperately hot under her skull brace.

'I see, yeah,' said Jack.

He wondered if he was doing this right. The doctor probably expected him to break down. Instead he was hovering an inch above his own emotions, not really feeling much except this kind of shadowy suspicion that what the doctor was saying might be true, impossible though it sounded.

'Do you understand what I'm on about? Given your dad's state, it might be best to keep all this between us.'

'OK. He's bad too, is he?'

'I'm worried about him,' said the doctor, placing his long, neat fingers together under his chin. 'Not *very* worried, but just . . . concerned. He looks exhausted, doesn't he? He's no spring chicken.'

There were noises from outside, from up and down the corridor, pure ambient scratch music, like something improvised in the seventies – the trundling of trolleys, jolly shouts of orderlies or nurses, squeaks and bleeps and trills and thumps. In here, Jack felt safer. He even felt that the doctor, with his kindly Indian eyes and effeminate hands, might be able to perform the miracle.

No, his mother would perform the miracle. She would show them all. And the doctor would be ever so glad. He must break this sort of news every day, Jack realised, but now it was as if he was doing it for the first time. And maybe he really did feel sorry for Mum. Jack felt a lump in his throat, not because of his mother, but because of this doctor's kindness, because of this drop of kindness in the great shambles of the NHS. He and Milly had offered Donald a place for Moyna in a private clinic, but Donald's pride had interfered. Donald had voted Labour for decades – the old decent Labour, as he would call it. This had not been usual among his fellow skilled workers in the EMI factory in Blyth Road. But after Moyna's accident at her factory, and the shameful attitude of the Tory owners, he had converted to socialism, a socialism streaked with fine flawed lines of the extreme right when it came to race or law and order. Anyway, it was hard for Donald, to sit in the hospital and watch the NHS at work. But this doctor – he was the saving grace, along with some of the nurses. While most of it felt like a massive orchestra getting by through sheer bluster, trying to drown out Death blasting away on the Hammond organ, this doctor knew it was all about more than fingering.

'How long do you think she's got, then?'

'A month, tops,' said the doctor. 'Maybe as little as a day. We just don't know, you see.'

'She'll be back here by Christmas,' said Donald, over a meal from the local Chinese that filled the house and probably beyond with its deep-fried smell. 'So you and Milly could spend it here. I don't suppose your mum'll be able to travel.'

'Who says she'll be back?'

'Well, obviously she'll be back by then. Her neck has only got a couple more weeks to go before it heals. She'll be glad to get that scaffolding off.'

'What about the infection?'

'Antibiotics. More rice, Jack?'

Moyna deteriorated very quickly. The doctor knew exactly what he was talking about, but it still surprised Jack. The weaker she got, with bouts of delirium, the less caring the nurses were. So, for the first time in his life, Jack combed her hair. She also requested a nail file, and Jack popped out to buy one. She was too weak to use the nail file, but let it rest in her cupped hands as if just holding it was something. She had always looked after her nails. Perhaps it was something to do with being blind, with the heightened sensation of touch.

He said nothing to his father about Milly. Milly was down in Hampshire right now, recuperating at the Hall, probably riding a lot. Moyna wondered why Milly wasn't visiting. She was perched in the straight-backed leatherette hospital chair – the hospital was unable to furnish one more suited to a patient with a weight of metal on her head, though apparently they'd looked. Her short-term memory was pretty well shot: it was easy to imply that Milly had popped by the day before.

'You were asleep, Mum.'

Moyna didn't know her short-term memory was shot, and got very angry once or twice, insisting that Milly hadn't been at all for ages. Which was, ironically, true. Certainly truer than the idea that the Earl Mountbatten of Burma had shaken her hand that morning and given her a prune, which she'd entertained on and off for some time.

Jack had been in Hayes a full week, now, and Milly had not got in touch from the Hall.

He had popped back to Hampstead on Monday to give the Thai girl her lesson, practising his cricket on the lawn and moping over the bomb passage in *Waters of the Trip Hazard*, still unable to find a place for the cymbal crash. The whole situation felt unreal, as if it had never happened – Milly would be coming back from work later on, gagging for a tipple; and then, on the lawn, he saw the glitter of broken glass, still sticky with Pernod and full of ants.

He had phoned Kaja immediately and postponed the rendezvous in Kensington Gardens to the following week, using his mother as an excuse. Kaja had said very little, merely that Howard was going to be away teaching in Sicily so there was no viola lesson next week.

'Sicily – yeah, of course. How nice. We'll stick to Peter Pan, anyway,' Jack said. 'I've bought a cricket set for Jaan.'

'OK.'

He had gone to Charles Tyrwhitt's in Jermyn Street to buy the type of long-sleeved polo shirt his father liked, chosen a pre-cooked meal at Fortnum's, and arrived in Hayes in time for a mournful bite to eat with his dad, at the table outside, to the trance beat of a car parked with its doors open the other side of the fence. The noise chased them inside, in the end.

'I could complain,' Jack ventured.

'I don't want two of you in hospital,' said Donald, pushing his *poulet de Bresse* about with his fork. 'Or in the morgue. When you were a baby it was mods and rockers. Then it was hippies and skinheads. Now it's raving lunatics in plimsolls.'

Jack chuckled, appreciating the joke – Donald wasn't given to jokes – but it turned out he was being dead serious.

Jack spent most mornings at the hospital, his sentence relieved by the odd break in its spotless, trendy 'brasserie' in the hospital's swish new 'Cartwright Centre' across a well-watered lawn. Jack was never quite sure what this 'centre' was, though the brasserie was generally full of doctors and nurses escaping the hectic shabbiness. The long list of private donors above the lobby's fountain included, Jack was surprised to see, 'Richard and Marjorie du Crane'.

Moyna hardly ate. If they forgot to bring in a menu to tick off in the morning, she got nothing. The first day Jack was there, it was beef curry and treacle tart. Moyna told the nurse to give it to Jack. 'He needs fattening up,' she said. The nurse, who was short, red-faced and shaped like a grapefruit, turned out to be from Latvia. She was strict and bossy, with no identifiable sense of humour, but she left the tray. Jack made cutlery and chewing noises, pretending to eat; in fact, the sight and smell of the curry made him feel ill. It was as close as food can come to looking like sewage.

'Enjoying it?' Moyna asked.

'Lip-smacking good,' said Jack. 'Quite spicy, though.'

'It all is,' said Moyna. 'It's all the coloureds in the kitchen.'

Donald came in to relieve Jack and helped himself to the treacle tart. It peeled his dentures from his gums and caused a minor fuss, which Moyna enjoyed as distraction from her own pain.

'I hope nothing's wrong between you,' she said, one morning about a minute and a half after Jack had arrived. Her voice was not weak so much as high and piping, like a caricature of someone very old. She was stock-still in her usual, hopelessly unadapted chair, head down low as if taking a bow.

'Between us?'

'Between you and Milly.'

'Why do you think that?'

'You think of everything, given enough time,' she said, staying bowed over with the weight of her scaffolded head. It must be pulling on her half-healed neck, Jack thought. And her eyes these days looked milkier, blinder. Before the fall, it was hard to tell from just looking at them: there were no panda-like burn marks around them, no scarred smoothness anywhere, because it hadn't been that sort of accident. The drips in her arm, the bruises they made, the saline solution and waste bags around her like her innards pulled out on wires: he felt deadened to it all, to the horror of it all. She'd once been a shop-floor supervisor in a sausage factory, bustling about, giving orders, laughing and scolding in a white coat with a clipboard and beehive hairdo, looking like a doctor. He had to remember this.

'Everything's fine,' Jack said, sensing a sob rise in his chest.

He could so easily break into pieces. He bit his lip until it hurt. The room, the ward next door, the corridors, the whole place, smelt of the body turned inside out. All those tubes and pipes and wires. Like the Pompidou Centre. He and Milly had visited the Pompidou Centre very soon after they'd met. He'd once had an early, strident composition of his performed there in a festival, before a vast flickering bank of televisions each showing a motorcycle accident in a race, the rider crawling away with flames on his back like the plates on a stegosaurus. Over and over again.

'I'm very glad,' said his mother, unable to see him cover his face with his hands. 'She isn't only what I call well bred, but kind and thoughtful with it.'

TEN

He thought that Milly would get over it, would come round to forgiving him, to acknowledging that what they'd had together for so many years was worth salvaging. He had no idea whether Marjorie and Richard had been told, but he guessed they must have been. They would try to talk her round to forgiveness, surely. They were not stick-in-the-muds. The du Crane history was full of illegitimacies and sexual scandal.

It was Monday again, at last, and still preternaturally warm, if threatening to be wet. He was on his way to Kensington Gardens via Hampstead and the awkward journey allowed him to think. He'd left himself an extra hour; he could do with a stroll, on his own, before meeting up with Kaja and Jaan. Afterwards, he would stay the weekend in Hampstead, in his own house. He had not been thrown out, not yet. He wondered what the legal position would be if Milly decided to chuck him, to enforce her threat about *him* leaving *her*.

He had decided to thrash a lot of this out with Kaja, to let her know exactly what was going on. If she were to fling her arms around him and say, 'Then come and please live with Jaan and me for ever, my darling Jack,' he knew what he would do. He would be resolute. He would say: 'Let's play it by ear.'

He could (he realised, as the Tube carriage swayed and rattled) shift the four bombs on baroque timps to sound *after* the cymbal crash, bringing in the choir's intoning underneath. For the voices, he was borrowing from Shostakovich's 'Tayniye znaki', or 'Secret Signs', one of his *Seven Romances on Poems of Aleksandr Blok*, Op. 127 – an allusive, personal reference that would be lost to most of the audience, even in the Purcell Room, but which had helped him find a way through, musically as well as emotionally. On the day of the bombs, at the moment they had gone off, he had been listening to that very work on CD. The score scribbled itself in front of his eyes, the woman opposite deep in *Il Codice Da Vinci* and unaware of what the staring was all about.

Jack realised that he had never read to his son. He didn't even know which books his son was reading. Kaja was no doubt seeing to the cultural and literary side of things. Jack felt like an appendage, uninvolved. Milly had told him recently that the second most used word in the English language was '*Coca-Cola*'.

'It ought to be *love*', she'd said. 'Or *care*.'

'As in *I don't care*,' Jack had quipped.

They'd wondered what it would have been in prehistoric times, and thought seriously about it and then had a laugh.

He missed her, badly. He missed her strength, her keeping him and the world in order, her failure to do so. He was going to the park via Hampstead in order to fetch the cricket set. It would have been odd to have taken a toy cricket set down to Hayes, it would have needed explaining, but now he regretted not doing so, wasting time as he was on the Northern Line.

Maybe Mill was right, he thought — seeing his reflection in the carriage's tunnel-barrelled glass: he did need a haircut. A complete revamp. A change of style. Dimmed flatteringly in reflection, his face seemed about the same as when he would look at himself in the school bus decades ago. Where had he got, since then? Anywhere at all? Could he ever find an instrumental equivalent for this awful, disembowelling sound of a Tube train's interior at full whining pelt? Cage would have used a tape, Cardew would have said it was enough to hear the real thing, but those times were over. The bombings piece was not a narrative, it was a meditation, a memorial. It was vertical, not horizontal. It must be chiselled out by his own despair: and thinking this, the score in front of his eyes immediately vanished, as if someone had rolled it up. He was not in despair, that's why. He was just . . . what was the word . . . dispassionate? The high white clouds passed over Middlesex, humming over his life, and then they were around him, part of him, and he was looking down on his own life. It had always been like that. He was going to explain all this to Milly. And to Kaja. Perhaps he already had done. So he would re-explain it.

The Italian woman looked up, her eyes so glazed she didn't smile back at him. Someone further along was testing the ring tones on their mobile. It kept trilling something very similar to James Last's *Zip-A-Dee-Doo-Dah*, slithering into Jack's head and staying there all day.

On opening his front door (was it still his? Had it ever been his?) he stepped on a letter that Marita hadn't put into the wicker tray. That meant she'd not been in since this morning. Marita would have appreciated having the house to herself for a week. The scent of cigarettes, rather sweet – maybe of joints – lingered in the back sitting room. Marita had found a Greek boyfriend who smoked dope as others drank tea. Milly thought he was disastrous, but as Jack had told her, she was not their ward and he was very rich. A used coffee mug sat on the mat in front of the fireplace, with a teaspoon stuck inside it.

The house felt strange, like a new edition of an old familiar book. He had an hour to play with before setting off for the park. He went upstairs and retrieved the junior cricket set from where he'd put it, under the couch in his study. He was looking forward to the expression on Jaan's shy face, the dimpled smile on seeing the cricket set, the realisation that it was his to keep.

The letter he'd stepped on was addressed to *Mr Jack Middleton*, in rounded handwriting rather like Milly's, but smaller. He opened it, sitting in the plant-fugged garden room with the doors wide open to the unseasonal sultriness, the junior cricket set leaning next to him. This is what the letter said.

Dearest Jack,

By the time you get this I will be returned to Estonia with Jaan. In fact, I will be in Haaremaa. This is where I want to bring up our son. My old friend I told about, called Toomas, the really fine carpenter, will be waiting for us.

Why am I doing this?

Because I know you will be only the weekend father, come and go when you wish, playing cricket or football once a week, keeping your wife happy – as I can understand. Maybe it's my fault that I can't support this. Jack, you are very English, very polite, taking what you want. Also, Jaan is not happy in London. Me neither. He is bullied and teased for his foot, and the air is bad for him. I am often taken for something I am not, because I am from the Baltic States and so-called blonde. I wanted you to see your son and then maybe . . . So I feel I have done OK by my duty.

Sorry about this. When Jaan wants to, he will know who his father really is. Right now it's Toomas, who he loves from a baby. For the present he will learn viola with a friend on the island, a retired professional musician, a bit old-fashioned from Soviet orchestra days but she is a honey. For three years or about that, it's OK. Then maybe we'll go to Tallinn on the coach once a fortnight. I will be working on the Haaremaa Radio, studying too. You soon can listen to the station on Internet.

Jack, I will send you photos of Jaan sometimes, if you would like that. This is the best way. To say goodbye is not possible.

'Which is the true key of the sky?' That's Jaan Kaplinski. I thought of you as a kid, looking and hearing the clouds in Heayes, when I read that. And there's Akhmatova: 'Secret is the source of the light.'

With love always,
Kaja

'But my wife *isn't* happy!' he heard his mind shouting. He looked at the junior cricket set in its clear plastic case like a stocking. He stared at it for a long time. He let the letter fall from his hand. On an ashtray next to his chair, under a succulent with scarlet tips on its leaves, lay the remains of three joints. He felt he could die like this, just let himself go, in a fatal trance until decomposition set in. Flies crawling over his face. But Marita would find him in time.

He experienced the weight of his mother's head brace, the sensation of its screws in his skull bone. He was sure she was not going to die today or tomorrow or even next week, whatever the doctor said. She was Jaan's granny. She was Jack's mum. Donald was Jaan's gramp. Donald was Jack's dad. It was all very clear.

And *he* was *Jaan's* dad. He wanted to teach him a bit of cricket. To take him to the Toy Museum in Bethnal Green, which apparently was about to close for a year. All very simple and clear. But he was nailed to the chair. The plants breathing all around him, withdrawing the air, pumping out new gases. The big limewood table that had cost a fortune, that had been scarred by life in the past, by past lives. A job to get it in.

He felt Jaan's absence in his chest. A great hole torn out of his chest. He felt afloat, floating, but shipped by this feeling he had in his chest. It was sending him under. Of course he would not have timps for the bombs! The explosion would start at the beginning and finish at the end. It was a millisecond extended into twenty minutes. It would be a cello in second position in C and over it would be the most terrible tearing of woodwind and boy trebles and soft Arabic percussion. He heard it all as he stared at the junior cricket set, its pale wood blackening and whitening alternately as his eyes played tricks, fatigued by the fixity – and by seeing the score penned carefully and clearly in ink, the ink gleaming like brain fluid on the unrolling sheets in his head.

In one sense, Kaja's letter made everything easier. In another, it made everything harder. This created cross-currents, of the rip-tide type, in Jack. He phoned Wadhampton Hall that evening and got a rather diffident Richard.

'Ah yes, Jack. I'm sure you want to speak to Millicent.'

Millicent?

'If I can.'

'I'll go and see.'

Jack felt like a vague, unwanted boyfriend, not a son-in-law. Richard was away at least ten minutes. Now and again Jack tried to call out into the phone. He imagined Richard wandering over the vast house, popping out into the grounds, slow and a little lame these days. He thought he could hear the rooks, the occasional far-off strike of mallet on fence post, the sighs of the freshness of the country air.

Eventually, there were hollow footsteps and a clumsy crackling and Richard came back on the phone.

'Hello?'

'Hi, Richard. Any luck?'

He'd got very nervous, as a jejune boyfriend might have done.

'No luck, sorry.'

'She's gone out?'

'Ah, well, I think she's not quite ready.'

'Ready?'

'To talk. You know.'

Richard was treating him as a bomb-disposal expert would treat a bomb.

'Can you tell her that they've gone, Richard? I mean, for ever?'

'Who's gone?'

'What's she told you?'

'Oh, that you've been having a spot of bother between you. I believe a nipper's involved. Not Millicent's.'

'Right. Just tell her they've gone back. For good.'

'Wilco.'

Jack thought he could hear someone talking urgently in the background. He didn't think it was Milly.

'And how's your *mother*?' asked Richard, as if – rather uncon-vincingly – he'd just thought of it himself.

'Pretty bad,' said Jack.

'Oh dear,' said Richard, equally unconvincingly. 'So sorry to hear it.'

Richard must have told Milly, in the end, because she came back the next day. Jack had spent the interim contemplating the darkness. That is, he had seriously weighed the possibility of death being a better option for him than life, as if he was choosing between two savings deposits. He felt the hospital had infiltrated his blood, his bones, his heart. It was tough watching his mother suffer, his father hope, while life went on in its random, violent, spurious way. On an impulse he'd looked in Mill's wardrobe and noticed that the little tub of their dead child's ashes had gone. She might have asked, he thought. If only people would ask. It had been labelled *Max Middleton*. But he couldn't blame her.

But he could blame Kaja. He would write to her once he'd got over his anger. She was unstable, he'd decided. No, she'd wanted to punish him. And she'd succeeded. He was really cross.

To see or talk to an old friend – Nick Bradford, say, or 'Breakdown' Barnaby (Howard was still in Sicily) – felt like a betrayal of his instinctive need to be alone. This made it all the weirder, then, that he ended up the next evening drinking champagne in Edward Cochrane's garden.

Right at the wrong moment, just when he was at his lowest, sitting in the twilight in his own garden, the front doorbell had rung. He had this wild notion that it might be Kaja.

Instead, it was Edward Cochrane.

'How-de-do!'

'I'm busy, Edward.'

'We're two of a pair, and don't deny it.'

Jack had forgotten about Edward's father committing suicide. Now, seeing the man's puppyish, sallow face, its pug nose peeled by the sun, he remembered it.

'Not necessarily. It's not like that.'

'My advice is, keep yourself busy. Get a job. Helping old ladies, serving in Oxfam, whatever.'

'I *have* got a bloody job, Edward. And I have been helping old ladies. My mum, anyway.'

Edward cocked his head to one side. 'I mean, involving other people. Not so much wanking time.'

'Thanks for the hot tip, mate.'

He started to close the door, but Edward held it open with a firm hand.

'Fancy a barbie? Just the two of us moping, muzzling some champers?'

'A barbie? It's the fag end of October in England.'

'It's Australia. Hottest recorded. Noticed? They're sunbathing in Yorkshire.'

'I don't, not really.'

'It's all ready to go. Stop you topping yourself. Prime cuts. Only bought them this arvo. Fresh as daisies. Marshmallows for afters.'

Jack felt hungry, suddenly. He hadn't eaten since breakfast – the hospital lunch had been curry again, curried eggs, mingling with the bleach smell; it had put him off food for several hours.

So it was that he found himself in Edward's tidy garden, full of water features, swirls of brick paving and tasteful classical statues, slipping into the sweet inebria of a Bollinger. He turned down his host's offer to put on the Rolling Stones as background ambience.

'Milly told me the gist,' Edward explained, breezily. He was clearly delighted by their troubles. 'Corker and son.'

'Why the hell did she tell *you*? That's *really* annoying.'

'I admit I probed. Mill and Lilian were great buddies, you know.'

'*You* weren't.'

'No, but I have a way with women.'

'Not with my wife, I hope.'

Edward laughed, prodding the glowing coals on the fancy

brick-built barbecue, his thighs emerging enormous from his jungle shorts. Leaves fell from the trees and flared into fire. 'Alas, no. Way above my game. She wanted me to keep an eye on the house. Neighbourhood watch. Very distraught, she was, underneath. For God's sake, you're even barmier than I thought. Fancy going off with a Baltic bimbo when you had free official access to Milly du Crane.'

'She wasn't a bimbo, but I agree with you.'

A sudden lurch of loss hit him through the fume of bubbly. He watched Edward coax the charcoal, trying to imagine him as a boy. It wasn't difficult. He was stunted, in some way. It explained a lot about him. The darkness was settling thickly now – or would have done, if the garden hadn't been lit like a runway by three outside halogen spots. Edward squirted barbecue fluid on the coals and they leapt up, charring the thick slabs of meat.

'Watch you don't squirt the food,' said Jack.

'Trust me, my man. This is bachelor country. We have to stick together. Whoosh! Fangyew, lads, fangyew.'

Jack heard the phone ringing faintly from his own house next door. He'd left the French windows wide open, which was probably unwise. Maybe it was the hospital, or his dad. Or Milly. Or even Kaja. He'd have to get a mobile. The last thing in the world he wanted was a barbecue with Edward Cochrane, and yet that's exactly what he was doing. Edward's house looked very smart after the revamp. Its owner didn't, or not in shorts. He filled his glass again. He needed to spoil himself. He wished he'd brought along a pullie. The day fooled you into thinking it was southern, when it was northern and already autumn.

'That thing about your father.'

'That thing.'

'Are you angry with him for doing it?'

'Probably,' said Edward. 'He was a vicar, so I joined the army.'

'Did you?'

'Seven years. Northern Ireland was a gas.'

He was turning over the meat. Jack tried to imagine him in

uniform, stalking the Falls Road, helmeted, sticking out of an armoured car like a jack-in-the-box. People were always so much more than the coffin you made for them.

'So you got back at him.'

'Absolutely. Slapped him in the face.'

'He was a vicar, and yet he committed suicide.'

'He was a vicar, *so* he committed suicide. Actually, he lost his faith. Careless, huh? He was something in the C. of E. admin line, in the end. Awful to my mum. Chain-smoker, but never touched a drop. Very selfish man.'

As if, Jack thought, Edward was not. But he had invited him round. A gesture of neighbourly sympathy. Or had Milly asked him to keep an eye on her husband as well as the house?

They were well into the marshmallows when, like a nightmare or a dream, Jack heard Milly calling him through the French windows the other side of the fence, beyond the trees and thick shrubs. Her voice sounded quavery, as if afraid of what she might find. He didn't usually leave the house with the French windows open, but he'd reckoned that as he was only just next door . . .

'God, sounds like the missus,' whispered Edward, tackling a melting marshmallow on his fork.

Jack had just bitten through the heat-crisped exterior of his, finding the sweet goo of the melting insides as provocatively delicious as when he was a kid in Scout camp. He was stuck to it by his mouth, and he engulfed the rest to get rid of it. It burnt his tongue.

'She's back,' he managed to say, more or less, swallowing.

'Seems like it. Yoo-hoo!' Edward called, too sozzled to think about asking permission first. 'He's over with me!'

'With you?'

'We're having fun!' Edward went on. 'Can't blame us!'

'Not true!' shouted Jack. 'I'm bloody miserable!'

He really had drunk so much more than he was used to that everything did seem to have its comic, devil-may-care side. Life was not a hospital after all. It was a place where quite ridiculous and extremely funny stuff could happen, if only you had the wit to see it. He found his own observation – that he was miserable – brilliantly funny, for instance. Now Edward was putting his hand on his – Jack's – knee. That was funny, too. As was – in fact, this was the funniest thing of the lot – the sight of a second marshmallow very slowly losing its form to gravity on Edward's upheld fork, like something gelatinous out of a horror film, and threatening to fall into Edward's lap.

'Ooo, your husband's knee is gore-djuss!' Edward roared, in the Welsh gay's voice from *Little Britain*.

There was no reply from Milly.

'Where's she gone?' asked Edward, just as the cooked marshmallow – or the ectoplasmic blob it had become – gave up and dropped smack onto Edward's groin.

The way Edward looked down at the result, genuinely taken aback in a sozzled way, was the funniest thing Jack had ever witnessed in his life. It made the best of TV comedy look wan. He was seized up with hilarity, rising from inside him in a great and unstoppable wave. He was shaking with it, or it was shaking him. And Edward had been infected by it, too, which made things worse. Jack's stomach hurt, his muscles, his jaw. The laughter was almost silent, just little squeaky noises right up in the palate, it felt like, before it roared out of his and Edward's bodies simultaneously in a great and stupendous release – tears pouring down their faces, the white blob on Edward's groin acting like the ON button, asphyxiating them with mirth. They all but rolled on the lawn, crouched down almost to the grass, their chairs on two legs, moaning, wanting it to stop, weak but mutually triggering it with each glance.

And it was at that point that Milly appeared. Of course, she had the key to Edward's house. Lilian had given it to her, in case of emergencies. In case the house caught fire and the children were inside when Lilian was shopping or at the pool.

'Sorry, sorry,' Jack managed, tears and nasal mucus wiped away unsuccessfully. 'It was . . . the . . . marshmallow. I'm really sorry. It . . .'

There was a strange suspension when nothing much happened for a few moments; his body was rippling of its own volition with the after-tremors of his laughquake, and Milly was watching him.

Then it went, just like that. The mirth left his body as devils leave bodies they've possessed. Something had exorcised it. He clutched his belly, which was sore, feeling very weak and shaken. Edward was raising a glass, similarly recovered, his eyes as red as if he'd been grieving.

'Milly, my love, sit with us and praise marshmallows.'

Milly was a few yards off, on the lawn, ablaze in the halogens. Her arms were crossed. She didn't generally find things funny. In fact, Milly's problem was that life was almost always a serious matter. Very serious. All about catastrophe, in fact. Jack struggled to remember what this meant. Composting dry toilets. Grey water. No more polar bears.

'Mill, come and sit down. I love you to bits.'

'Have some Bollinger, darling,' offered Edward, holding up the bottle. The white blob of marshmallow was still on his groin. 'If you wanna kid, babe, you have to do it *at least* three times a week.'

'Roger's dead,' said Milly.

'How do you know?' asked Jack.

Once again, he felt a bubble of laughter rise from his belly. A bit of the tickly devil had remained. The *way* Milly stood there, arms folded, glaring at him and telling him that Roger Grove-Carey, his dearly beloved old tutor, was dead . . . it was just *so* extremely offbeat. He thought of Auschwitz and Hiroshima and Rwanda. He thought of never seeing Jaan again. It made no difference. His belly shook from each burst of suppressed laughter, as if it was being hit by a fist, the reverberations going right up to his throat. The mechanics of it. Even they were funny. Global warming. Polar bears dropping off the melted ice. Plop plop plop. Milly was telling him that she'd heard from Claudia, that Roger had died yesterday, that she had something to tell Jack, in private, but that he was clearly too pissed out of his tiny little head to listen.

'I'm not pissed, Milly. I'm really, *really* miserable. This is compensation.'

'Constipation?' said Edward.

'Com-pen-sation.'

'I'm pissed, but he's not,' Edward pointed out. 'He's really miserable.'

Jack stuffed a fist against his mouth. Edward was hilarious. He was a natural. They both were. They were Laurel and Hardy, Eric and Ern. Fry and whatsit. Whoever. Roger was dead, but the laughter wouldn't stop pumping up from Jack's belly, throttled only by the fist at his mouth, like a tie on a fat balloon.

'I'd like to hit you very hard on the head,' said Milly.

'They've gone,' explained Jack, puffing his breath out as if he'd swum a few lengths. 'I phoned to tell you. They've gone out of my life for ever. Poof.'

'What's that you called me?' said Edward, blinking. Brilliantly funny.

'It's too late,' said Milly.

'Never too late,' Edward echoed, holding up his hand as if he was hailing a taxi. The white blob on his groin had slid off the shorts, down his inner thigh, onto the chair, leaving a gooey trail like a snail's. He had the fattest, ugliest knees Jack had ever seen in his life. 'Except for me,' Edward added, a bit of pink marshmallow stuck on his nose; Jack hadn't noticed it before. It moved with his nose, wherever it went. Edward was a clown, a comic genius. *Because he didn't know it.*

'You're really killing,' said Jack, jabbing a finger at him, 'because you *think* you're funny, when you're not.'

Milly was coming up to him and was hitting the glass out of his hand and was picking up the bottle of barbecue lighter fluid and Edward was saying, 'Zen, Zen, Zen,' like a fat monk, and then she was squirting the lighter fluid onto her skimpy top, her nice red skirt, as if it was insect repellent, and Jack found himself on his feet, staying steady with the help of the back of the chair, and he was saying, 'Mill, whassup? What're you doing? That's toxic. Highly inflammable. Really unecological. It's to light the barbie with. Mill, what're you doing?'

Then she threw the bottle away and picked up the cigarette lighter on the table and lit it. Its little flame steepled, then sank a bit, but it was still a flame. She held it in front of her chest, which was dark and wet from the lighter fluid.

'That's really dangerous, Mill,' said Jack.

'Put that down,' said Edward, in an authoritative voice betrayed only by his inability to stand up steadily.

'How nice to have your attention at last,' said Milly, her eyes gleaming with tears in the light of the tiny flame. 'I'd come back to have a sensible chat, that's all.'

'I *want* a sensible chat,' said Jack, his whole body burning inside with terror.

'I want, I want.'

'Mill . . .'

Edward said: 'Don't do it, Milly.'

'Don't,' said Jack.

'Men do it to their wives all the time.'

'Not in civilised, Christian countries,' said Edward.

'You wanna bet?'

'Mill . . .'

'Shuddup. Don't tell me what to do.'

'I'm not.'

'I'm not a dog. You're never going to see her again, are you?'

'She's gone. I told you. Back to Estonia. One-way ticket.'

'This is silly,' said Edward, with an exaggerated military bearing in his unsteadiness.

'I'm the planet,' said Milly, moving the tiny flame even nearer to her chest. 'You men are the flame. This is how close we are. You make war and poisons. I hate you all. This is how close we are, and you're doing nothing. In fact, you're holding the flame.'

'But I'm totally on your side, politically,' said Jack, who no longer found anything at all funny.

'I normally put my bottles in the bottle bank,' said Edward.

'You're holding the flame against Mother Earth's body,' said Milly. 'You're all destroyers. I hate you all.'

'Milly, please. Let's have a sensible chat. Please.'

'You're pissed.'

'I'm not pissed, honest.'

He was, but was fighting it off, albeit drunkenly with flailing fists.

'I'll never see her again,' he added. 'I promise. In the whole of my life.'

Milly looked at him steadily and then, instead of whooshing in a blaze, blew out the flame. Her eyes seemed to disappear, her hair shadowing her face from the artificial light.

'You can do whatever you like,' she said. 'You're a free man, now.'

The next day she said exactly the same thing.

Jack sat opposite her at the limewood table in the garden room. It was raining softly outside. The leaves were just about all fallen and it was cooler. Summer was giving up at last, way beyond time. Jack had spent the night at Edward's on one of the absent kids' beds, his feet going over the end, the sheets covered in characters from *The Lion King*, the pillowcase stained where the mouth usually went.

It wasn't just that he and Edward had felt it was safer, given Milly's state. After threatening to turn herself into a human torch, she had instructed Jack to come over for lunch, when he was sober, for a proper discussion. At that moment Jack knew that he had lost the house, the game, his wife. Then she had left them to themselves.

'Purcell's wife locked him out after he'd had a drop too many one evening, and he died of a chill at thirty-seven,' said Jack. 'I hope I die, too.'

'Not on my carpet,' said Edward.

Edward Cochrane then revealed – in a low, insistent voice – what he would do if he was President of Britain for life. It was

365

oddly close to the caliphate promulgated by the kind of people who'd bombed London's transport system. Women had a very lowly part in his ideal state, at any rate, and homosexuals would be gassed along with the mentally handicapped, illegal immigrants, lager louts who attacked old ladies, the shrieking 'Guardianista' class and poor old Trevor Norris, because Trevor Norris was a local pain in the arse who'd once opposed a Heath development Edward Cochrane had had an interest in. Jack half listened, dazed by drink and events. They'd moved from champagne to brandy. Women would be dealt with, at any rate. Kept to their proper functions. Veiled, even. Edward was no longer funny, even when he tried to be.

'You're a fascist, then,' Jack said, eventually.

'A realist,' said Edward. He had what appeared to be slime on his lip. 'I'm a man of the world. Listen to me, son. I've had a *much* more fucking interesting life than you. Three years in Dubai, for a start.'

Jack, some twelve hours later, felt terrible. Poisoned. And Milly said again, very much unveiled: 'You're a free man, now.'

'I'm sorry, Mill. I really am sorry.'

There was the dim sound of squealing tyres from the street. He wouldn't mention Max's ashes.

'Right. Here it is,' said Milly.

She'd gone out and bought a Marks & Sparks vegetarian lasagne and a couple of Louis's custard millefeuilles that would simultaneously spurt and disintegrate however you approached them. Jack fumbled with the lasagne's hard, vellum layers, his gorge rising at the cheesiness. Milly looked older, but not in a bad way. Someone had redone her hair to look somehow Russian, early twentieth century – he couldn't pinpoint why or whether he was right in thinking this. It was an impression.

'You can't go whiter than you already are,' she went on, 'so that's OK. Claudia and myself, we're going to sell up and buy in Italy. Maybe France. Grow vegetables. Sorry, but there it is.'

'Claudia?'

'Claudia, widow of Roger Grove-Carey.'

'Is he really dead?'

'At long last,' said Milly. 'He died last week. His funeral's tomorrow.'

'No one told me,' Jack complained, forgetting he'd made himself technologically unavailable.

'I just have. And I told you yesterday. But you were too pissed.'

Jack put his fork down and tucked his hands between his thighs.

'Vegetables.'

'Yup. Claudia and I are going to bring up her son together. Far away from here. In a big farmhouse. As a couple. Lots of vegetables. We could even start a little veggie restaurant, for a lark. You could come and play jazz on the piano now and again, as long as it was tuneful. I've not been listening to my inner self, until now.'

Jack bit the inside of his lip, which prevented his face betraying him with a spasm.

'Um, I require a bit of guidance on this,' he said, eventually. Because it was not the way he usually put things, it had a shadow of mockery in it.

He was inadequate.

'I think it'll do you good to face the world on your own two feet again. Fend for yourself a bit.'

He pushed his lasagne to one side, then put his hand back between his thighs again. He could bicycle round the world, he thought. Keep on bicycling round the world until he withered away in somewhere like the Gobi Desert.

'Right,' he said. 'OK. So, er . . . you're leaving the job?'

'I'm easy. If they want me to do consultancy work . . . You can work anywhere, these days. Open up in Italy or France. Extend.'

Jack nodded. Milly could do anything: behind a laptop against a crumbling wall of pale stone, lozenges of warm sun playing on her hands, the scent of oleander and wild thyme . . . no problem.

'I guess you should do what you feel is right,' said Jack, in a small, hoarse voice, his hands still tucked between his thighs, his head bowed as if awaiting the blade.

'All I wanted was quiet days making rice pudding with the children,' Milly said, dreamily.

There was a buzz at the door before Jack could reply. To his surprise, Milly almost leapt up to answer it. She seemed to have a surplus of energy, a flush in her cheeks, a bounce in her hair. He rose and followed her, dimly worried it might be Edward, but his legs were weak. He looked up the hallway where a man was standing, holding a bright red dog's collar.

'Is this yours?' the man said, out of breath. 'I'm afraid I've just had an accident on the road with a Labrador.'

'Jack?'

Milly turned to him. The man was very tall and dressed in black. A white patch instead of a tie. White to go with the red. A vicar. A faint scent of burnt rubber. Jack thought: *I've lost my wife, for good.* The vicar would never know, seeing only a contented couple in their glossy Hampstead hallway with signed landscape photographs by Art Sinsabaugh on the safe wall, the wall you couldn't see from the street when the door was open to the thieving, ravenous world outside.

'We don't have a dog,' said Jack, his voice rising more than he'd meant it to. 'My wife and I, we've never had a dog or a cat or even a goldfish called Cliff in our whole time together. Just a little teeny tub of ashes. And even that's gone.'

'I'm not your *wife*,' hissed Milly.

'There's always a first time,' the vicar called out, waving the dog's collar as he backed away, so that its tiny bell rang and rang over the dimly massed chords of London.

Jack slept alone in the house that night; Milly was comforting Claudia, looking after the baby. He sat up late in his study with the headphones on, sandblasting his mind with bands like Five Section Crass or Saxon and polishing off Richard's present to him from four Christmases ago: a twenty-five-year-old bottle of Highland Park. Now twenty-nine years old. Not even whisky stood still.

The next morning, which was suitably thunderous, several of Roger Grove-Carey's pieces were played in the gloomy red-brick crematorium, including the cacophonic and over-saxed 'Memoriae Without Permission' as the coffin slid into the unseen furnace: for all but the atonal diehards present, it was terrifying, hellish. The baby cried all the way through, its squeals bouncing off the brick and all but drowning Roger's voice in Jack's head.

You were so good once, you bastard!

Milly sat next to Claudia, helping out. Roger's first genera-tion of children were further along the pew, looking like bent lawyers, with their bedraggled-looking blob of a mother. Claudia seemed as if she was on a high, oddly. Jack sat in his own lone-liness and headache the other side of the room; the whole thing was as close to psychological torture as he'd ever got. There were loads of people he knew, which made it worse – from old, clapped-out atonals with hip problems to punky young students brimming with tears. He couldn't work out how Roger had done it: he must have shagged half the women here – and some of the men, too, probably. Jack had been convinced that the funeral would be embarrassing in its dearth of mourners. Instead, if the building had blown up, most of Britain's contem-porary music scene would have gone with it – including the friendly, silver-haired controller of Radio 3, who admired Jack's work and had once asked him why he didn't do more. The speeches made Roger sound like someone of biblical propor-tions; a wise, good man who had changed the face of humanity. It was depressing.

And it made Jack feel cross with himself, rather than guilty, for not visiting Roger in hospital. Everyone else, it appeared, had visited. They all kept saying how he'd looked like Lenin, lying in state. A waxwork, but alive enough to growl. A great man. An original.

He didn't stay for the noisy reception; he went straight back to Hayes. Apart from the usual overhead traffic, it was nicely quiet in the house, as if the air was sitting with pursed lips. He tried to find Radio 3 on the battered tranny in the kitchen, fiddling with the dicky plug at the back then giving up in a haze of crackles. The plug had been dicky for years, although Donald could find the connection in seconds with a tap of his finger. Why had they never thought of buying his parents a radio? It was always pointless, trendy, style stuff they bought, stuff that got put away because 'there's no room'. Really, it was because it would damage the integrity of the house, its mind-blowing, well-dusted dullness, c.1970. He remembered sitting in this same chair as a kid, watching the black-and-white test card for ages and ages, waiting for the pretty long-haired girl to move, the lines to take on colour, the wallpaper music to turn wild and weird. Sometimes it did.

Donald came in from the hospital, eventually.

'How's Milly?' said his father. 'Doesn't she miss you?'

'Things aren't all that brilliant between us, in fact.'

His father nodded, but said nothing for a few moments. He was making a pot of tea for two in the tiny kitchen, although Jack had offered. His hand trembled as he poured the boiling water in. The teapot was from Devon and overdone with autumn leaves in thick impasto relief, the lid awkward to put back on, making it look as if Donald was playing a strange percussion instrument.

Eventually his father said: 'A marriage is not just a summer-house. It's for all seasons. More like a conservatory.'

'That's a very good simile,' said Jack, surprised.

'But a conservatory's walls are of glass,' Donald went on. 'You can't go throwing stones. You have to take care.'

'I'm impressed.'

'"Thought for the Day", this morning. About respecting each other's faith. I thought of your mum and me, you see. Not about faith.'

He suddenly started crying. Jack put an arm on his shoulder. He hadn't touched his dad in this way for decades. Donald didn't like to be touched.

'Right now it's winter,' Donald managed, in a piping voice like a child's. 'But I'm not going to abandon her now, am I?'

'No,' said Jack, rubbing his dad's back through the sleeveless cardy scattered with scurf.

'Well, I'm blowed,' said Donald, his chin scrunched up like a little boy's. 'Sorry about this.'

'Don't be. Good to have a cry.'

'Better to have a laugh than a cry,' said Donald, who'd hardly ever laughed in his life. Or cried.

'Not always,' said Jack.

His mum died three days later, delirium followed by clarity followed by sleep from which she never woke up, sinking into death with an obstinate look on her face, daring anyone to stop her. Jack's visit coincided with the clarity. She couldn't be bothered to listen any more to her RNIB CDs, or to the radio, so Jack read to her. For this very possibility, he'd carried in his jacket pocket a book of poems by the Sufi poet, Rumi. He started reading them, and realised it was a complete mistake. He should have brought something side-splittingly humorous. His mother listened politely, though. His voice droned on, each poem ending too soon, so that it sounded pointless. A nurse came in, rather large around the waist, with a mug of tea on a tray. It was just before lunch. The tea was stone cold and milky.

'I've been asking for that since ten o'clock,' piped his mother, shrunk doll-like against the pillows in her chair. 'It's because they're all coloured. They don't know our ways.'

'She wasn't. She was as Aryan as they come,' said Jack. He could hardly tick her off for racial prejudice this late in the day.

'I know *that* one was white,' his mother fibbed. 'What about playing me one of your musical works?'

'I didn't bring anything. Stupid. I'll bring one tomorrow.'

He did feel stupid. He also felt touched. There would be a great, healing moment tomorrow. He might even tell her about Jaan, who he was missing not in his head but in his belly.

'That'll be nice,' she said. 'One of the calmer ones.'

'No problem,' said Jack. His father had all three of his CDs in a special drawer. 'I'd really like that.'

'What are you sitting on the lawn for? You'll catch your death.'

'I'm, um, not sitting on the lawn, Mum.'

'Don't fib. I can see now because it hasn't happened. Don't tell me it's happened already. You've got to get me out of here, you can't just sit on the lawn. There's too much wind about.'

'Mum, it's OK.'

'No it's not. Look at you, you're miles away.' Her head was bowed right over, her nose inches from her lap, like a drunken queen. 'All dreamy again. Sweet little charmer. D'you want a bicky, Jacko? You mustn't sit on the bare lawn like that. We've got to get to the other side. What are you looking at then?'

'You, Mum. You're looking great.'

'Them clouds, is it? All nice and white, eh? All fluffy? Like they've been through the wash with Daz? Muriel uses Persil. So does Daphne.'

'Yes,' said Jack, half mesmerised. 'The clouds are whiter than white.'

'Why don't you play with your ball, run about a bit? It's that washing line, Jack.'

'Oh dear,' he said, smiling. 'About to rain, is it?'

He remembered her popping out, leaving him to get the washing in if it rained. And how many times had he forgotten to? And the washing then had to stay out there until the rain stopped – staying for days sometimes, strung between the metal poles on a plastic cord that ran along the side of the garden plot. Bedraggled, wetter and wetter, like a reproach.

'Going round and round,' she was saying. 'Turning thing. What d'you call it? The thingummy that goes round and round? Like we used to have before my accident. Come on, tell me!'

'Round and round? You mean a revolving washing-line thing?'

'There's a name for it. A special name. Come on, Jack! You're so *useless*!'

He had never known her like this. Maybe this was what Moyna really thought of him. Maybe she was hitting some primordial layer of honesty, now.

'I can't think,' he said, helplessly.

'You'll know when you're older,' she said. 'Makes them noises. You love them noises, don't you? It's the washing line going round and round, making them noises. Mmmmmmmmmmm.'

Jack stared, open-mouthed. His mother was imitating the private sounds the white clouds had made. It was a crude imitation, but it was unmistakable. Bent right over, humming. Dying.

'Come on, what's that name? Don't be useless.'

'I don't know, but I'll look it up. I'll ask someone. It made that noise, did it?'

'Mmmmmmmmmm,' went his mum, rocking slightly in her almost doubled-up state, heavy with her crown, the healing fracture no doubt strained to breaking point. 'Round and round, on windy days. Mmmmm. Get it all in before it rains. What's that name? Come on, come on, you *ought* to know. You've a blinking brain, haven't you? Why have you come instead of Donald? Eh? If you don't know the name?'

'Look, I'll find out. Don't worry about it. Mum, please don't worry about it. I promise I'll find out.'

She raised herself a little, wincing, and then her head bowed down again under its terrible weight.

'When's your dad back then? I don't want you instead of him. You're no blinking use.'

'It's all right, Mum. It's all all right. Really. It is. I'll find out.'

He went to the desk, but the usual ward sister warned him before he could open his mouth that she had one of her migraines, while the two other young nurses were in a flap, and the phones were going, and the man in the room next to his mum was crying out louder than usual, and he could hardly ask them what you called a revolving washing line in the midst of all this life-and-death stuff. By the time he got back, she'd forgotten all about it and wanted him to comb her hair, which he did.

He asked Donald that evening about the washing line. Donald was on weirdly good form, almost cheerful.

'Our old rotary clothes dryer, you mean?'

'That's it. That's the name of it. It was on the tip of my tongue.'

'Why?'

'She was asking about it. She said it made noises.'

Donald smiled. 'It did make noises. Oh yes. It sort of hummed when it turned, if the wind was right. Not every time. You liked the noise. You reckoned it came from the sky. Like the Heathrow lot. You were tiny, of course. There you are, you see. You were musical right from the start.'

Jack stared at his fish finger. He felt his whole life was built on a misconception. Most lives were, probably. The cat was gazing up at him with eyes as big as saucers.

'Dad, why did you get rid of the rotary dryer?'

'Too difficult for your mum, after the accident. She had to locate it. You won't believe how hard it is to locate a rotary clothes dryer on the edge of the garden, when you're blind. I tried it myself, with my eyes shut, one day.'

'It's not exactly a big garden, Dad.'

'But it's a thin pole. And she'd bang her head on the poles sticking out. Much easier to feel her way along the flex from the house. And then just follow it back again. I made sure a bag for the pegs was hung at each end. She never had any sense of direction, you see.'

'She's still alive, Dad.'

'I know she is. And she'll be back.'

Jack was looking forward to telling Moyna the right name for it. Rotary clothes dryer. Show he cared. But a call came early in the morning. They had to rush straight over. She was unconscious. She was really dying, now, lying on the bed and reduced to the bony architecture of her face, which was dead white. By teatime, the gaps between each rattling breath were as long as those of that patient called Eileen had been. Then the gap wouldn't close up, one time. The silence went on and on. Donald had popped out to the loo. He was taking ages. Her hand was as cool as something left out all night.

Jack said, 'Mum, hang on, you've got to wait till Dad's back. It's a rotary clothes dryer. Mum, don't go off now.'

Then a little sigh came from the mouth. She wasn't yet passed away, thank goodness. And Jack still expected her to open her eyes and begin a long, slow recovery. He couldn't lose his mum. He wasn't prepared for it. He was still only about fifteen. Donald came back, washing his hands at the alcohol gel dispenser. Jack was relieved. There was another little bubbly sigh, apparently cut off in the middle.

Jack said, 'I think this is it, Dad. We'd better get a nurse.'

Donald sat down in the chair next to the pillow and said, 'Did they have any toilet paper? Of course not.'

'Dad, I think she's going. Any moment now.'

'Is she?'

There were no more sounds from her mouth after that.

It was the last day of October. November came in as normal.

The last thing he'd said to her while she was still conscious was, 'I'll bring my CDs tomorrow. Till then, Mum.' The last thing she said to him was, 'With a bit of luck, love. Ta-ta.'

So her last word to him was 'love', discounting 'ta-ta'.

'Mum' and 'love'.

This made it easier when he looked in the coffin at the undertaker's and saw her face as he'd never known it. Dolled up with pancake, tidied, it was tucked and pinned, the skin as smooth as paint. The eyes were closed, and he wondered if she could see, now, wherever she was. Now that her eyes were open somewhere else. But the overall impression was one of relief, on her part. She could no longer feel, no longer know she was blind, and curse it. She could sleep for good.

There was a Bible open under the fake electric candle in the windowless room. The tissuey paper smelt like sick, oddly. He turned the pages and stuck his finger at random on a verse. It was from Jeremiah: *'For a voice of wailing is heard out of Zion, How are we spoiled! we are greatly confounded, because we have forsaken the land, because our dwellings have cast us out.*' He felt a ripple of recognition travel up his spine, realising that no one would ever believe it was sheer bloody chance. And he knew his fate was sealed.

He leaned over the coffin and kissed her forehead, which was even colder than he'd expected. Cold from the hospital morgue. He wondered how the jaw stay closed, invisibly trussed.

The cold stayed on his lips for several hours, like a metal butterfly clip.

Right through the funeral a few days later – his second in under a fortnight – he could only picture the face in the coffin. Milly was there, of course, and they had to pretend. He half hoped she'd be sympathetic, but he'd had the vague impression, through the various phone calls beforehand, that she considered this whole death-of-the-mother business to be a deliberate ploy on his part to win her back. This was probably a ridiculous projection on his part, as she'd been very good to Donald, phoning him every day and giving practical as well as emotional counsel. She seemed to be living all the time at Claudia's, now, and still had a healthy flush about her face when she turned up, at the last moment, flustered by the traffic. Her snappy black outfit made everyone else look dowdy.

Jack would have liked to have helped carry his mother's coffin, but it was already there in the crematorium, waiting for them to the strains of 'The Piper's Lament' played on the flute by James Galway. He had helped to choose the music, but was cramped by his sister and brother. He had a tape of his first recorded piece, like a childhood memento, but they didn't feel it was 'quite right'.

'It's meant to be Moyna's choice, not yours,' said his sister, interrupting the minimalist tinkles and pings, turning them ridiculous. She'd always had this notion that Jack never missed a chance to push himself into the limelight.

But Moyna was dead, he pointed out.

They all three entertained this idea that she'd loved Frank Sinatra, which Donald vigorously denied.

'Val Doonican. Or Andy Williams. And she never missed *The Black and White Minstrel Show*,' he said, staring mournfully at the blank screen. Which was all Moyna would have seen of it, after the factory accident.

In the end, the coffin slid through the curtains into the furnace to the strains of a slow air from the Chieftains, recalling Moyna's origins. Since she avoided all mention of her origins – there was some dodgy business involving a drink-sodden uncle and abuse, quite apart from the grimness and poverty – this might not have been appreciated by her. Val Doonican would have been subtler. None of her Irish relatives turned up, perhaps because they were too distant, or hadn't been invited. Jack was disappointed. Moyna had lost most of her immediate family in the Blitz not long after their arrival in England, been placed in an orphanage at thirteen, and gone into service two years later. She'd worked at the Wall's factory in Hayes from 1952, meeting Donald at a factory club do. She'd erased her early past, which was probably sensible.

The family speeches recapped on this, on Moyna's bravery and suffering, her sense of humour, and – in Donald's Baptist brother's long-winded contribution – the remarkable achievements of the children. In his sister Julie's case, this consisted of marrying an Australian policeman whose shaven, cannonball head had never quite been able to encompass the idea of Jack. Jack's brother, Denny, had turned overnight from interesting hippy to computer geek sometime back in the early 1980s, and had an American weight problem which made him waddle and wheeze. He was a bachelor who had all but tied the knot three times, and was still hoping.

And Jack got on reasonably well with both of them, partly because they were so much older than him. He had been the baby brother, although he had no memories of being particularly spoilt or petted – not even by his sister, who now had five rather difficult kids of her own, the oldest being a twenty-four-year-old lifeguard convicted recently of assaulting an Arab tourist on a beach.

The idea that either might find out about the collapse of his marriage was anathema to him: they would gloat, if only secretly. They were convinced that he did nothing all day, except count his wife's money and whistle tunes.

Milly came and stood next to him in the front row. At the instant his eyes met hers, he felt desperate. He needed Milly. He needed his wife. Her face was gentle, not hard – not turned against him. She was beautiful and clever and tough. She was unique. She couldn't do this to him, not now. Not *now*. She touched his hand, but didn't take it, didn't squeeze it.

Amazingly, although he felt vaguely dizzy and unreal, he didn't cry once during the funeral. He half tried to and had brought along a wodge of tissues in expectation. The ducts didn't function. It was as if the engineering had gone wrong. In the little reception afterwards, with some twenty people crammed into the house (it was raining), Milly asked him how he was. They were in the hallway, where the overflow had spilled out. She was standing on the lower step of the stairs, and so was artificially taller than him.

'It hits me,' he said. The occasion had made him oddly excited, even high. It wasn't just the roach-killer red Julie had insisted on bringing over from Australia. 'At unexpected moments. I'm OK, then it hits me again.'

'It?'

'Everything,' he murmured, catching her eye with meaning.

'Life doesn't always time things well,' she said. 'Take the tsunami.'

He nodded, seeing bloated bodies and the grieving wives of fishermen. Milly had always tended to arse about with scale. He felt himself shrinking to a kind of silly bendy toy.

'That thing about making rice pudding quietly and stuff,' he said, not quite able to focus on the words, 'I reckon it might work now the whole situation's less awkward.'

'Are you drunk, or just sad?'

'Depends what you mean by sad,' he said. He remembered sitting on this step and almost suffocating on a biro top. Now his estranged wife's very smart Gucci heels were denting its runner. Not exactly sexy, talking in your parents' house. My father's house, now.

Sad.

And so she left early, hooted at by the estate's resident louts who'd noticed something going on and were hanging about in the rain outside to vex the invitees.

'Everything OK with you and Milly?' his sister ventured, with a fifty-year-old beautician's smirk, her sun-scorched skin now the subject of elaborate care and shielding. She had no trace of an Australian accent, unless it was interchangeable with Middlesex.

'Um, as ever. Pretty brill, in fact,' said Jack, faux poshly, sounding like Hugh Grant. And wanting to kick her.

He saw death everywhere, of course. He took a break for a day on the Sussex Downs and saw three ravens perched on a telephone wire. He felt vacuum-packed, somehow. He was nearly run over twice in Hayes and once in Hampstead, dazedly not looking, all three drivers equally elsewhere on their mobiles. One morning there were some magnificent white clouds piled up over the Heath, sailing overhead, and he thought about the rotary dryer in the wind and laughed. Passers-by thought he was a daftie, from the looks they gave him.

He had to fetch his mother's wedding ring from the hospital, a few days later, with Donald. A smart young woman with snappy high heels emerged from Relative Support, which was being redecorated: a man in white overalls was applying sealant above the door and they walked the length of a low-ceilinged corridor on builder's sheets Donald kept catching his foot in.

'Sorry about the mess,' said the woman, whose name tag said *Yvonne*, 'but it's got to be done.' She was not unattractive.

'It's all relative,' Jack joked, but Yvonne didn't respond.

The room they were shown to was a narrow, pretend lounge, with drab easy chairs in light green. Yvonne went off to fetch the ring. Jack and his father didn't say a word. The pictures on the walls were off-the-peg modern – trim landscapes of wintry, angular trees. Jack was sure he'd seen the same pictures in a hotel. The builders were whistling and laughing in the corridor outside. There was no daylight. The low, Formica table had a pile of leaflets on *What To Do After A Death*. Jack would have appreciated a leaflet on *What To Do After Death*, but no one knew what happened then, let alone what you did. There was no piped music, for once. Just the decorators.

The woman returned with a large brown A3 envelope marked *Moyna S. Middleton* and tipped it as though she were tipping out powder and something dropped into Donald's palm.

His father stared at the ring, as if it wasn't recognisable. It looked much smaller than when Moyna had been attached to it. Fifty-five years before, Donald had worked this over her knuckle and into her life; now he didn't know what to do with it, it was so very small – a golden sliver under the neon strip light.

Yvonne, in her kindly, counsellor's voice (as if she was encouraging him to perform a trick), suggested it went back into the envelope. He dropped it in and Jack took the envelope; he recognised that Donald was done, crumbling at the edges of his soul.

'Well,' she said, 'I think that's it, if there's nothing more.'

They mumbled their thanks and made their way out, squeezing past the metal ladder in front of the door where the man in white overalls was whistling. He was running the nozzle of the sealant plunger along the gap between the ceiling and the wall, the wall stripped to the ragged, patched glue of its original trim. The smell got down Jack's throat. It made him feel even more exhausted, as if he'd gone on a great journey that had taken them decades to accomplish.

'The lords of the ring, us two,' he commented.

His father didn't hear. He was so bewildered Jack had to take his arm. They walked slowly down the main corridor towards the blaze of light at the exit, with squeaking trolleys and harassed relatives passing the other way.

Jack wondered what Milly would do with the ring he'd worked over her knuckle twelve years ago, now it was redundant.

I'm in Hell, he thought. What I have to do is get out.

In Hayes, inside the big new grey Lidl-cum-aircraft hangar, getting basics under the neon glare, Jack was seized by a kind of grief fit. It seemed to come up from his toes, without warning, in the milk products aisle next to the yogurts – flowing through his knees and up via his belly to his throat. He covered his face with one hand and – there was nothing he could do about it – he sobbed. He would have liked to have howled, but it was not the place. He was sobbing for his mum, not for Mill – not even for Jaan. The metallic smell of the refrigerated counter, its glow and hum, reminded him of mortuaries, although he'd never been in one. He couldn't believe he'd never see his mother again. It was something to do with the wrapping-up of his childhood and youth, the performance finally over, with no applause. Just a pin-drop silence.

She preferred apricot yogurts, with not too many bits in. She'd lean right over the pot, holding the pot tight and aiming the spoon carefully in. Everything was a complex operation, except sleep. He could write a grief piece with the sound of the spoon scraping, the interesting internal acoustics of the yogurt pot, soft-blowing clarinets and rubbing timpani.

He wished he was twenty years younger, knowing all the things he knew now.

His whole body was shaking, but he couldn't stop it. A woman next to him, reaching for a tub of cream, said, 'Nice to see someone having a good laugh, for a change.'

He had been permitted to stay in Hampstead, as Milly was mostly down the road in Belsize Park. Slowly, reluctantly, he was removing the traces of his presence, starting with the study. It was surprisingly easy, as long as he had big enough boxes and didn't have to worry too much about what went where.

He felt cross and inadequate, dazed and tearful. He spent quite a few nights at Hayes, though, once his siblings had gone back to their respective continents. His father needed the company.

His brief performance in Stockholm was a surreal break. Among the reticent Swedes, a bright-faced young American lecturer told him he was 'like Bernstein run backward'. It was surprisingly cold and there were about twenty people in the hall.

He was starting to watch what grown-up folk called 'outgoings' fairly carefully. Milly was going for the whole hog, as she went for the whole hog in everything she did – from sex to diet to waste reduction. He felt a new pleasure in accepting a puny, underpaid commission from the Almeida Festival simply for the extra dosh it would supply. He offered his services as a hack reviewer to various music magazines, and readvertised himself as a composition and advanced piano tutor. He bought cheaper toothpaste. He borrowed CDs from the library instead of buying them. He took the bus and, a few times, his bicycle. He worked away at *Trip Hazard* without the help of wine gums, bringing back the Shostakovich reference, dropping the boy trebles as being too Britten-like, planing away at the Arabic hints until they were barely discernible. At first he reckoned that, one day soon, once the Hampstead house was sold, he would start looking for a bedsit in somewhere like Bounds Green. He could picture it: small, pale and bare, with the bed up on bricks and chairs made out of packing cases and spring sunlight through uncurtained glass.

He kept waiting for his mum to phone. He wanted to ask her about that revolving washing line.

Then his ideas changed. There wasn't a magic moment of recognition, a flash, a satori: it just evolved in a kind of cross-rhythm.

Milly and Claudia both came to Hampstead one afternoon, with the baby. Jack was watching children's TV on the box, his feet up on the table, an open can of ale in his hand, an empty can of ale on the rug. He felt like walking straight out, but stayed put, playing the miserable oaf, pretending – by looks alone – that he'd acquired a colossal cocaine habit. Or heroin, even.

Mill went straight off to the kitchen. Claudia smiled down at him, holding the baby. She was slightly less worn-looking, just as slim and attractive, her figure stencilled against the window light. Baby Ricco was pulping her sharp breast with a pudgy little hand.

'Hi, Jack.'

'Hi, Claudia.'

'What's this programme?'

'Down on the funny farm.'

'I hope we stay friends, y'know?'

'We could do a *ménage à trois*,' he said, pretending to be caustic but actually, for one weird moment, finding it not such a bad idea. He could bathe with them, watch them search for bath crystals in each other's cracks, before hoeing the fields or picking the olives somewhere where cypresses punctuated the view and the heat smelt of wild herbs.

She left. He heard a peal of laughter from the kitchen. Two peals of laughter, pretty mocking. He stayed resolutely staring at a singing pantomime cow nuzzling a young polo-necked presenter with hair like Perry Como. When they left, they didn't say goodbye.

Then Howard, back from Sicily, had phoned him one evening at Hayes. Jack had to leave the table in the middle of supper with his father, who didn't know most of it. He arranged to meet Howard for an early pint near Covent Garden the next day.

They sat outside among hearty office workers working steadily through several swift ones in lieu of facing home. Howard waggled his healed finger, only a little stiff, and Jack congratulated him. His friend had grown a moustache like the wings of a wren, and was patchily sunburned. As usual, he claimed this would be his last ever visit to Sicily.

'It's crazy,' he said. 'Completely rotted out by the Mafia. EU money pouring into its bottomless pockets. The decomposing heel of Europe.'

'But you're paid well.'

'But I'm paid well.'

'And the sun shines.'

'And the sun shines.'

'And there's lots of cock.'

'And Etna,' said Howard, wistfully. 'Great wastes of black lava. Did I say it?'

'What?'

'Makes the whole human endeavour feel totally and completely pointless? Not me.'

When Jack had filled him in on the long litany of consequence, he claimed to be baffled. '*Completely* baffled. Gutted, too. If I'd known, I wouldn't ever have suggested −'

'Hey, forget it,' said Jack. 'You were just her alibi.'

'Jaan? Planning to see him?'

'Well, I miss him.'

'Go see him. Pronto.'

Jack sighed. 'Maybe. Or maybe kids are better without their dads screwing their little heads up.'

'Yo,' said Howard, 'leave it to the stepfathers. Did anyone ever tell you your hair's just like Hitler's, if a bit more voluminous? By the way, don't be in any doubt that Jaan is going to be a *massive* viola player, one day,' he added, with an unusual seriousness in his voice.

Jack nodded, wincing at the elephantine bellows from the office workers. He wondered what it took to be a part of that. To be normal. 'Just as long as it doesn't erode a correspondingly massive canyon in his life, Howard.'

'Oh, he'll be much too busy keeping his viola in tune in the fucking *heat*,' said Howard, although it was now much cooler. 'I'm going to sue the Yanks for that. And the Chinese.'

'And the Brits,' said Jack. 'And everyone else bar Milly.'

'Oh, I wouldn't dare sue our Milly,' said Howard, pulling a silly, frightened face which annoyed Jack, although he pretended to smile.

'You know why Jaan limps, by the way? Why the club foot?'

Howard nodded. 'I do. Wait for this. Those nasty Communists gave his mum drugs before her gymnastics championships. A sad legacy of harm.'

'No, she told me. I knew already. I was just wondering whether *you* knew.'

Jack was feeling a twinge of jealousy, which probably showed in his face. What hadn't she told Howard?

He went back to sort out his things, one morning, and found Milly crying in the garden room.

'I'm so in need of *approval*,' she said, blowing her nose. 'All the time. I'm like something out of fucking *Dante*. Even when I'm *happy*. Like I am *now*.'

'Um, why Dante?'

'I don't care. I've put the house up for sale, by the way. We need to discuss it with the solicitor. Fifty-fifty on the gain, even though it was *all* my family's money, originally. The gain's incredibly massive, even in five years.'

'I don't want a bean,' said Jack, suddenly feeling very certain about this, as if he was on his own and composing and allowing in a savage shift, a real yorker.

'You what?'

'Ground zero. My mum's left me a bit. There's my stuff I can sell. I think the piano's mine. Ten grand's worth, for a start.'

'Are you just blowing off, as usual?'

'Money money money. Yuk. Fink on it, Mill.'

When Hampstead was sold in early December for, yes, silly money, he moved in with his father full-time in Hayes. Claudia and Milly, laughing and sporting with little Ricco in Belsize Park, were taking the odd flight over to Pisa to house-hunt; Jack found this hypocritical, ecologically speaking, but kept his mouth shut. Since they never asked him to open it, this was not hard.

His boyhood bedroom swallowed him up. He felt like the snow leopard in its cage, with the odd wispy reminder of the Himalayas. He had nowhere to put most of his books, or even many of his pictures – framed posters, portraits of favourite composers, a hand-coloured plate from Albertus Seba's *Cabinet of Natural Curiosities* he'd stumbled across in Delft as a student and blown a month's grant to buy. Everything Milly had bought him – small modern originals or limited prints by well-known artists he didn't really go for – he'd sold at an auction house in north Finchley, along with the piano. The antique oil of the woman bathing (for his thirty-fifth) was bought by a chippy gallery owner who called it 'rococo junk', but notched up a decent price. The early nine-teenth-century ceramic lantern, with its original candle, he did not sell. It was worth at least a couple of grand, but he felt super-stitious about parting with it. The rest went.

It wasn't easy to do this. Or rather, it was frighteningly easy.

The bed in his old room felt narrow and too short, although it was a normal-sized single; he remembered going to the stores with Donald and Moyna to choose it. He was, what, thirteen? He remembered the embarrassment of the huge bed depart-ment, with beds wherever you looked; it made him feel that sleeping was weird, that human beings were weird, that some-thing very private was being turned inside out and made public under the bright neon lights: couples testing the bounce on oyster-shaped doubles with padded sides next to posters of women in nighties and medical-looking diagrams of spines, everybody very serious about it because sleep is serious, except for a balding man who lay down on a Dunlopillo and pretended to snore. His parents were urging him to lie down on the mattress in front of a pretty shop assistant in high heels and he'd started to take off his shoes and the assistant had found this really funny, tapping the strip of plastic at the end of the bed, where you placed your heels, with her biro. Really amused, she was.

He was a natural curiosity himself. He'd gone on a long journey and come back to where he'd started out. He was the Ulysses of subtopia. Actually, it was an insignificant, pathetic journey. *You bastard.*

Donald came along to the Purcell Room for the performance

of *Waters of the Trip Hazard*. A few of the composers – including Jack – were interviewed on Radio 3. As usual, despite flicking through his *Selected Baudrillard* beforehand in search of some killer phrase for any occasion, he found the others wittier and more intellectual, freighted with arcane, encyclopedic knowledge about the history of music. Even the young Abigail Staunton defied her Top Shop look and sparkled with references to the Gerber Variable Scale, imperialist assumptions and her recent trip to Lebanon. Above all, they knew what they were doing when they composed. His reference to Shostakovich was mangled by nerves. If he'd been asked to spell him, he'd have probably got it wrong.

He was entirely dissatisfied with his piece the moment he heard it live during the scratch rehearsal. It was the only piece without anything resembling a bomb sound. It went on and on, his inspired ideas flopping about in the mud of the well-behaved but unworked-at performance. The mechanical bleeper sounded nothing like a hospital cardiogram, it just got in the way. Even the title looked somehow dated and pretentious next to the others, and his photograph – taken hurriedly with a digital by Milly three years back for one of his CDs – made him look in urgent need of the loo, which fitted the title perfectly.

The audience in the Purcell Room – he could sense this as if it was written above their heads – were very patient flowers during his sixteen minutes. He squirmed internally, clutching his chin in the back row. The whole thing was overworked, a mess. He would have to blow himself to smithereens and start again.

Afterwards, in all the usual revolting back-slapping, he was barely tickled. Tansy Davies came up to him and offered encouraging things, but no one else said much – including Donald. And then a new senior producer at Radio 3 called Gary Soames gave him a nuggety little commission, for the week up to St George's Day the following year.

'New music about England,' the producer said, beaming over

the champagne. A lot of people in Radio 3 beamed, these days. 'Recorded, not live. For a new heavyweight slot called *Air Chambers*. Reputed composers only need apply. Part of our commissioning end. Subject inspire you?'

'Um, *ancient* England, yes,' said Jack, rather automatically. 'Silbury Hill, green roads, harebells on the downs, ancient fertility rites, all that. Neolithic and mysterious. You know. Really dark, not folksy.'

He suddenly realised, as Gary Soames nodded with half an ear clearly cocked to George Benjamin saying something in a group just next to them, that he sounded New Agey rather than clever and original.

'Perfect,' said the producer, who was possibly younger than him but seemed more senior, with large, square teeth and a lazy eye Jack tried not to notice. 'That's absolutely perfect. Exactly what the others said, funnily enough. Length about ten, twelve minutes max. *Very* exciting. A little pre-recorded gossip with you, and then in.'

'Sounds good.'

'Think about it, Jack. Let me know. I'm sure you're amazingly busy.'

Jack's fractiousness, after his disappointment, suddenly burst into view. Despite the commission, Gary Soames was annoying him: 'OK, but please, a *silence* afterwards,' he found himself saying, his hand waving about. 'No ditzy comments cutting in from the presenter. *I'm sure you'll agree that was* . . . And all that. In fact, I'll write it in. The silence. At least five bars.'

Gary Soames was already turning to George Benjamin.

Later, Jack heard him explaining the commission at much greater length to Abigail Staunton. 'We've a spot every day for that week, miraculously. Early evening, peak time. Brilliant. And for God's sake make it challenging. Don't be afraid to shake 'em up, Abigail. Lean-forward radio, we are. They'll have plenty of the usual tuneful suspects on the actual day. Purcell, Vaughan Williams, Elgar, Finzi, all that. Birtwistle's got a slot, too, so it's not all cowpats and cornfields.'

Abigail laughed.

'The real drag,' Gary went on, encouraged, 'is having to avoid sounding like the culture arm of the BNP. You on the pop, my love?'

Abigail held her glass out, flashing a smile that got the producer's lazy eye watering. Jack left the South Bank deeply disgruntled. The secret to success was not to speak, and to look permanently hot for it.

He'd no idea when St George's Day was, but hadn't dared to ask. He googled it, afterwards. April 23rd. England's national day, this. The day of Shakespeare's birth – and death! How embarrassing. Like, *so* obviously arranged by a Tory, Home Counties God. Amazing, to think it had all been appropriated by football louts and fascists. Made into the equivalent of exposing your genitals.

He had a few months in hand. He would take it extremely seriously. It would be very pagan and green and dark and all about losing your mother, losing Mother Earth. Losing Moyna and losing Milly. Losing his eyrie with its view of the Heath. Losing Wadhampton Hall. Slipped through his fingers, just like that. The rooks, the soft thuds of the croquet mallet, the hidden ancient bones beneath. It would keep him occupied.

Donald was not in a good state, of course. He wandered about the house in Hayes as if searching for something, with a dulled look in his eyes. Jack had to do more for him than anticipated, including the cooking and the cleaning. In fact, Donald kept calling him Moyna by mistake. They even laughed about it.

Moyna was behind every door, about to appear. When Jack took very long baths, her voice was always about to wonder if he had drowned. When he watched rubbish on late telly, long after Donald had gone to bed after fussing about in the bathroom for ages, Moyna was always about to yawn noisily in her easy chair (now occupied by unread copies of the *Daily Mail*) and deny that she had nodded off. She was the Moyna of his childhood and youth, this phantom. She was his mum. At one point, cooking at the stove, he felt she had slipped inside him. He almost ticked Donald off for sniffing.

He was all but wearing her slacks; pulling down the sleeves of her cardy. When Donald fished out the housekeeping envelopes at the back of the cupboard, fumbling for coins for the gas, he almost put his hand out.

The weather turned properly cold and the last leaves were a mush among the dogs' doings in the meagre slips of green that Hayes offered up, these days. Jack took Donald out on trips in the car, getting stuck for ages in fume-laden traffic as they battled their way out to some form of reasonable country-side pocked by pylons, to some stately or interesting sight like Chenies or Cliveden or Stoke Poges, to some recommended country pub that usually turned out chilly in the corners and served up indifferent, overpriced nosh. But Donald wasn't interested, anyway. It wasn't his thing. He preferred airfields, plane-spotting, model-glider meetings in windswept fields full of cowpats beside car dumps or vast storage sheds. But when Jack heroically suggested driving him out to one of these, Donald never felt like it.

The England piece was stuck at the twenty-second bar. So far, it sounded like Britten bludgeoned into Pärt, and strained through a morris dance. All wrong. He drove out to Watership Down, not so far from Wadhampton, and stood on the grassy bumps of the ancient fort on Ladle Hill and felt barren and grief-stricken in the biting wind. Most of the downland seemed to have been nibbled away by arid-looking wintry fields, and there was some kind of ginormous antenna; walking through a bleak farmyard, he noticed a battered van in the distance turn a wide circle and head back towards him menacingly. It stopped and he stopped and a man with a nicely wind-pickled face leaned out of it and snarled at him about private property.

He got rid of all but the last bar, then tore that up as well.

There was a succession of days before Christmas, dragging into weeks, which stayed resolutely ashen. The sky was a sheet of impenetrable lead, not really a sky at all: no clouds were discernible. It was something exhaled by the colourless land, by the air itself, hardening into a depression and bolted to Jack's own heart – which actually seemed not so much to ache as to turn gaseous with grief. It hardly rained, and yet it was always about to. It was always about to spit, rather than rain, and one was convinced it was actually spitting, except that it wasn't. The light was so feeble that no hour of the day was differentiated from another: Jack felt it as a purgatorial, equinoctial stage that might usher in some kind of redemptive blaze, but the blaze never came, nor did the night. It probably never would. The days were down a well, a bunker. And through all this the traffic moved steadily and with a sinuous heaped motion onwards to no discernible place and for no discernible reason. Jack saw this through the spittled windscreen, or from the squeezed pavements of Hayes, and heard a harp. He had never heard a harp play what he was hearing it playing. It was playing the greyness of England. It was playing this weather. It was playing this English reality of ashen, utterly leaden futility. Of spoliation. Of flag-fluttering retail parks and commercial estates spread in a cancerous ring around every town. Of people with too much money and the people they'd taken it from, who no one cared a hoot about. Of the zillions that went into scuttling the green land and the clear air that must have existed once, not all that long a time ago.

He was on his way to Currys, situated in a retail park outside Harlington, to buy Donald a digital radio. It was Sunday. The estate's car park was almost full. It was, in fact, spitting steadily and people were hurrying with their wares from sliding glass door to vehicle – or vice versa with empty, needy hands. Jack looked at them from his father's rattly old Ford and thought: we are the damned. And the harp continued into another phrase, squeezing out the greyness onto the scored page in his mind. *This* is our England, he thought. This is our world. It is giving up. There is no sky. There are no white clouds. There is only loss, and Currys, and cars nudging their way towards nothing, and the end of polar bears. And no one cares.

You were so good once.

But this harp was crazy. It wasn't ancient or pagan or green or plangent. It was grey, that's all. It was the leadenness of this. It was the futility of this. It was this piss in the ocean. It was a harp playing grey and this scurrying into Currys. It was nonsense. It was it.

Donald would nap in the afternoon, in the easy chair, an unread newspaper or *Model Glider* sliding off his knees. He looked much older. He was considering moving to Australia, to live with Julie and Mike. Julie and Mike were keen, because they felt lonely without family. Jack thought this was their lookout. But Donald couldn't be unhappier in Australia than he was in Middlesex. In Australia, the only arvo was the afternoon.

'I'm thinking on it,' he'd say, on the phone to Julie. 'I *know* it's nice and warm, pet. I've got a head on my shoulders. Just about.'

Christmas had been just the two of them; Donald had wanted to skate over it, do the minimum, but Jack had cooked a turkey and overdone the Brussels sprouts and his father had all but choked on a walnut and his siblings had phoned. It was miserable and painful, but it fed Jack's piece for St George's Day. In fact, the piece was growing into several pieces: the Radio 3 broadcast would be an extract, just part of the middle section for solo harp in A minor. In A for April; and in B for Birth and D for Death, either side. B, A, D. Major and minor.

Jack knew, with a thrill in his bones like something stirring in the black sediment, that it was very good. He would call it: *Grey Days*. Everyone would know what it meant. The silences between the plucked notes were thrusting forward in a way he'd never achieved before. It was music for the blind. All music is for the blind – that we might see. At intervals, between the grey notes of the harp, hewn from the granite silence, he introduced a tranny in bursts of one or two seconds, distorted trash, agonised over the fence. Oh, it was very good. And everything, *everything* fed in. Even the humming of a revolving washing line turning in its socket.

Radio 3 hated it. They didn't say they did, but he knew they did. He sent them the whole score, marking where the extract began and ended in the middle section, and after a fortnight came a lukewarm thank you by email. They had found it 'very interesting and surprising, but we aren't sure it fits with the others in the series. Maybe it would suit a late-night slot, for our more serious, committed listeners.' Unusually for Jack, he sent back a furious defence of it, quoting the producer's over-heard request to be 'challenging'. They crumbled immediately. This is how it's going to be from now on, he thought. No compromise.

He would dodge the silly questions in the pre-recorded inter-view and say what he thought. He had to say what he thought.

The complete work was over an hour long.

He sent it to Howard, not all that nervously because he knew it was good. A week later, Howard wrote a proper letter on proper paper, three pages long in nice violet ink, proclaiming *Grey Days* to be a work of genius. He meant it, too.

'Thank you, Mum,' said Jack, lying with his hands behind his head on the bed, Howard's letter on his chest. 'Oh, and thank you, too, Roger. You bastard.'

ELEVEN

A group of men are waiting to board their return flight as I emerge into arrivals at Tallinn airport. Their identical yellow sweatshirts are emblazoned with big purple letters: *Bridegroom, Best Man, Usher, Chauffeur, Groom's Best Mate* and, in one case, *Poor Jilted Bastard*. They look like released prisoners still adapting to daylight and they all appear to be called Chris. They have very loud, if hoarse, voices. One of them wears a felt top hat marked with a St George's flag.

I'm staying just the one night in Tallinn. My hotel's the cheapest I could find, a grey lump smelling of BO and hair grease next to the railway in the ex-Soviet zone, but I can walk into the Old Town in a few minutes.

It's cooler here than in London – about the same as it was six years ago, although it's April now rather than October. There are a lot more tourists, and most of the houses have been stripped and painted, teetering on the edge of Disneyfication. I feel like a trespasser on my own memories. The café where I met Kaja, where this long phrase started cooking, has been entirely revamped into something very red inside with night lights on the tables, called St Petersburg. The façade's painted a subtle blue, with a gas light on an elaborate hook. Cardiac-challenging trance pumps out through the open door. *No Stag Parties Please Respecful Behaviour Only* is stuck on the window in elaborate computer-Gothic.

Not one trace of the Café Majolica is left, in fact.

I wander up to the pub, still O'Looney's, with a hand-painted wooden sign saying *Since 1994*. As before, music and shouting are in chromatic conflict through the open door. It's the very

same tweedling Irish folk tape (I picture it as a cassette) as in
'99, but the shouting is English, not Finnish. It sounds like
blood-up-the-walls fisticuffs, and I'm turning to go when about
ten of my compatriots spill out, yelling and guffawing. Despite
the cool spring weather, they're dressed for summer.

I back off, to the other side of the street, not wanting to be
started on. I am also fairly curious. Is their behaviour the same
as it might have been in Hayes or Harlow or wherever they
come from? One lifts up his T-shirt at his reflection in the
window, waggling his mammoth behind; another lies belly
down, pretending to have sex with the cobbles. Just like home.

The others gob and guffaw some more, then spot me loitering.
I pretend to be checking text messages on an invisible mobile
in my palm. My lifeline looks interestingly short. One of them
approaches, fat and ginger-haired rather than hard, with huge
fuzzy nostrils he seems to be looking through, and he yells, a
few yards off: '*Oi, what's the big issue, piss-face?*'

OK, I'm cross. As if I'm watching a foreign army rampage
through my own land. It isn't courage that makes me answer
back, it's blind and spontaneous anger. They're bombed stupid
on cheap beer and Tallinn vodka, I should let it go – but I can't
let it go. They're jeering at me, thinking I'm Estonian, or thinking
I'm at least not English and therefore of an inferior race. And,
at the same time, they're revelling in their ugliness, their brutish-
ness – there's something self-consciously comic in it, something
theatrical. It makes you think they wouldn't harm you, in the
end.

But that is a big mistake. I make that mistake. I'm not exactly
naive – I was brought up in the fag end of Middlesex, after all,
and saw a man's face pulped against a pub's floorboards when
I was eighteen – but I have lost my animal edge, my instinct.

So I answer back instead of hurrying away.

And it is, in fact, like everything I've wanted to say to myself
for years, rolled up into a tiny black ball and ejected at the
speed of sound.

'*Grow up,*' I scream, jabbing my finger at him and bouncing on the balls of my feet; *'Why don't you just grow up? Fat chance, eh? You're pathetic! Got that? Pathetic!'*

I fray my throat in a voice I recognise as lacking lumpen cred. I've been away from it all too long, in the likes of Richmond and Hampstead and Wadhampton Hall. I sound like a teacher. It echoes down the street with all the menace of a ping-pong ball.

A kind of swaying roar goes up, not so much a battle cry as this drunken inability to believe that anyone would dare to say what I have just said. And then there is a pause. There is even a silence. The kind of silence that occurs just before major battle is joined. The crack of banners. The odd distant whinnying of a single horse among the thousands lined up opposite.

They start moving towards me as one. I make to run off, but too late. Edward would like this story, I am thinking. Piss-up.com. We're taking over. Fear hasn't yet hit me.

They are drunk, but not that drunk. They can still shift: it's as if someone has cheated and placed them all around me. I put my hands out in front, like someone blind.

I wake up in a white room, seeing a girl in a white dress on a white shore, playing a viola. Then I realise I am in a hammam, filled with steam, like the one Mill and I went to once in Turkey a long time back. My nose is stinging, and something is digging a metal point into my lower chest. If I could only move, I'd be free of the man with the knife, sticking it in me through the steam.

The girl is a nurse, smiling through the fog.

The metal point is a broken rib. My nose has been reset. My upper lip is cut, swollen to twice its normal size. My ear is broccoli rather than a cabbage. My head feels like hot ice and hammers. I staggered about with blood on my face, apparently, then curled myself into a ball on the ground while the boots kept on coming. Then the police arrived and beat the drunken English oafs over their heads with Estonian truncheons. The police were appointed to deal with just this imported problem.

The oafs are in the cells, bleeding and moaning, and I can bring charges. Yes?

I shake my head. That would ruin all my plans. It would be England entangling me deeper in her briars.

'And your family? You have a wife?'

The doctor is young and friendly, with gold-rimmed specs. I say I don't want to upset my family, I'll be fine. I apologise for my fellow Englishmen. The doctor shrugs, tolerantly.

'Not polite and gentlemen these days,' he smiles. 'The world has change.'

'Telling *me*,' I say, indistinctly what with my swollen lip. 'Things haven't worked out as perfectly as some of us would have wished. Actually, this is the second time I've been hit in Tallinn. Maybe I ask for it.'

'Oh,' says the doctor, slapping his own bared lower arm, 'what is this in English?'

'Smack? Slap?'

'Smack, yes. You must not smack your nation too strong or you might be hurting yourself again.'

I leave the hospital after a couple of days. The various checks on my head have found nothing amiss. I give a brief statement to the police. A headache, nausea – but that's shock. My face will settle down to what it was, I'm told – even the ear. My rib will mend itself. The bruises are already less tender, turning purple and green as they should.

Milly would've told me how I *wanted* to be punished, I think, as I stare at myself in the hotel's cracked mirror. A psycho-physical urge to be thumped in Tallinn. Twice over. Oh, Mill.

I stay on in Tallinn a few more days, as medically advised, allowing my body and my mind to settle down before setting off for Haaremaa. I'm nervous in the streets, to be honest, my legs jellifying without warning, and I keep mostly to the upper town or to the massive library – where I finish *Anna Karenina* in between loafing about in the music section. Plasters over my nose and my forehead, hiding the stitches, provide something to stare at for passers-by. I avoid wherever I can hear shouting.

I walk past a quiet group of pale, menacing-looking blokes sitting outside a restaurant. They meet my eyes point-blank, but not out of friendliness. I assume they're mafiosi, well entrenched these days, here and everywhere else: porn, drugs, arms. Then I hear English, London English. Off I go, at a brisk pace.

All this has spoilt Tallinn for me. A mistake to come back. I'm upset, I have to fight self-pity and depression. I am forty-three, and washed up. It's an ugly age: too old not to know your dreams are an illusion, but not old enough to dismiss them. That's Dostoevsky, as far as I can recall. But my dreams aren't an illusion, like Dostoevsky's were. They can't be. Without them, I might as well be dead.

How far is St Petersburg? Not much more than a hundred kilometres, apparently. Everything close, these days. Finland just over the water. Riga.

Somebody has written in black felt pen on the painted rail I am gingerly leaning on, looking out at my favourite view: *Grab My Pretty Tits*. I picture the *easyJet* flight as a kind of sewage pipe, polluting the city with my country's effluent.

I stop by at the music shop and buy a sheaf of blank score-paper and a good dark pencil. I tell the owner – who recognises me from six years before – that I have fallen off a bicycle. The owner has aged drastically in the interim, his shaggy hair and beard turning completely white. But his eyes are still young.

I'll get to know him well, I think.

After a bad last night (the trains shovelling sleep to one side), I am on the coach and happier. I feel very emptied out and simultaneously very much on a high, as if I've consumed nothing but brown rice and water for a week.

It is the same rattly coach, and it is full. All I have is a battered rucksack and, straining it inside, the junior cricket set. The withered old woman next to me, in a spotted scarf, offers me a slice of black bread. The countryside looks much the same, flat and green and just as empty. A huge abandoned factory turns slowly in the distance, its filthy concrete slivered by barbed wire and covered in graffiti. I never noticed it, last time. Maybe I was nuzzling Kaja's neck, at that point. Each time I breathe deeply, my rib grinds. It's a reminder not to wander from my course.

The ferry boat serves black tea and I sip mine in a corner, wondering who I am and what I am doing. The lorry drivers keep looking at me from the opposite table; one of them wears a singlet on which is written, *I Am Fucker Champion If You Ask.* I don't think I'll bother to ask.

Then I remember what I am doing, and feel better.

The Soviet-era coach station, slapped up in unevenly pointed brick, is unchanged. It's only a ten-minute walk from the estate where Kaja's mother still lives, and I am half afraid of meeting her when I go into the centre of town for a bite to eat. It is very calm on the square. An estate agent's window in one of the low, Swedish-era houses advertises dachas and plots of building land that are relatively cheap – but not that cheap. I expected better.

Some of the photos show nothing but a grassy field, distant reeds, windswept trees and sky, each snap's colours faded by the sun. I stare at these for some time.

I buy a new map of Haaremaa. It's dotted all over with the at sign, showing where you can hitch up to the Internet. Otherwise, apart from one wider road in the south, a dual carriageway for a few miles, it's just the same.

I spend half an hour after lunch sitting on the artificial beach in the shadow of the castle, watching some young locals playing basketball. The brisk wind still makes hooting noises in the metal posts.

Setting off for the dacha with the rucksack on my back, I look like an ordinary hiker in the dark blue trekker's jacket I found on eBay.

It is cool, grey April weather, which I appreciate. I feel really calm and clear, inside. I walk up the wide country road, turning off when I recognise the right yellow sign. The lane winds like an English country lane, the spring vegetation starting to crowd up on each side, the air full of the sea and wet leaf mould and sap. I begin to feel pretty good. I begin to feel exhilarated, ideas leaping about in my head, fragments coming and going over the urge to turn them into something huge and improbable.

I approach the dacha at twilight, after taking a detour up a path that Kaja and I walked a few times. It's a long, winding path that ends where the cranes nest somewhere lonely and lovely near the waterline. I hover there by the reeds for an hour or so, listening to the sounds as I have never listened to sounds before. I wish the sun would come out, because it is cool and grey, but then I close my eyes and just listen.

The dacha is much the same, to my surprise.

The house itself is in darkness: Kaja always said that her parents never stayed after dark unless they were spending the night. The vegetable garden looks messier than I remember, and the big, wild plot next door is now a mown lawn with water features, gnomes with fishing rods, meticulous flower beds. Its owner – maybe the son of the old dead couple – has replaced its shed-like dacha with something that wouldn't look out of place in Hayes, and its security lights are blazing.

The hen run is still in place and, from the soft chortling sounds in the coop, still full of hens. I'm tempted to look for an egg, but it's too dark. I scurry as softly as I can on the far side of the long plot down to where the woodshed looms.

The cage is in the same position. A shadowy presence inside makes scuffling noises as it paces. I feel afraid of it, suddenly. The yellow eyes catch whatever light makes it down here from the neighbour's dacha; they look malevolent, like a psychotic's eyes.

I fish for my cutters in the rucksack and then fumble for the wire that fastens the cage door in the darkness. The animal stops pacing and crouches down at the end of the cage, treading on its feeding bowl. Whenever Mikhel fed it, six years ago, it crouched in the same way, as if used to being punished, and never made any attempt to escape. It's crafty, I think: it knows it would be useless to try.

Now, as I swing the cage door open, I feel that this is the moment the fox has been expecting after so many years. It always knew this moment would come. It has never given up on the notion that one day the door would be left open and no one would be there to beat it back.

I step carefully away for a few yards, waiting on my heels by the fresh new leaves of the potato plants. I can smell the cut wood in the woodshed, reminded of the sauna and the sweet thrashing of the birch twigs, of how paths diverge and meander and cross again. My rib bothers me and I straighten slightly. They might have killed me. They might have kicked my eyeballs out. They'll be sent back to live another day, perhaps chastened, perhaps not. The police shrugged when I said I didn't want to press charges. In one sense, I had provoked it. It happens every night in Hayes. Now I'll have to let it sink into the silt of everything else that has happened to me.

I sense the bulk in the cage – really, just a blacker shadow – rise and move, sniffing at the open door. The forest is not fenced off: the fox is about four paces from the forest's safe darkness and might slip into it in seconds. I think I see the glisten of teeth, the wet muzzle, the eyeball.

I wonder if I shouldn't urge the fox out, but decide against it.

Eventually – aware of my own sweat, the rustle of my clothes – I realise I might have to go before the fox can escape.

I might just have to trust that the fox will, at some point in the long night, find the courage in itself to leave where it has been for good and slip away into the great and complex darkness beyond.

I tramp about the island for five days, sleeping on the long and empty beaches or in barns. It's very cold at night, despite my mountaineer's sleeping bag, and the rustle of the waves keeps bothering me. I've not seen many people, find the odd shop for supplies in the lonely, modern-looking villages, grow very used to trees and getting wet. I also have stomach ache, probably from the radical change of diet, along with a shivery background suggestion of flu. I send postcards to my father and to a few friends including Howard, but not to Mill. I don't mention the beating-up. My rib hurts less when I breathe deep, and my stitches have dissolved. My nose is fractionally, even invisibly different, like the difference between Rex and Lance.

One morning – the third day, I think – I wake up among trees feeling sick and am fairly worried about delayed concussion, being a hypochondriac. But the sickness goes and I hurry out of the wood towards somewhere nearer people, out of my own silence, out of the fear of death.

I come across gun emplacements, tangles of barbed wire, mysterious concrete lumps in the middle of woods. This gets to me. There are very few cars on the wide grit roads, but each time I hear one coming I expect it to slow down, anticipate a cry of recognition. I half expect to bump into Kaja whenever I go into a village. I think a little boy by the shelves of sweets is Jaan. One day, quite suddenly, I break out of a straggly spruce forest to find myself facing the bareness of an alvar, stretched all the way to a glimmering strip of sea. It might be the same lichen-patched alvar we crossed six years ago, treading so carefully over the delicate habitat, when Kaja said how each life is an alvar, as if she was anticipating everything between us. Maybe the winds have blown it even barer, as they've half drowned stunted pines in sand off the beach in another place I think I recognise.

I am beginning to talk to myself, in a low, hushed monotone. I can watch a bird faffing about in the undergrowth, or a beetle on a twig, or the waves curling and sighing against the white sand for rather longer than I've watched anything before, not counting films, or concerts, or a computer screen, or Milly's face in sleep.

One night I sleep by a stream and in the morning, very early, from first light, I do something that I remember Cornelius Cardew suggesting in his little book, *Scratch Music*: 'Tune a brook by moving the stones in it.' I spend at least two hours

tuning the stream, the stones large enough to make a difference, released from the gravelly bed with a sucking reluctance,
displaced to change the music of the water.

I tune it to A, in the end. My hands get so cold I can hardly
move them. I stay all day by the stream, composing, scribbling
on the scoresheets I bought in Tallinn, sharpening my pencil
on my Swiss army knife and scribbling again. That night, I
dream of the dark wispy scorelines of wrack on the white
beaches and try to read their music before the foam takes them.

At the precise hour *Grey Days* is being broadcast on Radio
3, I hear it in my head, sitting alone in long grass on an island
in Estonia, with the stream's music moving through and over
and beneath.

By the time I arrive on Kaja's mother's doorstep, then, I look
less London-bleached, less urban. In fact, I'm looking pretty
messy. There's hay in my hair and sand in my nails. I am wearing
what were called, in my youth, bovver boots. My rucksack is
ex-army and frayed – I'd not wanted to go about looking like
something in a photo shoot. It bulges awkwardly: the junior
cricket set only just fits inside, along with the sleeping bag.
Above all, I've let my stubble develop, and it turns out to be
brindled. The only music I've heard – aside from piped radio
in the local stores – has been provided free by the wind. My
injuries are evident, if fainter. My ear is almost back to normal,
retrieving the blueprint from the bloodied lump it was.

I had hoped to spend weeks as a tramp, but five days is plenty.

There's a large bright hypermarket on the corner near the
estate – I can't even recall what it's replaced. Waste ground,
maybe. Wooden sheds. I wonder if this is the one built by Kaja's
ex-husband. I go inside and buy chocolates and a bottle of
wine. It's even more basic than Lidl, but brighter and newer-
looking. It cheers me up, which it shouldn't do.

'Hi,' I say, as the apartment door gives way to Kaja's mum.
'It's Jack. I've come to see you.'

Kaja's mother pulls a face. She looks quite a bit older. I

suppose *I* must look quite a bit older. I grin amiably, holding out the chocolate and the wine.

'Is that OK? I'm on holiday.'

I don't know how much she knows. It is a gamble. Jaan may even be with her. Or Kaja. I am improvising. I am walking and not looking where I am going, trusting to where I have just been.

'OK,' says Maarje, brightening. 'Welcome, welcome.'

The flat is just the same, except that there are more family photographs dotted about. A framed portrait of Mikhel stands on the kitchen table, as if she's just been studying it. The television is on, with poor black-and-white reception, showing what appears to be a badly dubbed American cop series set somewhere like Chicago. Maarje pulls out a chair in the kitchen and I sit in it; I'm glad it makes the same squeaky sigh as before. She makes coffee and fishes out some of her factory's buttery biscuits, hardly speaking. When she does, it is comments about the weather, all but using up her limited English vocabulary. I want her to switch the television off, but she doesn't, and I'm distracted by the nervous-sounding dialogue, the pulse of the talking music, the violence. I ask no questions, merely make inane, polite observations about the island, the flat, the coffee. We're padding around each other. We both know that someone is missing. Two people. Three, if you count Mikhel.

The oilcloth on the table, rippled by heat-rings, gleams from being obsessively wiped. The flat smells of loneliness.

'On holidays? Walk?'

'Yes. What a beautiful island.'

'Weather not so . . .'

'It's fine,' I insist. 'It's really perfect. Not *too* much rain.'

Maarje laughs. 'A miracle! What's your . . . hurt?' she adds, touching her own nose and forehead.

'Oh, just fell off my bicycle. And how's Kaja? And Jaan?'

Maarje studies her coffee cup. 'I dunno,' she says. 'Maybe you not see her.'

'How do you mean? That I *mustn't* see her?'

'Yah. You are Jaan's . . .'

I nod.

'Now Toomas,' she says, with a kind of resignation to it. 'Toomas is his pappa. Jaan beautiful boy. Live here when Kaja study. No problem. Is nice for us. Now Mikhel . . . Oh, yes. I *very* sad. Even his – in the – the animal . . . in the dacha . . .'

'His fox?'

'Yah. Even she go. Someone come. She – out. Kill.'

'Kill?'

Her fingers make little steps across the table, then take off to flick a strand of hair away from her eyes, then make grabbing movements while her upper lip shows her teeth in a vague snarl. I nod, looking concerned. I'm not sure what she means – that the fox was killed by some wild beast of the island? A lynx? I pull a face, as if I understand. Her rheumy eyes film over, but I don't feel any guilt. In fact, I feel glad. Better a quick death than that intolerable imprisonment. A few days' tramping has left me, not with mystical inclinations, but a hard, practical nub. I wonder if Kaja lives very near. Maybe not. Although nowhere is very far on this island.

In six years, Maarje has stepped over the threshold into old age. This is vaguely annoying, as if it's all her own doing.

'So,' she goes on. 'Now Toomas, very good man, her husband – he look after Jaan. Kaja happy – work for radio.'

Her eyes are shining, turning moist.

'Beautiful girl,' she adds, with a sigh.

I nod all but imperceptibly: I am here for Jaan, not for anything else.

'I thinking a lot, here,' she goes on. 'Too much thinking.'

'Brooding, in English.'

'Broa-ding?'

'Brooding. I could give you English lessons.'

She laughs, again. 'Very good!'

'It's hard on your own,' I say, pleased to be getting on with her so well.

She gets up with a grunt to make more coffee. The cop

series has finished and it's now the adverts. A blonde, laughing woman scattering Estonian washing powder over a lawn; a red car racing through an Italian piazza; a varnished McNugget trifling with the nation's new health.

My eyes find solace in a recent, glossier photograph of the family, taken in front of the lighthouse I saw on my tramp, right out on the end of a spit of rock. A foursome, counting baby Jaan in a pushchair. Mikhel, much the same, except he's got glasses. Next to this photo there is a close-up of Kaja, with a studio glaze about it, looking fourteen or fifteen. That was there before, I'm sure of that, but now it looks different.

She's smiling, but it isn't quite Kaja's smile. There are no dimples and one of her front teeth is slightly overlapping the other. She is dressed in something neat and dutiful, with a white collar. Otherwise, yes, it is the same Kaja. But not *quite* the same, not under the studio lamp, the fine lens, the glossy detail. I frown. She looks ordinary, not striking. And then I remember how people change in just a few years, how this is not Kaja at twenty-seven, but at the dawn of her adulthood.

Maarje is breathing heavily, head bowed a little, holding the framed photograph of Mikhel. She has a handkerchief over her nose. She is silently crying: the tears are darkening the cotton.

'Mikhel, half of month, very bad. Very, very bad. Blood from inside. Then nothing. Just cry in sleeping. Then white and he sleep for always. Like TV off.'

The male announcer on the screen is laughing, holding up a huge repro banknote in euros.

Maarje lets me accompany her to Mikhel's grave, next to her father's and her pan-wielding mother's; her great-uncles are buried in separate war cemeteries. It is ten minutes on foot: a small lumpy graveyard under cedars on the edge of town. She goes there every day. The wet grass makes squeaky noises as we tread on it, but there is no path. The dates are clear on the plaque: *1940–2003.* There are plants in pots, and a spray of tiny withered flowers picked from the spring verges. I know the spray is Jaan's little offering, even before Maarje tells me.

'Very close. Yah. Jaan put flower. Is better.'

'Much better,' I say, moved by her grief, by the reminder of my own.

Maarje snuffles, and I place a tentative hand on her shoulder. Roughly the same sort of shoulder as my own mum's.

We're a right pair, both of us, audibly snuffling away by the graves.

I can feel the flame rise in me again – that desperate need to see Kaja, to be with her.

But I am here for Jaan, not Kaja. I have to keep reminding myself of this. I am not quite there yet.

There are yellow crocuses on the grave, as on my mum's – and those pretty star-like flowers I can never remember the name of.

Kaja lives about twenty minutes by bike from her mother, in an old, thatched place originally belonging to Toomas's farmer-uncle, and which Toomas has spent the last six years restoring. I can borrow Mikhel's old bicycle, to get there.

But first, Maarje insists on me having a shower. Like a proper tramp, I have no change of clothes.

I undress in Kaja's old room, where we made love while Maarje was chatting to the aunt on the phone. Nothing has altered: the china squirrel's still begging us to stop on the windowsill. But we didn't stop. And Jaan was the result, of that I am pretty sure.

The dirt sticks doggedly – to my ankles most of all. After the shower, I can smell my clothes, much riper than I thought. But not unpleasant.

Maarje phones Kaja, after the shower; I hear my name embedded in the Estonian, repeated urgently several times with nods of the head, as if Kaja can't believe it on the other end of the line. Then I'm handed the phone. My heart thumping in my throat.

Kaja sounds worried, rather than surprised.

'Are you chasing me?'

'No.'

'No?'

'I just miss Jaan, Kaja. I did the hotel tissue test. My box is almost empty. My mum's died and my wife's left me.'

'Really?'

'Yes.'

A pause. She sighs. I think I can hear Jaan talking in the background.

'Oh God. I'm sorry about your mother.'

'Not about my wife,' I say, but keeping it light so she can hear my smile.

'Because of me, was it?'

'No, she left me because of *me*.'

I wonder how disappointed she is, to hear that.

'You aren't going to take him away?'

'I don't think kidnapping is my line, somehow. Look, Kaja, I've got something to tell you. It's completely crazy, but there we go. I can't tell you over the hooter.'

'The hooter?'

'The phone.'

'Toomas my husband knows about you. He'll be worried.'

'Tell him not to be. It's not *that* crazy. I don't want to get heavy about this, but I do have a kind of – well, um, I'm *allowed* to see my son, aren't I?'

'When it's your convenience.'

'Kaja, that's just not cricket. You'll see why that's not cricket, when I've told you what I want to tell you. Please?'

The bicycle is hung on a hook in the boiler room, like a giant pair of spectacles perched on a nose. It takes some time to get the tyres pumped up – one of them has a slow leak, from lack of use. The gritty roads mean I have to stop twice on the way, to get it tight again, and the saddle is loose so that I all but slide off backwards. The junior cricket set is slung across my back like a guitar, tied around me with twine. The odd passer-by stares. In my tramp's shapeless hat and stained trekker's jacket, I must look like the supreme English eccentric.

Or a complete git.

The house itself is off a main grit road, down a grassy track next to a big church destroyed in the war and partially rebuilt. I pass two or three other houses crouched along the green lane, with vegetable patches and battered-looking cars. An old couple raise their hands in greeting. One of the houses is derelict, holding itself together by a miracle of crossed beams and wattle, with a dark vault of a barn alongside. Five minutes further up, past a freshly sprouting birch copse and a couple of small meadows, there's a carved letter box in the shape of a steepled tower. You lift the steeple to put the post in.

A crooked, low-slung building with attic windows in its thatch; a leaning barn; a green yard. It's unpretentiously pretty. Wooden sculptures shaped like giant corkscrews give it a bohemian flavour. An old blue Saab with its passenger door resprayed in violet, like a subdued hippy wagon, reminds me of the seventies in Britain. The trees in which the place buries itself – mostly birch and alder – are leafing from their buds in droves. The sun shines fitfully and the air smells of grass and forest mulch and manure. A few hens scrabble about in happy freedom, and what I think are white ducks paddle about in a bath with a plank for access.

The house seems closed off to me, about its own quiet business, but not unfriendly.

They'll be waiting for me. Toomas is an unknown quantity, he might be difficult. On the other hand, he'll probably be a very open and easy-going guy with an earring.

My bum hurts from the loose saddle. I breathe in deeply and square my shoulders. I have to look in control.

I ring a tiny Pärt-like bell, dangling by the unvarnished door. This is like a fairy tale. Someone has collected red hips, hawthorn or rose, and put them on an old plate on a shelf in the rickety porch. They're as bright as blood, even after months. No one comes. I give the door a strong rap with my knuckles. Nothing.

As I open the thick door a crack, crouching and peering in, it disappears to be replaced by Kaja's chest. I straighten up clumsily and grin.

'Hi,' she says. 'My God, what a hat.'

'I rang, but . . .'

I am embarrassed.

'We had the radio on,' she explains.

'No, it's fine.'

'Well, please, come in.'

When I am inside, shuffling from foot to foot and wishing I had never come, Kaja puts her hands either side of her face and says, 'This is *so* mad!'

'Crazy,' I agree. 'I'm really sorry.'

'Your nose and head? Someone hit you *again*?'

I smile. 'Actually, I was going to say I fell off my bicycle in London. In fact, I did get hit. In Tallinn. By English drunks.'

'Do you *ask* to be hit?'

'Probably.'

'You were drunk?'

'A definite no-no. Sober as a judge.'

She frowns. It's hopeless. I shouldn't be here. I turn to go but she calls out for Jaan. No answer. She tells me to wait right where I am and goes off through a low door in the corner of the room.

I wait, feeling I am sculling softly over my own depths.

Everything in the room is dark and wooden, apart from the metallic gleam of a stereo. There is a peaty, earthy smell, perhaps of burned logs from the fireplace. It reminds me of the shallow bogs I've had to squelch through over the last few days, but it's not unpleasant.

'Look, Jaan, it's our friend from England. It's Jack!'

I find myself kneeling down and gathering Jaan in my arms and squeezing him. Then I unhitch the cricket set in its plastic sheath.

'Where's our pitch, chief?'

Jaan takes the set with huge eyes. I start pulling out the bat like a sword from its scabbard.

'It's yours,' I say. 'Oh, and so is this.'

I produce, from an inside pocket in my jacket, a somewhat crumpled sheaf of papers. Jaan's more interested in the cricket bat.

'What's that, Jaan?' asks Kaja.

'Music,' says Jaan, glancing at it, fishing with the length of his arm for the ball.

'It's a score,' I tell him. 'It's for you. It's called *Seven Cheers for Jaan* and it's basically seven practice pieces for solo viola.'

Kaja leans over to look. 'You wrote that?'

'Sure did,' I say, sitting on my heels. 'I wrote it this week. It's full of bird sounds and sounds of water and the wind in the trees.'

'That's wonderful,' says Kaja.

'It's my job,' I smile.

The floorboards squeak and Toomas comes in, drying his hands on a rag. I stand up, the score in my hands, sensing my body go apologetic under my stained shirt and trousers.

'Hello. I'm Jack.'

'I think he must see that,' says Kaja, with an ambiguous smile that flusters me for a moment. Her eyes examine my clothes for the first time. 'Hey, what have you been *doing*?'

'Tuning streams by moving stones,' I reply, feeling like a real intruder.

The first surprise is that Toomas is short and wiry and has no earring. The second is that he is extremely restrained in his welcome. He's clean-shaven, with a blond ponytail and a tiredness under his pale blue eyes, standing with the rag in his hand. Of course, he's known Kaja since school. He must be her age.

Toomas speaks very little English. His hand is like sandpaper when I shake it. There is fight in him, a kind of residual anger. I can feel it in the firm squeeze of his hand.

'Don't worry, I'm going to be learning Estonian,' I say. '*Tuletikk. Tikutoos. Välgumihkel. Rebane.*'

Toomas tightens his mouth in what might have been a grim smile. He says something to Kaja.

'He says Estonian is very purging for the digestion.'

I nod and smile, assuming this is a joke. But Toomas has already turned and left us to our own devices.

The first of these consists of a quick tour of the place. Jaan's viola is in his little room in the eaves. There is an action photo of me with the red ball, looking as if I have serious rickets, taken in Kensington Gardens. It is pinned to a cork board along with some other London snaps: a lopsided Tower of London; Kaja by half a Horse Guard; Jaan in front of the elephant cage at the Zoo. Jaan shows them off proudly.

'You liked London?'

Jaan shrugs, his eyes checking with his mother.

'Say what you think, Jaanie,' Kaja insists.

'I got hit,' says Jaan.

I nod, pulling a face. 'Yeah, I know the feeling.'

'Money, money, money,' says Kaja, suddenly. 'Nothing else. The only thing that's important, there.'

'Dead right,' I agree. 'Yup, *dead* right. Sad.'

Jaan tries out the first *Cheer*, having some difficulty at first with my handwritten score, the paper spattered with mud and rippled from an encounter with a leaking bottle. Within half an hour, with some coaching, Jaan has got it. We listen without stirring as he plays its four minutes right through. He has, I'm thinking, an astonishing sense of what is needed for every phrase.

And I didn't expect him to understand it so quickly – its mixture of the plangent and the joyful in its chromatic shifting, like a young child with an old face, a child who cannot die and maybe doesn't want to.

Of course, I have to pretend to be scratching under my eyes, afterwards, catching the salt moisture on my finger-pads. Then I blow my nose.

'Hay fever,' I say.

Kaja has her face turned away, towards the window.

'That was really swell, my Jaan,' she says. Her voice is pitched a little too high, as if something is constricting her throat.

We visit the yard. Their hens, Kaja says, are really lazy, and all twenty or so of the dacha's hens have been slaughtered by the fox, so they have to buy their eggs now from a distant cousin. It's hard to buy so many new hens on the island, these days.

'The fox?'

'That old sad fox in the cage. To keep the other foxes away. Someone let him out.'

I pull a convincing face. Convincing to me, at least.

'Why?'

'I dunno. Maybe kids did it. It's just a true foxy fox, of course,' she adds. She twirls a finger against her temple. 'But mad, maybe. Like an escaped prisoner. Blood and feathers all over the shop,' she adds in a murmur, out of Jaan's earshot. 'Not one left without an injury or dead. Horrible.'

I nod knowingly, feeling confused, feeling a strange dark confusion in my chest.

'Maybe it wasn't that actual fox.'

'Maybe. We just put two things together, though.'

I will buy them twenty more hens, somehow. Maybe first I'll have to do something about the fox. The thought of it vaguely scares me, or maybe the thought of having to track it down: its yellow eyes in the woods. Its slipperiness.

We stop in the barn to watch Toomas plane a huge beam, a battered ghetto blaster pumping out AC/DC. There is a hint of reefer in the perfume of sweet sawdust. He doesn't turn round, but it isn't an unfriendly back. It is a very concentrated back.

'I'll need to do something about his taste in music,' I laugh, as we emerge from the barn.

Jaan is bursting with impatience. He grips the cricket set to his chest as if it is his life raft.

'Unkalalunka Jack,' he says.

'Is that me? Wow. Sounds like a Zulu god.'

'We'll go to the beach and play cricket,' Kaja announces. 'Get your coat, Jaanie.'

At the end of the track, silent and invisible beyond a marshy meadow and an inlet of waving reeds, is the sea. The path turns right and continues for a hundred yards or so, following the coast, before it veers left, snaking along the head of the saltmarsh to cut through low dunes and out onto the beach. The sea's sighs and whispers envelop us suddenly as we clear the dunes, the marram grass biting at our legs. The sand is white and firm. There is a coolish wind and the light scuds in fits over the water. Trees flourish right up to the sand beyond the saltmarsh, the shoreline curving round into the far distance: poplars of a dazzlingly fresh green are waving in the sea breeze. It is exceptionally beautiful, if not quite real, like something out of an eighteenth-century oil.

Jaan is still hopeless at cricket, but it doesn't matter. He'll improve over the years, I'm thinking. We'll start an island team. My own bowling is hampered by nerves. I try overarm, surprised by the whiffs of my shirt. Kaja watches me as she fields in the slips. Then she bowls against me, underarm but rather expertly, and when I strike the ball into the creamy surf, she squeals like a little girl.

Jaan runs after the ball in his limping, cockeyed way, retrieving it as it is rolled up by the power of the sea.

'Here! Jaanie! Here!' yells Kaja.

She's jumping up and down, gesticulating wildly as I plod between the wicket – three times, four times, five . . . and finally let myself be run out, throwing myself forward into the sand as Kaja sends the long bail flying with an excited whoop. I can't imagine Toomas fooling about like this.

On the way back, I take Jaan's small hand and feel it flex with the need to have it held by a father. There is hope in it. It isn't just need. It makes me want to shout out loud, at any rate. I wonder when Kaja will break the news to Jaan.

This is your father, Jaanie. Your pappa.

We stop to admire the derelict house. It's hard to imagine in its present state, but Kaja tells me it was a rare example of the island's original architecture. The glass in the windows is blurred with cobwebs and the thatch is mossed over a dark green. Black plastic sheets flap and sway in the wind. A rusty bicycle with handles like antlers is smothered in decaying, creeping growth.

'That's really sad,' she says, 'about your mother.'

'Hit me left field, even though it was expected, you know?'

'Left field?'

'From the side, kind of unexpected.'

She nods slowly. I feel I am talking nonsense. Too much to explain.

And then: 'I used to visit here with my father,' Kaja says. 'An old lady with arthritis. She told us about the war. Bodies everywhere. Terrible things. Her whole family. Throats cut. Hung like meat in that barn.'

Jaan is bouncing the ball off the barn's crooked wall.

I let the silence ride, grow thicker as it travels. The silence congeals into history, as if history is a ball of silence that never goes away, but continues in your head.

There is Haaremaa sand in my boots, again. I feel at home. There is, for every single person alive, somewhere on earth that is their deep and unexpected home, even if glimpsed only from a train or a car. It feels right to have Haaremaa sand in my boots, again.

'They have really gone, now,' murmurs Kaja, at last. 'Where to, I dunno. They were ready, I guess.'

'Gone away?'

'I think.'

'To somewhere really good,' I nod, keen to encourage this. 'White clouds, maybe. White clouds, you know? Where the dead go.'

We look up. There is a wispy white and grey in swatches over the blue, not really what I meant.

'Maybe. I hope for that, at least.'

The sky seems to be moving in one mass against the tree-tops. I'm not quite sure who she's talking about, now.

'You know, it was like we . . . us two . . . we coincidenced,' she said.

'Coincided.'

'Maybe.'

Or perhaps she does mean that new word, coincidenced. I think how sometimes I feel I'm no more than a coincidence of this me and that me. Maybe it applies to the dead, too. Or our memories. Or other people we meet or just fail to meet or don't follow up. I am in a foreign country, on a lonely island, and the air is different. But I have a past here, already.

I notice she's not smoking any more. Maybe she only smoked in London, the number-one stressville. We watch Jaan run about with the bat, using it as a gun, making vague blowing-up noises. I want to comment on this, to make some clever comment about the state of the world, but feel anything I say would be an implied criticism of her mothering.

In front of the abandoned barn, whose smell of mouldering hay is as sour as cat's piss, I decide never to tell her about the fox, to confess my role in its release. Until we're very old.

She is looking at me with the corner of her mouth tucked in, as if she's reading my thoughts. It is an ambiguous look that I have to turn away from, to watch Jaan swipe the tender young grass with the cricket bat.

We're invited to Maarje's for supper. Before we leave in the old blue Saab with the violet door, I tell Kaja what happened between me and Milly. About the whole disaster, the tearing-up, right up to my island tramp – and what I now plan to do. I add that she must not take the blame, but she doesn't look as if she was planning to. It takes all of twenty minutes.

I'm surprised at her lack of surprise, at the way she listens as if she knows about it all already. She sips her green tea calmly as she listens. We can hear an electric saw whining from the barn through the CD she's put on the stereo – a sampler from a record label sent to Radio Haaremaa. Right now it's a song by Castledown, an obscure newish folk band I like. It's called 'The Attending'.

'I know this,' I say, surprised. 'Really delicate and ambiguous. Really nice steely plucked guitar.'

'I love it,' she says.

'It's sad, though. Another bitter-sweet song about love.'

She picks up the ball and rolls it to Jaan, who carries on bouncing it against the beam, playing catch.

'Hey, about your big plan,' she says. 'I have to tell Toomas.'

'Could be a problem?'

'I'm three-months pregnant. It's no problem.'

'Hey, congratulations,' I say, overeagerly. 'Toomas seems very nice.'

I realise, as she absorbs my bluster, that I sound like my mother commenting on a new spotty friend, years back.

'It's his thirtieth birthday coming, in a few weeks. We'll have a party at the dacha. You can come and meet a lot of people. People in your new life. A really huge big cake I'll cook. Guitar. Beer. Dancing. A summer party.'

'That's really kind.'

'You're doing this for Jaan, *not* for me. I know that.'

It is more like an order, the way she says it.

'And for my work,' I point out, hurriedly, surprised at how sick I feel in my heart at her news about her pregnancy. 'My music. I think I've just written my best piece, for English radio. It's called *Grey Days*. There'll be more, not necessarily grey. Lots of colours, in fact.'

She looks at me straight in the eyes. Hers are definitely blue-green, with a kind of grey edging, and they just about fill their space.

'I'm glad you say that. Now I'm believing you.'

I shift in the chair, I try to concentrate. 'Anyway, look, I think I'm much more sussed now, as a person. You don't need to worry. Milly's pretty happy, she's not planning to slice me into little pieces or anything. I can go back to England to visit my dad, my friends. Concerts. You know? Once or twice a year, for a couple of weeks, maybe. Maybe some engagements, I hope. It's just so easy from Tallinn. Cheap-break Europe, yeah? I don't want to pat everyone on the back too much, but I think – I think we're doing OK.'

'We have to be,' she says.

I study my hands on the table. My nails are broken and filthy; there are ingrained patches of beach tar on my knuckles. The indent of the wedding ring is almost gone, like a trace of something in wet sand. That's what happens to the past. My rib gives a sharp twinge, suddenly, as if in denial.

'I'm going to work pretty hard,' I add. 'I mean, just to live. To survive. To eat. I'm going to be forced to. That's fairly real for me. Haven't known it for years and years. Squelching around in money is a really bad idea. I think it kills everything, in the end. I mean, *everything*.'

She nods. There is a little pause, during which the ball ticks and tocks against the beam. We can just hear the whine of Toomas's saw, like an insect. I try to breathe shallowly.

'This is good,' she says, at last. 'You've gone the good way. I feel it. You know *why* you're here, on this earth. Not in the sky. On *this* earth. Here.' She absently rubs at a knot in the table with her thumb. 'You'll meet someone nice, on Haaremaa. You'll write beautiful music. You can do things for my radio.'

'No problem,' I say, glowing.

It's as if, walking without looking where I was going – walking backwards, heels first, virtually improvising – I have suddenly turned my head. I very much like what I see stretching out in front of me. It was always there, too, I just didn't realise it. It just needed a turn of the head.

'As long as I find somewhere close enough to bike from,' I go on.

'Don't fall off again.'

I grin, nodding, and my lip twinges where the two stitches were.

'And a half-decent piano. I sold mine.'

'There's the dacha,' says Kaja.

I assume she must be joking. We watch Jaan as he goes on bouncing the ball and catching it off the main beam. The frail song comes to an end. She switches off the stereo with the remote. She places the remote carefully on the table.

'There's the dacha,' she says again. 'For renting. Maybe. Where we sang the forbidden songs.'

'Well, OK, just for while I'm looking,' I agree, suddenly seeing how sensible this is.

'Looking?'

'I'm looking for a plot of land to buy, yeah. Something I could put a yurt on.'

'A yurt? Like a Mongolian?'

'You know, I'm not exaggerating: I don't have a lot of money, now.'

'A yurt!' She laughs, placing her hands either side of her face. 'You are *so* mad!'

'Bonkers,' I say. 'Stark raving. It only costs a couple of thousand to buy one. It's round. It's warm. It's perfect.'

'You're like you're selling one to *me*.'

'No, I'm not. I'm selling it to myself.'

'You can make it really . . . what's that expression?'

'Home?'

'Hip! Really hip!'

'*Hip?*' I shake my head. 'No way,' I assert, as she grins at me. 'No way is this whole dream of mine ever going to be hip. It's just going to be concentrated. That's all. We don't do hip,' I add, catching her grin.

Yes, I'm grinning myself, now. From ear to ear. But not Jaan. He's watching us, frowning, passing the ball without thinking from hand to hand. It's because I promised to give him another innings in the yard before we leave for Maarje's, and now he's impatient. Now he wants to start.

Acknowledgements

With many thanks to John Woolrich and Jonathan Reekie of the Aldeburgh Festival of Music and the Arts, where I was writer-in-residence in 2004 and where the germ of this novel was first sown. I am deeply indebted to Zoë Swenson-Wright for her dedicated close reading and notes; to Corinne Chabert and Bill Hamilton for crucial advice; and to the composers Felicity Laurence, Sébastien Damiani and James Ellis for their assiduous checking of the musical details and for general counsel. I am also grateful to Imogen Barford, Kiffer Finzi, Sean Martin, Josh Thorpe and Grit Orgis for inspired help with certain details, to my editor Robin Robertson for his guidance and encouragement, and most of all to my wife Jo for persuading me to write a love story in the first place – and for seeing it through.

www.vintage-books.co.uk